Downfall of the Blood King

Shaquilla Lunsford

An idea starts off as a dream...then someone trailblazes it into reality. Here's to the dreamers.

-S.M.L.

Also by Shaquilla Lunsford

<u>Fall of the Dragon King Trilogy:</u>
After the Fall of the Dragon King
Rise of the Phoenix Queen
Downfall of the Blood King

<u>The Forces of Nature Series</u>
Heart of the Forest

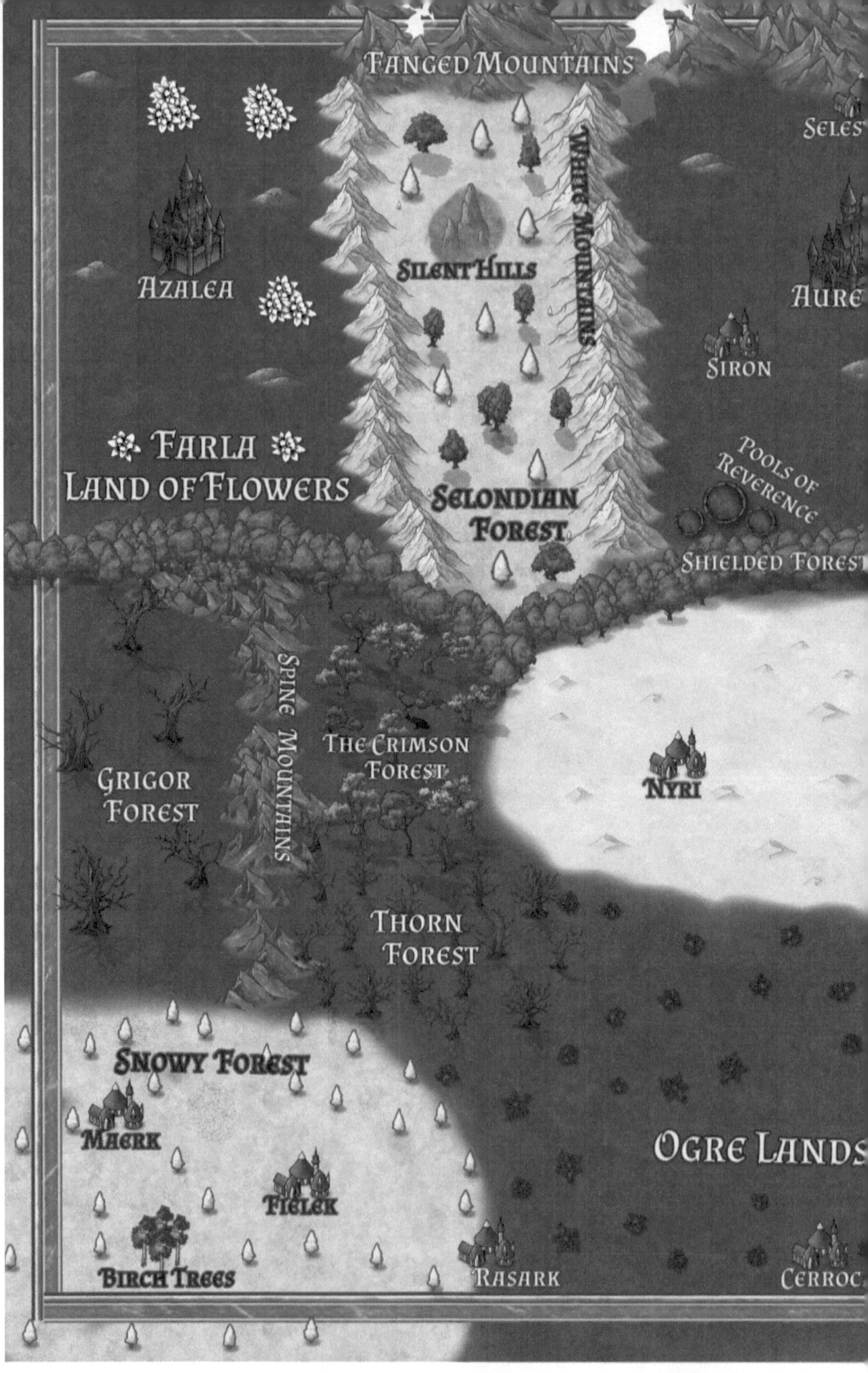

FANGED MOUNTAINS
SELES
WHITE MOUNTAINS
SILENT HILLS
AURE
SIRON
AZALEA
POOLS OF REVERENCE
FARLA
LAND OF FLOWERS
SELONDIAN FOREST
SHIELDED FOREST
SPINE MOUNTAINS
THE CRIMSON FOREST
GRIGOR FOREST
NYRI
THORN FOREST
SNOWY FOREST
MAERK
OGRE LANDS
FIELEK
BIRCH TREES
RASARK
CERROC

FENRIEL
GHIRIT
KRA
VALLEY OF WHISPERS
FOREST OF DREAMS
SEA OF NIGHTMARES
RIFKA
LAND OF THE WINGED
SILENT HILLS
MOUNTAIN PASS
HERCULE
HYRA
LAND OF GIANTS
UNA DESERT
BLACK FOREST
BLOOD CLAN
TERRITORY
RIVIA

Pronunciation Guide

Aoi (oy)

Aris (are-riss)

Aurevel:(or-ree-veil)

Aux: (ox)

Barak: (bear-eck)

Berus (bear-us)

Bohr Eagles: (boar) Eagle

Celena: (se-lee-nuh)

Cerrok: (sair-rock)

Dalacia: (duh-lace-ee-uh)

Dilek: (dye-lek)

Dolis (doe-less)

Dyrewolf: (dye-ur-wulf)

Eshara (e-shar-ruh)

Eztil Karlus (ex-til) (car-luss)

Farek: (fair-ick)

Fariel: (fair-ee-el)

Farla: (far-luh)

Faunus (faun-us)

Fenriel: (fin-ree-el)

Galaton owls: (ga-luh-ton)

Ghirit: (gear-it)

Ghost Lokswood: Ghost (locks-wood)

Gilus (guy-less)

Gonthar: (gone-thur)

Grigor: (grig-or)

Hemera (he-mare-uh)

Hesper (hes-burr)

Hira (here-ruh)

Hirkul (her-cule)

Hogar: (hoe-gar)

Hyra: (hi-ruh)

Ikari (ick-car-ee)

Isrella: (is-rail-uh)

Ivar (eye-var)

Kamuna Desert: (kuh-moon-nuh)

Kratos (kray-toes)

Larynnx: (lair-inks)

Liock: (lye-ock)

Lorik: (lore-ick)

Lyris (lie-ris)

Master Astral: (as-trul)

Master Daris (dare-ris)

Master Kure (cure)

Master Roark (roar-ck)

Master Zephia: (zeff-ee -uh)

Nyri: (nye-ree)

Raiden: (ray-den)

Rasark: (raz-ark)

Reece: (reese)

Reesik: (reese-ick)

Resisti: (ree-zist-tee)

Rifka: (riff-kuh)

Selondian Forest: (se-lone-dee-an)

Sicily: (sis-uh-lee)

Silivia Aria Briar: (suh-li-vee-uh) (are-ee-uh) Briar

Sirius: (serious)

Siron: (sigh-ron)

Teslia Sorrell: (tess-lee-uh) (sore-rale)

Toro: (tor-oh)

Tyrian Vorkan: (tear-ree-an) (vor-can)

Vanadei (van-uh-day)

Vedia (ve-dee-uh)

Zerath (zay-wrath)

Zerc (zurk)

<u>The Mountains We Climb</u>

We all desire to be on top of the mountain.
To feel that joy of success,
of making it.
But what is a mountain?

Our fears.
Our challenges.
Our hopes.
Our dreams.

It's tears cried in the night.
It's the laugh in that moment of sunshine.
It's good days
and...not so good days.
It's despair and hopelessness.
It's resilience and stubborn determination.
It's late nights
and early mornings.
It's everything that brought us to this moment.

We all want to skip to the top of the mountain,
But it's the pain,
the tears,
the laughs,
the growth,
the failures,
the journey
that allows us to stand on the mountain,
and remain there.

Don't knock the journey.
Knock the voices that say you won't make it.

-Shaquilla Lunsford

Prologue

The Blood King

I tapped impatient fingers on the iron throne's arm. It was a work of twisted, dark art accented with rubies set to appear as drops of blood. The red sat out in the deep black, and it matched my dark, demented soul. I'd come a long way from the useless male lost in his brother's shadow. Now, the shadows bent to my will. Or at least they would soon.

I considered the creature before me, her moon white skin and blood-red eyes accentuated by the tight black silk caressing her body. She was my equal, a queen of sorts, but I was growing impatient with her progress.

"Where is he?" I demanded.

The larynnx, demon that she was, smiled seductively at me. While any other time, that would have been enough to convince me to let her into my bed, this time, I simply glared at her until she lowered her head. Her eyes still held that teasing look, and I narrowed mine in answer.

"He remains at her side. Silivia has finally reclaimed the throne, but the tensions are still high in Rifka. It is unclear whether she will be able to hold on to her new title."

I said nothing, just considered my next move. I had no doubt the daughter of Fariel was capable of much more than the world gave her credit for. A fitting queen for the Dark King himself.

"Bring him to me, Ilara. He is the key to everything. If I have the King of Shadows under my thumb, the Phoenix Queen will follow."

And then Fenriel will finally belong to me, but I need not remind her of this. My bloodhound curtsied deeply even as her eyes never left mine, a boldness I only tolerated from her.

"He will not come quietly, Your Majesty."

No, the male of shadows never would. I'd been trying for centuries to claim him.

"Then trap him with that he cannot live without."

I'd thought in the past that capturing his fellow teammates would be enough, but now that he had a spiritbond, my hold over him would be that much more absolute. Ilara smiled wickedly.

"Use his mate to draw him in. Brilliant, Your Majesty." She curtsied again and flew from the room. No doubt, the idea of drinking some of the King of Shadows' power also motivated her. If that meant the male would finally bow to me, it mattered not.

The male was mine. I would have had him centuries ago if I'd known what slumbered under his skin. But then, maybe the darkness would have never manifested if everything hadn't been taken from him. His power may very well rival my own, which is why I must have him. It was a simpler task back when he was furious at the world, but now that mate of his tempered some of his dark rage.

No matter, the same thing that tempered him could rile him. Having them both under my thumb was a power I could not resist. Luckily, they didn't know who the Blood King was. I had to assume that Silivia's sister hadn't revealed my existence, or they would be hunting for me more frantically. But I was not under the misconception that an extended period away from me would not cause the block on her mind to deteriorate until she remembered who exactly had convinced her to attack her sister.

By the time she did, it would be too late. Fenriel would be mine.

Part I:

To Bind a Kingdom

Chapter 1

Silver and gold.
Snow and shadows.

Ghost

There were countless eyes on me–including furious ones worn by the council–but I only had eyes for her. My beautiful, stormy-eyed mate. Her ice blue dress was just short enough to allow the matching heeled boots to peek out, while a deep V-neck showed me a glimpse of the crest of her full breasts and soft caramel colored skin. The back was long, leading to a train that trailed behind her, snow falling with every step. Black strands weaved with diamonds painted the tight dress and continued down the train in a pattern that resembled the tail of the phoenix.

It was beautiful, but nothing was more beautiful than the black curls raining down her back, or the silver crown adorned with sapphires that sat upon them.

I wore my customary black etched in gold but had switched my normal tunic and pants for a close-fitted suit, just for her. Only ever for her. My queen. My love. My spiritbonded. I felt the silver bond within my core hum in confirmation, and my mist pooled at my feet.

Silivia must have felt it too because her lips lifted into a smile that nearly stopped my heart. Ever since she'd started down the aisle, those gorgeous blue-grey eyes had never left mine. And when she stood before me, her hand firmly in mine, I wanted to fall to my knees and worship her. I didn't deserve her, and when it came time to speak, I felt the truth of my words flow through my veins.

"Silivia, my queen. You have held my darkness, my very soul, in the palm of your hand from the first day we met. You gave me a reason to live beyond the darkness. You are my light in the shadows, my redemption, my heart. I vow to stand by your side always. To encourage you when you are down. To protect you when you need it and stand beside you when you don't. I vow to be here always in times of turmoil and times of peace. And although I do not deserve you, I vow that I will spend the rest of my immortal life loving you."

She took a sharp intake of breath, and my heart twisted to see the tears glistening in her eyes.

"Ghost, my King of Shadows."

My heart jolted again. Only she could ever make that title feel like an honor to have instead of something to fear.

"I have been yours since the moment you first danced with me with daggers and blades. You have always been there for me, even when you didn't want to be, and through you, I have found the woman I strive to always be. I vow to always stand by you on the good days and the bad. To be your light when the shadows become too thick. To hold your hand and remind you who you really are when you forget. I vow to love you with all my heart and to remind you every day that you are worthy of it."

I blinked back my own tears as I slipped a ring with bands of intertwining silver and gold onto her finger, its sapphire centerpiece and black diamonds reflecting the emotions I couldn't voice. Her eyes still didn't leave mine as tears flowed freely down her cheeks, and she slipped a gold and silver band onto my hand. I barely heard the priest as I stepped closer to her, wiping away her tears with my thumb.

"Whatever comes," I whispered, pressing my forehead to hers.

"Together. Always."

And then I kissed her deeply to the sound of thunderous cheers and whistles. We became lost in each other, the room falling silent in the wake of the female in my arms. She melted into me, her fingers gripping the lapels of my coat as I pulled her closer. It took several moments for me to pull away, still fighting the need to devour her and carry her to our suite to worship her properly. But first, we had to finish this ceremony.

With a soft smile, Silivia stepped away from me, our hands hesitant to separate, and I turned back to face the dais. The lead councilman now stood before me. I could sense his distaste even as he kept his expression indifferent.

"Kneel," he told me, and I did so. He lifted a golden crown with black diamonds and held it above my head. "Do you vow to protect and rule Rifka alongside our queen with fairness and truth until your last breath?"

"I do so vow," I swore.

"Do you vow to uphold the laws when required, and to develop new ones when needed?"

"I do so vow."

He placed the crown upon my head. "Rise."

I stood to my feet and faced the crowd. Silivia moved to my side and interlocked our hands firmly.

"All hail Her Majesty, Silivia Rosaletta Briar Lokswood, the Phoenix Queen and Queen of the Winged. All hail His Majesty, Daniel "Ghost" Merlin Lokswood, the King of Shadows, and now, King of the Winged of Rifka."

"All hail Queen Silivia! All hail King Ghost!"

A shiver ran down my spine, the weight of the title and crown on my head settling on my shoulders. I stole a glance at my mate. She smiled.

"Figured you weren't ready to be called Daniel by anyone else but me," she whispered, her eyes twinkling with mischief.

I grinned at her. How she'd ensured it was so was nothing short of miraculous. "You figured correctly," I whispered back, lifting our interlocked hands to kiss her fingers.

We turned back to the people as king and queen, a mix of snow and shadows dancing at our feet.

Chapter 2

I'd renounced all titles.
Denied my birthright.
But when you asked me
to stand by your side,
what could I say but
Yes.

Ghost

I folded my arms as I waited impatiently for the Resisti Seven to arrive. Where *were* they? There was plenty I'd rather be doing, and this definitely wasn't it. An annoyed huff came from behind me, reminding me of another's discontent, and I smirked.

One royal guard stood behind me, his arms also folded and his large, black, feathered wings almost touching the ground. Changelings were already known for their gruffness and love of protocol, so I knew he was still displeased with my refusal to let royal guards follow me everywhere. I didn't need the winged males to keep me safe, and I sure as hell didn't need them brooding at my back. In the end, to appease them–and the female with stormy grey eyes–I'd agreed to *one*.

I turned to the door as the Resisti filed in, glaring at Aux. One of my oldest friends, the warrior simply gave me a huge grin.

"You're late," I snapped.

The older male held up his hands, his unique purple and black eyes twinkling with amusement.

"Our apologies, Ghost." He paused, tapping a finger on his chin. "Or should we call you Your Majesty now?"

I bit back a grimace despite the hint of amusement. "Ghost is fine, Aux."

He nodded, a knowing grin on his face. I narrowed my eyes. I was used to being called King of Shadows. I was, after all, infamously adept at controlling the darkness and shadows that people feared. And their fear was warranted, considering I'd shown on multiple occasions throughout the centuries what happened when I let the darkness slip off its leash a little too far.

This new title of king, however... It would take some getting used to. Being King of Rifka, Land of the Winged, had its benefits, I supposed, but right now, only a couple of weeks after being crowned, I simply found it tiresome with the court politics. If it wasn't for the beautiful snow queen at my side, it would be utterly unbearable. But I'd been unable to refuse when she'd said my true name and asked me to be her king. Hell, there wasn't much I could refuse her. She was the only person alive who was truly unafraid of the darkness and the rage that filled it.

Aux only grinned as each of the seven sat down. Aux, the brothers Raiden and Barak, the assassin twins Hesper and Hemera, Rose, and the slippery Sirius. I glared at the yellow-eyed male, who only returned the look with a scowl of his own. Here were the seven warriors who'd answered our calls for aid during Silivia's final trial against the late queen. Rifka would have been lost to the clan and Isrella if it weren't for their bravery and loyalty.

It was the reason they now made up the core of our inner council –our inner circle – privy to all plans concerning the kingdom, Resisti, Blood Clan, and beyond. Aux, along with Tyrian and Teslia, were also a part of the royal council to help balance out the aged views of the members there. Silivia had removed the top few that opposed her on day one. My promotion to king only increased their motivation to behave.

"Where's Tyrian and Her Majesty?" Rose asked as she stretched. Her ever-flowing auburn hair shifted in an unseen breeze behind her.

"She went with Tess to meet with the royal guards about the latest accident. Tyrian should be finishing up with the new prisoners and joining us any moment." My darkness growled at the thought.

There had been an attempt to burn down the stables this morning while Silivia had been with the horses. Luckily, one of her guards, Farek, had seen the smoke in time to put out the worst of it. Not that she couldn't have put them out herself, but it had been fire formed with magic and not so easily smothered. Ty and a couple of others had chased down the culprits and now interrogated them.

"Do we know who they were?" Raiden asked, his fists clenched.

There were twin expressions of anger around the room.

"Clan sympathizers, unfortunately."

We all turned as Ty strolled in. He had splatters of blood across his dark pants and boots. Rose lifted a brow.

"Seems like they regret it now."

My brother-in-arms gave her a wicked grin as he took a seat at my side.

"Yes, but these attacks are becoming more frequent," Barak pointed out. "There have to be additional clan members still present in Aurevel."

"I thought between Sirius and Rose that we removed them all," Aux mused, a frown marring his face.

Sirius shrugged. "Aurevel, and Rifka as a whole, are large. As you see, they have sympathizers who could be hiding them, and not necessarily inside the city walls."

"Sounds like excuses to me," Barak muttered. Usually the easy-going one of the brothers, it was surprising to hear the level of scorn in his voice. Something else must be bothering him.

Sirius shot him a scalding look. "Got something to say, lightning boy?" he snarled.

Barak shrugged, but his hazel eyes flashed dangerously, and the air became charged. "Seems like to me the last person we should trust is one whose personality is as slippery as a snake is all."

Sirius shot out of his seat and growled across the table at him. "How about you stand up and back up those words, you spineless…"

"That's enough!" I barked. I glared at Barak. "Sirius and his men fought just as hard during the Battle of Aurevel as you and yours. That is the reason he is a part of this council. Unless he becomes otherwise, he is an ally."

I glowered at Sirius until he retook his seat before turning to the Hesper and Hemera. Neither had spoken during this time, but the twins rarely did unless necessary. They'd been making their way through the surrounding cities and towns, taking out concealed clan soldiers, but maybe it was time to station them closer to home. Both nodded a confirmation to me.

"If we are to deal with the threat of the Blood Clan in Fenriel, we need to first wipe out the issue in Rifka. We know they have been concentrated in Aurevel and Siron since their presence has been removed from most of the other overrun cities, thanks to the twins." I folded my hands together in front of my face, thoughtfully.

"Since they remain hidden, maybe their hunters should be skilled in such as well." I lifted a brow at the twins. Eventually, I would need them to travel even further, but for now, Rifka was our priority.

Both inclined their heads. "We'll take care of it," Hesper said smoothly.

I nodded. "Good, what's next?"

"What about the queen's sister? What is being done about her?" Sirius grumbled.

Barak tensed. "She's none of your concern," he said quietly. Too quietly.

Tyrian and I shared a look. So that was what–or should I say *who*–had the male so bent out of shape.

"So, you worry about my fake betrayal, but protect the one who *did* betray our queen?" Sirius mocked, a twisted smile on his face.

"She's being dealt with," Barak gritted out.

"Oh? And what exactly are you using to *deal* with it, Barak?"

Lightning shot through his eyes, and the air became supercharged.

"The queen's sister is not your concern, Sirius," I said sharply, letting my darkness slip out enough to warn both males to stand down. "Silivia will deal with her when she's ready."

Sirius held up his hands. "Hey, I'm just concerned about the queen letting emotions blind her to a known threat."

"You should be worried about the threat right in front of you if you don't stay in your place," Ty commented evenly, his fingers tapping on the table.

I hid my surprise, not expecting him to speak up on Silivia's behalf with the tension still between them. The yellow-eyed male glanced from Barak to Tyrian, and back to me. Whatever he saw between us made him pale and lower his gaze.

"I see. Forgive me. Obviously, it has been handled."

"Well, okay then," Aux muttered. He glanced around the room. "If we're ready to move on, what about the elders?"

"What about them?" Rose asked, frowning.

"We should speak to them if we're thinking of taking on the Blood Clan for good. They are over the entirety of the Resisti, and we're going to need as many of them on our side as we can get."

I grimaced. We weren't on the best of terms with the elders at the moment. Not when we'd recruited Resisti to fight in a battle without consulting them. Then again, Silivia wouldn't have wanted them involved anyway after Master Marcus had blindly sent her to Rifka for the organization's own agenda. They'd needed the winged kingdom free of Isrella and the clan's influence and had been willing to sacrifice my mate to do so. Of course, if you were to ask Marcus, he'd say he knew she wouldn't survive in the end, but that didn't make what he'd done any more forgivable.

I was indebted to the male for what he'd done for Ty, Tess, and me in raising and training us after we lost everything, but he'd burnt a bridge with my mate I wasn't sure could be repaired.

"What if the elders don't agree to join us?" Raiden pointed out. He'd been watching his brother's responses closely up to this point, concern shadowing his eyes. "They've been against a direct approach to handling the clan for centuries now."

"We're already at war," Tyrian argued. "It has to end at some point, whether they believe we're ready to face them head-on or not."

"They just want to resolve this without unnecessary bloodshed," Rose said bitterly.

"I don't think that's an option anymore," Aux pointed out. "The clan has become too powerful. We saw what happened to Rifka. And it isn't just here. All of Fenriel is under attack. If we wait too long to act, there may not be a world to protect."

"He's right. Somehow, we need to convince the elders to join our cause," Ty said thoughtfully. He glanced at me. "They're going to want to test her first."

I scowled. "As if she hasn't been tested enough," I grumbled.

"You knew it would come to this eventually," Ty pointed out. "Only Marcus has met her as of yet, but with the prophecies…"

I grimaced. Yeah, the prophecies that told of the rising of the legendary blue phoenix–Silivia's spirit animal–and of the fate of Fenriel depending on the combination of her snow and ice…and my darkness and shadows.

"Fine. Aux, can you reach out to them and find out when and where?" I gritted out.

He inclined his head.

"One more thing, before we call it," Ty said, lifting a hand. He glanced at me. "We need to get the other kingdoms on board. The Resisti are scattered within them as well, and Rifka can't stand against the clan alone. We'll need their help."

I grimaced again. "Meaning we'll need to travel to both Farla and Hyra. We need Rifka under control before that can occur. Aux, I want you to travel with Sirius to Siron. We need to start flushing the clan out of there. The twins will be there soon to take out the rest. Raiden and Rose, you continue helping Tyrian with the interrogations and ensuring the royal guards and Rifka soldiers are prepared.

"The assassin twins will be in the shadows here as mentioned, while Teslia and Reese will use their combined charm to flush out anyone within the court who may be concealing clan followers. Barak, you will continue with the security of the queen's sister and your other assignment. Silivia and I will be handling the other political side of things."

I bit back a sigh and glanced around the table. They all nodded in acknowledgment.

"We'll take care of it," Raiden declared, though he glanced curiously at his brother.

Seemed as if Barak still hadn't told him the other reason I'd assigned the younger brother to watch over Dalacia. I'd hope he could connect with her in a way the rest of us could not and convince her to reveal clan secrets. But even if he could only convince the wayward female to reconnect with my mate as her sister again, I would take it, regardless of how I felt about her betrayal.

I nodded and stood. "Then let's reconvene at the end of the week for an update. I need to go check in with our queen."

Everyone rose and shuffled out of the room until only Ty and I remained. We were quiet for several moments. Things had been tense between us for months, but I knew it still wasn't as bad as the tension between him and my mate. I didn't regret Silivia finally choosing me as her mate, but I did regret that our hesitation to admit our true bond had caused mixed signals between her and my brother. He was still hurt, rightfully so, but I looked forward to when things settled among us.

Ty sighed. "Gods, I look forward to a day when the only problem we have is whose turn it is to cook. Preferably during a vacation back at the cabin."

I chuckled. We were definitely overdue for our yearly trip to the Selondian Forest.

"We get through this war, and I'll be the first to sign you up."

He bellowed out a laugh and slapped me on the back. I smiled, praying that day would come sooner rather than later, and that my family was intact when it did.

Chapter 3

A cage is a cage,
no matter how pretty.

Dalacia

I *hated her*. I hated that Dad had chosen her over me. I hated that the clan only wanted me so they could claim her. And most of all, I hated that despite the fire in my veins and a year of torturous training, I had still been bested by her.

I glared at the rooms that had become my prison. A fancy one, but a prison, nonetheless. Yes, the floors were soft, spiraled hardwood that flowed from room to room and was accented with luscious fur rugs. Yes, the living area featured sickly, comfortable couches and chairs of deep burgundy tastefully positioned around a fireplace. Yes, there was a balcony and windows with a beautiful view of the distant Fanged Mountains.

Yes, there was a small study with a library with yet another sickly, cozy fireplace. Yes, the bathroom was the largest I'd ever seen with an in-floor tub equipped with jets big enough for four people easily, *annnd* a giant shower. And of course, the bedroom featured a king-sized bed with the same dark burgundy sheets that were like sleeping on clouds and bed curtains out of a fairy tale. But each room had a downfall that I would never be able to forgive.

I raised my hands in front of my face from where I sat crosslegged on the bed. I focused hard, gritting my teeth so fiercely I thought they would crack, but no matter how hard I tried, I couldn't summon the flames...not even an ember. They'd coated this room with iron not long after I'd been defeated.

When asked why I'd been removed from my previous iron prison, my guards had only shrugged and said, "You're the queen's sister."

Queen. Not only did she have Dad's favor and the clan's desire, but she was also queen of our father's kingdom. A title that should have been mine. Not because I wanted it–I didn't–but because she got everything else. Why couldn't I have something too? I screamed in fury, tossing one of the many pillows adorning the bed across the room.

"My, my, my. Someone's fiery today."

My head shot up to meet the most intense, honey brown eyes I'd ever seen. Occasionally, a streak of lightning would shoot across them, similar to the lightning bolt scar that cut from his left eyebrow to his right cheek. His auburn hair was in a mohawk, shaved on the sides and long down the middle with a curled piece that tended to fall into his eyes. It fit him well. So did the daggers and blade down his back, which I heard was shaped like a lightning bolt as well. He wasn't as big as many of the lumbering males around here, but I'd seen for myself how capable he was in battle.

Barak. One of the Resisti warriors who stood with my sister in her fight for the throne. Even with that too smug smirk on his face, he was still the sexiest male I'd ever seen...not that I would tell him that.

I twisted my face into a disgusted scowl. "Go screw yourself."

He snorted. "That's all you got? You must be distracted today. Usually, I get at least one name cursed at me." His grin bordered on cruel as he continued to lean against my door frame, his arms and ankles crossed.

I ignored how his muscles bulged, making the veins along his arms pop. See, *sexy*. My eyes narrowed.

"Trust me, I can come up with all kinds of names for you." I sighed dramatically, holding my hand against my forehead. "But alas, I was raised to respect my elders."

Barak snorted a reluctant laugh, and a spark of triumph flashed through me, but the amusement didn't quite reach his eyes.

"Nice try. I may be two centuries your senior, give or take, but that's never stopped you in the past."

I stared at him silently, unable to conceal my surprise. I kept forgetting that Fae lived so long...that *I* was fated to live as long. Despite my mother being human, Dad was very much Fae and a powerful one at that, meaning I followed Fae rules. I scoffed to myself. Except the Fae in Fenriel didn't welcome halfbreeds who were part human. Grow up in the human world, and you're no better than animals in the forest. Sounded too familiar a concept to me.

"What do you care?" I snapped, still disgusted by the prejudice still present despite leaving the human world behind.

He shrugged. "I don't, but the queen likes weekly reports."

Right. *The queen* would want to know how her little captive was doing. Try to kill a person a couple times, and they give you a rotation of four Resisti warriors *and* four changeling guards to watch you nonstop. So sensitive. It was nothing personal. Except it very much was and is. Only this one ever actually entered the room, though. It made me wonder what he'd done to get burdened with watching over me.

"Well, you can tell sister dearest that if she really cares to know how I'm doing, she can come see for herself," I told him sweetly. I fluttered my eyelashes for emphasis.

"The queen has better things to do than come see the person who attempted to kill her and burn down Rifka." His eyes narrowed, and lightning shot across them. I could feel the charge in the air despite the iron that should smother it. "If I had it my way, you would still be an ice cube, or deep down in the cold, iron dungeons, not pampered in the royal suites."

Ahh. There was the hatred his teasing could never conceal. I glared back. "A cage is a cage, no matter how pretty," I snapped.

"Yeah, and a murderer is a murderer no matter how pretty."

"Aww, you think I'm pretty." I winked at him, and he bristled, the air in the room becoming even more charged. I waved a hand. "Besides, I didn't murder anyone."

"Not directly," Barak said through gritted teeth.

I scoffed. "There are always casualties in war, and I never *directly* killed any-one." I hadn't. I'd simply set the fires that burned down villages and cities. What happened afterwards was never my problem.

"Just because you try to justify your actions, doesn't make the lives you helped destroy go away. People *died*. Mythical creatures *died*. Your *sister* almost *died*."

He was fuming now, his hands in tight fists. I knew he'd been waiting to say this to me for a while. Could feel it in the casual way he'd spoken to me that he was simmering underneath. I'd seen the fury in his eyes despite the easy smirks he threw my way. In all my guards' eyes. They loathed me and loved her.

"Why should I care? They never cared about me and my family. Where were they when the Blood Clan killed both my parents and burned our house down? Where were they when I was kidnapped and tortured for months, forced to do the clan's bidding? Uh? *Where. Were. They?* So, why should I care if some people got to experience what it feels like to have your entire life go up in flames?"

At some point, I'd risen to my feet, and by the end of my rant, I was almost screaming in his face. Barak was silent for a while, his rage barely restrained. Then, he turned his back to me.

"You are nothing but a jealous, spoiled brat. Your world was destroyed, and yet you learned nothing. If you had, you would know inflicting misery on others doesn't change your own. It just feeds the plague. Until you learn that, you will always be the pawn in someone else's war and destined to remain in a cage."

Then he walked away. I heard the door slam, but I remained standing where I was. I screamed with pent-up rage, destroying everything I could reach until I was surrounded by destruction. It would be cleaned up by the morning, like every other time I'd destroyed the room. I was being smothered with kindness. Never had I wanted my flames as much as I did now. Maybe then I could use it to burn away this growing kernel of dread that maybe...just maybe...I'd been wrong.

Chapter 4

Trauma
leaves behind everlasting scars.
But scars are beautiful.
They mean you survived.

Barak

"You should stay away from her."

I turned away from the punching bag I'd been hammering mercilessly for the last half hour. Raiden glanced pointedly at my bruised and bleeding fists. Yeah, probably should have bandaged those.

"I'm one of her guards, remember? Can't exactly stay away by order of the king and queen." My tone was mocking as I walked over to the water pitchers, poured one over my head, and another half over my fists before drinking the rest.

"Yeah, but no one said you had to talk to her."

I scoffed. Talking to her was a strong enough description of our interactions. It felt more like a summer storm whenever we were together. One of those quick ones with thunderous clouds and lightning that drenched the world before blowing over like it never happened...minus the damage it left behind.

I scoffed. "You can always be the one to check in with *Her Highness*," I sneered. Yet, my stomach twisted uncomfortably. Somehow, the thought of my brother being the one to deal with Dalacia didn't sit well.

Raiden held his hands up in surrender. "Naw, I'd rather observe from a distance. That girl is a wildfire ready to happen."

That's exactly what she was and, unfortunately for me, a gorgeous one at that. I wish I didn't notice how she kept her long, dark brown curls half up and framing those angry blue eyes and smooth caramel skin. I definitely wish I didn't notice the way her body was like a dancer–or a flickering flame–graceful and curvy.

Gods. That's what made this so damn hard. I was furious that she could destroy her family's kingdom. Furious that she could spit on the importance of family so royally that she would try to kill her own sister. And I was furious with myself, because despite all of that, I saw her pain hidden behind all that anger, and a small part of me wanted to take it away.

"She has a reason to be," I muttered bitterly.

Raiden raised a brow incredulously. "Are you defending her now?" he asked in disbelief.

I sighed. "No, I'm just saying…" What was I saying? That she was right to give in to her jealousy? The Blood Clan? That she had a right to be a part of so much suffering over the last few months?

"I'm just saying there's always two sides to the story," I finished lamely. I had to give my older brother credit. He's open-minded enough to accept that comment. I mean, had we not been through enough hell ourselves growing up? Had we not witnessed the hell Reese went through with the late queen, his mother? Trauma changes people. Didn't mean it had to remain a negative change.

Was this why Ghost had specifically asked me to get close to the princess? Did he think that having an older sibling would make me more relatable? Or was it because he somehow knew about my past and thought I could reach her through her scars?

I thought back to the pain I saw beyond those blazing, blue eyes. Dalacia hadn't had an ally, a true friend, since her parents were murdered. What if the way to reach the princess was to give her the one thing she'd never received? Acknowledgement of who *she* was. In order for that to happen, someone had to stop and listen long enough to learn who that was. What if that someone was me? I glanced up at the knowing look in my brother's eyes.

"Going to listen to her side?"

I stared him down. Did he know, or had he simply guessed? He had the uncanny ability of reading between the words I did say to those I didn't.

"A fire doesn't rage without someone first lighting it."

Raiden considered me for a second, then nodded once. "If anyone can walk into the fire and not get burned, it'll be you."

I grinned wickedly, lightning flashing across my eyes. Fire didn't fear fire after all.

Chapter 5

They wanted you,
You said to me.
Save her,
You pleaded.
But what if,
she doesn't want to be saved?

Silivia

Long live the queen.

I stared out over the balcony at the garden and forest below. Oh, how I wished that my only worry was getting lost in the hedge maze as I hid from all the responsibilities of this crown. I thought I knew what I was getting into when I completed the five trials to convince the world that I was the late King Fariel's true heir. I thought I was ready to be responsible for an entire kingdom. I thought I was ready to face my sister...but I was wrong. *Gods* was I wrong.

I tried not to think about how my sister now lived in iron-padded rooms until I built up the courage to deal with her, because deal with her I must. But how do you deal with blood that attempts to kill you multiple times? How do you balance her punishment with your dying father's wish to save her?

So instead, I avoided her. What kind of sister did that make me? It'd been a month since I turned her into an icicle, and yet I couldn't bring myself to do more than get a report from Barak about her status every couple of days.

I sighed and turned away from the window. I could use the attacks on the city as an excuse. The fire earlier this week could have been worse than it was. I could blame the reworking of the council, or my training on running this castle, this kingdom. But there weren't enough excuses in the world to make what I needed to do less daunting...or less necessary.

I gritted my teeth and strolled to the door. Swinging it open, I met the questioning glances of my guards, Farek and Uther. Their large wings shifted slightly, already preparing for my next move. The royal guards were all changelings, warriors who usually guarded royalty or important people. They were ruthless in battle, and considering most had special abilities as well, they were valuable allies. Apparently, the royalty protected now included me. Go figure.

"Heading out?" Farek asked.

He and his older brother, Lorik, were my main guards. While the captain had a full head of dreads, Farek chose to shave the sides and only have dreads in a mohawk down the middle.

I closed my fists and opened them again as I considered how to answer him. I took a deep breath. "Yes," I finally managed. "Take me to see my sister."

Both males tensed. To say many weren't fans of Dalacia would be an understatement.

"As you wish, Your Majesty," he said quietly with a shrug.

"We talked about this, Farek," I reminded him, ignoring the rage I could see rumbling just under the surface. That was not something *I* could remove.

He grinned. "As you wish, Silivia." I smiled back, but it quickly faded as he led me to the other side of the castle, where she was kept. Too soon, we were stopping in front of her rooms.

"Silivia," Barak greeted me, surprise on his face. "Wasn't expecting you today."

"Hi, Barak. It wasn't planned, but I can't avoid her forever."

"Fair enough." He put a hand on the door as the other Resisti warrior and two royal guards shifted out of the way. "Ready?"

I took a deep breath and nodded. He swung the door open, and he, along with my own guards, followed me in. The others remained outside. I indicated for Barak, Farek, and Uther to wait at the door as I walked further into my sister's living space. Despite their obvious hesitation, they nodded and leaned against the wall, their distrustful gazes lasered on my sister.

The female sitting crosslegged on the couch with a book in her lap could be mistaken for the innocent little sister I grew up with. At least until she lifted her head and irate peacock blue eyes glared into mine.

"Oh, so I finally warrant a visit from the great Phoenix Queen herself," she taunted. "Whatever have I done to deserve such an honor?"

The males at my back stiffened, and I heard multiple soft growls.

"Hello to you too, sis. Glad to see you've had some time to cool off," I said smoothly.

Her eyes flashed. "My, my. Give her a crown, and suddenly she has all the confidence in the world," Dalacia sneered.

"You know nothing about what comes along with said crown, little sister. There's a reason one of the oldest, not the youngest, is chosen."

She narrowed her eyes. "Surely, you're not claiming that so-called brother of ours."

"Why not? He's been more like family in the last few months than you have," I replied with a shrug.

"He tried to kill you."

"No, his mother did. The sibling-on-sibling attempted murder title is still firmly in your hands."

"But did you die, though?"

I glared at her, feeling ice on my tongue, but unable to let it out. I really detested the feeling of the iron.

"No thanks to you!" I snapped. "One would think you wanted to stay in these rooms forever."

"What? Are you offering to let me fight by your side if I repent?"

"You could have *been* fought on my side, but yes, if you repent of your crimes, you can work to erase the reputation you've formed for yourself. You can use your newfound abilities for something good this time."

"And why would you offer that?" she scoffed skeptically.

"Because, regardless of what's happened over the last year and a half, you are still my sister."

She was quiet for a long time and just stared at me. I hoped she was considering my offer. As angry as I was at Dalacia, I was angrier at myself because it was indirectly my fault that she'd fallen into the clan's hands in the first place.

"I'll think about it," she said eventually. "But don't expect me to embrace brother dearest."

"I don't," I assured her. "But I do hope you decide to get to know him. May find that you like him more than you think. I did."

"I'm not you, big sis. I think that has been made abundantly clear," she muttered bitterly.

My heart clenched, but I shrugged. "Even still." I turned and exited the room, Barak and the guards with me. I exhaled heavily as the door closed.

"Well, that went better than expected," Barak mumbled.

I glanced at him and lifted a brow. He didn't say anything more, but I got the distinct feeling there was more going on between the male and my sister. Who knows, maybe she'll find her spiritbonded too, and he can help guide her home as mine has.

"Siblings will be siblings," I stated, walking away. And someday, if God willed it, we will act as sisters again.

Chapter 6

Bind me.

Judge me.

But you will not break me.

Dalacia

"What are those?" I stared down at the iron bracelets Barak held in his hands. They were thin with an intricate design, almost as if someone had tried to make them pretty.

Barak looked uncomfortable holding them, but stared at me with a wicked gleam in his eyes. "It's your ticket out of this room. The queen commissioned them so you can explore the castle and the grounds without concern." He shot me a look.

I rolled my eyes. In other words, I wouldn't have access to my abilities, but I could wander around. Seemed like someone was feeling guilty after their little visit a few days ago. Oh, whoopie doo.

Barak grinned as if reading my mind. "I could always find some iron chains instead. I do love the sound of shuffling irons in the morning."

I sneered at him, but I wanted out of this room, so I held out my wrists. "Not like I have a choice," I spat.

He winked. "Nope."

The last place I expected him to take me was to the gym, but it was a welcome sight. I didn't realize how desperately I needed an outlet until I was wrapping my fists and hammering it out on the punching bag. I did so for several minutes, distantly aware of the male leaning against the wall as he watched me, and the guards who'd followed us. I expected Barak to rush me through the tour of the rest of the castle, but instead, after a while, he moved to the opposite side of the room and started this intricate, controlled dance with his long blade. Turns out, it really was in the shape of a golden lightning bolt with an ebony handle.

He moved with more feline grace than I expected of a man with over six feet of muscle, but his every strike, step, and slide was indicative of the warrior he was. I didn't even realize I'd stopped my workout to watch him until his blazing gaze met mine and held. A slow, knowing grin lifted his lips as he straightened and rested his blade on his shoulder.

"Like what you see, princess?" He asked with obnoxious male ego. I snorted and turned back to the punching bag.

"Not even close," I answered, continuing my one-two strikes. "I was just looking for any weaknesses to take advantage of."

It was something I should have been doing, instead of watching how his biceps tightened and shifted, how his hair fell into his face, and the scar there stretched while he concentrated. I definitely shouldn't have been thinking of tracing said scar with my fingers or feeling the shift of those muscles underneath my hands.

I shook my head to clear it. You would think him being my enemy would be enough to keep my libido under control, but it felt like there was this irrational pull towards him. I despised him with all my being, if only because he followed my sister, but something deeper wanted to answer the call his presence seeped into my blood.

Barak chuckled. "Whatever you say, fire girl." I spun to face him, feeling said fire brimming under my skin, fighting to get out.

"You better be glad this 'fire girl's' power is contained, or she'd roast your tail so well you wouldn't be able to sit for a week."

His eyes darkened as he stalked towards me, a wicked grin on his face. Suddenly feeling like cornered prey, I retreated until my back hit the punching bag, but before I could scoot around it, he had me pinned with a hand on either side of my head.

"What would you know about roasting tail?" he growled, then scanned me up and down. "And do you have the moves to back up that fiery mouth of yours?"

I growled back at him and shoved his chest. He didn't move an inch, and his grin widened, becoming more deadly. I fought the shiver rolling down my spine, and the air became charged as lightning shot across his eyes.

"Want to fight, Princess?"

I glared back at him, refusing to back down despite my powers being locked. I'd been trained for the last year and a half in more than fire work.

"You're not ready to fight me," I sneered.

His eyes assessed me again, and I bristled at the look that said he found me lacking. He stepped away with a snort of disgust.

"No, it's you who's not ready to fight me. I'm over two centuries old. There are many things you've yet to learn."

I scoffed. "And what? You're going to teach me?" I turned away from him, purposely giving him my back, even though it went against every instinct in my being to do so. Regardless of all my training, he had been fighting longer than I'd been alive. That didn't mean I didn't have a few tricks up my sleeve, but it did mean I needed him to let his guard down. It was the only way I would successfully escape this castle.

So, I ignored him as I unwrapped my hands. When he'd still said nothing, I turned back to face him. He was considering me, his arms folded, but I couldn't tell what he was thinking. Then he shrugged.

"My queen will want to know what you're capable of anyway, and I need to keep in shape. Might as well kill two birds with one stone. We'll add daily training to your schedule. First thing in the morning. Think you can handle that, *Princess*?" He turned and stalked away.

I sneered at his back. The last thing I wanted to do was train every day with this bastard, but it would give me an opportunity to assess his skills. And I did need to stay in shape for when I got out of here. I sped after him as he left the room and headed down the hall, the guards moving to shadow us.

"Sure. It'll be a great opportunity to see if you're really all that you think you are," I teased mockingly.

Barak shot me a look and then faced forward. "We start tomorrow."

We spent the rest of the afternoon touring the castle and its grounds. He pointed out the royal suites in the eastern part of the castle, although he didn't take me there. I was told it was essentially an entire house all on its own with three massive bedrooms, a library slash office, a sitting and dining area, and a balcony that let out into a private garden.

There were three other suites in the castle. The north, where I stayed, just so happened to also house the Resisti Seven and any other Resisti members within the castle. I was under more guard than I knew. I gritted my teeth in frustration at the thought.

The south housed the castle guests, and the west, the rest of the staff. I was shown the massive throne room with several large platforms for winged beasts such as dragons to perch. One such platform sat right above the twisted metal thrones where my sister and the King of Shadows likely sat. I fought the wave of fiery rage at the thought, but took in the intricate designs weaving the pillars of the room, admiring the artwork that went into its décor despite myself. They depicted various winged creatures, of which only a few I was able to identify, such as the dragons and griffins.

I was then shown the kitchens where many were busy at work preparing the meal for dinner, and then the dining hall where all residents of the castle, from the staff to the guests, were encouraged to mingle. One large oak table sat along the back of the room with two massive chairs directly in the center, likely for the king and queen. There were ten other chairs there, for my sister's companions, the prince, and the Resisti Seven. Although, Barak explained, they tended to sit wherever they pleased during meals.

Next was a library with winding bookshelves that reached the ceiling, tall windows that allowed fresh air and the vining plants to thrive, and another giant platform for winged beasts. There were countless other rooms that I soon lost track of before we wandered the grounds briefly. Off the courtyard were the horse stables on one side and the winged stables on the other.

The winged stable was so large that it went further than my eyes could see as it wound around to the other side of the castle. It was also positioned higher up since most of the winged didn't like camping on the ground. Barak explained how each stall was equipped with a sliding ceiling so the winged could fly out at any point to hunt or exercise, and was triggered by their presence so that it opened when they returned.

There were several gardens that we didn't have time to explore, but the last thing he showed me was the training grounds where many of the royal guards and soldiers were busy doing drills. Throughout the tour, I couldn't help noticing the repairs being done after the battle that had taken my freedom.

I also noticed an increase in the guards with various wing colors, but similar rugged clothing, patrolling. They hadn't been present when I'd first visited the castle while Queen Isrella still ruled. I didn't miss the glares of distrust and hatred thrown my way as we moved throughout the castle. I had a feeling that if Barak wasn't by my side, many would happily show me their opinion on my decisions over the last few months.

By the time we finally returned to my room, my feet hurt, and I was so tense I thought my muscles were going to freeze up from holding them so tightly.

"What was the point of that?" I snapped at Barak as soon as we entered my suite.

His eyes were cold as he met my gaze. "To give you a tour of the castle as your sister requested." His eyes darkened menacingly. "And to remind you that you're not with the clan anymore. You won't get away with that BS that you've been relishing for the last few months. Your actions have consequences, and there are many here who would love to show you which ones."

I folded my arms defiantly. "And is that supposed to endear me to dear old sis and convince me to join her side?"

He turned away with an obvious display of dismissal. "No, but if you insist on refusing the olive branch my queen has so generously offered you, you will spend the rest of your miserable life alone, surrounded by the reminder of the hatred you nourished and continue to nourish with your misplaced hostility and loyalty. Think on that, Princess."

And then, he was gone with a slam of my door, and I was once again left alone in the middle of the floor with no idea which way was up.

Chapter 7

Silivia

"The lords are restless and uneasy. Likely due to fear of whatever changes you will continue to make now that you're queen. Remember, they've had a loose leash for a long time."

I sighed as the council member explained the state of our alliances within Rifka. He frowned down at the lengthy paper detailing their concerns. Apparently, it was too big an ask to have a smooth transition. No, I was still dealing with the consequences of removing the council members who'd so openly opposed me, not trusting them at my back or side. The elder who'd led them was a foul one who still made his displeasure and loathing known despite no longer holding the position. I knew there were others around the table who still sought him out. Although they didn't make my life as difficult as some of the others who downright refused to follow me. It was why major discussions and decisions were only made within my inner council and brought to the royal council afterwards.

Unfortunately, to keep the favor of the people, I couldn't remove everyone I didn't like from Rifka's council. The knowledge had me grateful for the royal guards at my back— at least I'd won their loyalty–and my brother and friends. I glanced over to my right to see Reece frowning as he nodded at something the council member was still explaining. My brother appeared relaxed, but the turbulence in his eyes behind unruly, black hair gave him away. He was as displeased as I was to find the level of corruption he'd been living with, but never acknowledged.

I knew he still felt guilty for blindly following his mother's decrees without questioning the suspicious decisions she and the council had been responsible for. But then, she had been his queen, and more importantly, his mother. Despite the abuse she'd inflicted on him all his life, I couldn't blame my brother for being desperate for the motherly love she'd cruelly withheld.

I glanced to my left to find Tyrian scowling, his fist clenched as he studied the crimes some of the lords of Rifka were responsible for. They'd knowingly allowed clan soldiers to come in and kidnap power users and destroy villages and cities under their protection. Much like Ty's own family had been attacked when they should have been safe behind Rifka's shielded forest. The betrayal did not sit well with the burly warrior, and I couldn't fault him for the anger marring his face.

Same as I couldn't fault him for his newfound hatred of me. My heart clenched painfully, and I met Teslia's gaze across the table. She gave me a sad, knowing smile as she glanced between Ty and me. I fought a sigh. I didn't know if the male and I would ever be okay again, but I admired his ability to put aside any animosity between us to stabilize Rifka.

"What would you have us do, Your Majesty?"

I blinked, realizing I'd stopped listening and now every expectant gaze around the table was on me. I swallowed, uncomfortable as I fought the desire to squirm under their scrutiny. I shot pleading eyes to Ty. I was crap at this battle talk, and I knew the team had already discussed an approach for this. He must have been feeling merciful today because he turned and explained our plan for flushing out the clan supporters.

"And the lords whom we know have supported the clan? What is your plan for them?" one of the female councilmen asked, her hands steepled on the table as she addressed me.

Her expectant look reminded me that I may not be good at every part of being queen as of yet, but I needed to stop shying away from the authority I now held, or I would lose it. And my friends and I had worked too hard to win back my father's throne for me to lose it now.

I sat up straighter and met her gaze. "They will be given a trial. If they are found guilty, depending on the severity of their involvement, they will either serve their time assisting the rebuild of Rifka, or be exiled."

There were murmurs of acknowledgment and reluctant approval around the table.

A male with red eyes and long spiraling horns pinned me with a speculative look. "I am surprised you wouldn't simply lock them away in the dungeons or have them executed," he said evenly. "Not all will take to their punishment peacefully."

I nodded to the toro, impressed that such a quick-tempered species held a spot on the council. That reason alone was enough to protect his position. We underdogs had to stick together after all.

"I will not have that be our only options, but yes, I realize some will have crimes too severe for release at all. They will be dealt with as needed."

The toro nodded in approval. Thankfully, the meeting wrapped up pretty quickly after that, and I stood and spoke to anyone who wished to until no one but the toro and my friends remained. Reece rushed off with a promise to catch up with me later.

"Well said, Phoenix Queen. You have matured surprisingly fast in your role."

I turned to face him and inclined my head. "Thank you, Gilus. I take that as a compliment."

The sound of tumbling stones filled the room as he chuckled. "As you should. I realize we have not made it easy for you since you became queen. You thought yourself only human, not too long ago, no?"

I nodded. Hard to believe it had only been about a year and a half. It felt so much longer.

"You should be proud of all you have accomplished so far. You have much more ahead of you." He eyed my friends and the guards behind me. "Remember to lean on those who have your back in the coming times. It is not a weakness to need help, but to refuse it when it is offered."

I bowed to him in respect. "Thank you. I will remember your wise words."

Red, intelligent eyes studied me closely. "I believe that you and your mate are about to turn this world on its axis. I look forward to seeing what remains when the ash settles."

Shivers of apprehension raced down my spine as I stared with wide eyes as he strode from the room.

"Well, that was intense," Tess breathed.

Understatement of the century. I fought another shudder. His words clearly referenced the prophecy that could either be the end or a new beginning for Fenriel as a whole. I prayed that it was the latter.

Chapter 8

I hated her,
not just because of what she'd done,
but for the reminder
of what *I'd* done.

Barak

Her cries of frustration were music to my ears. Seeing her fight to keep her cool was beyond entertaining. Although I could tell she had indeed been trained, she had the confidence of one who'd never truly fought a seasoned opponent.

"Come now, Princess," I mocked. "I was under the impression you were trained by the best. Were they holding back to let you win all that time?"

I saw a flash of pain before dark rage masked it, and she was swinging wildly at my face. I dodged it, only to be quickly met with a roundhouse kick. I barely dodged that before I was dodging another and another. She became a whirlwind of kicks and punches until I was raising my brows in surprise. She had speed that some masters couldn't manage, and it was graceful and controlled. Correction. Maybe it was *she* who'd been holding back. But why? *Wait.*

I quickly dodged out of her way, moving faster than she was prepared for, so that I came up behind her. Before she knew what had happened, I had a dagger to her throat and another to her side.

"Cheater," she spat, chest heaving as she kept herself still to prevent the blade from cutting into her.

"I never said I wouldn't use them. Only that you couldn't," I reminded her sweetly. I froze in surprise when I felt something poke between my legs.

"Oh, so is now a bad time to mention I stole one of your blades?" she replied just as sweetly.

I glanced down to find her threatening my manhood with my own dagger. I blinked, grudgingly impressed. I snorted. "Well played, Princess," I muttered, letting her go. My eyes narrowed at Dalacia spun to give me a wicked grin, spinning my dagger in her fingers.

"Bet you didn't see that coming, uh?"

I lifted a brow. "I'm more interested in why you felt the need to hold back in the first place."

She shrugged. "It's not my fault you underestimated me. I told you that they spent time training me specifically."

A darkness crossed over her eyes, and something inside me clenched in answer. There was more she wasn't saying, but what?

"Oh yeah? Who trained you? I may need to challenge him to a fight."

Her eyes grew even darker and distant...but also hazy as if they'd glazed over into a memory she'd rather forget. Oh yeah, there was definitely something else going on here.

She waved a hand dismissively. "Don't worry about it. You wouldn't know him."

I narrowed my eyes, but hers had cleared again as if she'd wiped the pain from them with sheer will. Interesting. Needing more time to consider how to convince her to talk, I decided to call it a day. I needed to go on patrol in the city anyway.

"Come, Princess. You get to keep your secrets for a little bit longer." She scowled at me, but I only laughed as I led her back to her rooms.

"Do you get the feeling that this is the quiet before the storm?" Raiden mused.

I turned to him as we strolled through Aurevel's streets a few weeks later. Everywhere you looked, you could see the damage Queen Isrella and the clan had inflicted on the city. Yes, we were rebuilding, and the blood had mostly been washed from the cobblestones, but the scars remained.

You could see it in the wary eyes of the people who watched us as if we would defect to the clan's side at any moment. It didn't matter that we wore the symbol of the Resisti on one sleeve—a phoenix holding an olive branch—and of the winged throne on the other. Even the ancient symbol carved into the wrist of every Resisti warrior, meaning ally, did little to ease their distrust. It was something that would take time.

I frowned as one of our men assisted an old Fae female with rebuilding her destroyed stand. There was a mixture of gratitude and unease as she did, as if he would build it only to destroy it again. The story was the same no matter what we did or said. I couldn't stop the tightness in my chest, knowing that many others continued to suffer simply because they didn't trust us to help them.

"Barak?"

I blinked, realizing I'd never answered my brother's question. "Sorry, Raid. I'm a little out of it today."

He studied me worriedly. "Because of her or because of this city?" I fought the grimace but didn't quite master it before he was nodding knowingly. "Yeah, figured as much." My big brother eyed me, his dark eyes pensive. "You going to tell me about this secret assignment now or what?"

I sighed. It wasn't what was bothering me at the moment, but maybe it would help to talk it out.

"I wasn't hiding it from you on purpose. Ghost and Silivia didn't say I couldn't tell you."

Raiden frowned. "And yet you haven't."

"I thought you'd figured it out already."

He shrugged. "I believe I have, but I still want you to tell me yourself."

I grimaced, scanning the streets for people who seemed out of place. The citizens will feel better—as will I—when we've finally removed the clan members still concealed in our city. It still boggled my mind how Isrella allowed them to implant so deeply. It was a betrayal I wouldn't soon forgive. Just like another such betrayal.

"They wanted me to get close to Dalacia and see if I could convince her to reveal clan secrets. The locations we don't know about. The agendas we haven't accounted for. And most importantly..."

Raiden lifted a brow. "And most importantly?"

I glanced at him, finally speaking out loud what had really started to bother me. "Don't you find it odd that *she* was chosen specifically? She said she was separated from the clan soldiers and trained extensively, but I think there's more to it than that."

Raiden frowned as he considered the implications of what I'd implied. "We know she was trained to kill Silivia," he pointed out.

But I shook my head. "See, that's what I don't get. The clan wants Silivia on their side, not dead. Her kind of power is what they live for. I think Dalacia was actually meant to bring her sister back. I think more went on during this training than we know."

Raiden suddenly froze in the middle of the path. He turned to me with wide eyes. "You think she was trained by whoever leads the clan. The same one who's been after Ghost all these centuries."

I nodded slowly, the tightening in my gut telling me I was right, even if I'd been unable to unearth any other information to support it.

"I think it's the same one who's to blame for taking Dalacia in the first place. Their men screwed up by taking the wrong sister, but I don't think it was a coincidence that Silivia's sister was used against her."

Pained understanding crossed his face, and he took a step towards me. "Barak..."

Shouts went up around us as a band of clan soldiers spilled onto the street, scattering the city residents as they did. Blood splattered the ground as they cut down anyone who got in their way.

"What the hell? Where did they come from?" Raiden exclaimed as he drew his blade.

I drew my own and spun it, lightning shooting down the shimmering metal. "Does it matter?"

We raced into the fray, the others behind us, as we directed the residents away and met the clan soldiers head-on. There were roughly fifteen of them and five of us, but it was over much quicker than I would have liked. My blood was still screaming for theirs when the last one was cut down before me. Well, all but one.

"Where are the others?" Raiden demanded from the Fae male kneeling before him.

Another Resisti warrior held a blade to his throat, but the clan soldier only speared my brother with a hateful glare.

"I'll tell you nothing but of your pending doom, Resisti bastard, so you might as well slit my throat now," he spat.

"You sure you don't want to rethink those words?" Raiden replied through gritted teeth.

The soldier grinned. "You sure your so-called queen is safe in her bed at night?"

My eyes widened in shock, and I couldn't stop the male if I wanted to as he slit the soldier's throat then and there.

"He could have told us more," Raiden snapped.

"Or he could have continued to spew trash about our queen," the warrior argued. "Trust me, I doubt Ghost or Tyrian will fault me."

He wasn't wrong. In fact, I thought the soldier got off easy in comparison.

Raiden snorted in disgust and waved his hand at the bodies now littering the once clear street. "Let's get this cleaned up so we can report to the king and queen."

But as I listened to the moans and groans of the injured, and stared at the dead males before us, I wondered if we were fighting a losing battle.

"Barak?"

I lifted my head to find my brother watching me worriedly again. I blinked in confusion. When had we returned to the castle?

"Are you alright?"

I wasn't, but what right did I have to be freaking out right now when others had it so much worse? So, what if everything lately kept tossing me back into memories I'd rather not relive?

I hated the look in my brother's eyes. The look that said his little brother was losing it again. I couldn't afford to. So many more people depended on me now. I was a part of the dream team. I worked with legends like the Shadow King himself. I couldn't afford these setbacks.

But their screams. The blood on the streets. Another town long ago the same. Another time when it had been *my fault*.

"Go, little brother. I'll handle the report. Get your mind right."

I nodded, not able or willing to discard the olive branch he extended. I knew he would come by later to check on me, but for now, I needed a moment to remind myself that I was no longer that helpless male who'd almost lost it all. And Aurevel wouldn't fall, not if I had anything to say about it.

Chapter 9

I hear him.
The voice in the shadows,
encouraging me to rule.
To Destroy.

Ghost

The shadows ebbed and flowed before me, but they did not feel like my own. There was a presence there that wasn't mine, but with a taste of the darkness I was used to feeling. I edged closer, wondering if this was my mind telling me something, or my power as it truly was. This ominous presence that whispered for me to do what I willed...what I wanted. That familiar pull to just wipe the board clean.

What if that was what it took to finally weed out the evil that had seeped through my home? It had taken so much from me, and it would take so much more if it could. It was the reason I'd become the shadows, the darkness. To face it head-on. To defeat your ultimate enemy, you have to become worse than they were. At least... that's what I used to think.

I looked down at my feet and back at the shadows, seeing the many battles I'd fought, the damage I'd wrought, and I reveled in it. But I frowned, because unlike before, it felt...empty. Like I'd been fighting for the right thing with the wrong mindset.

"No," the shadows whispered. "Not empty. Your right. They deserve to feel your pain. They deserve to *die.*"

My right. *My brows scrunched, unsure. I would never regret the clan soldiers I'd killed. Never lose sleep over their blood coating my skin like a badge of honor. But the innocent...*

"Not innocent," *the shadows whispered again.* "Tainted. Corrupted. Destroy."

It would be so easy. So very easy to do. All I had to do was remove the leash from my full power. The darkness that always roiled in my core was only ever unleashed slightly to devour my enemies, but it wanted more. Needed *more. What if I was wrong? What if I needed to let it go? What if...*

"Yessss," the shadows cooed. "Desstroy."

My power shifted, hearing its call, wanting out. I could feel it leaking out around me, my hold on it loosening as my resolve did.

"Step away, my son."

I froze. It couldn't be. He was dead. *Taken from me when I was still too young to know him. Too young to save him. Too weak, just as I'd been to save my mother and sister.*

"Look at me."

The shadows implored me not to, but I spun to face powerful, golden eyes. The only other pair I'd ever seen in all of Fenriel was in the mirror. Seeing them mirrored back at me in a much older face with short, black hair and long black wings was unnerving. Over four centuries dead, and he was still the most imposing male I'd ever seen, and I'd only seen him in paintings and as statues.

"Father?" I asked, feeling as if I was that little boy again, huddled in the trunk of a tree waiting for the clan to finish destroying my home.

"Daniel."

My heart clenched, and I felt tears pool in my eyes. No one had called me that since I was a child...not until I gifted my true name to my mate.

"My son, you have to step away."

I frowned and glanced back to see just how close I was to falling into the mass of shadows still whispering for me.

"They are not your own, and if you fall into them, you will be lost. Step away, Daniel."

"But..." I couldn't help whispering. Would that be so bad? I wouldn't have to feel this centuries-old guilt and pain. I could forget. I could stop them.

"You would lose more than your pain. You would lose everything. Everything you have fought for. Everything you value. Every good thing you've created by destroying those who would see this world watered with blood and tears."

Those last words jolted me, reminding me of a familiar phrase. The prophecy.

"And you would lose her." *I turned to face him.* "I regretted not being able to raise you as I wanted, and maybe someday you will understand why, but I will never regret my love. Even with all the pain in the world, she and my darling children were always worth it."

I studied the darkness around me, considering his words.

"She sees you, my son. When the world becomes too dark. When the shadows speak, she *sees you still* and does not run. What does that tell you?"

I frowned deeper, my eyes imploring him to tell me because I knew I was missing a key detail here that I desperately needed.

"You are the King of Shadows, but you are not lost to the darkness. You command it, not follow it. They are your weapon of choice, not your yielding hand. She sees your light and nurses it with her own. But if you fall into those shadows, my son, you lose her forever."

The silver bond screamed in my core, the very thought too much to bear. I'd thought I'd lost her already once before. I'd felt the residual pain from what it would feel like to have a spiritbond break, and that had been debilitating. I never wanted to feel that again. I never wanted to feel that empty again. I stepped away from the shadows until I stood at my father's side. I was as tall as he was now, so I met his gaze head-on.

"What are they?"

His golden eyes darkened with sadness and regret. "A mistake I should have destroyed long before it touched you. Promise me you will always fight it. If not for your own sake, then for your mate's."

The silver bond hummed, and despite my confusion, I nodded. "I swear."

He smiled at me then and turned away. "I am proud to call you my son," *he said over his shoulder.*

I closed my eyes, letting the truth of his words wash over me. When I opened them again, I was alone, and the foreign shadows were gone.

I jarred awake, sweat slicking my skin as I panted, gripping the sheets in a desperate attempt to settle the unease racing through my veins. I wished I could say that was a dream, but I knew I couldn't. It wasn't the first time I'd felt the pull of darkness that wasn't my own, but this was the first time it had felt almost desperate, as if it was losing its chance to sway me. But seeing my father...

I glanced at Silivia at my side, her hair fanned out across the pillow, her mouth slightly open as she slept. Peaceful. Unaware of the battle within my mind. A battle I was afraid of losing, because this time I had so much more to lose. I will fight like my father bade me. I'll fight for the sake of the beautiful, snow queen at my side who'd wiped my soul clean. And I'll fight for myself, because I'd found something worth living in the light for.

Silivia shifted, a frown marring her face even as her eyes remained closed. "Ghost?" she whispered as if hearing my turmoil.

Smiling slightly, I lay back down beside her and pulled her into my arms. With her head resting on my chest against my heart, she settled again with a sigh, and I let her presence ease me back to sleep.

Chapter 10

I want to forget
because when I remember
I'm forced to face the truth...
I. Did. Nothing.

Dalacia

I could hear their screams. Dad was fighting back as the robed man behind me clutched me roughly. Another robed figure was wrestling with Mom.

"Mom!" I cried, watching them backhand her so that she hit the floor. The cry distracted Dad, and I watched as they stabbed him in the gut. "Dad!"

He still fought though. He was outnumbered, but he still fought with all he had. Even Mom was fighting, her fists and feet kicking as they beat her. And what did I do? Nothing. I stood there helpless. Useless. There was nothing my mom could do against the many hands ripping her clothes and slicing at her arms. I didn't know when it had started, but the fire around us raged on as the battle continued around me.

"Get your hands off her!" my dad roared, tearing them off her just for them to attack him again.

It was in slow motion that I watched the blade enter him from behind. My strong, unrelenting father fell to his knees. His bloody lips still cursing the monsters around us, his eyes only for my mother.

Not once did he look at me.

My mother screamed, and I spun to face her as I watched one robed figure backhand her so hard, something snapped. The fight instantly left her, and the anguish that tore through me was mind-numbing. I couldn't even make a sound as I watched the men drop her unceremoniously to the ground. As they stabbed my father once more for good measure, until he collapsed, still reaching for her.

I did nothing as they dragged me away from them. From the broken, lifeless body of my mother and the heartbroken, bleeding body of my father. He didn't look at me as they dragged me out the door. Why would he? I'd let them into our home, and I hadn't fought back. I hadn't known how. Whose fault was that? Mine? Theirs?

Finally, realizing they were taking me away from my family, I screamed. I couldn't stop even when they growled at me to do so. Even when they dragged me to the forest that used to be our refuge. Even when they tossed me into a black carriage so that I fell against the unforgiving floor. Only then did I fight, trying desperately to get out of the carriage.

"Silvee!" Where was my sister? Why hadn't she helped me? Why hadn't he looked at me? It was my last thought before something hard met the back of my head and everything went dark.

I could still hear the screams as I bolted upright in bed. I couldn't breathe fast enough. Couldn't get my heart rate to slow for anything. I needed out. Jumping from the bed, I quickly threw on some pants and a shirt. Then I was racing for the door, banging on it with all my might. I didn't care what time it was or if he hated me or not. I needed him to be there.

Please be here, I thought desperately.

The door flung open, and I jumped back as Barak burst in. He sneered down at me, taking in my attire.

"What!" he snapped irritably.

I didn't care. "I need to go to the gym." I sounded unhinged even to myself, but if I didn't get out of this room right now, I was going to explode. "*Please*, I need to go right now."

He frowned. Maybe it was the plea and lack of my normal attitude, but he stared at me for a second before giving a single nod. A shot of relief went through me as he gestured for me to come along. As we made our way through the wing to the gym, I didn't miss how he told the rest of the guards to stay. They didn't seem happy about it, but being in the king and queen's inner circle, he outranked them. He didn't say anything to me as I nearly jogged to the gym, and I ignored him. He'd already done what I needed him to do. He could go to hell now for all I cared.

I'd barely entered the room before I was strapping on the boxing gloves. I was panting, and I hadn't even hit anything yet. I still couldn't get enough air in. I couldn't stop my heart from pounding out of my chest. I couldn't stop the scenes from playing in my head. They were giving way to memories of my training with the clan. I gritted my teeth against the ache building, crushing my insides. I had to make it stop. I *needed* it to *stop*.

I hit the boxing bag hard, but the ache grew. So, I hit it harder and harder, but as I hammered into it, I could feel the pain clenching in my chest. It was so hard to breathe around it. The grief choked me. I hit harder. Harder. If I could just hit hard enough, then that night would go away. The pain would go away. I felt like screaming. Like if I didn't release this pressure somehow that I'll die. Maybe I should die. Who would miss me? They'd never come to rescue me. Never. No one reached out to me in *my misery*.

I couldn't see anymore. Tears clouded my vision, and yet I still punched. I could feel the heat rising. Rising. Rising. Until my blood dripped onto the floor. Until strong arms were wrapped around my waist, pulling me into an unforgiving chest. I fought him, punching my fists against the arms holding me, but he only pulled me closer, enveloping me in his warmth.

My throat felt raw just like my chest, and I realized I had been screaming. The screaming turned to retching sobs. I hadn't felt this raw in years. The clan had been sure to beat it out of me those first few months. Tears were a weakness. So was caring. Love. Regret. I was alone. Always alone.

Another jagged sob tore through me, and I stopped fighting him. I just crumbled in his arms, barely registering when he turned me around and pulled me against his chest. I clutched onto him like he was a life raft, desperate for...for... I wasn't even sure what I needed anymore. I didn't deserve to be comforted. To be relieved of my pain. Not after what I'd been doing since coming to this world. But

I couldn't let him go. I could feel the charge bouncing off his skin and running along mine, soothing in some odd way. I didn't deserve to be soothed.

"I fucked up," I whispered. Barak tightened his grip but didn't say anything. "You hate me, and you should." Another sob shook my body, and I pulled him impossibly closer. "They hated me." I knew he didn't know who *they* were, but I couldn't stop my next confession. "*I* hate me."

He was quiet for so long, I was sure he hadn't heard me. Or he simply didn't care. Just didn't want the queen's sister to...what? Lose it?

He lifted my chin to meet my eyes then. His were the most beautiful hue I'd ever seen. Golden brown blending with streaks of yellow and green. I didn't want to like them, but I couldn't help the way they drew me in. I expected to see his hatred flashing across them in those lightning bolts he was known for, but instead, he searched my eyes with a look I couldn't identify. Why was he looking at me like that? What did he see? Why did he care?

"I don't hate you," he said softly, his eyes still hard but unreadable.

Another river of tears escaped, and his eyes didn't leave mine as he wiped them away, his thumb stroking the scar on my left cheek. I flinched, but he held me still as he leaned forward. I froze, not breathing as he kissed the scar. His lips on my skin were electric–pun intended–and I felt heat that wasn't my own flush my veins along with this insistent hum deep within my core.

"You're only as much a monster as you let yourself be," he said against my skin.

Then, he pulled away, and I wondered if he had somehow felt that thrum because his eyes held an emotion I still couldn't identify. I couldn't take my eyes off him, my body still in shock, but he glanced down to where my hands still clenched him to me. I followed his gaze to see the tears and blood I'd stained his shirt with. I frowned. How had I burned through the gloves? A quick glance at him showed the same confusion on his face.

Then he stepped away. "That's enough for today." He inclined his head towards the showers off the training room. "Get cleaned up and I'll return you to your rooms."

And just like that, he'd shut me out again. I didn't blame him. I was still reeling, my insides raw, so I disappeared into the showers. It wasn't until the cold water was washing the blood and tears down the drain that I realized that he had eased the ache. Instead of that all consuming need to scream, there was this charged humming that made me feel warm inside...and just a little bit less alone.

Chapter 11

To acknowledge her demons
would mean embracing my own
and I've buried them too deep
to want to face them again.

Barak

This was a bad idea. I was getting too close...but then it was my job to get close. I had to convince her to join her sister's cause so that she could be free. The queen wanted her sister back. But...but I could *feel* the pain Dalacia harbored. Watching her the night before as she fell apart did something to me, and I hadn't been able to stand there and watch her fall without catching her.

Then there was that weird, warm hum. I was aware of spiritbonds among Fae, but it was rare and only between true mates. The fact that Silivia and Ghost had one was a blessing. The thought I had one with Dalacia...

No, that couldn't be. Not only because the likelihood of two rare spiritbonds appearing at the same time was low to none, but also because I would never feel that way about her. I understood she went through an ordeal. Hell, so had I, but I hadn't tried to kill my brother. I hadn't tried to destroy my father's home. I hadn't tried for a throne that wasn't my own. I hadn't let the clan use me...not like that.

But maybe I was being too hard on her. She hadn't known a thing about our world. She'd had to watch while her parents died and had been tortured into summoning an ability she knew nothing about. Who could blame her for snapping?

But that wasn't enough. I knew heartache did things to people. And maybe it truly had been grief and guilt that had crumbled her yesterday, but there wasn't an excuse large enough for what she'd done. There was no bond between us, and there never would be. I would get Dalacia to join Silivia's side, get her to reveal clan secrets, but I would never claim her as mine.

"Okay, what happened?"

I started as Raiden threw himself into the seat in front of me. We were in the smaller sitting area for the king and queen's inner court. The wing held rooms for our entire team and happened to be adjacent to the royal wing itself. It was an honor to be considered so highly, but all I could currently think about was that I'd rather be anywhere but here.

Hell, I'd rather be sweating my balls off hiking through the Kamuna Desert or freezing in the Snowy Forest than be here, but I only had a few more weeks left before we were to visit the other Fae kingdoms. I was feeling that deadline with every charged beat of my heart...and stupid warm hum in my core. The last thing I wanted to do was tell my brother about any of it. That being around the queen's sister kept unburying memories I'd rather forget. Kept making me feel things I shouldn't feel. Not for her.

"Barak?"

I refocused on my brother, realizing I hadn't answered him. His previous teasing tone was replaced with concern again, and his brows were knitted as he studied me.

"What happened?"

I shook my head. "Nothing."

He lifted a brow. "It's not nothing. I can feel that something's different. You're not falling for that fire witch, are you?"

I snorted in disgust, anger sending electricity down my veins. "Never in a million years!" I spat. "Just tired of the job is all. I know we need her on our side, but does she truly deserve to be?" I expected him to agree with me, but he only studied me with an odd look on his face. "What?"

"You can empathize with her, can you not?" My heart clenched, and I fought the electricity trying to escape my skin. "Don't think I don't know being around her has brought forth things you'd rather forget."

"I was never like her!" I snarled. "I would have never done what she did."

He glanced away. "You don't know that," he said quietly, and I fumed. "I'm not trying to make excuses for her."

"Sure sounds like you are," I interjected.

"I know I'm the same one who gave you hell when you said you could connect with her and convince her to join our side, but I'd be remiss if I didn't remind you that you don't know everything she went through." He looked at me then, regret in his eyes. "You were saved, Barak, but she was in their hands for a long time."

I flinched. I knew my brother blamed himself for not getting to me sooner, but it wasn't his fault. The clan had continuously moved me to prevent escape and rescue until they broke me. I wasn't naïve. I know I was lucky that he and Reese had gotten to me in time. It could have been so much worse, and he was right, Dalacia hadn't been rescued. She'd had to endure the clan's torture for far longer than I.

"She could have been rescued in Nyri," I reminded him.

He shrugged. "Maybe. Or maybe she was already so scarred from being with the clan that she couldn't see that."

What he said made sense, and it angered me that he was being so reasonable.

"What happened to you and Reese hating her, too?" I growled, but I was losing steam.

Raiden eyed me again as if he were seeing something more than I wanted him to.

"Reese knows she's his half-sister, and even if he's pissed at how she treated Silivia, you know as well as I that he won't just dismiss her as family."

No, he wouldn't, not when Silivia and Dalacia were the closest thing he had left of his father. He wouldn't simply give up hope that she was lost without trying first. He'd done the same with his mother for decades before he'd finally accepted her for the evil witch she was. Blood ran deep after all.

"And I may not trust her, but I'm not stupid enough to believe that she isn't still considered family. Once she starts acting like it, maybe I'll be inclined to treat her as such."

I snorted, but I'd seen how Dalacia perked up at the mention of her sister even while she sneered at her name. She missed her, even if she wouldn't admit it.

I sighed. "I know," I relented. He raised a brow.

"So, are you going to tell me what the issue is then? You were just saying that someone needed to listen to her side. Why are you suddenly completely against this mission of yours?"

"I'm not, it's just more challenging than I imagined." I glanced away, praying he would drop it. He was quiet for several moments.

"If things change for you, don't automatically assume it's a bad thing. Maybe it's a blessing in disguise." I spun to face him, wondering if he was referring to what I thought he was. There was no way he knew about it. But then, we were brothers. His eyes gave nothing away as he stood. "Just something to think about, Barak. You more than anyone deserve to have one." His eyes softened, and then he walked away, and I had no words left to stop him.

Chapter 12

I feel like an imposter
in my own skin.

Silivia

I was drowning. Something big was coming, and I knew it was going to take everything we had to defeat it. I couldn't shake the feeling that being queen was just the tip of the iceberg, but I couldn't put my finger on what was bothering me. Well, there were actually many things bothering me, but this one was elusive, like I was waiting for the other shoe to drop.

My nineteenth birthday had come and gone a couple of months ago, a grand celebration that had overtaken the castle for a week. Guess that's what my other birthdays would have been like if I'd grown up in Aurevel. It had been bittersweet if not heartwarming to be surrounded by new family. Birthdays had always been a big deal back home, and this was now the second I'd celebrated without my parents and sister. I hadn't mentioned it to Ghost, but I was worried. Fae came into their power by this time, yet my power still seemed to simmer, just short of boiling over. Could I hold on to a crown, a kingdom, without my father's level of power to protect it? Was I equipped for what came next?

Gritting my teeth against the migraine forming, I weaved through the shelves of books in the massive library. Somehow, I'd convinced my guards to wait outside its giant wooden doors and give me some much-needed breathing room. The council was suffocating. The impending fight with the clan was suffocating. My relationship troubles...also, suffocating. How had I lost a sister and a best friend at the same time that I gained another best friend/mate? What was this world playing at? Dalacia, I could understand. She was likely still brainwashed and angry from being with the clan too long. Tyrian...Tyrian was one hundred percent my fault.

Anyone who thinks love triangles are romantic has never lived one. Hell, I used to think they were great, until I was forced to choose between the two males who meant the world to me. I remember thinking it was stupid when I watched Bella in Twilight refuse to let Jacob go, even as she held on to Edward. How she couldn't see she was hurting both men, I didn't understand. Then, I'd gone and done the same thing, but worse. I'd shown interest in both. I'd played them against each other. Males who'd been friends and brothers for centuries.

I'd turned them against each other because I'd refused to acknowledge how I felt. I could blame Ghost's hesitance to embrace our connection after losing his family, but that wouldn't be fair. I should have withdrawn from both of them until I figured out my crap. Instead, I'd allowed them to compete for best male. Instead, I'd let them believe they both had my heart when I knew all along who did. And worse, I'd let the late queen's challenge be the only reason I'd finally told the truth.

I slapped the bookcase in front of me with disgust. Gods, I deserved for both Tyrian and Ghost to hate me forever. I despised how selfish and immature I'd been. Now, I didn't know if the males would ever reconcile. I doubted Ty would ever truly forgive me. Even Ghost watched me sometimes, like he feared I would run away again.

I could feel the ice on the tip of my tongue and was tempted to freeze the entire room. Only the concern for the books stopped me. I punched the bookcase again, then kicked it for good measure.

"What the library ever do to you, Cowgirl?"

I spun around to meet amused, if not a little reserved, violet eyes.

"Tyrian," I said softly. I glanced at the books and back at him, embarrassed. "I...nothing. You weren't supposed to see that."

He smiled slightly and lifted a brow. "We've moved on from dummies to bookcases. Is it still Bookcase infinity and Silivia zero?"

I couldn't help it. I laughed, remembering him having to teach me how to strike at the dummies in the early days of my training.

"I wasn't keeping score, but yeah, something like that," I replied, still chuckling.

He smiled slightly, his hands in his pockets. "It looks good on you." I frowned, brow raised in question. "Love. Spiritbond. Queen. It looks good on you." I glanced down at my feet, feeling the regret flash through me, and tears prick my eyes.

"Tyrian, I..." I lifted my gaze to meet his again. "Tyrian, I am so sorry. I was selfish and careless. I saw what I was causing between you and Ghost, and I did nothing to stop it. I let my fear of losing both of you, of embracing the bond, prevent me from doing what was right. And I lost you anyway." Tears were running down my face now, and I didn't bother to wipe them away.

"I know you may never forgive me. I don't deserve for you to. I know Ghost is still angry and hurt about it. I don't deserve to have you as a friend. I wouldn't be surprised if you decided to leave, but I would miss you as desperately as I have these past weeks. I'm...sorry." I finished the last bit in little more than a whisper. It was quiet for so long, I was sure he would just walk away.

"I can't leave in the middle of a war," he said. "We need all the allies we can get."

I swallowed the lump in my throat. "Is that the only reason you're staying?" I whispered.

He took a deep breath and regarded me for a second. "No, that's not the only reason, Cowgirl," he replied finally. I took a shaky breath. "You hurt me...badly, when all you had to do was tell the truth, but instead you let Queen Isrella force you to do so. Did you think I would hate you?"

"Yes. I thought if I couldn't have both of you, then I could have neither, and because of fear, that almost happened." I wiped the side of my face as more tears fell.

"I love you, Silivia. I thought you loved me." Ty sighed. "It's my own fault. I could see you two had a connection. I just couldn't stop pushing. Stop hoping."

"I *do* love you, Ty," I insisted. "I just realized that I love you more as a very close friend." I cringed, knowing that nobody wanted to hear their unrequited love compared to that of a friend.

He nodded sullenly. "I know this, and if I'm being honest with myself, I knew it a long time ago. Likely even before you did." He smiled sadly at me. "Don't get me wrong, Silivia. I'm happy for both of you. I am. But it's going to take some time before I can move past this."

A little flicker of hope fluttered in my chest. "Do you think there's a chance that we may...you know...be friends again?" I asked softly.

"I want us to still be friends. I do. I just...I need some time. To take it slow. But believe me when I say that I'm not going anywhere. We're still a family even if things are a work in progress between us." His stare was intense and determined.

I swallowed again, trying to stop the tears. "Thank you. I...I really am sorry."

He nodded. "I know. I am too." He rubbed his hand against the back of his neck. "I said some things I shouldn't have. Treated you harsher than you deserved. A fact that Tess was quick to remind me." I stared at him in surprise. "We'll work on it, okay?" I nodded, still in shock. "Good. Now that that's settled, I have some advice."

I shook my head and wiped my face with my shirt. "Shoot."

He lifted a brow in slight amusement. "I think you need to travel to the other factions in the kingdom. You have won the dragons, Bohr eagles and Galaton owls, Kra and Aurevel, but the majority of Rifka still do not know you. They may have realized by now that your sister was working for the clan that destroyed their homes and friends, and they're probably wondering if you're anything like them."

He raised his hands in surrender at my murderous expression. "Hear me out. You need to put these rumors to rest, meaning you need to show them your face, what you're about. Right now, they know you're King Fariel's daughter and heir. They also know you completed the trials, killed his wife, and claimed the throne. They know *of* you, but they don't *know* you."

"So what? You want me to win over key cities in Rifka by proving I'm worthy of ruling them?" I said with barely concealed distaste. I was sick and tired of always having to prove this title was my own.

"Precisely. We'll need to get Rifka on board before you travel to the other kingdoms."

"Do we really need to involve the other kingdoms?" I asked halfheartedly.

Ty gave me a disapproving look. "Silivia, we're good, but we're not that good. The fight for Aurevel was no small feat. The downfall of the clan will be a much larger ordeal. We need allies. We need the Fae kingdoms to stand together instead of fighting each other as they did in the past."

I sighed. He was right, of course, he was. "I thought the kingdoms barely tolerated each other," I pointed out. "How the hell do we convince them to work together?"

"We have a common enemy. If we can show them how you united Rifka after its fall, it will go a long way in securing their support. Especially when they see that a good number of the Resisti stand with you."

I paused, understanding hitting me as I followed his train of thought. "That's why you all discussed talking to the Resisti elders."

Tyrian nodded. "The elders lead the Resisti all over Fenriel, but it helps that at the end of the day, the Resisti of Rifka answer to you. You're one of us, and being united with the top three warriors of the organization, and now the Resisti Seven, means they will follow you unquestioningly. The others around Fenriel...not so much. We'll need the elders' support for that."

I sighed heavily and rubbed my temples. This was intense, and I'd thought the last few years of my life had been bad, but I suppose that's what came with being queen and facing a war.

"Tell me honestly, Ty," I said, glancing at him. "Can we win this?"

He was quiet for a while as he considered his next words. "I'm not going to lie to you, Silivia. This isn't going to be easy. In fact, a lot of people will die before this is over."

How encouraging, I thought somberly.

He must have read my expression because he gave me a sad smile. "It's inevitable, but I believe in you. I believe in our family. If anyone can bring the clan to their knees, it will be us. We just have to play our cards right."

I bit my lip as I considered. He was right. I had to believe we could do this, or we would fail. A lot was riding on us doing this right. An entire world in fact. This went way beyond taking care of my sister. I now had a kingdom to protect. Friends, allies, brother, mate. They needed me to go in with everything I had. If I'd learned anything in the last year, it was that doubt and fear only yielded indecision and pain. They didn't need a reluctant princess. They needed a brave queen.

I stood tall as I turned to Tyrian, who gazed at me with pride. "Then, let's get planning. We have a world to save."

Chapter 13

I have lost much,
but I refuse to lose you.

Ghost

"We need to talk."

My brother-in-arms gave me a dirty look and returned to staring at the world map spread across his desk.

"Do I want to know what about?"

I gritted my teeth and tried to keep my darkness at bay. This had to stop. I missed my brother. I sighed heavily. And my mate missed her friend.

"You know what this is about, Ty. Hell, we're going into war, and we're still fighting battles among ourselves. When are we going to stop?"

"I'm not fighting you," he answered, but his eyes didn't leave the map.

"Look at me. Tyrian!"

"What?!" he snapped, his eyes flashing as they met mine.

"*Gods.* What will it take?" I stretched my arms out. "Do you want me to let you get in a few good hits so you can burn it off? Do you want me to beat the hell out of you? What? What will it take for us to get back on the same page?" I sighed again, shoulders slumping. "I'm not naïve enough to think we can just go back to being normal, but fuck Tyrian. I miss my brother. I miss my best friend. We've never let anything get between us. Ever."

"She's not just anything."

Gods, did I know it. I still couldn't believe that between the two of us, she'd chosen me. I wasn't worthy of her. I may never be, but I would spend the rest of my immortal life working to be so. That meant, regardless of what went down, I needed to repair this relationship between Ty and I, and hopefully move it along between Ty and my mate.

"No, Silivia is everything." I stepped towards him so that we were only a few feet apart. "But you are my brother. I still need you. *She* still needs you. I'm not trying to dismiss what happened, but the bottom line is it did happen. I wish I could say I regret it. I don't. I could never regret being spiritbonded to my mate. But I do regret allowing our rivalry to get out of hand."

He was quiet for a long time, but he finally exhaled sharply. "I miss you too, brother," he muttered softly. "I hate that we let this get between us as well." He glanced away and then back at me as he rubbed the back of his neck. "If I were being honest with myself, I had a feeling who she would pick. Anyone with eyes could see you were meant for each other. I...I just couldn't help hoping she would pick me."

"Don't get me wrong," he held his hands up in surrender as I stiffened. "I'm happy for you, mate. If anyone deserves some light in their lives, it's you. I just hate that I let myself get in so deep. I should have backed out when I realized you two loved each other."

I frowned. "When was that?"

He smirked at me, a little of the mirth I'd been missing flashing in his eyes.

"Oh mate, you were whipped from the start. I just didn't know if you would pull your head out of your ass long enough to realize it." I scowled, and he laughed. His eyes softened as his laughter died off. "Like I said, I miss you too. Honestly, I forgave you a long time ago."

I tensed at what I saw flash through his eyes. "You can't keep blaming her," I growled.

Ty scoffed. "She led us both on for a long time, Ghost. I could tell you were all in when you took that bet in the Selondian Forest, even if you were still unsure of the outcome, but Silivia...she jumped between us for months, mate. *Months.*"

"She had a lot going on in case you forgot," I snarled, my fists balled and the mist around my feet building.

"Yeah, and we were with her every step of the way. We suffered too, Ghost. You can't tell me you appreciated being jerked around like that," he snapped.

He was right. I hadn't. It was something we still dealt with on occasion, despite her being completely mine. There was always this voice in the back of my head that said that if things became difficult, she would hesitate again.

"See. I can tell that it still bothers you. You can't expect me to just forget it happened."

"I don't. I just...she needs you, Ty. *We* need you. This war is going to be hard enough without us all in it together." I took a deep breath and released my balled fists. "I'm not asking you to suddenly go back to how you were before. I understand that it'll take time. I'm asking you to try...to still be her friend."

He turned to glance out the window, a contemplative frown on his face. Finally, he turned back to me and nodded.

"I can't promise that things will go back to normal. In fact, I know it won't, but I won't remove my friendship. You're right. We need to be a unified force more than ever. All I can promise you is that I'll work on it."

It was all I could ask for. I nodded. "We're good?"

He gave me a small smirk.

"Always, brother." I smirked back. Ty gestured at the map. "Ready to help me look at this?"

Moving to his side, I felt a small weight lift from my shoulders. Now, if only I could stop the force that was no doubt headed for us.

I gritted my teeth in frustration as I fought not to snap at my mate. I knew the decisions she was forced to make weren't easy. Hell, she'd been thrown into the deep end. It was barely two years ago that she entered Fenriel for the first time.

Now here she was, truly my queen and the queen of Rifka. I'd known it would cause opposition, same as I knew that a war was coming, but knowing it and dealing with it were two different things.

We couldn't afford to be a divided unit, not now. It was why I'd spoken to Tyrian about his aloofness towards her. I didn't care if he had a grudge towards me; we'd always managed to work together despite them in the past. But this time it involved my mate, and she couldn't focus on what she needed to if she was still grieving my best friend's attention. Even if that grief made my darkness snarl possessively.

"Tyrian says I need to make my presence known. Not just in the castle, but within the kingdom too."

I started. "When did he say that?"

She didn't turn to face me, just continued to stare out the window into the garden. "Last night."

I blinked in surprise. He'd let me lecture him on being a united force when he'd already started talking to her again? I scowled. Of course, he had.

"You disagree?"

I shook my head and moved to her side. I let one arm wrap around her waist and pulled her tightly to me. Just because I was pissed with her for taking on one of the clan threats alone without telling any of us, it didn't mean I didn't need to be touching her as much as possible. I'd denied myself for too long to continue to do so. She tensed in my arms before relaxing into me.

"I don't disagree," I told her, my lips pressed to her temple. "I just loathe the idea of you in danger. I loathe that you believe you still have something to prove." Why else would she still be out looking for trouble when she had warriors who'd gladly remove it for her?

She stiffened again. "I do still have something to prove, Ghost. They may have crowned me queen and you my king, but I see the way the court watches me, like they're waiting for me to fail. Like I'm just a temporary presence they have to endure until someone better comes along."

I growled low. "You have nothing to prove. You will not fail, because you were born for this. Not because you're Fariel's daughter, but because you're you." I turned her so she faced me, studying the doubt and uncertainty in her eyes. I lifted a hand to cup her cheek before sliding it down to her chin. "Silivia, your father had two other children. I didn't see them entering a new world and overcoming it in such a short time."

I could see her rebuttal forming on her lips, but I shook my head. "Reese is different. He's been here all his life. He's had time to build the alliances and make the waves you developed in a short time. Your father didn't even have the call over as many of the winged as you do." I cocked my head. "In fact, I think you probably can call more of them than we know."

"How can you think all that?" she whispered, her hands on my chest gripping my shirt.

Uncertainty shone in her eyes, and all I wanted to do was cart her away and keep her safe from the world. But she didn't need me to keep her safe. She needed me at her side and to step in in times when she fell short. It was still a new concept for me, being part of a bond that was only whole when both of us were there, but I would do anything for her.

"Because I see you. I've watched you mature and grow into the queen you are today, and you will no doubt grow to be an even greater queen. So, it's not what I think, but what I know."

She gave me a small smile. "Even if you don't want me to travel to the different parts of our kingdom?"

I snorted and leaned down to gently press my lips to hers. Her lips were so soft against mine, and I felt her melt further into me. I'd meant the kiss to be a tease, but then her hands shifted so they braced behind my neck and pulled me closer. Her tongue demanded entry as it traced my lips, and I couldn't deny her. Several minutes later, we pulled apart to catch our breath.

"It's the right decision, but I know what it'll lead to and I'm not ready to face it," I told her after a moment. She waited, a question in her eyes. "We need to stop the Blood Clan." She nodded in confirmation. "To do so, we need allies, both in Rifka...and out."

She inclined her head. Ty must have changed her mind. She'd been against the idea when I'd mentioned the inner council's suggestion before. "We need to talk to the other Kings and Queens."

I nodded solemnly. I had no interest in speaking with the royalty of Farla and Hyra. Hyra's king was a brutal, ruthless male whose appetite for violence normally complemented my own, but that didn't mean I wanted it aimed at the queen in my arms.

Farla's queen, on the other hand, was quiet and contemplative, and although King Ivar made the final decisions, I knew Queen Magnolia was the one who whispered them into his ear. Neither kingdom would agree to work with my queen easily. And yet we needed them if we were to finally wash the tainted stain of the Blood Clan from Fenriel.

"I have Teslia, Tyrian, and Reese," she stated firmly. "I have the Resisti Seven and hopefully the rest of the Resisti soon." She slid her fingers through my hair and down my face before stopping a hand over my heart. "Most importantly, I have you. I think we've proven by now that we can do anything together."

Gods, I loved this female. I pulled her tighter to me.

"I can't lose you," I told her sullenly, my words coming out choked. I knew where our journey took us would have worse risks than the ones we'd faced before.

"And I can't lose you, so I guess we'd better figure this out together and make sure we don't fail."

I laughed darkly. How did this switch from me comforting her to her comforting me? I kissed her deeply.

"Then let it rain snow and shadows, my queen. And wash this world clean."

She grinned wickedly as that snow mixed with the mist playing at her feet. The world wasn't ready for both of us.

Chapter 14

I respected my elders.
But what would it take
For them
To respect
Me?

Silivia

To say being in the room with all the elders of the Resisti wasn't intimidating would be a bald-faced lie. Seven Fae made up the leaders of the Resisti: four males and three females. They sat in a semicircle in front of Tess, Ty, Ghost, and I. Master Marcus, the elder who had taken the four of us in and trained us, sat at the head of the table to my right. It was in his house, at his meeting table, that we sat. I didn't bother to look at the white haired male, still too salty about his attempt to control my life.

The second most powerful elder, Master Astral, sat at the opposite end. There was no doubt she was gorgeous with her deep auburn hair that was almost black, and honey colored skin. She was the kindest of the masters as well, with gentle eyes that reminded me of my mother.

The others I wasn't so sure about. Master Zephia was a female with long, wavy black hair and olive colored skin. Her mismatched brown eyes were fierce as her cheekbones, and I couldn't meet her glare for very long. Master Kure to her side was equally harsh, but he had a brutal handsomeness. His dark hair came to his shoulders but was tied back. The quiver on his back showed arrows as dark and sharp as he.

Next were Master Roark and Master Daris, the twins. Both had brown hair, but Roark wore his in a half-messy bun, half hanging down fashion, while Daris's hair was cut short to his head. They looked like vikings, and I couldn't help but wonder if they'd helped train Tyrian.

The last was Master Lara. She, too, had white hair, although hers was in tiny braids that fell down her back. Her narrow, deep-set grey eyes seemed to stare into my soul, but I couldn't tell if she liked what she saw.

All in all, I found myself wishing desperately to be anywhere but here, but one didn't plan to recruit the Resisti for a war against the Blood Clan without talking to the leaders of said group.

"So, what you are saying is that after you trained the female from the prophecy, you recruited members of the Resisti to kill Rifka's queen, and then had Fariel's heir crowned queen without thinking to consult any of us," Master Kure stated bluntly.

How he had summed up the last several months of my life into that one sentence, I would never know. He acted as if we'd had time for the bureaucracy that would have taken place if we'd waited for them to make decisions. Especially with said prophecy hanging over my head. I fought a shiver.

"When the land shudders and is watered with blood and tears, only then will she be born. Risen from the ash as ice and flames, all that is winged will answer to her call. And only when the shadows and snow bond as one will the land be healed again."

Words that had haunted me for the last year as I completed the trials to reclaim my father's throne, but I'd come to accept that what was meant to happen would happen, ancient prophecy or not.

"We had the orders of Master Marcus," Ghost reminded him flatly.

I could feel his anger festering through the bond. His mist was calm at our feet, but it wouldn't take much for it to turn into deadly shadows. Not that Ghost would attack the elders. He knew we needed them, but that didn't stop his irritation over how they treated me. I'd forgiven him for his role long ago when I'd learned he didn't agree with the elders deciding the course of my life.

"The orders allowed for you three." Master Zephia gestured at Ghost, Teslia, and Tyrian. "Not once did you gain permission from us to include warriors under *our* jurisdiction."

A low growl built in my mate's throat, but he bit it back. "There was no time. We reached out to those we had worked closely with in the past. It was their decision whether they helped or not. We did not force them. But Silivia's life was in danger. Rifka was in danger. We needed to act."

"And people died as a result!" Master Roark snapped. "Casualties that wouldn't have occurred if you had waited for the proper chain of command."

"There was no time!" Ghost roared, jumping to his feet as a deep growl built in his chest.

"Ghost, control yourself," Marcus ordered.

I glanced over to see my mate's eyes were bleeding towards his deadly black with a gold ring. I placed my hand over his balled fists, not caring about the eyes taking in the gesture. Ghost glanced at me, his face twisted in a snarl. I sent my snow to stroke the bond between us, knowing this discussion was bringing back the fear he carried of losing me like he had everyone else. We'd come too close during the trials. I also knew he felt responsible for the loss of those warriors as much as I did.

He took a deep breath to calm himself and reclaimed his seat. Slowly, the gold bled back into his eyes. Ghost turned back to the masters, who all watched us with a mixture of curiosity, contemplation, and contempt. They thought they could use our bond to their benefit, but only Ghost and I chose what moves we made.

"You have trusted me in the past to make executive decisions on behave of the Resisti. We have never failed you." He gestured at his sister and brother-in-arms. "I made an executive decision that required us to build an army without Queen Isrella discovering our plans. She already had the Blood Clan on her side. We couldn't risk waiting to see if help would come. They may not have been in time to help Rifka."

He paused, letting that sink in. "It does not matter now. What's done is done. One prophecy has been fulfilled, and the other is in motion, whether we like it or not. The Blood Clan grows stronger, and unless we nip them in the bud, it won't just be Rifka in danger of falling next time. It will be Hyra and Farla, until all of Fenriel is in flames."

Master Zephia snorted, and Ghost shot her a dark smirk lacking any mirth. "Dramatic, I know, but we all knew this was coming for centuries. Isn't it time the Resisti finally did something about it?"

The elders were silent, then Master Lara glanced at me. "You believe you are the one from the prophecy?"

I bit back a disgruntled sigh, but inclined my head. "I don't have to believe it. The events up until today have shown that I am. Same as they have shown that Ghost himself is a part of it. Not knowing how to complete said prophecy does not change the fact that parts of it have already come to pass."

She nodded thoughtfully. "And what of your sister?"

I stiffened. "What of her?"

"Is it true that she orchestrated the destruction of Rifka?"

I swallowed hard, trying to calm the ice building on my tongue. It was Ghost's turn to send a comforting wave of darkness down the bond.

"My sister was kidnapped and forced to train under the clan. She then helped them attack the people of Rifka and tried to kill me." I gave them all a stern look. "I'm not blind to her actions, but I also don't plan on removing Rifka's princess when she herself was a victim. She is being handled."

"How exactly is she being *handled*?" Master Daris asked, his head tilted as he stared at me, as if I were prey he was trying to decide whether to devour.

I swallowed hard but held his stare. "All you need to know is that it's being handled."

Master Zephia snorted again. "And you expect us to accept that? She should be handed over to the Resisti to be dealt with."

Oh, I *really* didn't like her.

"The Resisti do not rule Rifka. I do. Ghost does. Her crimes occurred in Rifka and will be handled in Rifka."

"Rifka is nothing without the Resisti that live there, child," Master Kure reminded me.

The "child" comment rubbed me the wrong way, but I fought to keep my words composed and firm as I answered. "And the Resisti is nothing without the powerful warriors within it, including those sitting across from you. What do you think would happen if they were to no longer assist you?"

My friends and mate said nothing, didn't even flinch at my threat, but the masters bristled.

"You dare to threaten us!" Master Zephia spat. "How dare you! We trained these warriors. We trained you. You do not get to decide whether to help our cause!"

"We do actually, because to take our choices away would make you just as bad as the Blood Clan."

Silence. Approval shot down the bond, and I fought a smile. I held my hands out in front of me, trying to placate them.

"We do not seek to separate from the Resisti. Our goal is one and the same, and we need each other. But Dalacia is *my* sister, and with all that I've been through, I believe it is not unreasonable for me to request that you allow me time to see if she is truly a victim or an enemy before we condemn her."

"It is not unreasonable, Silivia, but you do understand what must happen if you are not successful?"

I turned to Master Marcus and nodded. "I do."

He inclined his head. "Then we will allow you to deal with your sister for the time being." He glanced at all four of us. "As for the other events, I must admit that it wasn't what I meant when I said to reclaim the throne. But, I would be lying if I said I didn't expect you to have *some* opposition. Overall, you all appeared to have resolved it as best as you could have. The next steps will need to be handled a little more...delicately."

He gave us a knowing smile, and I saw sheepish looks cross my friends' faces. "I assume you didn't just come to be berated about your past decisions. You have a plan, yes?"

I glanced at Tyrian, who sat up straighter.

"We need to ensure all the factions of Rifka are on one page," he explained. "And then we need to travel to Hyra and Farla to get the other kingdoms on board. This isn't just a Resisti issue, and we need their support in the times to come."

"I'm guessing you four will be the ones going?" Master Astral said, speaking up for the first time.

Ty nodded. "We're using the same group who completed the final trial, so Prince Reese and those known as the Resisti Seven will be assisting as well. I'm sure by now, tales of what happened in Aurevel have spread across Fenriel. It will be good for them to see us still working together, and it gives us more manpower to divide and conquer."

Because with how large Fenriel was, we would need every one of our allies to pull this off. While Reese and Teslia would remain in Rifka to ensure it remained running in my absence and to eliminate any remaining clan soldiers and followers, Rose and Sirius would go off to recruit some of the minor lords outside of the three Fae kingdoms. Aux and Raiden would recruit the major lords. Meanwhile, the assassin twins Hesper and Hemara would travel to the clan territories to gather intel. That left Ghost, Ty, and I–and hopefully Dalacia and Barak–convincing the Fae royalty. It was ambitious, I knew, but it was our best chance.

We waited anxiously after Ty finished explaining the plan to see how the masters would respond. They'd sent us out of the room while they deliberated, and I couldn't help pacing back in forth across the living room. They most likely wouldn't like that our plan centered around the people whom we'd recruited for the trials, but they were trusted and tested, unlike the Fae in the meeting room. Finally, we were called back in and took our seats in front of them again.

"We can see that we cannot deter you from this course of action," Master Astral said finally. "You are right in thinking the clan must be removed. We will allow you to recruit as you see fit, as long as you ensure we are kept in the know this time." She glanced pointedly at each of us, and we nodded.

"We will gift you something that will make this easier," Master Astral continued. She indicated a dozen disks in the center of the table. They looked like mirrors the size of both my hands together. "These are vision mirrors. They will allow you to stay in contact with the members of your group wherever you are. Simply visualize their face and name, and the mirrors will connect you."

I stared at the oval objects in surprise. So, facetime in the magic world. Cool.

"Good luck, and hopefully, sometime in the future, we will meet in a time of peace."

We inclined our heads before departing. As we climbed onto our dragons to fly back to Aurevel, I couldn't help but dream of a world free of blood and tears.

Chapter 15

Be it naivety.
Or youth.
I do not wish to condemn you.
Unless remorse is beyond you.

Silivia

I stepped over a crumpled piece of the wall. It had been about four months since the fifth trial, and most of the repairs to the castle were underway or almost complete. There were still a few spots that reminded me of the fight for my new home. Isrella partnering with the Blood Clan to hang on to the throne wasn't something I could have foreseen. I knew the late queen was ruthless and cruel from meeting her and talking to Reece. But allowing the worst organization in existence to take over the kingdom, so she could hold on to a throne that didn't even belong to her, was something else altogether. I couldn't even say she was brainwashed. No, the queen had been aware of the destruction the clan created across Rifka. She just didn't care.

I studied the gardens around me, the wall where one of the dragons had crashed to his death. I'd yet to have it repaired when there were so many parts of the city more important. I stared at the crumpled pieces of rock among the flowers and wondered how I was supposed to rebuild the foundation so that the people believed that I wasn't like my predecessor. That I had their best interests in mind. I snorted in disdain at myself. I'm sure Isrella had convinced them of just that on more than one occasion. How could I show them I wasn't her?

"There would have been more."

I spun to find Reece standing behind me, one hand in his pocket and another on the hilt of the twin dragon blades at his side. Both sets of our royal guards stood a few feet away, their hands crossed behind their backs as they stood tall. Lorik, the captain of the guard, met my gaze, and his giant wings shifted slightly as he inclined his head to me. I turned back to my brother.

"What do you mean?" I asked.

He gestured the hand on his blade to the destruction around us. "This. It would have been worse if not for you."

I sighed, my shoulders slumping. "It wouldn't have happened at all if not for me."

Reece tilted his head slightly and gave me a disapproving look. His unruly hair had gotten longer in the last few months, but didn't quite conceal the stormy, blue eyes glaring at me.

"Surely you've learned by now to stop blaming yourself for the actions of others. My mother was a monster. Eventually, the Blood Clan would have overrun the capital, and Rifka would have been lost." He walked over to the wall and fingered some of the blue roses that still remained.

"We lost some, but if you had not stood up for Rifka, we would have eventually lost it all. Unfortunately, there lies the burden of the crown." He threw a sad smile over his shoulder at me. "Bet you're wishing I was the heir now, uh?"

I chuckled softly. "I don't think you'll look as good in a dress," I teased.

Reese burst out laughing, the darkness in his eyes lightening. I could have sworn I heard a couple of snorts and coughs from the guards behind us. I smiled slightly.

"That's better," my brother said as he fought another smile.

I frowned. "What?"

"That smile. I haven't seen it much lately. Which is a crying shame for someone who was mated and married to their spiritbonded not so long ago. Plus, gained a brother whom they couldn't *possibly* live without."

I laughed again. "Thinking highly of ourselves, aren't we?" I smirked, shaking my head.

Reece grinned. "Well, I am royalty after all."

I rolled my eyes, but then grew serious. "Repairing the rift in Rifka isn't going to be easy," I said sullenly.

"Were you expecting it to be?"

I came to his side and palmed a rose, breathing its soft scent in. "No, but I know nothing about running a kingdom, Reece. Now, we have to travel to the sky cities and unite the people. We have to finish repairing Aurevel, and we really need to ensure this retaliation for replacing the council doesn't grow out of hand." I had no doubt some of the recent disturbances were their doing.

Reece scowled. "Replacing the council needed to occur. We wouldn't get anything done otherwise."

"I agree. But did you really think they were going to take it lying down?" I pointed out.

He shook his head and indicated I should walk with him. I sensed the guards moving into position behind us as we strolled through the garden.

"Oh, I knew they wouldn't. That's why we need to ensure you have the people's support. It was one of the reasons I came looking for you. The other reason being that I wanted to check on you."

"About our sister? Or everything else?"

He scowled. There was no love lost between my brother and sister. "Everything else. Although if I were a better big brother, I would inquire about our dear little sister's incarceration." I lifted a brow, and he sighed. "Fine. How is she?"

I shrugged. "Still convinced that I'm the worst thing to exist since peas and carrots." Reece scrunched his nose in revulsion. "Do you think Barak is right? That he can convince her to open up and see that she was brainwashed?"

Instead of speaking out of his loathing, I saw him consider before speaking. I loved him for the act alone. "It's possible. She was with them a long time, and if she really was with the inner circle, she could have been tortured in ways we don't know about. The Blood Clan has ways of breaking people."

He said the last part softly, and I wondered if he was hinting at a certain prince of lightning who wore a haunted expression sometimes after speaking to my sister. I nodded, biting my lip.

"If only we could figure out who was leading them," I muttered thoughtfully. "Then, we could cut the head off the snake instead of the tail."

Reece nodded in agreement. "First things first. We get Rifka united again, and then we take on the clan."

I swallowed nervously. "What did you have in mind?"

"The people need to see you. Yes, they saw you at the inauguration and the wedding, but they need to see you in the city."

I considered him. "Doing what exactly?"

"What you're already doing. Caring. Helping with repairs. I heard you and Ghost visited all the families of those who were killed during the battle for the castle."

I cringed and felt my heart squeeze painfully at the mention of those lost. Reece gave me a sympathetic look that said he understood and agreed. He, too, had gone to visit their families; Tess had accompanied him. I was grateful that my brother and sister-in-arms had become a support for each other, despite their history. I was hopeful that it was developing into something even deeper.

"The people need to see more of that. Even if all you do is walk through the market and speak to the patrons."

I nodded. I could do that. I glanced at him and found him tense. I frowned. "What else, Reece? It looks like you're sucking on a lemon."

He chuckled humorlessly. "You're not going to like it, but they also need to see justice being served."

Now I was really confused. "By justice you mean…"

"A public execution of the clan members who destroyed their homes."

I stopped dead in my tracks and stared at him in horror. Reece turned to me, his stance unforgiving.

"Have you lost your mind?!" I snapped. "We don't just go around killing people! We're not the clan."

"I know that. But these men cannot be released back into society. They will commit the same crimes again. They killed, robbed, and raped their way across Rifka. Do you really think they've repented of their ways just because they were caught?"

"But you're asking me to murder them in cold blood in front of an audience!" I couldn't believe he would ask this of me. It was one thing to kill someone in battle, and quite another to order their death. I'd always assumed those who couldn't be trusted would remain in the dungeons. I'd even made sure not to explicitly say I'd execute them when the council asked. Maybe that made me weak and naïve. Reece definitely didn't approve, if the look he was giving me was any indicator.

"You are queen now. You simply have to condemn them. You have a king for a reason, Silivia. You think Ghost won't take on the darker side of ruling if you needed him to?" Reece pointed out.

I knew he was right. Ghost would gladly take out the clan soldiers, so I didn't have to. In fact, he would probably enjoy it. I shook my head in denial.

"I can't just order the death of a group of men without giving them a chance to redeem themselves," I insisted.

Reece scoffed, anger twisting his features. "Dear little sister, if you were to speak to these males during interrogation, you would realize they do not wish to be redeemed."

I lifted my chin and stared him down. "I will determine that for myself."

Reese considered me for several seconds, then nodded. "As you wish, my queen."

I scrunched my nose in revulsion as Ghost, Reece, Teslia, and Tyrian descended into the dungeon alongside me. It was dark, wet, and cold, just like every dungeon I'd ever heard of. I just never thought I'd be in one. Let alone holding someone prisoner there.

Two of the royal guards walked in front of us, with four more at our backs. What they thought would attack us down here, I wasn't sure, but with the prisoners being clan soldiers, it had been impossible to convince the winged warriors to remain behind. Ghost's fingers slid across mine, and my gaze shot to his.

"*Are you okay?*" he said down the bond. "*I can feel your ice raging.*"

"*I'm not a fan of being down here,*" I answered. He waited and I sighed. "*I'm also not a fan of what Reece is asking me to do.*"

He was quiet for a few seconds. "*I know you don't want to, but after this meeting, you may come to the same realization as we have.*"

"*What? That they deserve to die?*" I retorted sharply.

"*These are really bad people, Silivia, and sometimes difficult decisions have to be made for the good of the kingdom.*"

I knew that. I did. I still didn't like it.

"*Judge for yourself, my love. And whatever you decide, I'll stand by you on it.*"

I bit my lip but nodded. We came to a stop in front of a group of cells full of fifteen dirty males in total. They all scowled at us, hatred radiating from bodies coiled to attack. One spat on the ground, almost splattering my boots.

"So, the new queen had finally deemed us worthy of a visit," one said, stepping forward. His hair was tangled and filthy, and the soldier uniform he still wore was torn and bloody in places.

"Trust me, there is nothing you are worthy of from our queen except a slow death," Tyrian snarled.

The soldier tsked him. "Still a little salty about me spearing your friend, uh?" He shrugged. "How can I be blamed for him falling onto my sword?"

"That's enough!" Ghost barked as Tyrian snarled and moved towards the cell. Something must have passed between them because Tyrian conceded a step. My mate turned back to the men in the cell. "For someone who finds themselves at the mercy of their enemies, you would think you would be playing your cards better."

The soldier snorted. "What? You're going to let us go if we play nice and give you information on the clan? Join your side instead?"

Ghost shrugged nonchalantly. "What do you have to lose? You can continue to be a hardass and stay in this cell until you rot, or I get so tired of your face that I feed you to my shadows. Or you can give us something we can use and maybe, just maybe, you'll get to see the sun again."

The soldier seemed to consider his offer for a moment before his eyes rolled over to me. A wicked, disgusting smile lifted his lips. "You're the one they sent us to claim. The one who will help bring Fenriel to its knees." His eyes shifted to Ghost, and then back to me. "Of course, he requires both the night and day to do so."

I fought to keep my expression indifferent even as my stomach twisted. "Who's he?" I asked instead.

The soldier let his eyes drift over every inch of my body and licked his lips. I felt a wave of revulsion and had to fight the urge to vomit. Ghost growled low and menacingly next to me as his shadows built around our feet. I didn't bother stopping him.

The soldier laughed. "I can see why he wants you. You'll make a delicious addition to his collection. Can't blame the King of Shadows for claiming you as his own." He shifted closer. "If you ever get tired of his royal darkness, I'll be more than happy to take the edge off. A hate fuck is the best kind."

He choked suddenly as wisps of darkness squeezed around his neck. Ghost was still and collected at my side even as I felt his roiling rage down the bond.

I tilted my head and eyed the soldier as he fought for breath. None of his comrades moved to help him. "I'll ask again. Who is this he you speak of? What does he want?"

Ghost loosened his grip slightly so that the male could speak.

"He is more powerful than you will ever be. His reach is great. Absolute. Everything he desires, he will have. He is a *god,* and this world will fall to its knees and worship him."

"Sounds like a delusional nutjob to me," Teslia said with a shrug. "What makes you think he will succeed?"

He smiled despite the darkness still wrapped around his windpipe. "He'll succeed. Once he has these two, his power will grow beyond that which can be comprehended by your feeble minds. Then, he'll reward those who stood by him."

"So, what you're saying is if we were to let you go, you'll simply go back to doing his bidding? You will not renounce your loyalty to him?"

I had to ask. Had to be sure before I let my dark king put an end to the wickedness festering in this cell. I saw the same malicious, twisted smiles and mindset mirrored in every male in the cells around me. They were not repentant. They would happily continue on killing and raping females and children. I could not let it stand. But I needed him to confirm what I'd already realized.

"You don't renounce the winning team, sweetheart, especially when the benefits are so great." He licked his lips again. "I told you. Hate fucks are the best fucks. Especially when they're screaming."

The lanterns went out, and then the soldier was the one screaming. When I managed to light them again with my blue flames, we found his twisted form staring wide-eyed at the ceiling, blood pouring from every crevice. Ghost was panting heavily next to me, his eyes black with a golden ring. His darkness was unleashed, whipping and raging behind him.

Fighting to showcase a calmness I one hundred percent did not feel, I sent a wave of snow and ice down the bond to try to ease him as I faced the rest of the men in the cell.

"Come dawn, you will stand for your crimes. Let's see if your god deems to save you." Then, I grabbed the fuming king beside me by the hand and marched out of the dungeon. No one said anything as we raced to get back up to the daylight.

The entire walk, I fought to calm my raging mate as I also tried to ease the rolling of my stomach.

It wasn't until we were exiting the dungeon into the hallway that it hit me why Ghost had lost it. What the clan soldier had hinted at doing to me on more than one occasion. Ghost's own mother and sister had been beaten, raped, and then thrown into the fire of his home when he was still a child. Their screams still woke him some nights centuries later, and the captive had hinted... Had done it to females and children regularly.

I turned and vomited into a flowerpot. No one said anything about that either.

Chapter 16

I will be your avenging angel.

Ghost

I could feel her apprehension as we watched the fourteen clan soldiers line up before us in the city square. Their iron chains dragged across the ground as they walked, and despite the utter reluctance to execute them radiating from my mate at my side, I knew from their hate-filled glares that these males were beyond redemption. But my lovely mate could not bear to kill them, and I would gladly take that burden from her. I did not mind the stain of their deaths on my soul. Not when the stains on theirs were so much greater.

Females and children. These bastards went after them like it was a sport. Just like they'd done to my mother and sister. I balled my fists at my sides. I couldn't save them, same as I couldn't save those the clan has continued to hurt. Taking out these males was only the tip of the iceberg. It didn't make up for the countless lives they'd destroyed, but maybe it could bring some justice to their families.

A hand slipped between my fingers until they were clasped tightly around mine. I glanced at my mate, my queen. Over my dead body would I allow them to take her. To taint her with their darkness. It was bad enough she had to contend with mine.

"Together," she whispered just for me. "We'll avenge them together."

Because she understood me better than anyone ever had. She didn't condemn me for my need to kill as many clan members as possible in hopes that it could even the score somehow. No, she embraced it. After all, they had stolen her family as well. I lifted our clasped hands and kissed hers, trying to convey with the act alone just how much I loved and appreciated the female at my side. It had taken hours for me to work out the dark rage last night, but her screaming my name in pleasure, holding her tightly through the night, had helped wash away the memories taunting me.

"Shall we get this over with?" I asked her finally.

Silivia took a deep breath and inclined her head. We stepped forward together, our hands still clasped, to address the crowd below us. The residents of Aurevel stared up at the platform. Their eyes took in our clasped hands and the prisoners behind us. Different emotions were worn by the Fae before us. Pain, anger, curiosity, distrust...and even some fear and admiration.

"People of Aurevel," Silivia proclaimed, her voice strong and steady. "These males before you have been accused of heinous crimes across Rifka. They have raped, robbed, and destroyed, and have made it clear that if released, they will continue to do so."

The crowd roared with horror and rage, making their displeasure known. I held up a hand, and they instantly quieted.

"For these heinous crimes, I, Silivia, the Phoenix Queen and Queen of the Winged, sentence them to death."

There was silence after this statement as the crowd waited in anticipation. This was where I came in. Spinning to face the males behind us, I lifted a hand.

"Any last words?" I asked, daring them to challenge me. They only stared back in loathing. "So be it. I, Ghost, King of Shadows and King of the Winged, also sentence you to death."

I waved a hand and loosened the leash on my power, letting the darkness weave around them from their feet upwards. Loathing turned to apprehension as the darkness started to squeeze, and then straight fear as it seeped into their mouths. Some tried to scream around it as they convulsed and fell to their knees, but a couple fought on. One, just as the darkness reached his neck, bellowed into the crowd.

"The Blood King will rule! He will flood this world with blood and tears until it drowns in his power, and then he will rule over a new world! You will not win...you will not..."

He choked as the darkness took over, and then he was convulsing on the ground with everyone else. Finally, the prisoners stiffened, and I drew the darkness back into my core. I turned back to the crowd, feeling the panic and realization building down the bond.

"Let it be known that the King and Queen of Rifka will stand against tyranny and the Blood Clan. Let it be known that the Resisti stand with us. We fought for Aurevel and Rifka and removed their hold on our home. We removed the queen who willingly let them within our borders to reap and destroy. Hear me and hear me true. We will bring an end to the Blood Clan and cleanse this world of their stain. Stand by us and help us ensure that they will never set foot in Rifka again. That they are uprooted from Fenriel forever."

The crowd cheered and chanted earnestly as the royal guards surrounded us to escort us back to the castle. "Long live the Phoenix Queen! Long live the Shadow King!"

A piece of me reveled in their acceptance of me. But I couldn't focus on that for long, not when something had become very clear. The bringer of blood and tears in the prophecy was never my mate. It was the Blood King. The ruler of the Blood Clan. And if that was true, only the two of us, the shadows and snow, would be able to stop him. Unfortunately, we were also exactly what he needed to destroy the world for good.

Chapter 17

Does having a name for your fear conquer it?
Or feed it?

Silivia

"Oh gods. Oh gods," I chanted as I paced back and forth in the dining room of the king and queen suites.

It was where my friends, brother, and I ate when we wanted it to be just us. We ate just as often in the giant dining hall. It served as a way to build connections with the other Resisti warriors who remained in the castle, as well as Aurevel's army, staff, and visiting guests. Tonight, the Resisti Seven would just have to hold down the fort for us, because I was too stressed to eat with a large crowd.

Tess and Reece shared a look before glancing at me again. Ty was muttering something to Ghost on the side. I wasn't sure what they were talking about, but I was too freaked out to berate them.

"Sis, I know you're freaked out, but can you have a meltdown after dinner?" Reece reached for a breadstick and stuffed it into his mouth.

I turned and glared at him. "How can you be eating right now?"

He shrugged. "I'm hungry. Executions and dealing with the public build an appetite."

My stomach rolled as I stared at him in horror.

Tess scowled at him. "Not funny, Reece," she snapped.

My brother glanced sheepishly at her. "Sorry. Trying to lessen the tension." He glanced at me again. "I know today wasn't easy. It's never easy to order someone else's death, but you did the right thing."

I waved a hand dismissively as I started to pace again. "I know. I know. It doesn't change how crappy I feel, or the fact that we discovered the clan is under the rule of supposedly "the most powerful Fae king"." I stopped and glanced between them. "Has anyone ever even heard of him?"

Everyone shook their heads.

"I mean, we figured they had to have someone leading them," Ty pointed out. "They were too organized. Too efficient at what they were doing. I mean, look at how fast they gained a foothold during the Great Fae Wars."

"Okay, but how has no one known he was a king? The Blood King? Like what the hell." I could feel the panic rising in me again. I wasn't even sure why. Just that having a name for our enemy seemed to make him more real or something.

A strong arm wrapped around my waist, and I felt a wave of shadows wrap around the bond. "Take a deep breath, Silivia," Ghost told me, turning me to face him. I did as he asked until my heart rate steadied again. "Having a name is a step forward in the right direction, not a reason to panic. Now we know a little more about who we're dealing with."

"But do we, though?" Tess asked. We turned to her. "Silivia's right. Why have we not heard his name until now? Why has he been hiding?"

"Maybe he's not as powerful as he would like us to believe," Reece suggested. "Maybe he needed to wait until he'd gained enough followers to make his move."

"Reece is probably right, but we shouldn't underestimate how much power he holds," Ty suggested. "He's likely smart and was keeping hidden until his cards fell just so."

"Okay, but what cards exactly?" I asked, knowing the answer but needing someone else to say it.

Ty glanced at me apologetically. "Honestly? I think he was waiting for you. He's been trying to get Ghost for centuries, and now we understand why. He needs both of you on his side, because together you have the power to destroy him."

"How would he know that, though?" Ghost mused, a frown on his face. The hand around my waist stroked the sliver of skin exposed by my top soothingly, even as he contemplated. "He's been trying to recruit me since before we knew how great my power was. He sent men to the human world to claim Silivia."

He glanced down at me. "Even with Isrella telling them where to find Fariel, he would have needed to know to ask about you in the first place. How did he know Fariel had a daughter, and why did he wait so long to go after you?"

All good questions that we had no answers to. I could feel a migraine forming and looked around the room to see the same frustration and worry mirrored on my friends' faces.

"I don't like this," Ty growled. "We're just coming into the game with the realization that our adversary is not just a few steps ahead of us, but centuries. We need to even the playing field, and fast."

"Wait. How long has the prophecy been known?" Reece asked, twirling the wine glass in his hand.

At this rate, I could drink the entire bottle. Everyone turned to Ghost. He was the oldest in the room after all. My mate looked up at the ceiling as he deliberated.

"It's old. I'm not sure how old. I faintly remember my mother talking about it on a visit to the city." A flash of grief crossed his face, and I hugged him, but he continued. "She was obsessed with prophecies and fate. I remember Marcus mentioning that particular prophecy again during our history lessons years later." He frowned. "I believe it was spoken by the royal seer back when my father still guarded the king."

Ghost's father, Gonthar, was a famous changeling warrior who guarded my father and happened to be his best friend. He was unfortunately killed by the clan when Ghost was still young. For the prophecy to have been spoken even before then meant it was far older than we knew.

"But how would the Blood King know it? Do we have spies in the castle?" Tess asked.

Reese shrugged. "I wouldn't be surprised if someone heard the prophecy and was gossiping. But consider that it would have been placed in the Book of Prophecies. Any prophecies the seer deemed world-changing were placed in the museums so that all may know them."

"Why then, do I get the feeling that the Blood King knew about the prophecy close to when it was first spoken?" Ty muttered.

"So, there was a spy." I slipped from Ghost's embrace and sat at the table. He joined me and grabbed his glass of wine. "Okay, so we've determined that he knew long before Ghost gained his abilities, and I was even a thought. What does that tell us?"

Everyone was silent as the rest of us finally began eating. It wasn't until the servants had come to clear the table and we were working on only the wine that Ty shot up. We all glanced at him in surprise as he barely caught the wine bottle he'd hit.

"You good, bro?" Reece asked.

Ghost stared at his brother-in-arms like he'd grown a new limb. Ty stared right back like he'd seen a ghost.

"Uh, Tyrian?" Tess pushed. "What's wrong?"

"What if this goes deeper than we know?" he said quietly. "What if he set things in motion?" He still hadn't stopped staring at Ghost.

We all glanced at Ghost in confusion. He stared back at Ty blankly. Then his eyes widened, and his jaw dropped. His hand clenched around his glass so tightly, I swear I heard the glass groan. I placed a hand on his to ease it.

"What's wrong?" I asked them both.

"You...you think he sent the clan after them. To trigger my abilities."

Gasps went around the table, and I felt like I could drown in the amount of pain washing down the bond right now.

"You think that's why they tried to take me. To recruit me even before my power came to full fruition."

"But if that's true. Then he knew when Silivia would be of age to use hers," Tess pointed out, eyes wide.

Ghost still hadn't looked away from Ty. I knew he was waiting for his best friend to confirm that the worst day in his life...in both our lives...was *orchestrated* to control a prophecy.

"Yes," Ty said quietly. "I don't know how he knew. Maybe he has some type of ability where he could sense these things. But yes, I believe he set in motion both of your journeys so that he could manipulate you into joining him."

"Oh gods," Tess whispered.

Ghost didn't say anything. He just stood up from the table and walked out. A wall slammed down on his side of the bond, blocking me out.

"This is so fucked up," Reece said, swallowing uneasily. "How do we defeat someone who's held all the cards for longer than we knew there were cards to hold?"

Ty stared somberly at the door my mate had walked out of. "I don't know," he said quietly. "But if we don't figure it out quickly, we're going to lose. And there is far too much at stake for us to do so."

Chapter 18

Ghost

Orchestrated. My entire life had been manipulated just so I couldn't fulfill a prophecy I hadn't even known about. How far back did it go? My father's death? Before I was born? Was that why they had hunted so long for me when I'd run away?

They had come for me that day. The clan could have simply taken me and left my mother and sister behind. Hell, they could have quickly killed them and taken me, but instead, they'd made me *watch* as they tortured and raped them. Made me *listen* as the most important people in my life screamed for mercy. Made me *feel* the heat of the fire that burned them alive.

"Daniel! No! Please, he's only a child!"

Had she known? Had my mother known why the clan was there? What they were planning on doing?

"You don't know how special you are," she'd told me only the night before. *"You are meant for more than this small city. These simple people. You are meant to be a king."*

Had. She. Known?

I couldn't focus past the shadows and mist whipping around me. I couldn't even form them into a coherent form. I was barely preventing the darkness from lashing out at the world around me. Distantly, I remembered that I was supposed to have a royal guard following me. I'd given him the slip when I misted away. No one needed to be anywhere near me right now. No one needed to witness the destruction I was likely to cause at any moment. Arctic knocked on the bond, trying to reach me, but I pushed him away in a dark rage. Would I have ever met my bonded dragon if that night hadn't happened?

On the other side of the silver bond, I could feel the ice and snow stroking the wall I'd thrown up, trying to coax me to let it in, but I didn't want to be calmed. I wanted to rage. I wanted to destroy. I wanted...I wanted...my mother.

Tears flooded my eyes and rained down my cheeks as I bellowed to the sky. I screamed until I was hoarse, and still the pain did not cease. It had been four centuries since I last felt her hug me to her chest. Four centuries since I saw her smile. Heard her laugh. Sing. Four centuries since I played hide and seek with my sister in the forest. Every day, I wondered if this would be the day I no longer remembered their faces. Their voices. All I would be able to remember for eternity...was their screams.

I knew she would find me. Even when I didn't want her to, she somehow did. No one else had ever had that ability. She didn't say anything, just stood there, letting her snow and ice twist with the darkness and shadows. The pain was still clenching my chest painfully. I could barely breathe. She shouldn't be here. I could hurt her. Be used against her at some point in the future. Maybe I was naïve in believing I could have such light in my life.

"He killed them," I whispered hoarsely. "He killed them to make me into darkness." I swallowed the tears clogging my throat. "How could he think that I would blame anyone else but him?"

"He probably figured that if he raised you, he could make you see him as your savior...your father. You wouldn't despise him then. Or maybe you would, but you would be loyal to him."

I laughed bitterly as I glared at the ground between my knees. "I wonder if I would have ever developed my abilities if he'd left me alone. Or was I always destined to lose it all?" I would have gladly stayed powerless if I could have kept them.

"Does it matter?" she answered softly.

No, it didn't. What ifs didn't change the past. What was done was done. But I couldn't temper the rage, the grief. It was a tsunami building into something destructive within me.

"You should go. I can't...I can't control myself right now. I don't want to do something to you I'll regret," I warned her.

"Ghost."

"Go, Silivia!" I growled. "Please," I added on an angry, choked sob. Tears blurred my vision again, but not enough to block out the blue-grey eyes that met mine as she kneeled in front of me and palmed my wet cheeks.

"No, Daniel, I won't."

It jarred me every time she spoke my real name. At first, I'd thought I disliked it, but now I realized it felt like she was somehow keeping the memory of family alive by reminding me of the male I'd buried long ago.

"Go, Silivia," I tried once more. "I can't come home right now. I...I need to hurt something."

"Then take it out on me."

I blinked at her in surprise. "What?" I choked out. Did she know what she was saying? I wouldn't be able to hold back.

"Take it out on me. I can handle it." She stared up at me with such determination and love.

I wanted to kiss her desperately, but I had to be sure.

"I can't be gentle. I can't go slow."

Her gaze didn't waver. "I didn't ask you to."

Gods. Could she be any more perfect? I should convince her to leave. If I were a better male, I would, but I was the King of Shadows. I was darkness, and I needed to devour her light.

I crushed my lips to hers, one hand moving to wrap around her waist to hold her to me as the other gripped her hair. And then I devoured her. Our teeth clashed as I dove my tongue into the warm wetness of her mouth. I pulled her even closer, my hand grasping her breast and twisting the nipples to the point of pain. She groaned into my mouth and returned every drop of desire I thrust her way. Her tongue battled with mine. Her nails dug into the skin of my shoulders, and I still couldn't get enough. Pulling away, I gestured at her clothes.

"Take this off," I demanded, already pulling my shirt over my head.

She didn't hesitate. She simply pulled her shirt off, unbuttoned, and slid her pants down her long legs until she was kicking them off along with her shoes. My eyes trailed over the black lace adorning her, her long curly hair falling to frame her breasts. But it was her eyes that truly drew me in. They were stormy with desire to match my own. She was exquisite. And she was all mine.

I swallowed harshly. "All of it," I said hoarsely, taking my pants off. "Now, if you don't want me to rip them off you."

She gave me a mischievous look even as she shook her head in reproach. "You wouldn't dare."

My eyes flashed, and I grinned wickedly at her. "Try me," I growled. Luckily, she didn't hesitate to slip the lace off until she was bare before me. "Beautiful," I muttered.

And then I was on her again, pushing her back until she was sprawled out on the ground below me. I couldn't hold back. I knew I sucked, bit, and twisted her breasts too roughly. I pierced her with two fingers without warning and took her fast and deep, rubbing her bundle of nerves with my thumb until she was a writhing mess, and still, I couldn't stop. She didn't try to stop me either. I had long lines of claw marks going down my shoulders and back as she gripped me to her. She arched into me, as she bit my bottom lip so hard it bled. It wasn't long before I had her screaming at the sky, panting as she spiraled back to earth. But it wasn't enough. Not nearly enough.

I didn't warn her before I was thrusting all the way to the hilt. I roared and groaned, reveling in the connection. At some point, I must have lowered the wall around our bond because I could feel everything. Every ounce of pain, understanding, anger, and love.

"Do it," she panted. "Take what you need."

And then I was driving into her. Short, hard thrusts that had her coming apart beneath me in seconds. She was barely coming down before I was lifting her legs to my shoulders to thrust into her harder, deeper. Two more times she screamed my name. Two more times I adjusted her. Pounded her harder. Faster. Deeper. Our power was a tornado around us. Anyone who dared to approach us now would be destroyed. That's what this love was doing. It was destroying and remaking me into something new. Something greater.

Hot tears poured down my face, but the pain was receding. And then I couldn't hold on any longer. Every part of me tightened as my eyes rolled to the back of my head, and when she fell over the edge again, screaming my name, I followed her, bellowing my release to the night sky. I collapsed on top of her, barely catching myself before I crushed her beneath me. We both panted heavily as we clung to each other.

I opened my eyes to find her already staring back at me. She reached up to wipe my tears away, and I closed my eyes briefly before reopening them. She wore the face of a female who'd been thoroughly satisfied. I doubted she'd be able to walk. Forget misting. And she'd settled me. The darkness was leashed, the mist once again playing at our feet.

When I could finally breathe, I slowly pulled out of her and shifted so that she lay half on top of me, my arms wrapped securely around her body as her leg rested between mine, and her arm hugged me back. We were filthy. Covered in dirt and leaves, but I wasn't ready to let her go. She was almost asleep when I felt her kiss my chest.

"My Daniel. My Ghost. My King. My Love," she whispered, and then she was sleeping peacefully in my arms.

I stared up at the stars, trying to understand. I had lost so much at the hands of a demented king. I would be damned if I let him take anything more from me.

"You don't know how special you are. You are meant to be a king."

My mother was right. It didn't matter that the Blood King had set my life in motion. I was always destined to be who I was. I was just as powerful, if not more than he was. I was the Shadow King. There could only be one true king.

Chapter 19

Once, I only ruled the shadows.
But then I met the mistress of the light.
And became co-ruler of the dawn.

Ghost

Two days later, Silivia, Tyrian, and I strolled through the marketplace. I could feel the tension and slight guilt still haunting my mate, but she pasted on a brave face as she smiled and chatted with everyone we passed. I stood at her side, her equal, a king, still uncomfortable with the concept but no longer willing to hide from its meaning. I knew the people feared me and loved her. They'd had many centuries to hear of my dark deeds. If it kept them in line, then I would continue to wear my dark reputation on my head like the crown it was, but I knew fear only got a monarchy so far. A rapport of trust and loyalty was much more effective..

We would be headed to the first of the sky cities, Belus, City of the Griffins, tomorrow morning. We'd only lingered this long in the hope that we could have Aurevel well on the way to recovery before we left it. The main parts of the city were repaired, the castle mostly restored, and even some of the normal daily activities had resumed, like this marketplace we strolled through. The people were cautious even as they called out about their wares and completed their shopping. But despite how much my mate loathed having to do it, the public execution had gone a long way in strengthening resolve and trust.

They eyed us warily, but I saw many with looks of hope and awe as we passed. I offered greetings of my own and spoke to any who wished to speak to me. I still left the smiles and laughter to the glowing queen at my side. The children loved her, especially as she made it snow all around them. Their parents looked on with reluctant smiles at the easy acceptance of children. They didn't want to admit it, but it had been centuries since this much peace was seen on the streets. Isrella had not been a kind nor just queen. In only a few months, Silivia had reintroduced a time not seen since her father reigned.

"Your Majesty! Your Majesty!"

Startled, I glanced down at the hopping, elven boys in front of me. I smiled at their eager expressions even as I noted their parents' horrified looks in the background.

"Can you do it, King Ghost? Can you please?" The three boys implored.

I frowned down at them. "Do what, young ones?" I asked, lifting a brow.

They glanced at each other and then gestured for me to lean down. Kneeling on one knee, I let them circle around my ear to whisper their request. I pulled back and pretended to consider, then shrugged.

"Why not?" I replied with a wicked wink.

With a wave of my hand, I summoned my mist higher and weaved it until it formed into three giant dyrewolves, my spirit animal. The boys screeched in joy that only amplified when each wolf flattened to the ground to allow them to climb on. Before long, they were racing through the square on the back of shadow wolves, yipping and hollering for all to see. Their parents looked like they didn't know whether to pull them off or laugh along with them.

When I finally called the shadows back to me, the boys all hugged me earnestly, too excited to worry about looking mature in front of their friends, and raced back to their parents.

"You know you just gave them the story of a lifetime," Tyrian commented, smiling after the boys.

I couldn't help a grin of my own even as I slowly became aware of all the attention I'd garnered.

"To think you've never let anyone ride them before."

"I was never in the mindset to let them," I answered absentmindedly, a little uneasy with the differing looks aimed at me.

Sensing it, Silivia slipped her hand into mine. I glanced down at her gratefully.

"You just showed them that even the King of Shadows knows how to have fun. They'll love you forever for it," she mused.

I snorted. "It's you they adore, my love," I corrected. "But I'll take them being slightly less fearful of me."

She pulled us along, and this time, more people greeted me as they greeted her. One little stunt, and suddenly Aurevel was seeing me as more than their dark king. I shook my head in awe. The wonder of children.

"You're wrong."

I glanced at my mate again to see her gazing at me lovingly.

"It is not just me they love. After all, it wasn't just me who saved their city. You have been protecting them long before now. The difference is, you are more approachable and able to see the awe hidden below the fear."

"Is that really what you believe?" I asked her, surprised, thinking of all the past visits to my home's capital.

She leaned her head against my arm and squeezed my hand. "It is what I know. I mean, how could they not?"

I glanced over to my best friend to see if he was buying this, to find him watching us with a sad smile.

"She's right, you know." I lifted a brow in shock. "I'm glad others can see you the way Tess and I always could."

I shook my head at both of them, but as we continued visiting the city that day, I felt more at home than I ever had before.

Chapter 20

Sometimes I wish I could fade away
Like a long forgotten memory

Dalacia

Was I a fool for letting my guard down around my captor? Maybe. But every time I stared into his hazel-colored eyes, I found myself adrift at sea. It didn't matter that we couldn't stand each other. I took one look at those eyes and had to fight the impulse to kiss him. I also still couldn't help but want to trace that thunderbolt scar with my fingers...and then my tongue.

"Gods," I swore, giving myself a vicious shake. What was wrong with me? I was a prisoner in my sister's kingdom. It didn't matter that, thanks to the special iron bracelets around my wrists, I could now travel with an escort. Whether secluded in my room or roaming the capital, I was trapped.

I could barely see the flowers and trees surrounding me. Forget enjoying them. I slipped underneath a willow tree with willows so long, they formed a curtain around me, blocking me from view. It didn't matter that I knew *he* was still watching. I sat down on the bench wrapped around the tree trunk.

I stared down at my hands, wishing I could burn the pieces of metal from my arms. Hell, I'll take being able to summon sparks. I would have never thought having my fire abilities blocked would make me feel so...incomplete. It was like a piece of my soul was missing. I'd hated it at first as it had only been a weapon for the clan to use to capture my sister. *My sister*. As if I were still not enough and never would be. But then the embers had filled in the hole left from the loss of my parents. Without the flickering light, the hole in my chest felt darker, larger, like a black hole that could swallow me at any moment. A tightness I couldn't fight squeezed around my heart, and I leaned over my knees, trying to breathe past the pain. I gasped for air desperately.

"You cannot fall apart. Not here," I told myself, but tears built in the corners of my eyes until the world was blurry, and all I could see was a green haze beneath my feet. I couldn't breathe. My chest was too tight. Too empty. The darkness and misery too much. I needed my fire. I needed my parents. Gods, I needed...I needed...

A firm hand squeezed around the nape of my neck, massaging even as the dominance in the gesture radiated. I felt a warm presence near me, like a warm fire, but it gave off flickers of electricity, and I knew who'd joined me.

"Breathe," he told me firmly.

I choked on a retort. What did he think I was trying to do? But then his fingers started massaging my nape firmer, and I could feel his other hand rubbing circles along my thigh. He knelt at my feet. I could see his black pants in the haze of my tears. I tried to breathe. I really did. He pressed deeper, and I felt shots of electricity tingle my nerves. I gasped.

"Deep breath in. Hold it. Deep breath out. That's it, Princess. Again."

I followed his instructions, barely flinching at the title that rolled so effortlessly off his tongue without the usual mocking tone. When was the last time someone walked me off the ledge? For the first year of my life in Fenriel, I'd been punished and left to suffer until my panic attacks passed. My nightmares replayed on repeat so much that I forgot what it felt like to sleep peacefully.

"Stay with me, Dalacia," Barak told me, bringing my attention back to his instructions.

Slowly, my heart rate slowed, and the pressure in my chest eased until I could take in the male before me. His eyes held understanding I was unprepared for. With a start, I realized my fingers had his shirt in a death grip and one of his hands still held the nape of my neck while the other...the other wiped tears I didn't know had fallen. He was so tall, he was eye to eye with me despite being on his knees. As I stared into the liquid pools that had lightning sparking across them occasionally, I felt a different feeling building in my chest. It was like a hum you would get from sticking your tongue to a battery, and it felt like it was connected to the male in front of me.

I noticed his frown as if he could feel it too, but I didn't pull away. I should. He was my sister's ally, which made him my enemy. By principle, I loathed him. So why did I feel drawn to him more than ever? Why was I leaning forward as he did the same? Had he realized he had? His eyes flicked to my lips before meeting mine again, and he opened his mouth to say something. But then, he was shaking himself out of the daze we were in and standing to his feet. I felt his loss of touch like a phantom wound and berated myself for such a display of weakness.

Needing to shake off the feeling building within me, I jumped to my feet and balled my fists. "I'm surprised you didn't just let me be. Since when do you care?" I snapped.

Barak eyed me, considering, but he simply turned away. "I wasn't going to just watch while you drowned, Dalacia. You may be happy with just fading away, but I'm not."

He walked away, leaving me underneath the willow tree. What did he mean by that? And why had the hum in my chest grown louder at his declaration?

Chapter 21

I am no Romeo.
You are not Juliet.
You cannot be mine.

Barak

I'd wanted to kiss her. Seeing her tears as she fought the panic attack overtaking her had jarred something in me. For a second, I had caught a glance of the person Dalacia kept concealed. I think we'd all forgotten what she'd been through. Instead, just chalking her actions up to the jealousy and anger over her sister's success. I should know from experience that things were never that simple. No one had asked the full extent of what had happened to her over there, but I could guess. If I opened up about my own experience being a prisoner of the clan, would she expel their secrets?

No, I was lying to myself if I said that was the only reason I wanted her to confide in me. I sensed a kindred spirit in her, and maybe that's why her betrayal of her sister hurt so badly. I would never betray Raiden, no matter what the clan did to me. But what if they had done more to her than what had been done to me? What if the mind games had gone deeper?

I didn't have the late King Fariel as a father. I controlled lightning and could call forth storms like my brother, but I wasn't important enough for the inner clan court to take notice. And I had no doubt that that was who'd confined the fire princess of Rifka. She had most likely been in contact with the leader we sought, but what if... she didn't remember.

I frowned. Wait. What if that was it? What if she didn't *remember*? Could it be that she was coerced into attacking her sister? It wasn't unheard of. Few Fae had the power required to manipulate thoughts like that, but it wasn't impossible. It would explain how sibling jealousy had manifested into destruction of her father's kingdom. What if she simply had to be reminded of which side she belonged to? No doubt she'd gone through hell under the care of the clan. What if I showed her the opposite? Wasn't it my responsibility to ensure all threats to the crown were removed?

The Resisti Seven...I snorted at the name...minus Sirius, had become an unstoppable team over the final trial. While being Reese's friend had initially brought us together, I could feel the friendship forming with the others. Even more, I felt it forming with Tyrian, Teslia, and especially Silivia and Ghost. I'd never thought I would be working so closely with three of the most powerful warriors in the Resisti, forget calling them friends. Now I knew that despite the displeasure of the Resisti elders, my loyalty lay with this group–*this family*–first. Plus, sometimes the elders were stuck in their ways and failed to see how their plans affected the individuals.

But was it just my loyalty to our little team that made me want to convince the wildfire that was Silivia's sister? A hum in my core caught my attention. It crackled and flowed, much like a fire might. I knew what it could mean, but I never expected it to be an option for me, and most definitely not with a female who was determined to be my enemy. Except...except if I had kissed her in the garden this afternoon, I had no doubt she would have let me, and I didn't know what to do with that.

"I'm sorry, what?" Raiden said, blinking in shock.

They all stared at me in disbelief around the meeting table. I understood why. Hell, a part of me agreed.

"Did I hear you correctly? You want to bring the female who tried to kill our queen with us as we shop for allies. The same female, who may I remind you, is allies with the enemy we're trying to build an army against?"

I gritted my teeth even though I knew Aux was correct. "Reece designed the bracelets to hold her power," I reminded him.

"She still has her tongue and training intact," Sirius stated.

Now I wanted to jump across the table and knock him shitless. Except that wouldn't help my case. I was the same person who, weeks ago, was calling for Dalacia to be thrown into the dungeon. Now I was advocating for her joining us on a mission of life and death. The irony wasn't lost on me.

"Last I checked, it was always the plan to convince her to come to our side," I pointed out. I met each of the gazes around the table before focusing on the blue-grey eyes of the queen. "How can we expect her to see us differently from the clan when we treat her as the enemy?"

"That's because she currently *is* the enemy," Aux reminded me. I threw him a glare. "Don't give me that look. She may be Silivia's sister, but that doesn't wipe the damage she's done to Rifka's people and the queen herself."

"She didn't kill anyone," I threw back, my fists clenched.

"No, but she allowed for others to do so in her negligence," Rose retorted.

I glared at her next, but she shrugged, that annoyingly always perfect hair of hers flowing in a nonexistent wind. Meanwhile, my locs were always getting in my eyes.

"I'm just saying, on purpose or not, she caused a lot of pain."

"Isn't the saying, keep your friends close and your enemies closer?" I glanced around the table again, desperate for their agreement for some reason. "We are about to travel to other kingdoms. Would it be wise to leave her here in Rifka?"

There was silence as everyone considered my words. I could feel a dark gaze on me and turned to meet Ghost's eyes. He studied me as if he knew there was another reason I wanted their agreement. Maybe a part of me hoped he did. Maybe then he could explain this feeling squeezing my chest.

The King of Shadows considered me for a few seconds more before turning to his mate. "He's right, and we both know you want your sister at our side."

Silivia glanced at him with a look that held regret with a hint of anger. "She's not ready to be at our side, Ghost," she answered bitterly.

"Give me until we leave for Hyra," I propositioned, and both of them glanced my way. "If I can't convince her to at least give us a chance by then, we'll go without her." There was a sharp pain within me at the thought.

Ghost glanced at Silivia again. I knew the male would happily remove Dalacia from the picture if it came to it, but I appreciated him considering his mate's feelings first.

"It wouldn't hurt to let Barak try to work on your sister's alliance while we get Rifka settled. Whether we like it or not, your sister has power of her own, and we may need her for the war ahead. If he can convince her to trust one person in our party, it will make our job easier in the long run."

Silivia bit her lip, obviously unsure about this.

"We can't afford for her to rejoin the clan," Tyrian cut in. We all turned to him. "Barak's right. If we can show her why our side's a better option, it could give us a lift in the battles to come. Think about it. She was likely within the inner court of the clan."

I nodded my agreement, glad the warrior had come to the same conclusion as I. He gave me a single nod, and warmth filled me at his show of support.

"If we turn her back to our side, she can share what she knows. Gods know we've been trying to determine who led the Blood Clan for centuries. The answers could be locked up in her head." Literally, but I didn't say that part. I wanted proof before I presented such to the group.

"We could always torture it out of her," Sirius offered with a shrug.

I bit down a growl and once again felt Ghost's eyes on me. Yeah, he could definitely tell something else was going on.

"You touch my sister, Sirius, and I'll let Ghost's shadows play with your mind before I freeze them permanently into your bloodstream."

The room went silent. The threat was said so calmly, one would think the queen nonchalant, but the room had dropped several degrees. Ghost chuckled, breaking the tension in the room.

"Please, Sirius, continue to talk out of your ass. I would love to see my mate put you in your place."

Me too, I thought with wicked glee. Honestly, I didn't know why they allowed the slippery male to remain in their inner circle, but his loyalty had remained steadfast despite his tongue. The yellow-eyed male held up his hands in defeat.

"It was just a suggestion," he assured us. "Of course, I wouldn't touch the princess without permission." He said princess like it put a bad taste in his mouth.

"You won't touch the princess at all, Sirius," Ghost stated plainly. "Or our queen's threat becomes a promise."

Sirius muttered incoherently under his breath but said nothing else. Everyone was quiet for a long moment.

"Okay, so what are we doing?" Teslia asked, breaking the silence.

All eyes zeroed on Silivia. It was her sister, so it was her decision. She turned eyes tinged with hope to mine.

"Do you really think you can turn her back?"

The pain reflected in that question alone. I knew without a shadow of doubt that the queen before me was just a sister missing her sibling. I could relate to an extent, so I nodded.

"I will do my uttermost best," I swore.

She nodded. "Fine. Barak will work on my sister here, while the rest of us work on the rest of Rifka. When we're done, we meet up in Siron, and hopefully together travel to Hercule to proposition the King and Queen of Hyra."

And with that, we separated.

"Barak." I stopped at Ghost's call, turning to watch the powerful warrior stroll down the hall towards us. He halted and stood in front of Raiden and me. He glanced at my brother before turning to me. "Can I have a word?"

Raiden's brows shot up as he glanced at me, but I nodded once. He didn't look pleased at being dismissed and would likely accost me later, but he nodded to both of us and disappeared down the hall. I turned back to the king. Ghost inclined his head, indicating I should follow him. We made our way out of the castle until we were traveling down a path alongside the forest. He finally stopped when we reached a stream snaking through the trees. It was quiet and peaceful here, and although I knew his royal guard was somewhere out of sight, I figured he wasn't close enough to hear this conversation. To ensure just that, I sensed a wave of darkness blocking our words from the outside world. Only then did Ghost turn to face me.

"You're spiritbonded." I choked on my spit and coughed to clear my airway. When I could breathe again, I stared at him in shock.

"What?" I sputtered. He only studied me calmly.

"You're spiritbonded," he stated again. I shook my head, eyes wide.

"No, I'm not," I insisted. "I just know a little about what she's been through. She needs someone to see her and not the enemy or sister label she's had to cart around." Ghost nodded in understanding.

"Like the label of Fariel's daughter, or heir, or prophecy bearer."

"Exactly." Both sisters had been burdened with too much pressure since entering Fenriel. They needed people to simply see *them*.

"You care about her, then." I shrugged. I didn't want to admit how, with each day, I disliked her less and less.

"She was given a crappy hand, and she *is* Silivia's sister. They deserve to have someone care enough to fix their sibling rivalry." Ghost wasn't budging, though. He studied me as if he could see that annoying hum permeating my core.

"I was just like you, you know," he said finally. "I tried to deny how I felt, too. I wanted to stay angry and just do what I needed to out of disgruntled duty." He chuckled darkly. "Fate didn't allow it, and being around her didn't either." I shifted uncomfortably.

"What are you saying?" He gave me a knowing look.

"I'm saying it's okay to hate her, to begrudgingly care. I'm also saying it's okay if that changes." I blinked at him, not sure what to say.

"Are you going soft on me, Ghost?" I teased, but I was off kilter. He chuckled again.

"No, I assure you, I'm not. She may have rounded out my edges some, but I'm still the ruthless King of Shadows you all know and love. I'm just saying it's not bad to want someone to temper you."

"She's supposed to be the enemy," I reminded him weakly, as if I hadn't just spent the meeting fighting to prove the opposite. He nodded his understanding.

"And by your own admission, she may have been coerced. Who's to say she can't be your mate as well?"

I couldn't form a reply, and he didn't need one. He'd said what he meant to. He left me by the stream to consider his words. My mate. My spiritbonded. Could I really have found my other half in the hands of the enemy? The humming in my core told me what it thought, but I wasn't ready to give my heart to anyone. The last female I'd done so, sold me to the clan. How much worse could one trained by the clan's inner circle hurt me?

No. I would convince Dalacia to join our side because this war and her sister needed her to. But I would never be spiritbonded. Not to her. Not to anyone.

Chapter 22

I am no longer the child
huddled in the corner
waiting to be saved.
I am the queen.

Silivia

There was a level of nostalgia traveling across Rifka again. Although before it had been on horseback and by foot, and this time we flew on dragonback, I still felt awe filling me as I took in the landscape below. Rifka was beautiful. From its mountains to its forests, to the rolling hills, to the people who called it home. Every aspect of it hummed in my soul, telling me I was home.

But as we left the landscape behind to fly higher into the clouds in the southernmost part of Rifka, I grew apprehensive. By the time the mountains in the sky came into sight, I was fighting all out anxiety. Something told me the people of the sky wouldn't be as welcoming as those of the land...and they hadn't exactly rolled out the red carpet.

The massive, grey mountain range painted with snow sat on a sea of clouds, and in its center, in a valley inhabited by a city made of ancient stone, sat a small castle. As we flew through the valley, I took in the pillars and overall architecture and couldn't help thinking it reminded me of what Olympus would look like. The Fae even walked around in clothes common in Greece, like chlamys and togas. How they managed to ride the griffins that lay sprawled across various buildings and the mountainside itself, I didn't know. The massive half-lion, half-eagle creatures varied in color, but all looked menacing and likely to rip anyone to shreds with those massive talons. I gulped.

"Welcome to Belus," Reece said with distaste from beside me.

I shot him a look, but he was scowling down at the residents who stared back with equal disgust. I frowned at the name, remembering something from what Dad had made me read.

"Does Belus happen to mean..."

"City of the gods? Yeah, it does," Tess confirmed as we landed in the courtyard.

The castle rose up on giant stone pillars that truly looked like it housed a god.

"And is it the city of gods?" I asked, not really putting anything past Fenriel at this point.

Ty scoffed. "They wish."

Ghost snorted as they came to my side and glanced at me. "Remember how Reece said how the sky cities believe they are greater than those on land?" I nodded. "Well, Belus thinks it's the greatest of the sky cities."

"Why?" I watched as royal guards marched from the castle to meet us.

Our own guards quickly moved to surround us. In my peripheral, I noticed Lorik tense, his giant black wings shifting as if readying for a fight. It was he who answered.

"They are of the opinion that since the griffins claim these mountains as their own, then their city must be the greatest. After all, the eagle is king of all birds and the lion king of all beasts in the human land, no?" I nodded, a slight frown on my face. "Then, if combined, it can be understood why they are considered such formidable beasts."

I shrugged. "I mean, I guess." I glanced at the griffins along the castle wall. They ignored us as they slumbered or lazed around.

"I'm partial to dragons myself," Ghost commented.

Everyone but the changelings mumbled their agreements–*they* could fly–and then went silent as the guards stopped in front of me. They bowed, one hand over their hearts. I couldn't help noticing their wings were more of a dark brown than black.

"*They're not a part of the elite royal guard,*" Ghost explained when I asked him down the bond. "*Those with black or dark grey wings are usually the strongest and have proven their skills above all else. Their wings change colors to reflect their status.*"

Interesting. There was still so much for me to learn.

"Your Majesty," the lead one said, rising. "I am Captain Hirkul, leader of the royal guards of Belus. It is our honor to welcome you to our great city and to escort you to Lord Zerc and Lady Hira."

I blinked. Then blinked again. Was it just me, or was his name similar to Hercules and the others to Zeus and Hera? I must have been silent too long because Reese cleared his throat at my side. I blinked, then shook myself internally.

"Lead on, Captain," I said finally.

Before long, we were strolling into a massive meeting hall, and in two chairs sitting as if they were indeed god and goddess, were Lord Zerc and Lady Hira. They stared down their noses at us as we approached, not once making a move to bow or acknowledge us as everyone else in Rifka had begun to do. You would think I was still just normal Silivia, but Reece had always been their prince. Where was their respect?

"The Phoenix Queen, Silivia, The King of Shadows, Ghost, Prince Reece, and the Resisti warriors Tyrian and Teslia," Hirkul announced before bowing to us again and stepping to the side. Noticeably leaving out our titles of King and Queen of the Winged and Rifka.

I noticed that my guards stood tense and ready, hands hovering close to their weapons. Obviously, there was no trust or love lost between land and sky. Odd for a kingdom where all its people celebrated the winged.

The lord and lady were both silent as they appraised us, content to let us stew in the awkward silence. This may have bothered me a year ago, or even a few months ago, but after dealing with various people and warriors during the trials and the council afterwards, I was more than happy to stand and let them stew right back.

"*Apparently, they didn't get the memo that the monarchy is under new rule,*" Ghost said bitterly. "*If they had, maybe then they'd realized not acknowledging their king and queen was a punishable offense.*"

I fought to keep my face indifferent even as I felt their disrespect rubbing me the wrong way. *"Yeah, well, Reece did warn us they were going to be a handful."*

I felt his growl vibrate down the bond as the mist whipped around our feet. *"And you wonder why I never cared to interact with them or deal with court politics."*

I fought a smile as I sent a wave of snow to mix with the mist. *"Don't worry, my dark king, if they become too much, you can always feed them to the shadow dyrewolves,"* I crooned sweetly. He snorted, but I could sense his reluctant amusement.

Lord Zerc and Lady Hira's eyes narrowed as they took in the power swirling around our feet.

"So, it is true," Lord Zerc finally spoke, his deep voice sounding too loud as it bounced off the walls of the room...likely by design. "The King of Shadows has found his mate in the Bringer of Blood and Tears."

Instantly, ice froze every vein as I fought not to let my rage and shock show, but I could barely contain a wince. Ghost growled aloud this time as our guards shifted, but it was Reece who spoke.

"Careful," he warned quietly, his tone coated in silent wrath. "That is your king and queen you speak to, as well as my sister. You would do well to watch your tongue."

Lady Hira inclined her head. "Forgive us, Prince Reece. It is still difficult to reconcile the female who is prophesied to be the cause of the destruction of Fenriel with the one who is supposed to save it. Add on the King of Shadows, and it becomes highly unlikely."

Reece narrowed his eyes, and I felt everyone behind and beside me tense further. Tyrian shifted closer even as the guards tightened their hands on their weapons. Ghost's mist grew more agitated as his lips pulled back in a silent snarl. Even Teslia had her hands on her staff, ready to jump in as needed. I held a hand up, and they all settled. Both the lady and lord's brows rose in surprise.

"Let's jump past the bullshit, shall we," I said calmly. "You don't see either Ghost nor I as your king and queen, and unless we prove ourselves worthy of the title, you refuse to bow to us. Despite the trials revealing I was the rightful heir. Despite my defeating the murderous queen, who allowed the clan into Rifka to plunder and destroy. Despite the answer of the dragons, Bohr Eagles, and Galaton Owls to my call."

"Unless I pass some test of your making, you will not accept our rule and join us in preventing the Blood Clan from taking over Rifka and the rest of Fenriel. And don't think just because you live in the sky that you are exempt from their greed and wrath. You act as if they too cannot find winged creatures to attack you even here. You are not the only city I must visit and rally. Nor are you part of the only kingdom that I must do so in. So, what will it be? What test must we complete to earn your loyalty?"

The entire room was silent, friend and potential foe alike staring at me with a mixture of shock, respect, and amusement. Lord Zerc and Lady Hira sat with their jaws to the floor and eyes wide, likely not expecting me to call them out with confidence I'd most definitely lacked only a few months ago. When no one had said anything for several seconds, I raised a brow in question.

"Well?"

Shock quickly morphed into fury as they glared at me.

"There is nothing you can do to earn our loyalty," Lord Zerc spat. "You are not of our world and do not belong here. You are no queen of ours, no more than this male of darkness and death is our king." He gestured wildly at Ghost, who only crossed his arms.

"You didn't mind my darkness when it was defending you in battle," he said smoothly. "You didn't mind it when it prevented the clan from overtaking Rifka either. Funny how now that the threat is neutralized, you find fault with my darkness."

The lord sputtered in indignation.

"And you say I'm not of this world, even though you know Fariel was my father. When have you known a human to call the winged and command a blue phoenix?"

They paled at the mention of my spirit animal. "The blue phoenix is a myth and does not exist," Lady Hira argued, but her voice betrayed her doubt.

I shrugged. They could believe what they wanted. I did not come here to flaunt my power. "Then I will win over a creature you do believe in." I saw the moment they realized what I meant.

They glanced at each other and then burst into laughter.

"That is as unlikely as you summoning the blue phoenix," Lady Hira laughed. "No one commands the king and queen of griffins."

"Wanna bet?"

They abruptly stopped laughing as they took in the serious expressions of my companions and I. They glanced at each other again, wicked delight flickering in their eyes. They sat back against their makeshift thrones.

"Fine. If you are able to command the king and queen of griffins and bring them into the city, Belus will bow to you and follow you in whatever endeavor you see fit."

I nodded. "Deal."

Their smiles widened. "But if you fail...we get the crown."

Gasps filled the room, and tension magnified tenfold. I stiffened, trying to keep my indifference, but this was a risk far greater than I'd anticipated. And yet...if I didn't agree, we wouldn't be able to get the sky kingdoms in line. In my peripheral, Reece shook his head once. Even Ty was trying to catch my eye, but Ghost, despite the rage buffeting the bond, said nothing, trusting me to make the decision. This could either go horribly wrong, or really right. I had to trust in our abilities. In our fate. In our bond. So, I stood tall and nodded once.

"Deal."

Chapter 23

Stories are memories written, spoken.
Legends are those memories magnified.

Dalacia

"Tell me again why we're strolling through the market?" I asked, trying to conceal the curiosity rushing through me as I eyed the various wares of the patrons around us.

"Because I needed a break from the castle and wasn't going to let you stay within its walls without me present."

I shot the disgruntled warrior at my side a questioning look. He studiously ignored my stare as he took in the market. Behind us, two royal guards and two of the Resisti followed. Apparently, despite Barak's status, they weren't going to allow me to move throughout Aurevel without extra eyes.

"What? You didn't consider simply locking me up in the dungeon?" I asked sweetly, grinning at him.

Electric eyes glared at me, but there was a hint of amusement in them. "It crossed my mind, but I didn't want to deal with the other patrons' complaints about your presence."

I snorted. "They would deem themselves lucky to be in the presence of the fire princess, thank you very much," I said, lifting my chin high.

He chuckled and shook his head. The animosity between us had started to fade long before I'd realized. I wasn't going to tell the stubborn male, but I actually enjoyed our verbal matches as much as our physical ones.

"Glad to see your confidence wasn't boxed up with that fiery power of yours."

I narrowed my eyes but smiled sweetly at him. "Yeah, it remained untethered just like my fiery temper."

He snorted in amusement. "Oh, I know. I see it every time I wipe the floor with you after all."

I scowled, and his feral grin grew. "Last I checked, you've been on the mat a few times yourself," I reminded him.

He shrugged. "You got lucky a few times, so what?"

I scowled again. "Lucky? A few times? Just you wait, I'll..." I was cut off by a commotion up ahead. Curious, I tried to see over the crowd amassing in the middle of the square. "What's going on?" I asked, glancing at Barak.

He studied the group and continued towards them. "Looks like one of the traveling elders is about to tell a story."

I eyed the crowd again, excitement building. There was nothing I loved more than a good story. "Really? Can we listen?"

His gaze shot to mine, a brow raised in surprise, but then he led us through the crowd until we stood before an ancient faerie with silver hair and tree bark colored clothes sitting atop a giant boulder. His opaque wings were tinged with pink and fluttered lightly behind him.

"Come. Come. Hear the tale of the Great Fariel. Come. Come. Hear the tale of the Dragon King."

My heart clenched at the mention of my father, but a part of me was desperate to learn more about the side of my dad's life that I never had the chance to see.

"I tell you the tale of when he defeated the White Witch. It was a dark time, and our king was still young, still only a prince. Rifka was plagued by rumors of a white shadow that came in the night. It danced through the villages. Stalked through the forest. Haunted the cities. Shrouded the hills. And whenever it came, it would play the most beautiful music that you will ever hear."

"Those who heard it could not help but seek it out. It drew them in until young males and warriors alike drifted from their homes, the taverns, the fields to reach it. And once they did, the shadow revealed itself as a female dressed in white, a siren of the moon. Then, the males would grow desperate, for only one could have her, and they would fight for the right as she drank her fill of their violence. Our king heard the tale of this siren of the moon, and so with his loyal friend Gonthar at his side, they rode out into Rifka to hunt her down."

The story continued to explain how my father and the changeling traveled from village to village seeking the White Witch, always just missing her, until finally they happened to hear the music. Gonthar, unable to resist the call of the siren, started towards it, a haze in his eyes, and fearing for his friend's safety, my father knocked him out and tied him to a tree. Continuing on, my father came upon the siren sitting atop a tree stump, the males of the village fighting at her feet.

"He snuck up behind her, fighting the pull of her song, but for a second grew distracted, for she was as beautiful as her music. It was then that the siren noticed him, and claws grew from her nails as she screeched a warning, sending the males after him. He fought them off, careful to only knock them unconscious. But then his twin dragon blades were knocked from his hands as the siren slammed into him. She held him against a tree, slashing her deadly claws across his chest."

I held my breath, eyes wide as I waited to hear how my dad would get himself free. I could feel Barak's attention just as riveted as the rest of the crowd as the storyteller gestured dramatically throughout the tale.

"It was then our prince, our king, felt under his skin, a power rising. And with a mighty roar, he placed a hand on the siren's chest, sending her flying backwards in a wave of flames. Her screams filled the night as she burned until nothing but ash remained and was blown away on a silent wind."

"The males in the clearing awoke then, a pounding filling their heads along with confusion, but Fariel sent them home and returned to free his friend. And so, the Dragon King came upon his first power. The power of fire, and the White Witch was no more."

There was thunderous applause, and I clapped so hard, my hands hurt, my eyes still wide in amazement. Finally, the crowd dispersed, and the storyteller disappeared between one blink and another. I turned to Barak in surprise.

"Where did he go?" I asked.

He shrugged. "He goes where he wants. He is a wanderer after all." He turned to head back towards the castle. "If we're lucky. He'll be back to tell another story tomorrow."

I hurried to catch up to him. "Can we come back to hear it?" I couldn't keep the excitement out of my voice. I felt like a child again listening to my mother tell tales of mythical creatures and legends. I was desperate to hear more about this world besides what the Blood Clan had told me. I expected him to scoff, or laugh, or shrug me off, but instead he gave me a true smile that had my heart stuttering in my chest.

"Of course. And every day after as long as he's here."

My answering grin could not be contained.

The next day, I was sloppy during our training, and after Barak had knocked me to the floor for the tenth time, he finally called it a day with a shake of his head.

"You're already in the marketplace listening to the next story, aren't you?" he teased.

I shrugged. "What can I say. He's sooo much more interesting than you," I tossed over my shoulder as I quickly returned my wooden sword. I was eager to get going, and luckily, he took pity on me because soon we were heading out of the castle. We arrived at the stage just as the ancient faerie called out.

"Come. Come. Hear the tale of the Great Fariel. Come. Come. Hear the tale of the Dragon King."

I bounced on my toes after we'd weaved our way to the front. Barak shot me an amused smirk.

"Relax, Dalacia. You're like a child in the candy store."

"Shhh," I hushed him. "He's about to start."

"Come. Come. And I'll tell you the tale of the Serpent of the Sea of Nightmares."

"Ahh, this is a good one," the male beside me commented with a nod.

"Shhh, lightning boy," I reprimanded.

Barak scowled. *"That's prince of lightning to you,"* he muttered under his breath.

"Our king was still young in his reign when he set out to map the Sea of Nightmares. It was known for claiming those who dared sail its waters, but the fish captured there were bountiful and had meat so rich some still braved it. But during this time, tales began of a creature beyond the deadly sirens, the massive squids, and the ruthless sharks. No, this creature was rumored to be as large as a mountain with an appetite to match, and it had a vendetta against any ship that dared enter its territory. Wishing to learn the Sea of Nightmares and hopefully prove the legend of the serpent within it as just that, our king set out into the deeps."

The storyteller went on to describe all the creatures that attacked my dad's ship. The storms that raged for a week, causing even the most seaworthy male to lose his stomach. But despite the storms and the bloody battles, there was no sign of the legendary serpent until he came across a giant island in the middle of the sea.

"This island was not marked, you see, and no one had ever mentioned it before, so King Fariel ordered his warriors to drop anchor and take a boat to shore. This island was unlike any they'd ever seen. The ground was hard and cracked like the Kamuna Desert. The trees, tall and deadly, with massive thorns sticking out of the ground. And the smell was of death and fish."

"Uneasy, our king examined it closer, and when he touched the ground, he realized why it appeared so odd. It was too late to yell a warning before the island was shifting. The ground rolled from beneath their feet so quickly, they had no time to react before they were thrust into the sea. And there, King Fariel came face to face with a living mountain, the Serpent of the Sea of Nightmares."

"And what a nightmare it was. Its roar was deafening, and their ship was no match for the beast. It was not long before our king and his trusted guardian, Gonthar, were the only ones who remained. Gonthar fought valiantly, but soon even he was left injured, floating in the sea."

"When all seemed lost, the power rose in King Fariel once more, growing until he began to change. The water churned, and even the serpent paused as a creature larger than even it rose from the sea. One roar and the serpent was turning in a desperate bid to escape. One swipe of deadly claws and it was sinking to the bottom of the sea. And so, King Fariel discovered his second power. The power of shapeshifting."

The crowd broke out into applause again as he finished, and just like the day before, he was gone before I could blink. But it didn't matter. I would be back tomorrow even if I had to drag Barak along.

The next day, I couldn't even pretend to care about training. I took so many hits that any other day I would have effortlessly blocked, that Barak finally sighed.

"Why don't we head to the market early today? We can grab breakfast there."

I was already screeching in excitement and racing back towards my rooms before he'd finished speaking. I heard the guards chuckle as they hurried after me. They were used to my antics at this point, and I couldn't help but feel like they were warming up to me despite fighting to keep the wall up between us. A wall I myself was finding it increasingly difficult to maintain.

By the time we had stocked up on blueberry scones and cava, I was seconds from dragging Barak back to the square. Luckily, he got the memo, and we arrived in time to be front and center again. The old faerie smiled down at me with a wink before he called out.

"Come. Come. Hear the tale of the Great Fariel. Come. Come. Hear the tale of the Dragon King."

Distantly, I felt the royal guards circle around protectively as the crowd surrounded the stage.

"Come. Come. And I'll tell you the tale of Dragon King's title."

Finally, I would learn about my father's final gift. The power to call upon the dragons. A gift I'd heard was considered so rare it was even more extraordinary that my sister had a more powerful version of it.

"There was a time when grigors overran Rifka. Their populations so great that no city stood a chance. With their six-foot jumps, no one was safe from their deadly, twisted bodies as they pillaged and destroyed."

"Pleas were issued to our king, imploring him to bring the grigors to heel. Reluctant to leave his young wife, the king sent his warriors out to battle in his stead, but with every report of those lost, it became clear that King Fariel would need to face the beasts himself. But how could he rival the half lion, half dragon beasts? His fire and shapeshifting would not be enough. And so, he journeyed to the Fanged Mountains."

The faerie went on to tell of my father's perilous trip from Aurevel into the Fanged Mountains, Gonthar fighting at his side. He fought all manner of beasts like the terrifying banshee and countless grigors before he finally reached the destination he sought. A nest of dragons.

"You would say our king was insane, jumping from one vicious beast to another, but King Fariel had a skill you do not know. One that stemmed from his ability to shapeshift. He could sense the bonds of most creatures around him, and although he could not sense one with the grigors, he'd always felt a connection with the mighty dragons."

"He called upon this connection now. Wrapping his power around it so that the bond and himself became intertwined. The beasts roared. They expelled their weapons of choice, and Gonthar held them all back, giving our king the time and the strength to complete what is considered the greatest feat of his rule. With one quiet command, he bid them to stop. And they did. Bowing to our king. Some say he ordered the dragons to do his bidding from there. Some say he controlled them like puppets. But I tell you that the bond was not one of control, but of communication. He did not force them. He *asked* them. And they complied."

"It was with the dragons' aid that the grigors were driven to the place we now call the Grigor Forest, and Rifka was at peace again. And it was in this way that King Fariel discovered his final power. The power to command dragons, giving him the title you know so well. The Dragon King. Long and peaceful was his reign. May he rest in eternal peace."

The sentiment was echoed by the crowd. And then the faerie was gone. I had a feeling he wouldn't be back tomorrow, or even for a few days. There was a shade of sadness in his voice when he'd bowed his head at the end in remembrance of my father. Sadness as if he'd personally known him. I'd seen it reflected in the crowd even as he disappeared. These people had loved my father. Had missed him when he was gone. If these stories were anything to go off of, my father had loved them too, and yet had left to protect my sister and the woman he loved. Had remained to protect them, myself included.

But his people...*my people*...had been left to survive without him. And I'd dug into their wounds by attacking them. How much more did I spit on my father's legacy if I continued to stand against them? I may not be his heir, but I carried a piece of his power. A power he had used to protect. To help Rifka prosper. What had I used it for? Destruction. Revenge.

But...what if I chose not to anymore? Was it too late to walk in who my father raised me to be?

Chapter 24

Barak

It had been two weeks of taking a run in the morning, training either on the training field or in the gym, before bathing, eating breakfast, and heading out into the city. We'd wander around a bit before finding our spot, just as the storyteller would appear. Each tale riveted the crowd as much as the next. Sometimes he would tell one. Sometimes two, but regardless, I couldn't help but revel in the joy it brought the female at my side. Her sky-blue eyes were always wide in wonder and awe as she devoured story after story.

She would lean forward as if she itched to be running, fighting, or dancing with the characters painted with words and hand gestures. Her joy reminded me of happy times sitting around the fire as my grandmother weaved mind blowing stories after dinner. When the princess had asked to come day after day, I hadn't hesitated to humor her. The guards enjoyed the storyteller as much as I did, and it was no real struggle to say yes. But as I listened to her babble about all the stories we'd heard throughout the day, I couldn't help wondering if I was getting a glimpse of the female buried under the clan's torture.

Even now, she spoke animatedly about the latest tale of King Fariel's battle with the clan that had lost him his best friend. His stories filled his daughter with nothing but amazement. Was this the real Dalacia? The one that made her sister take hit after hit instead of striking her down? I had to say, if it was, I understood. I understood wanting to preserve the fire in her eyes. Her inerrant curiosity and appreciation of the legends of old. I found myself wanting to encourage it myself day by day.

After a while, she caught me staring at her for the millionth time today as we stopped to grab bread and liock on a stick for dinner.

"What?" she asked as she bit off a piece and licked her fingers clean.

My favorite part twitched in my tight pants, and I quickly glanced away from her mouth. Gods, I did not have time for the thoughts now running through my head. Thoughts that encouraged me to lick her fingers myself, and then those full lips of hers.

I shook my head and gestured back towards the square. "Nothing. It's just interesting seeing your excitement for something besides trying to knock me to the mat during training."

She snorted. "Trying? Are we really going to have to debate this again?" She fluttered her eyelashes at me. "Did you not get *real* acquainted with said mat this morning?"

I snorted a laugh. "Didn't you, every other morning this week?"

She shrugged. "Sure, let's compare my many times to an experienced warrior who fell once."

To be honest, Dalacia had been trained well and continued to improve with our daily exercises, but not enough to take me down. I'd been distracted just as I was now, trying not to imagine how it would feel to kiss that smirk right off her face. It was becoming harder to ignore the hum vibrating in my chest that grew warmer with every passing day I spent around her. I knew I should take the time to consider what Ghost had said, but I wasn't ready for that. Didn't mean I couldn't partake in other things.

It was because of this thought and her continued taunts that I missed the attack until it was almost too late. One of the guards cried out a warning, and suddenly I was pushing Dalacia behind me as my blade met the attack of the males before us. Screams sounded as the crowd ran to escape. I snarled, pushing the male back and striking him across the chest. He fell, only to be replaced with another. I glanced down at his bicep just as I met his swing, and my eyes widened. A red dripping B on black cloth wrapped around it. Clan soldiers.

"Give us the princess and we'll let you live," the foxling growled, his teeth jagged and dripping with what looked like venom.

No normal foxling then. I pushed him back.

"How about you surrender now, and I'll make your death quick," I offered in return, baring my teeth.

The foxling growled again, and a roar from my side showed several toros and even an ogre mixed in with the other Fae. Who let them into the city? There was no way they'd been here all this time.

I swore as I barely missed having my gut sliced open, and cut the foxling down, only to get my side opened up from another's blade. Hissing with the pain, we parried until I finally cut him down. A scream from behind me had me spinning to find Dalacia fighting off a toro with only her fists as the guards defended her against the others fighting to get to her.

"Get off me, you bull-headed freak!" she screeched, trying to wrestle out of his iron grip on her arm.

Unrelenting rage filled me, and electricity crackled through my veins until they sparked between my fingers. The guards glanced my way, no doubt alerted by the charge in the air.

"Duck!" I snarled, and with quick, efficient movements, they dodged to the side.

Dalacia broke away from the toro just as I sent ribbons of lightning across the ground to every clan soldier surrounding us. Roars of agony and fury rose and then ceased as each one hit the ground. I panted hard, electricity still racing through me as I ensured they remained down, and then, slowly, I took a deep breath and eased my power back.

I lifted eyes, likely still charged, to wide blue ones. She gripped her arm where the toro had held, and I fought the new surge of fury racing through me. Biting it back, I turned to the guards.

"Clean this up. I'm going to get her to the castle."

They nodded in agreement, and I rushed Dalacia forward with a hand on her lower back. We didn't speak until we were back in her rooms with additional guards at the door. I spun to face her.

"Are you hurt?" I asked, fighting to keep the growl out of my voice as I scanned her for injuries. "Your arm?"

"I...no. I don't think so," she stuttered, likely in shock.

I just couldn't tell if it was fear of me or the clan soldiers that showed in her eyes. "Let me take a look." When she didn't fight me, I lifted the sleeve of her shirt to see a massive hand-shaped bruise on her upper bicep. A growl did escape then, and she flinched. I cleared my throat and stepped back. "You should be fine, although that may be a little sore for a few days. I can have a healer send up a salve." She nodded but didn't say anything. Needing some space, I turned to leave her. "I'll go make sure that's taken care of."

"Barak."

I paused, not used to her calling my name with that soft of a tone. I turned slightly to face her.

"Are you okay?"

"Of course," I managed, trying to get my muscles to relax, but I was still itching for a fight.

She moved closer to me, glanced down, and then back up to meet my gaze. "You sure? You're bleeding all over my floor." I glanced down at the cut on my side I'd forgotten about. "Here. Sit down. I'll clean it up."

In a daze, I did as she requested, sinking into a chair as she hurried to the bathroom and came back with a towel and a bowl of water. She rushed to her bedroom and returned with bandages and some salve likely leftover from her own injuries. I watched in silent fascination as she had me hold my shirt up so she could dress the wound. She did so with intense concentration and a gentle hand as a curl persistently fell into her eyes. I had to clench my hand at my side to keep from reaching out to brush it behind her ear.

"There, you should be good now." I still said nothing as she started cleaning up the supplies. "I guess I should thank you for saving me," she said quietly.

It hadn't even occurred to me that she might have considered the clan soldiers as rescuing her, but this definitely dismissed that idea.

"I understand you could have just let them take me, and then I'd be out of your hair. Or I guess you couldn't do that because I'm a liability and whatnot."

She still hadn't looked at me, and I couldn't stand it. I grabbed her hand. She froze, but I pulled her towards me. She really was a little thing, especially when she made herself shrink down. I lifted her chin so those expressive eyes met mine.

"You're not a liability," I told her softly. "You're family. And family looks after each other no matter what."

A tear escaped from her eyes, and there was a hurt there that had lingered for a long time. Maybe someday she'll tell me about it, but right now...right now, I needed her to understand that she had a place here.

"I won't let the clan take you, not because you're our prisoner. Not because my queen orders it. But because I won't let them destroy another person." I stood up then because the emotions racing through me needed an outlet. I needed to make sure there weren't any other clan soldiers hiding out in the city.

As I reached the door, I heard her whisper, "Even after what I've done?"

My hand tightened around the doorknob. "Even then."

"Why?" came her pained whisper. "Why protect me when I've caused nothing but suffering? What if I wouldn't do the same for you?"

I swallowed past the lump in my throat, still fighting to keep whatever emotions raged within me settled.

"Because that's what families do. They protect. They forgive." And then I left and raced into the night. I let the lightning in my veins free, determined to ensure that the clan never stole from me and mine ever again.

Chapter 25

With every challenge, I grow stronger.
But I also grow further away from you.

Ghost

"Shit. Shit. Shit. Shit." Reece repeated as he paced back and forth. He was so riled, dragon scales were popping up all over his skin.

Not that I was much calmer, I was just better at hiding it, minus the mist whipping agitatedly around my feet.

"What were you thinking, sis?" he snapped, spinning to face my mate.

She stood staring at the fire, her arms crossed as she bit her lower lip. Despite the anxiety rushing through my veins right now, I couldn't help the flash of arousal the sight gave me.

"That's just it. You weren't thinking!"

When she failed to speak, he growled and started pacing again.

Tyrian glanced at the agitated prince, then back at our queen. "He's right, Silivia. That was a huge risk. If you lose the crown, we won't be able to use the armies to fight the clan."

Finally, she spun around. "You think I don't know that?!" she shouted. "You think I don't know that I may be in over my head? The truth of the matter is we need as many allies as we can get, and that means getting the sky kingdoms in line. Is that not what you said?"

Ty raised his hands in surrender. "Of course, but the crown? I hate to say it, but what if you fail?"

"If I fail at this, then we might as well throw in the towel for the rest of this war, because if I can't convince the citizens of my *own* kingdom to follow me, I sure as hell can't convince the rest of Fenriel."

She was right, and they knew it. The room went silent for several seconds, then she turned to me.

"What about you? Do you doubt me too?" she asked bitterly.

I shook my head. "This has nothing to do with us doubting you, Silivia. It was just a huge risk to agree to, especially when we have no idea what is required to win over the griffins."

She sighed in defeat, and her shoulders slumped. "I know," she said quietly. "But a power play wasn't going to work with them. I could feel it."

I nodded. I could too, which is why I'd supported her decision. I walked over and wrapped my arms around her, pulling her snug against me as I laid my chin on her head.

"Then you made the only decision you could have given the situation, and we'll figure the rest out."

"Just don't forget that you are not alone in this. You don't have to make nor carry these big decisions on your own. We are one after all," I reminded her through our bond.

She was stiff for a moment, then hugged me back with a slight nod of acknowledgement. It would take time for us to learn to fully lead together after being at odds and alone in our pain for so long. But our bond was worth the fight, and we'd come too far to stop doing so now.

Only when her tension melted away did I step back, still holding her close to my side with an arm wrapped around her waist. I turned to our friends who watched our exchange with expectant gazes. By now, they were used to our silent conversations. The price of being around a spiritbonded pair.

"So, what do we know?" I asked the group.

Reece growled in frustration and then finally sat down on the couch next to Teslia, who sat with her legs crisscrossed under her with a book flat across her knees. She glanced up.

"Well, while you males were grumbling over a decision already made, I was researching more about griffins."

Ty and Reece shot her an annoyed look, but she ignored them. Shaking my head, I gestured at the book.

"What did you find?"

Tess glanced down at the book in the pages again. "Well, it looks like the King and Queen of Griffins live in the center of Mount Beur, similar to the King of Dragons in the Fanged Mountains." She traced her finger across the page. "Now, it says here that many centuries ago, there used to be an ancient artifact that belonged to none other than King Reesik himself. He supposedly gifted it to the griffins, and in doing so, they answered his call."

"What happened to the artifact?" Reese asked as we all listened intently.

Tess frowned in concentration as she continued to read. He sat close enough that his leg brushed against hers, and I saw the slight smile she threw his way before she continued.

"Apparently, a thief broke into the griffin nest, stole the artifact, and then tried to run with it."

"Damn. It could be anywhere," the prince groaned, slumping on the couch.

Tess shook her head. "Not anywhere. It's still here." We glanced back at her in surprise. "The thief tried to cross the River of Tears, but the griffins attacked him, and it is thought to have sunk and fallen into the Cave of Despair. No one has seen it since."

"The River of Tears. The Cave of Despair," Silivia scoffed. "Why can't these places have more friendly names like, I don't know, The River of Candy or Cave of Rainbows?"

I shot her an amused smirk. "What fun would that be?"

Ty snorted sarcastically. My mate sighed and glanced around the room.

"Guess we're heading to Cave of Despair then, uh?"

There was a collective shrug, and she sighed again and glanced at Tess.

"I'm guessing you know where it is?"

My sister-in-arms grinned and held up the book, showcasing a map of the mountains. "Yup. Sounds like we're going on another trip."

"Tell me again why you insist on going on trips where we dragons are not welcome?" Celena growled, her tail flicking back and forth in irritation.

Tyrian ducked as it almost took his head off and glared at the dragon. She ignored him, her midnight blue scales reflecting the light as she shifted her silver wings next.

"And don't assume the other dragons aren't as peeved as I."

I glanced at my ebony black dragon, who glared down at me, his fiery eyes flashing. Oh, Arctic was peeved, alright. Puffs of icy air flew out of his nose as smoke came from Celena's. I lifted a brow, and his eyes narrowed further. I couldn't blame him for his agitation.

Ever since I'd been sent to collect Silivia those many, many months ago, I'd been with him less. Not to say our bond had become any less important to me, but my world had expanded further than just us and my brother and sister-in-arms. Sometimes, I missed the times when Arctic and I would fly for days, battling monsters and clan soldiers in a desperate attempt to silence the pangs in my chest. And maybe we would have that time of uninterrupted flying again someday...this time with our mates at our sides.

But for now, all I could do was send an apology wrapped in shadows down our bond to the seething dragon. I grimaced when a growl was his reply.

"As anyone else noticed how our dragons are the opposite of our abilities?" I asked, trying to ease the tension.

The dragons all turned to glare and snarl at me. Obviously, they weren't moved, but my friends all raised their brows in surprise.

"Uh. He's right," Reece agreed, glancing from Celena to Arctic and back.

"Now is not the time to comment on my ice ability matching the Phoenix Queen, when she and our king insist on placing themselves in danger without backup," Arctic raged, his deep voice more gravelly than normal in his anger.

"Sooo, is this a bad time to mention that we have to get to the cave before the full moon sets or we won't be able to find the entrance and will instead be washed down the River of Tears to our death."

We all shot Tess an incredulous look.

"And you're just mentioning this *now*?" Tyrian said in exasperation and disbelief.

She shrugged. "I wasn't expecting the flight here to take so long, and then you all started fighting with the dragons."

I gestured at Eclipse. "You act as if your own dragon isn't just as annoyed with this arrangement."

Emerald green eyes flashed as said dragon glowered at her rider. "Exactly," Eclipse snarled, and Tess rolled her eyes.

"Oh, for gods' sake!" Silivia exclaimed, throwing her hands in the air. She pointed at each of the four dragons. "You all act as if we do this on purpose. Like we want to be traveling without your powerful scaley behinds. We don't. Trust me, it's much more preferred that we don't, but alas, so is life," she said sarcastically. Her eyes softened as she met the silver ones of her dragon. She placed a hand on the uneasy dragon's snout.

"I know you're worried, Celena, and I promise we'll stay in contact, but you must know that this won't be the last time we are separated. I am not only the queen of dragons."

Meaning she wouldn't always be able to ride just Celena, or even a dragon. The blue dragon stared back for a long moment, then tossed her head at the royal guardians.

"Then, you will at least take them."

My mate scowled, and honestly, I agreed with the sentiment.

"We can take care of ourselves, remember," she reminded the dragons.

"Yes, but as you just mentioned, you are more than just Queen of Dragons." Celena glanced at me. "And you are more than just King of Shadows."

I blinked, surprised. Silivia huffed and grumbled under her breath.

"Alright, how about this?" Tyrian cut in. He gestured at the dragons and half the guards. "The dragons and some of the guards remain here to secure the entrance to the cave. We can't assume we'll be the only ones searching for the artifact, especially not now."

Now that we knew the Blood King had been orchestrating our fate for longer than we'd been born. I fought the wave of darkness raging against its leash at the thought. My brother shot me a look that said he knew where my thoughts had gone.

"The dragons are right. We can't go about as we once were, because hate it or not, all our statuses have been elevated, especially yours." He gestured at Silivia and me. "Meaning, whether you like it or not, your guards need to come, even if it's the normal amount each."

I growled under my breath and folded my arms. I could take all of them out with merely a thought, with both hands tied behind my back.

Farek must have read the thoughts on my face because he bowed his head at me. "We do not guard you because you are incapable of taking care of yourself. We guard you because you are, and so you don't always have to watch your back. Consider us your breathing room."

I narrowed my eyes. I really hated it when he was so reasonable. Made it harder to hate the changeling bastard. I huffed but turned to my mate.

"Just let them come so they'll get off our backs already. I don't want mine per usual, but they are nothing if not incessant." I glanced at Lorik's third in command, Obsidian, who led my guard detail.

He grinned knowingly at me. His dark eyes flashed in challenge. "We'll just find a way to follow, Ghost. Better to skip to the inevitable now."

I scowled at him. Why couldn't they be less likable? Silivia groaned, drawing our attention back to her.

"Fine. Whatever. Let's go before this stupid cave decides to flush us down the river."

There were several snorts of amusement, but it quickly grew serious as Lorik and Obsidian chose the male to join them and arranged the rest, interspersed with the dragons, to guard the area. Farek looked especially irritated about being left behind, but he was the highest ranked guardian after his brother, and so was needed here. Finally, we all stood along the riverbank.

"Shall we?" I asked, extending a hand to my mate.

She gave me a nervous grin and placed hers in mine. As one, we jumped into the river. The current tore at us, feeling thicker and slimier than actual water, but we used the protruding rocks to pull ourselves along until we stood at the entrance of the cave. Dark emotions spewed from it, and I fought the shiver of despair that traveled down my spine. Around me, I could see everyone else doing the same. I glanced up at the waning moon. We had to do this now or not at all. I met each person's eye before leading the dive into the darkness where not even the moon could penetrate.

Chapter 26

Beware, beware
the cave of despair.

Silivia

I gasped for air as we all surfaced within the cave. I could feel the relief that we'd made it inside passing through the group, but it was quickly washed away by the gloom of the cave itself. I swam to shore through the inky black water and took Ghost's hand as he hoisted me up and out. As everyone joined us, I took in the cavern around us in confusion.

It was...beautiful. Flecks of crystals were embedded in the black stone and made everything glisten. The cavern itself was enormous. Its ceiling was several miles above us, and its walls extended as far as the eye could see. It could easily fit the golden King of Dragons and his horde. But while the cave itself was beautiful, there was still this air of despair that hung thick around us.

"Obsidian," muttered my mate.

I glanced at Ghost, thinking he was speaking to his lead guardian. Instead, his eyes were trained on the walls. I looked at said guardian to see him nod. It was indeed his namesake. Interesting.

"I thought obsidian was supposed to be rare," I commented, tracing a hand down the glossy crystal.

Reece studied the cavern with reluctant awe. "It is, but it also only thrives in the darkest of environments," he explained. "It's likely why it's doing so well here. What's darker than a place named the Cavern of Despair?"

I glanced back at the dark male, his bright green eyes standing out against his dark hair and attire. Seems the guard was a better fit for my dark king than I thought.

"Okay, next question," I said, glancing around as we moved deeper into the cave. "Why can we see?"

Reece blinked at me in surprise before frowning and glancing around. It was only a soft glow, and it reminded me of the moon peeking faintly through clouds, but it was a glow, nonetheless.

"Magic?" Tess replied, glancing around uneasily. She shivered as a chilling breeze brushed past us. "Let's hurry up and find this artifact and get out of here."

We all nodded eagerly as we marched deeper.

"Remind me what we're looking for again," Ty commented, tracing a hand along the wall and staring down at the debris on his fingers with a frown.

"Not sure. It's supposed to have a presence that makes it undeniable," Tess said skeptically.

"Great," I muttered. I glanced at my mate. He and Obsidian seemed the most at ease in this creepy cave. Getting an idea, I turned to him fully. "What do the shadows say?"

Everyone froze, surprised, and turned to him expectantly.

Ghost lifted a brow incredulously. "What? You think I can just reach into the shadows and *ask* them to tell me where the artifact is?"

I shrugged. "Hey, wouldn't be the oddest thing to happen to us."

He chuckled and shook his head. "I've never done that before, but fine, I'll try it."

He closed his amused, golden eyes, and I could feel his dark power reaching out to the darkness in the cave. Maybe it was because I was so close to him or because we were bonded, but I could feel as the darkness shifted, answering his call.

"Woah, anyone else feel like this cave just got creepier?" Reece whispered uneasily.

"Yeah, I could have sworn the shadows over there just shifted," Lorik growled, his hand on his blade at his side.

"Ghost?" I whispered, edging closer to him. I was only comfortable with his shadows and darkness because they were a part of him. They'd never once tried to hurt me. But this... The darkness here didn't have the same reservations. In fact, I had a feeling that if it wasn't for the King of Shadows at our side that they would have already devoured us whole.

"I don't like this," Ty grumbled, his hand reaching back for the broadsword on his back. "It feels like it's inching closer. Ghost, whatever you're doing, you need to hurry."

"Ghost?" I called again, as the darkness definitely started to creep closer. "*Ghost.*" I was seconds away from jumping into my mate's arms, if only to no longer be touching the cavern so determined to have us for dinner.

Then, he opened his eyes. "Found it," he exclaimed. He glanced at the anxious looks all around him, and then his golden eyes flashed. "Be gone!" he growled, his power rising up like a wall around us.

Just like that, the darkness eased away from our group until we all took a collective exhalation of relief.

"*Gods*, I've never been gladder for your shadows, mate," Ty breathed, eying the room warily. "Lead the way quickly before this crazy cave changes its mind."

"It wouldn't dare," Ghost growled, gripping my hand tightly as he led us deeper into the cavern.

My unease only grew, the darkness seemingly even darker the longer we trekked through the obsidian caves. I was almost ready to beg Ghost to find another way to win over the griffins when he finally stopped in front of a pond.

"There it is. The amulet of the gods."

I glanced over to see, on a stone pedestal in the middle of the pond, lay a golden amulet engraved with black diamonds.

"Beautiful," Tess breathed. "It looks ancient...and powerful."

"No doubt it is," Reece agreed. He eyed the water skeptically. "Now to get it."

"I got it," I whispered. "Ghost has been teaching me some new tricks." With a wave of my hand, I summoned my snow. We all watched as I willed it to flow over to the amulet and lift it on a snowy cloud before floating back to me.

"Got it!" I exclaimed, grinning broadly. Except, as soon as it landed in my palm, all hell broke loose.

Chapter 27

Fire calls to fire.

Barak

"Where the hell do they keep coming from?" my brother growled as we again slipped through the night on a hunt for the clan.

I bristled. "I don't know, but I, for one, am tired of them outmaneuvering us. I don't want to have to explain to the top Resisti warriors, *plus* the King and Queen, how we failed to protect the queen's sister and Aurevel."

Raiden scowled. "Yeah, but it would make it so much easier if we knew how they were getting in and how many still hid."

"I wouldn't be surprised if some of the removed council members are involved," Rose added, flipping her long hair back.

I rolled my eyes but nodded. "I hope the others are having more luck locating them than we are," I mumbled.

The rest of the Resisti had split into teams to scour the city. The royal guards were on standby with an extra ten protecting our fiery princess. I ignored the unease in my gut over leaving her without my protection. That was what the changeling guards were for. They were adept at their job, especially when they didn't have a malicious queen restricting their movements.

I'm definitely getting too close, I thought begrudgingly. But how else would I get the fire princess to spill valuable clan secrets? And yet... it hadn't been that duty that had pushed me into a panic to rescue her when the clan soldiers had ambushed us. No, that had been the hum that had grown hot in my chest as if in warning.

I rubbed my chest absentmindedly as we dodged the waste of the slums. I scrunched up my nose. "How did we get the short stick? This place stinks." I glanced over to find Raiden's focus on the hand still rubbing my chest. I quickly dropped it. The look he shot me said we'd be discussing this later. Great. Just what I wanted.

"So, what's up with you and the princess?"

Or we would be discussing it now. I glared at Rose, begging her to drop it. She was the last person I wanted to talk about this with.

"You mean besides the fact I'm one of her personal guards and messenger to the queen?" I hinged, stopping to help an elderly elf up the stairs to her home.

She patted me gratefully on the hand before hobbling inside. I grimaced at the location where she found herself living. Queen Isrella had let the city rot away in King Fariel's absence. The money that in the past had gone to help areas such as these was transferred to those lords and ladies of the cities and villages that supported Isrella instead. I fought the nausea rising at the smell of the waste covering the once neat cobbled streets. The light here was dim to almost nonexistent with the mandate to limit the glowworms used to light the city. Beggars and inhabitants alike wore tattered clothes over barely filled bellies.

I gritted my teeth in rage, fighting back the lightning charging my veins. The only thing that made it better was that once Silivia had taken over as queen and conquered the council, she'd immediately begun reversing many of the decrees on the city. Being on the council, for the first time in my life, I could ensure others didn't grow up like Raiden and I had. I'd asked to be in charge of areas like this, where people were often forgotten. Knowing the reason, my brother had quickly requested the same. Considering we'd lived on the edges of the slums growing up, we'd had a relatively good life, especially once the Resisti got word of our abilities and took us in to train us.

I had to stop beating myself up. The rot of this city was not my fault, and it would take time to reverse, especially if we couldn't find all the clan members who were still hiding in our midst. Plus, there were the repairs that still needed to be done all over the city.

"Fenriel to lightning boy. Come in, lightning boy."

I scowled at the grinning redhead. I swear if she wasn't sleeping with my brother, I would send her shooting through the sky with said lightning, but then Raiden would lose his shit and we'd likely cause the city more damage with our fight.

"Fuck off, Rose," I snapped. "And why the fuck doesn't your hair ever stop moving, uh? Answer me that, and maybe I'll tell you about me and the princess."

She wouldn't though. Her hair flowing on a nonexistent wind was part of her power. A power she'd never fully disclosed and obviously had no intention of doing so.

She pouted. "Raiden, your little brother sure is snippy these days." She grinned wickedly as she wrapped her arm around his much larger one. "Maybe it's because he needs to get laid but can't close the deal with our fire princess." Her grin grew wider as I fought the lightning trying to escape from under my skin.

"Fuck off, Rose," Raiden echoed, though his words held more affection. I grimaced and rolled my eyes. "This isn't the time for games. Or have you forgotten that Silivia would have our heads if her sister was hurt under our watch? Which will happen if we don't hurry up and find these clan bastards."

She straightened, suddenly growing serious. "Trust me, I know, but parading with the level of tension radiating off Barak isn't going to get the job done." She stared me down. "So, I ask again. Are you too compromised to do what needs to be done?"

I knew what she really asked. If Dalacia proved to be working against us again, would I do what it took to either apprehend or end her? I swallowed as the hum within me shot pain through my chest.

"I'll do what needs to be done," I told her firmly. Even if I had no idea what that entailed right now.

She nodded in acknowledgement and turned away, but Raiden still studied me.

"You good?" he asked when she'd gone some distance away.

I wasn't, but I nodded. "Let's finish up so we can get at least some sleep tonight."

His lips thinned, but he didn't push me as we followed after Rose.

"Anyone else getting a bad feeling?" Raiden whispered, his hand on the hammer strapped to his back.

I glanced around us, trying to see into the shadows coating almost every corner. We'd left the slums but were still in a poorer part of the city. The lighting here should be better, but instead it was just as dark as the area we'd left...if not darker. I swallowed, reaching a hand for my own weapon.

"Something's wrong," I muttered, still scanning the night.

"What was that?!"

We all turned to where Rose was looking off into an alleyway. Her deadly whip lay curled at her feet, ready for whatever came next.

"Damn it. It's gone."

Movement in my peripheral had me spinning again. Nothing was there.

"We need to move," Raiden snapped. "Now!"

We drew our weapons and broke into a brisk jog, fast enough to hopefully get ahead of whatever was cornering us, and slow enough to react if they thought to attack instead. We'd almost reached the next section of the city when a whistling had me dodging sharply to my left.

"Watch out!" I shouted as several arrows flew at us.

With a flick of her wrist, Rose snapped them all in two with her whip, sending them clattering to the cobblestones. She continued to do so as wave after wave came from our right. I barely registered the next attack on our other side until it was too late.

"Barak!"

I swore as I dodged the long, thin darts. They fell to the ground. Where they touched the plants, the leaves sizzled until the entire plant shriveled to nothing. I swore viciously again. This time, Raiden blasted wind, sending the darts back towards their owners. Using my blade, I cut down any darts or arrows that made it past either of them.

"They have to run out eventually," I growled, dodging another dart as an arrow caught me on my left arm.

They didn't answer as we all continued to cut down the arrows Rose was increasingly starting to miss with the sheer number being shot at her.

"We need to move!" Raiden yelled and then swore when an arrow lodged in his shoulder. He growled and snapped the shaft. "Go!"

Just then, the ground shook, and we lost our footing as the cobblestones shifted under our feet. The waves of darts and arrows halted, but the reprieve was short-lived when battle cries came from the shadows and fell upon us. We fought hard, the darkness and occasional shot of a poisoned dart or arrow keeping us from stopping the attack as quickly as we should.

"Barak."

I risked a glance at my brother. He panted as he bled from several wounds.

"Do it."

Unlike his, my power could be more accurately aimed. If I could catch my breath long enough to do so. I roared and pushed the clan soldiers accosting me back. Then, I called upon the lightning already racing down my veins. The shadows finally disappeared as I lit up the area, revealing far more clan members than there should have been still in the city. I roared again, sending my fury racing across the cobblestones and into the shadows. There were screams, smoke, and then nothing but ash.

Not stopping to rest, Raiden rushed to my side as my energy plummeted. "Let's go. We're in no shape to take on more."

It felt like a lifetime before we made it back to the castle; my brother supported me with one arm around his shoulders all the way back. Once we had though, the hum in my chest grew unbearable, pulling me towards the north wing.

"Go to the infirmary. I need to check on something," I told Raiden, pulling away from him.

He shot me a disbelieving look. "Are you crazy? You also need to go to the infirmary, you idiot!"

I waved him off. "I will. I swear. Go."

He still stared at me with worry and confusion until Rose pulled at his arm.

"Come on. He can take care of himself, and if he doesn't make it there, you can always come back and drag his ass there instead."

As she managed to get my reluctant brother to head away, I stumbled and weaved my way towards I didn't know what. Actually, that wasn't quite true. I wasn't surprised to find myself at Dalacia's door, but the guards patrolling the area were. Especially as I sent them to guard the front of the wing despite my blood dripping onto the floor. I suppose the fact that up until this point I'd been holding myself upright despite my injuries, and that I still had lightning crawling under my skin, kept them from refuting me. But then I was entering her room to see her shoot up from her seat by the fire.

"Barak?" Dalacia said in surprise as horror spread across her face. "What happened?"

The world was spinning, and suddenly every injury I'd sustained cried out at once. "Wildfire," I whispered, and then the ground was rushing up to meet my face.

Chapter 28

When did we stop being enemies?
When did we become friends?
And when...
Did we become something more?

Dalacia

"Wildfire," he whispered, and then he collapsed onto my floor.

Shock only paralyzed me for a second before I was rushing to his side. "Barak? Barak!"

He didn't respond, but he was covered in blood, and was that an arrow shaft sticking out of his leg? Fighting the panic building in my chest, I raced to my bathroom to grab the first aid supplies I'd used on him not so long ago. I placed it by my bed, pulled the blankets back, and then raced back to the prone warrior on my floor. Now I just had to get him up.

Biting my lip, I scanned him, trying to figure out how the hell I was supposed to lift a male twice my size. He would just have to help me. With a grimace, I raised my hand and smacked him hard across the face. He groaned but didn't stir.

"Come on, you good-for-nothing, charged bastard," I snapped. "Get up!" I slapped him again harder, and he groaned and opened his eyes.

"Haven't you heard of bedside manner?" he whispered groaned.

But I was already pulling at his thick biceps. "Yeah, yeah. I know it sucks. I'll be nice if you get up and help me place you on the bed," I growled, fighting his deadweight.

He moaned again and almost slipped back into unconsciousness.

"No, you don't. Get up, and I swear I'll reward you later."

His glazed eyes cleared slightly to focus on me. "Whatever I want?"

I hesitated. He was out of it, so it was unlikely he'd remember this later, so I nodded.

"Whatever you want, but you have to get up."

With a soft growl that sent shivers scattering down my spine and a deep groan, he managed to get to his feet and shuffle the few feet to my bed with my support. He collapsed onto the mattress with a grunt, and I made quick work of removing his clothes so I could get a better look at the damage. I wasn't sure if he was still conscious when he had his eyes closed, but I made sure not to linger too long on his anatomy just in case.

I swore colorfully when I saw the number of gashes and the arrow indeed buried in his leg. "How the hell did you even walk here?" I muttered in horror. Another moan was his only answer, and when I placed a hand to his forehead, he was already too warm. I swore again and then went to work.

I wasn't sure how much time had passed, but eventually I'd managed to bandage his chest, left bicep, and leg. I cleaned up the other cuts marring him, and wiped away the blood and grime with a wet cloth. Somehow, I'd convinced him to drink a solution from the healer to bring his fever down and counteract the poison slithering through his system. The healer had offered to have the lightning warrior moved to the healing suite, but I'd refused, some part of me wanting to care for the male who'd come to me instead of the hospital wing.

Exhausted, it was late into the night when I finally crawled up into the bed and lay at his side, careful not to jostle him. I awoke to the shine of sunlight on my face, but I refused to open my eyes just yet. The bed was especially warm and comfortable today. It felt like a heated blanket covered me, and it filled me with such comfort that I relaxed even more against the firmness beneath me. To make things better, it smelled like the forest did right after a summer shower with a hint of smoke. Mmm.

Wait a minute. Firmness? Summer shower? My eyes shot open to find a tanned, muscular chest covered in bandages under my cheek and hands. I was half splayed across his body, with my leg in between his and his arm wrapped securely around my waist.

Oh gods. Oh gods. Somehow, I'd been drawn to him in my sleep. I had to rectify this situation before he woke up and discovered me. I'd never live it down. Slowly and carefully, I tried to disentangle myself from his body, but then his arm tightened as he groaned. I froze as half-slitted, hazel eyes met mine.

We stared at each other for several seconds, the steady rhythm of his heart under my palm, along with the charged hum growing in my core, tempting me to lie back down and let him hold me just a little bit longer. I couldn't though. I shouldn't. We were enemies. Weren't we? The lines were getting blurred, and I couldn't ignore the fact that we were drawn to each other.

"Why did you come to me?" I whispered.

His gaze shifted to my mouth and lingered before rising to mine again. He knew what I meant. Why hadn't he gone to a healer? Why had he come to the female who was supposedly his enemy? I could have taken the opportunity to run... to hurt him...instead, all I could focus on was ensuring he didn't bleed out on my floor. He took a long time to answer.

"I don't know," he finally replied, his voice rough from sleep and probably last night. His eyes dropped to my mouth again. "I felt myself drawn here." He glanced up again. "I shouldn't be."

I knew what he meant. It was the same feeling that had me unconsciously relaxing against him again.

"You could have left," he muttered, his arm tightening around me slightly.

"I know," I whispered back, not meeting his eyes as I traced the edge of the tattoo I could see peeking past his bandages. It depicted a line of text in a language I didn't know in the shape of a lightning bolt. Likely the ancient language.

He stopped my hand, bringing my eyes back to his. "You helped me instead." I swallowed, seeing the question in his eyes. "Why?"

"I don't know," I answered honestly.

Barak studied me before swallowing. "I know what reward I want."

My brows rose in surprise. He remembered. His wicked grin told me he knew I'd hoped he hadn't.

"I want a kiss."

I blinked. He must still be out of it with the meds.

"A kiss?" The warrior nodded as I shook my head, incredulous. "I'm not going to kiss you."

He grinned wickedly at me again. "You promised. Thought you were a female of your word, Princess." He winked. "Don't worry. I'll let you control this one. If I were to kiss you, we'd never leave this bed." I rolled my eyes at his obviously inflated ego. "Come on. Just one little kiss. I promise I won't bite. This time."

I scowled at the tease in his eyes. He didn't think I would actually do it. Well screw him. I won't be labeled as someone who couldn't rise to the challenge.

"Fine," I snapped, and then before I could change my mind, I pressed my lips to his. I froze.

His summer storm scent flooded my nose, making my eyes flutter shut. I hadn't expected his lips to be so soft. As promised, he didn't move, letting me decide how far this would go. The thought made me feel powerful, and a little daring. So, I traced his lips with my own, pressing a little harder. I let my tongue peek out, tentatively touching his lips. He opened for me, and I pressed closer, curious to find out what he tasted like. I bit back a moan as his other hand drifted into my hair in between the strands. He didn't pull, just held me there as I explored his mouth. When my tongue touched his, his deep moan had me pulling back abruptly.

I stared down into his heated expression. We were both panting, and I could tell from the tenseness of his body under mine that he was fighting to keep from launching himself at me and taking over. A deep part of me wanted him to do just that. To take charge and show me what it felt like to be dominated by a male who was in it for both our pleasure and not my pain. But the sheer fact that I so desperately wanted it was exactly why I needed to get away. I didn't deserve to have the pleasure this charged male could most definitely give me. I didn't deserve anything good after all I'd done.

I pulled away from him, and he let me. Barak sat up carefully, a worried expression on his face. I didn't deserve that either.

"Dalacia…"

"You should go get checked out by the healer," I interjected. "I'm going to jump in the bath. I'll meet you for breakfast shortly." I rushed towards my bathroom, grabbing clothes as I went.

"Wildfire…"

"No, Barak," I told him, shooting him a pleading look even if the nickname filled me with warmth. "Please, just go."

He swallowed, the reluctance plain on his face, but he nodded and shifted off the bed to grab his stuff. I hurried into the bathroom and shut the door, and only when I'd heard the front door of my suite click shut, did I finally slip to the floor and let the tears fall.

Chapter 29

I am Queen of the Winged.

Silivia

Lord Zerc and Lady Hera stared in horror as we stood in front of them. Maybe I would take pity on them if it wasn't for the sheer annoyance racing through my veins.

"You look like you didn't expect us to return," I commented coldly. "Were you planning on telling us that the King and Queen of Griffins were not in fact on Mount Berus like they were supposed to be, but stuck inside the Cavern of Despair?"

Both continued to gape at us, mouths opening and closing as they tried to formulate a response.

"Or were you expecting them to *kill* us after being *trapped* in that cave for so long that they were overcome with despair?" Reece growled, his arms crossed and eyes hard.

The lord and lady of Berus glanced at each other and back at us.

"Or were you hoping that we would travel to Mount Berus and wander aimlessly until we were either attacked or admitted defeat after not finding said griffins?" Tyrian added, glaring at both of them.

"No, no. Surely you're all incorrect," Teslia said, her death glare the opposite of her sickly-sweet tone. "Surely, they assumed we would figure out the legend of the missing artifact needed. And *surely,* it just *slipped their minds* that there would be not one, but *two* delightful *banshees* living in the Cavern of Despair."

The Lord and Lady of Berus paled significantly. There was nothing remotely delightful about banshees. No one knew what they looked like, and their presence was always accompanied by a piercing cry that froze the fear and blood in your body. Most didn't survive past that cry. I'd had the honor of barely escaping one during my first year in Fenriel. Only Ghost bravely facing off against it in the night had saved us both, but his blood had been infected with its ice for days.

It had taken my icy flames and Ghost's darkness to hold them off long enough for us to kill both of these ones with our guards' help. Not to mention the others had been fending off the two griffins at the same time. Apparently, between the cavern itself and the banshees, their minds had been too warped to recognize they'd had the object of their desire within reach after all these centuries. It had taken us letting them chase us out of the cavern itself before they regained some semblance of sanity. Even then, it wasn't until I'd spoken to them as I once had the King of Dragons himself that they stopped.

No one said anything, but the lord and lady's wide eyes went to the blood we all continued to drip onto the floor, too ready to end this to worry about wounds that will heal in time. We'd hastily wrapped the worst ones and raced back here on the back of fuming dragons.

Ghost snorted at my side, his eyes black with a golden ring as they often were when his power was off its leash and his emotions were heightened. They'd been that way ever since we realized we'd walked into a trap. Rightfully so, the fear of the Fae in front of us grew to epic proportions until they were shaking uncontrollably on their makeshift thrones. And they thought themselves more King and Queen than us? Pathetic.

"No, you're all wrong," my mate said quietly, and even my friends and royal guards froze. We all knew that tone. When Ghost went quiet, you'd best fear for your life. "Lord Zerc and Lady Hera didn't know about any of that. In fact, I know they didn't ask for the crown because they thought that little group of clan soldiers was enough to stop us if the cavern wasn't."

Because that was the worst part about it. Despite their insistence that they valued the great griffins, they'd knowingly allowed them to be trapped *and* opened their city up to the very people trying to destroy it.

"I know for a fact that they weren't trying to *kill my mate*." Ghost tilted his head as he considered them. "Isn't that right?"

Both looked like they were ready to slit their own throats to avoid the simmering wrath of the male next to me. I placed a hand on his arm to soothe him.

"They wouldn't dare. Not when we are the only ones preventing them from being captured and killed by the clan," I said firmly. My power slipped from me and mixed with Ghost's agitated mist at our feet. "And most definitely not when I command that which they supposedly care for most."

Lord Zerc's eyes widened in shock. "You don't mean?" he breathed, finally finding his words even as he shook in his seat.

I lifted a brow. "Don't I?"

"*Come*," I commanded down a new bond that glowed a warm brown.

There was a stir, and the once silent room filled with shouts of awe and praise as an ebony and a white griffin twice the size of normal ones flew through the room and landed with thunderous flaps behind us. Both roared at the ceiling, their feathers glossy and clean after a thorough wash in the River of Tears. Their golden eyes flashed as they shifted restlessly on giant taloned feet.

I turned from the Lord and Lady staring aghast at the colossal creatures, and made my way over to the griffins just as they folded their wings to their side. I lifted a hand to each and they bowed their feathered heads to greet me. I said nothing as I stroked them, and they calmed their restless movements. Nor did I say anything when the rest of the griffins in the room stepped to my side. And when they all, including the King and Queen of Griffins, tucked in a leg and bowed deeply to me, only then did I turn back to the makeshift thrones. My companions had split into two, creating a walkway, and Ghost moved back to my side.

I lifted a brow and gestured at the majestic creatures behind me as they stood tall and shifted to flank both my mate and I. "You were saying?"

Ghost snorted in disgust as the Lord and Lady of Berus fell to their knees with frantic apologies, and the rest of the room bowed. Reece shook his head in disbelief while Tyrian muttered something nasty under his breath that made

Teslia smack his arm even as she barely hid her own disdain. The guards all shared equal looks of scorn as well, but I only waited for the royals' mumbling to cease.

"Forgive us, Your Majesties," Lady Hera pleaded, glancing up at Ghost and I. "Forgive us, for we knew not what we did."

"Actually, you did, but it's fine. You'll make it up to me by lending your army for the battle ahead," I said nonchalantly.

Lord Zerc's eyes flashed, but then he noticed the shadows creeping towards him, and he bowed his head to the ground again.

"Of course. Of course, Your Majesties."

I smiled as I gestured at the griffins again. "Wonderful. After all, based on your words, you can't refute I'm the Queen of Griffins now." There was a flash of pride down the bond, and I glanced over to find Ghost smirking wickedly. I turned and made my way out of the room, feeling my companions follow behind. "Be ready to march."

I sighed as we watched the King and Queen of Griffins fly back to their home on Mount Berus for the first time in centuries. They'd stay there until I called for them. Hopefully, afterwards, they'll be able to enjoy the peace they so deserved.

"Well, that's one city down," Reece muttered. "No doubt, word of your accomplishment has already started to spread throughout Rifka."

We'd taken the time to rest and address our injuries the night before. I knew we were all still tired and sore, but Ty was right. We couldn't afford to linger.

"Will it be enough?" I asked, watching the griffins fly fluidly through the sky.

"It'll have to be. We can't linger in Rifka forever while the clan continues to absorb the rest of Fenriel into its ranks," Ty replied solemnly.

I nodded resolutely. "To the southern sky city."

Ghost gripped my hand firmly in his, his eyes finally back to normal. He kissed my knuckles as he eyed me lovingly. "Whatever comes, my brilliant queen."

Reece rolled his eyes and snorted, but he couldn't hide his smile as we all climbed aboard the dragons and soared back into the skies.

Chapter 30

A bond of the spirit is undeniable.
Eventually, the spirits will be drawn to each other.

Barak

I couldn't get that kiss out of my head. It had been a few days, and besides ensuring I checked in with the guards watching her, I'd avoided seeing the fire princess. The healer had signed me off that same day, my Fae healing kicking in with Dalacia's expert treatment of my injuries. Even the healer had been impressed. Made me wonder how she'd learned such skills.

I could have continued our daily training the next day, but I'd taken breakfast in my room, trying to get my head screwed on straight. Besides a check-in from my brother, I'd been left relatively alone. Except by my thoughts. By the ghost feel of her plush lips on mine. The glide of her shy tongue as it explored my mouth. The sweet taste of her. The smell of a campfire mixed with the alluring scent of roses. On anyone else, it would have been revolting, but on her, with her soft skin pressed against the hard parts of me...

I gritted my teeth and tried to focus on the punching bag before me. Gods. It had taken everything within me not to take over. To not push her back on the bed and ravish her. To show her just how charged this warrior could be in bed. How good it would feel to wrestle in a different way as I brought us both pleasure. I would have buried my nose into her neck to get a better breath of her scent. I would have nibbled all along that neck on my way down to those perfectly round breasts of hers. They weren't overly large, but they would fit perfectly in the palm of my hands, and I bet they would taste amazing too.

And then while she was moaning with my mouth wrapped around her, my fingers would continue to explore down, until I could feel just how well I was pleasuring her. I'd slipped one finger in, maybe two, and watch her fall apart under my mouth and fingers. And when neither of us could take it anymore, I would slip into her warmth and take her until we burned the room down, either by fire or lightning alike.

"No!" I exclaimed, ripping myself from the pleasant daydream. I hit the bag so hard it went swinging farther back than it should, and I caught it before it pummeled me to the ground. With a groan, I laid my forehead against it, trying to ignore the throbbing of my favorite member.

"Someone's worked up."

I spun to see Aux watching me. He leaned against the gym wall, his arms folded and mirth dancing in his eyes. "

Am I right in saying that a certain female is to blame?"

"Fuck off, Aux," I growled, fighting a grimace. I should have worn looser pants.

The older warrior chuckled, his odd violet and black eyes twinkling. He gave me a look that said he saw way too much for my liking.

"Come, lad. You think no one has noticed you've been charged for a fight ever since the attack in the city?" Aux lifted a brow. "You remember our training. Letting it simmer leads to an explosion you can't control. And when your power is electricity..."

I grimaced. "I don't want to talk about it," I grumbled, knowing he was right.

The huge male shrugged and moved to grab a blade from the barrel. "Then don't." He settled into position and lifted a brow.

I sighed but moved across from him. We were still for a moment, watching each other for movement, but my patience was thin. The flow of arousal and frustration from my daydream still raged, so I attacked first, executing a series of moves that would have taken any normal soldier down in seconds. But Aux wasn't normal. He was older than even Ghost and with more tricks up his sleeve than I'd ever learned in all my centuries working with him. I wouldn't be surprised if he became one of the Resisti elders at some point.

Right now, he was having too much fun making me sweat. I growled, dodging a move that had my balance compromised. I jumped back, trying to give myself room to readjust, but he followed me, pushing me further into the room. I could feel the charge building in my veins as frustration grew. No matter what I did, I couldn't make any leeway. He kept me on defense so effectively, it would be embarrassing if any of our team could see us now.

"You're distracted, Barak," Aux warned me, slicing at my feet. I dodged away, barely getting my blade up to meet his next move. "Distraction gets you killed."

"I know that!" I barked, pushing him back. Another series of moves had him on the defense as my lightning grew and grew.

"Maybe you should just claim her already," the male said, dodging my blade. My eyes widened in surprise. "That's the problem, right? She's your mate, and you don't want to claim her?"

My vision went yellow as electricity sparked along my hands and blade. "I will never claim her! She's my enemy!" I roared, attacking him with all the power of a whirlwind.

In a move I would have never expected in a million years, he gripped me around the neck and pressed a hand against my chest. With a choked gasp, all the electricity vanished. I'd forgotten that he was a conduct. My charge didn't harm him, and he'd counteracted it. He whispered in my ear.

"You are only enemies as long as you two fight the bond within you. She needs you just as you need her. Stop fighting the truth and walk in it, Barak. You are better than this."

And then my eyes widened as he short-circuited my entire system. With a gasp, I collapsed to the ground. When I came to, he was squatting beside me.

"Only the truth will set you both free," Aux said quietly. "Maybe it's time you let each other in for good. Or your mission will fail." He stood and walked away. "I'm rooting for you, kid." And then he was gone, leaving me to lie on the floor and contemplate his words.

Eventually, I stood to my feet, every part of me sore from his attack. It wasn't until I was sinking into the hot waters of my bath did I realize that not once had I denied that Dalacia was my mate. The hum within me grew.

Chapter 31

He likes me.
He likes me not.

Dalacia

After several days, it became apparent that the Prince of Lightning was staying away because of me. Not once had I been allowed to wander the castle grounds and train without him, but now I did, for almost a week. Instead of lightning, the prince of thunder was the one currently marching at my side, careful not to walk too close as to touch me, but close enough in case I tried something.

I fought the frown trying to form. I hadn't realized how much leeway Barak had started to give me. He'd walked next to me like I was just another person, despite the enchanted iron bracelets around my wrists. He'd even started talking to me about his past adventures as both a child and under the Resisti. How had I missed that our relationship had been changing? Sure, we still threw snide comments at each other and battled like we hated each other on the training mat, but that had turned into more companionable ones instead, consisting of *"I'll burn you up alive"* and *"I'd like to see you try"* attitudes.

I shifted uncomfortably, the stroll through the gardens not holding any appeal today. I changed directions and veered towards the library instead. Stepping between the doors, I felt an immediate comfort surrounding me and took a deep breath of that alluring book smell. This was one thing my sister and I never disagreed on. Our love for books. But as I slipped from aisle to aisle, I still couldn't help wondering why a certain male wasn't here. Was he sick? Injured? I bit my lip almost hard enough to bleed. Or had he been so appalled by the kiss when he left that he never wanted to see me again? The thought affected me more than I liked.

Needing to know, I turned abruptly to face his brother, who still trailed me even as he scanned the shelves around us. "Where is he?"

Raiden stopped immediately, eyes darting to mine. His were darker, fiercer compared to his brother's. He lifted a brow. "Who?"

I scoffed in annoyance. Like he didn't know. "You know who. Your brother. You know, the one who shoots lightning out of his butt."

Both brows went up now, and I heard a couple of snorts from where the other guards waited.

"Last I checked, they came out of his hands, but who knows, he may have picked up a new skill from hanging around you."

His tone was straightforward, but I could hear the amusement in it and see the same in the slight uplift of his lips. Uh. Maybe Raiden didn't hate me as much as I thought. I narrowed my eyes.

"So, if he's so skilled, why are you here and not him?"

He shrugged. "What? Don't think I can handle the fire princess? I assure you, I can." He shot me a feral grin. I scowled, and he laughed. Then, he grew serious. "Why do you care? Want to do more of what has him destroying punching bags left and right?"

So, he was alright. Or maybe not fully if he was raging against inanimate objects. But I hadn't done anything...nothing except kiss him. I swallowed, suddenly uncomfortable. Was he avoiding me because I'd kissed him? He'd asked me to. Had it been that bad? Suddenly, I was furious. If he couldn't face me after one tiny kiss that meant nothing, then he was less of the male I thought he was.

"Uh oh. I know that look," Raiden said, stepping back.

I glared at him. "Take me to your stupid brother," I snarled. "We've got something we need to talk about." For a moment, I was sure he would refuse me, but then he shrugged.

"Hell. Why not? Maybe seeing you will pull him out of his slump." He glanced at me. "Or he can take it out on you instead."

I scoffed in disgust but followed him as he led us back to the north wing. I ignored the jump in my stomach at the thought of him "taking it out on me". We stopped at a door that could only be his room. With a glance at me, Raiden banged on it.

"What?" came the gruff reply.

"It's me," Raiden answered back.

There was grumbling that couldn't be made out, and then the door unlocked. He glanced at me again before slipping in and shutting the door. Anxious all of a sudden, I tried not to fidget while also trying to decipher the harsh whispers being thrown back and forth behind the door. Finally, Raiden came out but held the door open for me. I lifted a brow in question, but he only gestured for me to enter. Swallowing past the lump in my throat, I did, trying not to flinch when he shut the door behind me, leaving me alone with his fuming brother.

Determined to ignore the male pacing angrily in front of me, I explored what I could of his suite. The living space was similar to my own, with colors of burnt orange, black, and white. Befitting of the male who wore all black with streaks of burnt orange regularly. Not to mention the wicked blade on his back. I noticed one wall was lined with various weaponry he'd likely collected, unlike the books that adorned mine. There were various daggers and blades with intricate metalwork. There were even a few I didn't recognize.

I smoothly glanced into his bedroom to find a massive king-sized bed with dark ebony sheets and comforter with the sheer curtains of the canopy pulled back. I swallowed again, pushing back thoughts of him lying in such a bed that surely smelled like a summer storm. Not daring to get caught snooping in there, I moved to the window and looked out into the garden below.

"You wanted to see me?"

I glanced back to find him watching, his arms crossed and face carefully blanked. What was going on with him?

"You went from guarding me nonstop for months to suddenly avoiding me for days." I shrugged nonchalantly. "I was starting to think you'd fallen terribly ill or something." His eyes sparkled with a hint of mischief, and I scowled. "Not that I cared," I snapped. The mischief grew. Damn it.

"Of course not," he said, stepping to my side and looking out. I watched him in my peripheral, scanning him for injury, though I found none. "I had some planning to do. Just in case you were wondering."

"I wasn't." But I was, and I had. Surely, whatever plans he'd been working on wouldn't have prevented him from seeking me out. Should I mention the kiss? I shook myself mentally. No. It meant nothing, and he was obviously not going to mention it, so I'll just pretend it didn't happen. I swallowed. Even if the sight of his bed summoned images of him pinning me to those silky sheets, and this time dominating the kiss.

Barak's nostrils flared, and I fought to temper my growing arousal. Stupid Fae senses. Luckily, he didn't call me out on it.

"In fact," he continued. "I've decided that you should help with such plans." Was it just me, or was his voice slightly huskier?

I turned to glare at him. "What assignment have you sacrificed me for now?" I snapped.

He spun to face me, his face suddenly hard. "You're going to help clean up this city. Help feed its people so we can reverse some of the damage the late queen has allowed to flourish."

I could feel my face heating with the tinge of accusation in his eyes, his words. "Are you blaming me for the failure of your crappy city?"

His eyes narrowed menacingly. A look of animosity he hadn't shown me in weeks flared in them. "In case you forgot, you are partially to blame for the state of *our* city. Or did you suddenly become a different king's daughter? No? Then, this city, this kingdom, is as much yours as mine. Meaning you should be more than happy to help those in need."

I wanted to hide from the pain and rage in his eyes. Pain I'd helped put there. Like it had increasingly since my sister captured me, guilt and regret thick and cold, rushed through me, drowning me in their potency. I couldn't deny that I'd caused some serious damage in the last year. Away from the center of the clan and surrounded by people who openly cared and supported each other, it was becoming progressively difficult to see why it was worth it.

Did I even want to rule, or was I just mad at my sister for not rescuing me before the scars became embedded in my soul? But for some reason, it hurt seeing just what the male in front of me thought of my transgressions. Maybe because we'd been moving away from the hostility and hatred. It hurt so much more to see it back tenfold. What had he seen in his last trip to the city to turn him against me so? What damage had I done that he'd unearthed to turn his reluctant smile to a grimace at my presence?

He must have been surprised that he'd let me kiss him...me, the enemy. After the meds and adrenaline had faded, he would have remembered with immense disgust and horror why he shouldn't let me touch him...especially not intimately.

Why did these thoughts make my heart ache so badly? Why did that hum in my chest send a wave of agony through me? I hated that look on his face most of all...more than even the look of betrayal on my sister's, so I lowered my eyes to the ground and let my shoulders fall.

"Fine," I whispered, and then I escaped from his room.

He didn't stop me. His brother didn't speak to me. And no one else cared when I slipped into my room, slammed the door, and fell to the floor in tears.

I woke up the next morning feeling numb, but I made quick work of getting ready and eating the breakfast a servant had delivered. When Barak came to collect me instead of his brother, a part of me was relieved until I saw the same coldness in his eyes that I'd seen yesterday. Had I imagined the mischievous looks? Or had he simply forgotten how much he despised me for a moment? I kept my gaze turned away and silently followed him as we left for the city, this time on horseback, with several horse-drawn wagons behind us.

Barak nodded and even spoke fondly to those who greeted us, but I tried to keep my head down and avoid the eyes that said they knew who I was and what I'd done. The deeper we traveled into the city, the worse the conditions of the area around us became... and the heavier the animosity. It'd never felt this intense all those days in the marketplace. Maybe because the people here had suffered the most.

"Are you sure it's safe to be here?" I finally asked, apprehension sending cold shivers down my spine. It wasn't even the clan soldiers I was worried about now.

At first, it seemed like he wasn't going to answer, but then Barak shifted in his saddle. He didn't meet my gaze when he spoke.

"The slums are where the poorest live. They're not all horrible people, just the product of the hand they'd been dealt. A hand that used to be accommo-dating and caring under the rule of King Fariel, but became harsh and binding under Queen Isrella. Many were left to fend for themselves in a kingdom that had more than enough to support them. They barely have food, water, or even adequate light to discourage the shadows from overtaking them. They've had to fight off clan soldiers alone on top of their other troubles."

He gestured at the people around us. "I was once just like them. My brother and I fought for our lives, too, but we were rescued. Traveling through here the other day reminded me of my vow to do better by the people here." He then gestured at the guards at our backs. It was odd seeing the winged soldiers on horseback, but they rode them with fierce grace. "These people don't have the luxury of guards to watch their backs. No, they live with the risk of danger on their own every day. The least we can do is make their lives better."

He was right, of course. Despite their distaste and distrust of me, the guards at my back had sworn to keep me safe. Despite what I'd done, they still, to some extent, treated me like the princess my birth deemed me to be. The thought only increased my guilt as I took in the people less fortunate than I. People I'd helped hurt, along with a queen who was supposed to protect them. Damn this guilt. Barak was right. I didn't deserve the title of their princess.

So, I didn't complain as we dismounted next to a few decrepit houses. I just followed the lead of the people around me who had come to help Barak clean up this part of the city. It blew my mind to see big, burly warriors sweep the streets, help repair homes, and interact kindly with all the residents. Even the winged guards helped as they guarded me. I couldn't help the sadness twisting my gut as I took in the unsure and surprised gazes as we worked.

My muscles were screaming with exhaustion after hours of work, but I found myself glad. Was it enough to make up for my part in their suffering? My stomach twisted again, and I fought back tears as I watched the children study me from behind their parents' legs. No. I had a feeling it would never be enough.

What had I done?

I'd accused these people of being responsible for all that I'd lost, but what about them? They had no idea I existed until recently, but I had knowingly and willingly attacked them or opened doors for the clan to come in and make their lives miserable. Why? Because I missed my family? Because I'd been kidnapped and tortured until only the fiery rage of my flames remained? I'd blamed them for losing everything, and then turned around and helped others take it from them. While I'd lost my father, they'd lost their king a long time ago and were still suffering from it. How was I any better than those who'd burned my home to the ground?

I stood to the side, feeling as if I was intruding on a kingdom I had no business calling my own. Who was I to demand the throne when I'd done nothing to show that I actually cared for its well-being? I felt as Barak stepped to my side. His clothes were filthy, but his eyes held pride, the lightning in them flashing with his passion. He'd seen a need...had remembered where he'd come from and reached back to help instead of destroy. What had I done besides try to burn down all my father had built? I now fully understood that phrase "misery loves company".

"I think I screwed up," I whispered into the fading day. It was growing difficult to see without the special solar lights or glowworm lamps seen in the rest of the city, but the males still worked. Barak glanced at me, his arms folded over his chest.

"What do you mean?" he asked gruffly.

He'd barely spoken to me all day, only stopping to give me directions every now and again and to ensure I ate. I couldn't blame him. I wouldn't want to be associated with someone keen on destroying those I cared about either. I frowned. And yet... had I not helped them do just that? My head began to pound, flashes playing in my head...a feeling, like I was missing something. Forgotten something. Had I always hated my sister so? Or...had something else happened since I'd come to Fenriel?

"I have this feeling that... I don't know. Like I forgot who I was." I shook my head, frustrated. "I don't really know how to explain it, but the more I see this city, its people." I gestured at those around us, shutting down for the night. "The more shame I feel. I've always said I never directly hurt anyone, but now I think I used to say that to make myself feel better. To ignore that voice in my head telling me that something was wrong. That what I was doing–was *becoming*–was wrong." I swallowed past the lump in my throat.

I turned to him, the guilt eating me up alive, the darkness starting to pull me under. "I...I think I screwed up, Barak, and I don't know what to do to make it right."

He studied me for so long I was sure he'd turn and walk away, but instead he untied a bag from around his waist. He held it out to me.

"You can start by using fire to wash away the night instead of filling it," he said softly, gesturing at the lamp posts the males had finished placing.

I glanced at him and down at the bag. "What if I no longer know the difference?" I whispered. He stepped closer, and I glanced up into his steady, strong gaze.

"Then, let me show you, Dalacia. Let me show you what it means to choose the light, to choose your family."

The hum in my core grew louder, pulsing through my entire body at his words. Words that held a deeper meaning for both of us.

"You say that as if you know what it's like," I replied tentatively, afraid to hope.

"You'd be surprised," he said softly. "You're not the only one they tried to turn against their family." My eyes widened in surprise. Barak shook his head. "I'll tell you another time, but for now, let's fix what we can control." He held out the bag to me again, and this time I took it.

Taking a deep breath, I did my best to ignore the gazes of everyone around me as I traveled lamp post to lamp post until finally every last one was filled with glowworms. I saw tears on many of the Fae around me as the streets were awash with light for the first time in decades.

"Thank you, Princess of Fire."

I turned to meet the gaze of an old Fae woman. Her skin was wrinkled, her back stooped, but her auburn eyes were bright with knowing.

"I didn't do anything," I told her, shaking my head, shoulders slumped with shame. "I am the one to blame for this."

The old female smiled knowingly at me. "No, my child. You were trained in the darkness but loved in the light. The light will prevail as it always does... if you let it."

I frowned in confusion but bowed to her. I thought about her words long after we'd returned to the castle, and I lay in bed. Was she right? Was it as simple as deciding to no longer hold the grudge I did against my sister? Was it as simple as walking in who I was raised to be instead of conditioned to be? The hum in my chest, filling me with warmth despite the absence of my fire, said yes. As had the small smile of a male of lightning.

Chapter 32

If you sit back and watch them fall
does that make you wise?
Or a coward?

Silivia

"So, what's the name of the creature in this city?" I asked as we landed on the clouds—that would never get old—in front of the giant silver gates of the southern sky city. "And can someone please explain to me how there are forests...in the sky?"

Before me was a place like no other city I'd ever seen. Besides the stone walls surrounding a city with a castle made of glass, the area within and around it was carpeted with a field of white birch and cherry blossom trees. The area smelled amazing, and with the mixture of purple, blue, and white blossoms instead of the normal pink, it was a forest straight out of a fairy tale. This sky city also had a lush green mountainous region in the distance.

"Well, dear sister. Welcome to Vedia, city of the Ikari," Reece said, gesturing at the land around us.

I still stared with wonder as the gates were opened, and winged guards strolled towards us. "And what exactly are Ikari?" I asked, turning to Ghost."

He gave me a secret smile. "It'll be easier to show you," he replied with a wink.

I scowled. "Or you could tell me now," I grumbled. "I don't get why all of you are being so secretive about this creature."

"It's because seeing the Ikari is a rare treat," Tess explained. "It's well worth the wait."

"Yeah, but it's already been a week and a half," I grumbled irritably."

"Come now, Silivia. A queen shouldn't frown so much. It'll give you wrinkles," Ty teased.

I growled at him, much to Ghost's amusement, but I couldn't be too upset when Tyrian was slowly treating me like a friend again.

"Keep growling like that and I'll have to show you some other things besides the Ikari," Ghost promised down the bond.

I fought a shiver at the sensual caress. *"I learned from the best,"* I crooned, turning to meet the guards bowing in front of us.

A dark, hungry growl vibrated down the bond, and I bit back a laugh.

"Queen Silivia. King Ghost. Prince Reece. We are honored to have you in Vedia," the lead guard greeted, his long, braided hair flat to his back as he bowed. "Along with the famed Resisti warriors, of course." He bowed again to Teslia and Tyrian. We inclined our heads in answer. "Please follow me and I'll take you to see Lord Faunus and Lady Vanadei."

I lifted a brow at Reece. "Is there a reason why both sky cities have rulers named after gods?"

He chuckled. "Told you they think highly of themselves."

I shook my head in disbelief. It only grew as we walked through the glass castle with transparent windows and opaque walls and floors. Only the rooms contained walls of solid stone. It was beautiful, if not disturbing, to be walking in something so breakable. Although when I'd trailed a hand along the walls, it didn't seem to be like the glass from Earth.

"The glass of Vedia can withstand the force of a dragon and still stand tall," Lorik explained, noting my questioning stare. I glanced at him in surprise.

"And was this tested?"

He smirked. "Yes. The forest around it and even the stone walls faced extensive damage, but the castle stood strong."

I narrowed my eyes, a smirk twisting my lips. "Let me guess, you were on one of those dragons."

Lorik laughed, drawing questioning gazes to us. It was always a treat when the usually stoic guardian lowered his walls. We both knew the changeling guards much preferred their own wings to those of other flying beings. Considering the powerful males and females could match the speed of dragons—there had to be some magic involved there—one couldn't blame them.

"No, my queen, but my father used to tell stories of how our late king was sent to teach the Lord and Lady to respect the crown despite their...elevated position in the sky." I smiled at his choice of words, and Farek winked from his place at his brother's side. "The castle stood, but after having to recover from the damages done everywhere else...and to themselves, the lord and lady quickly learned they were not the god and goddess they believed themselves to be."

I could sense the tension in the guards leading us, even as the ones at our backs continued to smirk and chuckle to themselves. I shook my head in exasperation.

"More Fae politics?" I whispered to Tess, who mimicked my expression.

"More Fae politics," she confirmed.

I sighed. Here we go again. We were quiet as we were led into a large room. Once again, two Fae sat upon a throne as if they were the actual king and queen of Fariel. Lord Faunus was in a rustic brown tunic and pants with a sideways black cloak like a gladiator. Lady Vanadei wore a tan dress with slits on either side and her midriff bare. They both studied me with barely concealed contempt as we approached. Unlike Zera and Hira, they still rose from their seats to bow and curtsy to Ghost and I.

"Your Majesties. Our Prince," they greeted.

"Lord Faunus, Lady Vanadei, it's good to see that at least one of the sky cities hasn't forgotten how to address the rulers of Rifka," Reece said bluntly.

Ty smirked, his arms folded over his broad chest. "Someone's not holding his punches today," he muttered under his breath.

"Can you blame him?" Ghost muttered back.

With tensions still high, I bit my tongue, wondering how this was going to play out.

The lord and lady stood straight again, glancing quickly at each other before turning back to us. "Of course, we recognize that King Fariel's heir is the new ruler." They glanced at Ghost, a flash of fear crossing their eyes before they hid it. "And the King of Shadows himself."

"Good. That means we can jump several steps ahead to the reason we're here," Reece replied, his voice still holding a warning.

They glanced at each other again.

"That's starting to get on my nerves," Ghost growled.

I sent a comforting wave of snow down the bond. *"Well, to be fair, not all have a spiritbond to communicate with my dark king,"* I teased.

He snorted, but his darkness tempered.

"And why are you here?" Lord Faunus asked. "Surely you're not expecting us to raise an army to join you against the clan."

I raised my brows in surprise. "You know why we're here, but it sounds like you're saying you'd rather stay out of a war that will spread across all of Fenriel," I said evenly.

Faunus opened his mouth to speak, but I held up a hand to stop him.

"You see, I've already heard all the arguments in Belus and across Rifka. You believe that because the clan didn't harm your cities up in the sky when Isrella let them into Rifka – which may I remind you is a security risk we are still working to mitigate – that they won't come for you later. Once again, you fail to realize that the clan has access to winged creatures and winged Fae as well."

"Staying out of it will not save your city. In fact, I would argue that this is the mindset that allowed the clan to spread so quickly across Rifka in the first place. You live the closest to the shielded forest. If the sky cities weren't so insistent that they are better than everyone else in the kingdom we all inhabit, maybe they would have taken the initiative to help their fellow citizens and prevented some of the damage I am now blamed for."

The room went deathly silent. Gaping expressions were worn by many as they absorbed my words, but I was with Reece. Beating around the bush wasn't going to solve our problems, nor would Fae too high and mighty to do something about the threat they complained about.

"What would you have us do, Your Majesty?" Lady Vanadei said softly, but not weakly. "We have avoided fighting in the rest of Rifka's wars for centuries."

"And how has that worked out for you?" Tess interjected. "You've still managed to get into battles that have caused irrevocable damage to Vedia. Obviously, your approach doesn't work that well."

Lorik, Farek, Obsidian, and the rest of the royal guards shifted slightly, sensing the latent hostility in the room.

"We admit, we haven't been...successful in avoiding everything, but you are asking us to walk willingly into a war we may not survive," Lord Faunus pointed out.

"If you insist on doing nothing, you may not survive anyway," I stated coldly. "You really think the clan will leave you alone if we fail? They won't. They'll come up here and burn your city to the ground. Last I checked, the way glass is made is also how it can be destroyed."

Lord Faunus squeezed the arms of his chair as he said through gritted teeth, "Is that a threat, Your Majesty? Will you use your icy flames to end us?"

I shrugged. "That was merely a warning. Do with it as you will."

The room was silent again for what felt like ages before they finally seemed to come to a decision.

"If you expect our support, you will first need to win over the Ikari. A feat done by no halfbreed before. You are more likely to be defeated by the clan than for they to reveal themselves to you, but we wish you the best all the same, *Your Majesty.*"

I gritted my teeth against the pointed insults. I did not miss the dismissal in their voices, but decided a quick getaway was needed before Ghost decided to destroy them where they sat. Already, his shadows were whipping in agitation at our feet. I inclined my head and followed the guards to our accommodations.

Chapter 33

Sacrifices are often needed to succeed.
But never sacrifice who you are.

Ghost

"Well, that went well," Tyrian grumbled, slumping into a chair.

I folded my arms and leaned against the wall, still stewing. I had to agree with my brothers-in-arms. Lord Faunus and Lady Vanadei were on my short list.

"Actually, it did surprisingly," Reece said, leaning back against the opposite sofa.

Tess snorted. "If that's what we call going well, we're in for a fun time in Hyra and Farla," she scoffed.

Reece shrugged. "Honestly, I expected them to send the guards after us. Remember, the sky cities aren't the most compliant."

Silivia rolled her eyes as she slumped beside him. "And the rest of Rifka was?"

"Touché," the prince returned with a smirk.

"Okay, but where do we even start?" Tess said with a frown. "Our ever-so-gracious hosts had a valid point, even if they phrased it incorrectly. The Ikari have not revealed themselves to anyone since long before King Fariel left this land. If it was as simple as his heirs showing up, then they would have revealed themselves to Reece a long time ago."

"It'll take a very alluring act for them to reveal themselves."

We all turned to eye Obsidian. His gaze was on my mate, and a low growl slipped out before I could stop it. Amused green eyes flashed to mine as he gave me a wolfish grin. I narrowed mine, and he lifted his hands in placation.

"If you're done baiting our king, you should tell us what you mean, Obsidian," Lorik snapped at his third. The dark male inclined his head to me before continuing.

"The Ikari are known for revealing themselves during impactful moments: sacrifice, acts of love, birth. They revealed themselves to our late king when Ghost's father, Gonthar, sacrificed his life to protect him."

My chest clenched at that familiar loss of a male I never had a chance to know. A wave of comforting snow swept down the bond. I gave my mate a grateful half smile.

Obsidian lowered his head in a more respectful manner this time in acknowledgment. I returned the gesture, and he continued. "It will take something similar to convince them to come out of hiding again. Though it would help to know where to start."

A shuffling outside the door caught my attention, barely a brush of wind, but those in the shadows could not hide from me. Misting, I appeared behind them, where they had an ear pressed to the door. They didn't hear me as I took the doorknob and turned it, causing them to fall headfirst into the room. Everyone fell silent and eyed the faerie on the floor with surprise. The guards' hands were already on their weapons as they glared at the now shaking female.

"Please," she pleaded in a high, singsong voice, her iridescent wings fluttering fearfully. "I meant no harm."

I stepped into the room and closed the door, leaning back against it as I watched her.

"So, you weren't spying on us to run and tell your lord and lady later?" Tyrian growled.

The faerie cowered under his glare. "I...I was curious about the new queen," she said, turning pleading amber eyes to my mate. "I...I wanted to know if she was like her father or...or Queen Isrella." A grimace crossed her face.

Silivia glanced at me. I shrugged.

My mate stood from the chair and walked over to the cowering female. She held out a hand. "Come. None of us will hurt you if your intentions are indeed good."

The faerie took her hand carefully and rose to her tiny feet. She curtsied deeply. "Thank you, Your Majesty," she sang.

"What is your name?"

The faerie stared at her in surprise. No wonder. How many high Fae had deemed to learn her name?

"Lyris, Your Majesty."

"Lyris, what can you tell us about the Ikari?"

The faerie glanced nervously back at the door, meeting my gaze imploringly. I considered her for a moment, my eyes carefully blank, and then I raised a wall of darkness around us. I gestured at it.

"You may speak openly now," I told her.

"Thank you, my king," she sang excitedly. She turned back to Silivia. "There is a forest within a forest on the easternmost side of Vedia. It is there that the Ikari reside." The faerie grew somber as she glanced at everyone in the room.

"But beware, my queen. To reach their home, you will have to face the forest."

I frowned. Something about her warning sounded familiar, but maybe I was too exhausted for it to register in that moment.

Silivia took the faerie's hands in hers. "Thank you, Lyris. You have been a big help. Do not tell the lord and lady what you have shared with us today, and I will make sure you are rewarded when we are successful."

The faerie's wings fluttered excitedly, even as she threw nervous glances around her. "Even a place in Aurevel, Your Majesty?" she asked softly.

Silivia frowned in confusion. "Why Aurevel? Are you not from Vedia?"

Lyris shook her head. "My family abandoned the capital when King Fariel disappeared, fearful of the way the late queen treated us lesser Fae. Now that you and the Shadow King rule, we would like to return, but the lord and lady will not permit it."

"Of course they wouldn't," Reece scoffed. "Probably can't stand the thought that anyone wouldn't want to remain in their precious city."

"If you do not betray our trust, we will ensure your family can return home," I told her adamantly.

Grateful eyes filled with tears as she spun to face me. "You are as kind as you are merciless, my king. Thank you!"

Unsure how I should take that, I simply waved a hand, removing the wall of darkness, and stepped away from the door to allow her to leave.

"We should call the others," Tyrian said once she'd left, and I'd lifted another wall of darkness. "If what the faerie said is true, we'll be headed towards Siron soon. They should head that way to meet us."

"Sounds good." Silivia went to her pack and pulled out the oval vision mirror. I stalked towards the couches, and we gathered around as she placed it in the center of the table. She closed her eyes. "Show us the Resisti Seven."

The mirror shimmered, and a thin mist rose into the air until the image of Barak, Raiden, the assassin twins, Rose, Sirius, and Aux appeared.

"How goes it?" Aux greeted us.

"As well as can be expected," I answered. I gestured around the room. "We managed to wrangle Belus, and we should be finishing up soon in Vedia."

Surprise and respect flashed across their faces.

"Impressive," Sirius grumbled. "I was expecting them to put up more of a fight."

Tess snorted in annoyance. "Oh, they put up a fight, alright. Like Ghost said, we're almost done. Gods forbid we complete a task without having to complete challenges to do so. But alas."

Amused chuckles and smirks were shared by all.

"How's everything on your side?" Silivia asked.

Hemera shifted slightly. "We have neutralized those leading the clan in Aurevel and the surrounding cities. We left those who remained to the other Resisti." Blue-grey eyes met mine immediately.

"Do you think they actually managed to do so?" she asked down the bond.

I considered the male and female's twin blank expressions. *"It's the reason we sent them. If anyone could do so, they could."*

I turned back to the mirror. "Good job, Hemera, Hesper. You may head back towards Siron. Rest up. As soon as we arrive, you'll be headed out to start scouting the clan territories."

They bowed.

"Well, between the twins, Sirius, and I, Siron has been secured," Aux continued. "It was nasty here for a while. Those a-holes didn't want to relinquish the city." He gave me a pointed look. "We had to lock up the ruling lord and lady in the dungeon when they sent the clan to ambush us in our sleep."

"Good, they can remain there until this war is won," Tyrian growled.

Aux threw him a wicked grin. "My thought exactly, old friend."

I hid a smirk as I shook my head at the older male.

"It's the least they deserve," Sirius grumbled. "Should have let me slit their betraying throats."

Rose's hair fluttered wildly with her scowl. "Agreed, but rotting in that cesspool will have to do."

"Raiden? Barak? How's Aurevel?" Silivia asked, turning to the brothers who'd been quiet up to this point. We all knew what she was actually asking. The brothers shared a look, and I stiffened.

"Overall, it's going as well as can be expected," Raiden said reluctantly. "The clan's hold was deep here, similar to Siron, but we have made progress. Their attacks have been unorganized and desperate at best, thanks to the twins, but I still worry there are others who sympathize with them."

"The city has suffered under Isrella's rule, though," Barak interjected, and Raiden scowled at him. The younger male ignored his brother as he continued. "If we could have access to more resources, we could do more to reverse some of the damage in all parts of the city and not just near the castle."

Silivia and I shared a look before she turned back to him. "You may use whatever you need to bring Aurevel back to its prime. You are better equipped to do so since you both are from there."

"Thank you. You don't know how much that will mean to those in the lower city," Barak said thickly.

My mate nodded. "And my sister?"

Another hesitation. Another shared look between the brothers. I narrowed my eyes. It was my turn to send a comforting wave down the bond as the room grew colder with Silivia's anxiety.

"Barak," Reece cut in. The brooding male met his best friend's gaze. "Tell it to her straight."

Barak grimaced but turned back to Silivia. "I need a little more time. She is making progress, but I'm waiting for a sign that she's all in."

"We need to head out soon, Barak. We don't have time to wait for her forever," Tyrian growled.

The lightning male's eyes didn't leave my mate. "Not forever. Just...give me a little more time. She's on the cusp, Silivia. I can feel it. She just needs that little push to fall over the edge. We'll meet you in Siron if it's the last thing we do."

Silivia bit her lip, torn between hope and despair. Sullenly, she nodded. "You have until we reach Siron. But if she doesn't show any signs of joining our side by then, we have no choice but to move on," she said somberly.

Barak put a fist over his heart. "You have my word that I will do my utmost best to bring your sister to you."

They stared at each other for several seconds before she finally offered him a smile.

"If that is all, we'll see you all in Siron in the next week or two."

Goodbyes were shared, and then the mist twirled down until it disappeared into the vision mirror. Shifting to my mate's side, I pulled her into my arms. She slumped, allowing me to support some of the weight on her shoulders. I held her closer, and she wrapped her arms around me in return.

"Let's get some rest," I told everyone after a moment, my arms still wrapped around my mate. "We have a long day tomorrow if we're to find and win over the Ikari."

Chapter 34

You are great.
not because of what you do on the outside
but who you are on the inside.

Silivia

It was a relief to leave the glass castle early the next morning. It was beautiful, but I couldn't help feeling that its opaque wells reflected too much of the ones who ran it. Just enough about their intentions hidden so you weren't sure whether to trust them, or prepare for the floor to shatter beneath your feet.

As we traveled outside the gates and made our way towards the eastern side of Vedia, I couldn't help the feeling of déjà vu. Turning to gaze at the terrain around us as it shifted from open fields to deep forests, I called out to Celena.

"*Hey, how are you and the others?*"

My dragon showed me a vision of sitting close to Arctic, Eclipse, and Thistle as they slept and ate around a gorgeous waterfall.

"*Must be nice,*" I breathed, jealous of the peace they'd found.

Celena snorted. "*We're taking advantage of the quiet away from the courts,*" she said teasingly. The silver eyed dragon grew serious. "*Things will get complicated and chaotic in the next few weeks. War changes things. This may be the last slice of peace we see for a while.*"

I sighed. How I wished she wasn't right, but from the resistance I'd seen from just corralling Rifka's people, facing Hyra and Farla was going to test everything I'd learned up to this point. It would take everything I had to stop the Blood King once and for all. And I wasn't sure I was ready for it.

"Remember that you are not alone, Silivia," Celena cut into my turbulent thoughts. *"I may not like that you have to face so many challenges without me at your side, but you* are *Queen of the Winged. I am not the only winged ally you have, nor overall. Lean on your mate, your friends, and your family. Let them share your burdens and lend their strengths as you have done for them. What is that saying you and Ghost speak?"*

I smiled, feeling the silver bond in my chest hum in acknowledgement. *"Together, always. Whatever Comes."*

Celena hummed her agreement. *"Yes, remember this. Remind your mate of this when he forgets, and we will make it through this war."*

"Thank you, Celena. I don't know what I'd do without you."

She sent a wave of warmth down our bond. *"You would do just fine without me, but I am grateful to be a part of your life nonetheless."* Her presence withdrew from my mind as she cozied up to Arctic, and I refocused on those around me.

"Good, my queen?" Farek asked, glancing down at me from where he walked at my side.

I smirked at him. "What have I told you about formalities, Farek?"

He chuckled, his grey eyes twinkling. He inclined his head with a smile. "Apologies...Silivia," he corrected.

I grinned broadly at him. "See. Isn't that better?"

He shook his head, his smirk still in place. "You're the only royal I've ever met who disdains being addressed by her title."

I shrugged. "When you grow up in a much humbler environment where you're forced to do your own chores and train as a warrior in between doing your homework, you don't emphasize such things," I explained. "I was raised as Silivia Briar of Dogwood Lane. Not Princess Silivia Briar of Rifka."

"And now Queen Silivia Lokswood, The Phoenix Queen of the Winged of Rifka," Farek added as he lifted a tree's branches so I could duck under them.

I shivered at the title I'd never expected to hold. "Yeah, I never expected to be queen, and definitely didn't see being mated and married before I was twenty," I mused.

An uneasy feeling flushed through me as I remembered what else was supposed to happen by now. My power didn't feel any different, and whether that was due to my mixed heritage or being raised in the human world, I wasn't sure. Celena's words from before about leaning on those around me came to me then, and I sighed. Maybe I should talk to Ghost about it. It wasn't like he would judge me for my fears. If I did, maybe he would share what fears had been keeping *him* restless at night.

I noticed Farek giving me a look mirroring the concern now weaving down the silver bond. I gave both males a reassuring smile, but I think even my royal guards were getting to know me better than I knew.

"Not all gain it at nineteen."

I turned to see that Lorik had shifted from his position further at my back to my side. Out of the corner of my eye, I saw Farek shift back to replace him. Knowing dark eyes met mine as his wings shifted. They partially extended as if offering me the comfort the stern male himself could not.

"I didn't say anything," I told him, trying to hide my smile...and worry.

For a male who'd treated us like the dirt beneath his feet when we'd first met, he was warming up to our group fairly quickly.

"You didn't have to. I'm sure your comrades have all been wondering whether your power would manifest more than it has already." Lorik raised a brow. "I don't think it is a question of if, but when. You and the Shadow King have already proved that you do not follow the normal rules. Why should this be any different? Your power will come when it's needed as it has before."

I stared at him in surprise. "Why, Lorik, are you being encouraging right now?"

The tall male snorted, but his lips twitched. "I simply give credit where credit is due," he replied.

"Yeah, which doesn't happen often," one of Reece's guards threw over his shoulder.

The changelings all laughed as Lorik scowled at him. He grumbled something rude under his breath, and I giggled.

"Thanks, Lorik," I offered. "I'll cherish this moment forever." I winked at him, and the others laughed again as the grumbling male retreated from my side. My spirits lifted, I picked up the pace to join those up front.

The next day found us still traveling through the forest towards this mysterious forest at the center of the Ikari's territory, but the deeper we went, the more the unease in my gut grew. I wasn't the only one. Ghost stuck close to my right side, and Reece to my left. Ty and Tess even slowed their steps so that we traveled in a more compact group, the guards fanned out around us. What were we missing?

I kept thinking I saw things in my peripheral, the bloody grin of a velvet fox there, the hunkering body of a hogar there, but every time I turned to look, nothing was there. I shivered, not interested in meeting the ogres with hooved feet, rat tails, and horned, hog faces any time soon. I was starting to feel like I was under the hallucinations of the hypnotic viper. Its venomous bite fed off its victims' fears. Last time I'd felt its bite, I'd thought Ghost was out to kill me and feed me to ogres. He'd had to knock me out when I attacked him. I hadn't been bitten by anything, and yet I knew I was seeing things that weren't there. The question was.... were the others?

"Ghost?" I whispered, still eyeing the forest nervously. Golden eyes glanced at me, the indifferent mask barely concealing the stiffness in his stance. "Are you by any chance seeing things you can't explain, or am I going crazy?"

"Hard to go crazy when you already are," he retorted, but the teasing smile told me he was kidding.

I fluttered my eyes at him with a teasing grin. "But you would get sooo bored if I didn't drive you crazy at least once a day. However would we keep our relationship fresh otherwise?"

He rolled his eyes, and Reece snorted. "Sis, even I know you treat messing with the King of Shadows as a form of art," he pointed out with a grin.

It fell as I noticed the trees swaying ominously beyond him and frowned. He followed my gaze, but once again, nothing was there.

"To answer your question," Ghost continued. I turned to see him eyeing the shadows warily, something worrisome for someone who commanded them. "No, you're not the only one feeling like something is off."

Tyrian growled, and Teslia's hand went to her signature staff at her waist. "Is it just me, or are the trees changing?" he said, reaching a hand back to the broadsword down his back.

"It's not just you," Tess replied tightly as our group stopped.

The trees were indeed swaying, a menacing twist to their form that wasn't normal. Their branches seemed to reach out for us before withdrawing as if they couldn't decide whether to wrap us in their deadly embrace or simply trail along our skin.

"This isn't good," Lorik growled. "Farek. Obsidian. Protect the King and Queen."

"Don't even have to ask," Farek replied, drawing his blade and wrapping both hands around its hilt.

Obsidian did the same, eyeing the darkness with the same distrustful glare as Ghost. If both males of the shadows were uneasy by its presence, whatever was coming was most definitely not for the faint of heart.

The air temperature suddenly plummeted, causing our breaths to come out in puffs, increasing our anxiety.

"Silivia?" Reece asked, shivering already as he threw a look over his shoulder. "Please tell me that's just your ice escaping with your anxiety."

I shivered as fear flooded my veins. "It's not me," I whispered.

Ghost stepped closer to me, his mist rising up his legs and mine.

"Then who...?" My brother was cut off as a screech that froze the blood in our veins reverberated through the forest.

"Oh no," Tess breathed.

If the call of the banshee was our only problem, it would have been a blessing.

"Shit," Obsidian cursed.

I spun to see why and found us surrounded by twisted dragon-like creatures covered in rusted armor and deadly claws. Grigors. I blinked. And hogars. I blinked again. And more twisted creatures than I could even recognize slipped from the trees to surround us. Several screeches deeper than before had me almost peeing my pants. And more banshees.

"Ghost," I whispered, fear saturating my veins as the forest grew ever colder. "This doesn't feel right."

"I agree, but until we figure it out, everyone stay close and try to avoid getting killed."

The banshees' screeches flooded the forest, and as one, the deadliest creatures imaginable attacked.

Chapter 35

Barak

It would take months to get Aurevel back to stable times...and Rifka even longer... but in the last few weeks, at least we'd made progress. After the call with Silivia and the others and gaining permission to use resources as I saw fit in their absence, Raiden and I had been able to push the lower city from its sluggish crawl to furious anticipation. It was all hands on deck as, section by section, the city was repaired.

It was amazing to see how many pitched in to help. Even the remaining Resisti who had no ties to Rifka besides the alliance to the king and queen helped. Homes and shops were repaired. Walls that had fallen during the battle were finally resurrected, dragons and others used to pull them into place. Several Fae traveled through the lower parts of the cities, refilling the lamps that had sat empty for decades. Residents watched in awe as, for the first time in a long time, the shadows over their lives diminished.

Even the streets were washed clean. Water sprites came in waves, first flushing the clogged streets of their clumped-on waste. Others behind them came with brushes and scrubbed viciously at stubborn material before another wave came through to wash the remaining waste away.

And in areas where food was scarce, wagons had been stationed daily to pass out much-needed food, water, and medical supplies. Healers from the castle itself treated those who'd been without medical care for far too long. There were always Fae who didn't heal as quickly or effectively as those of us with power in our core. No longer were they neglected.

Several members of the Resisti passed out weapons, teaching their carriers how to use them safely. It'll be a useful skill to have while we continued to get the hidden clan sympathizers and adversaries of the crown still attacking unsuspecting individuals under control. Plus, with the upcoming war, they needed to know how to protect themselves. If only for the peace of mind it brought.

All in all, for the first time in my life, I felt like I was finally holding up my promise. And maybe this wasn't the only thing I was making progress on.

I glanced over to Dalacia to find her helping one of the shop owners set up her wares for the day. It was something she'd started doing at least three times a week. Training before sunrise so she could bathe and dress before coming here to the marketplace to help with setup for the day, before we traveled to do repairs in a different part of the city. I wasn't sure if it was because of the elder storyteller who always appeared around lunch to guile the crowd with ancient tales. Or if she just generally enjoyed interacting with the people...her people, but the marketplace had become her favorite place to be.

I watched the fire princess laugh at whatever the red-haired elf told her, her curls falling gracefully down her back, her blue eyes shining with mirth and joy as she threw her head back. The elf winked at her, and Dalacia gave her a smile that filled me with a burning ache to have that smile turned on me...caused by me. She was beautiful. A hot-headed, fiery hearted female, but it was that passion that made her so.

Every day that I watched her loosen up and interact with her people with care and determination, every day that I watched that wall of disdain crack and crumble, the more my own wall of loathing did the same. I'd doubted she could change even if I was committed to helping her do so, but now I wasn't so sure I was only doing so for Silivia.

"You're doing it again," Raiden mused, making me jump.

I hadn't even heard him approach. Sloppy and unwise in the dark times we were facing. I did a quick sweep of the marketplace, but the royal guards and the Resisti were patrolling as usual.

"What?" I asked finally, giving my older brother a questioning look.

Raiden raised a brow and inclined his head towards the fire princess, who had now moved on to the next shop, a little book and herb store. I'd noticed that it was something that both sisters shared...the love of a good book. I wondered if Dalacia realized what an oddity it was for the shop to be open at all. It had been too long since the skittish, young nymph who owned it felt safe enough to do so.

"I'm not sure I know what you mean," I said, realizing I was staring again.

Raiden snorted. "Gods, you have it bad, little brother." My gaze shot to his, a denial ready on my tongue. He gave me a knowing look that had me pausing. "Come now, Barak. I know you too well not to notice when your focus has been captured."

It was my turn to snort. "You forget that it's my job to be focused, Raid. It became so when we joined the Resisti and then the inner court of Rifka. I'm responsible for the queen's sister for gods' sake. I have to be focused."

"Yeah, and you're not using that as an excuse to avoid admitting that you care about her more than you let on?"

I turned to glare at him, bristling even as the truth burned in my core. "No, I'm not, because I don't care for her any more than this job requires. My presence is a means to an end."

Raiden lifted a brow, unbothered by my flaring temper or the electricity sparking between us. "So, your defense of her, the little freedoms you give her, and the way you watch her when you think no one notices is just what? A coincidence? I'm not stupid, brother. I can tell that you..."

"Stop! Whatever you're about to say, just stop. I don't care about her beyond her being Silivia's sister. I don't care about gaining her trust beyond ensuring she doesn't try to destroy our kingdom. And I don't care about her period, beyond ensuring she joins our side so she isn't just another fiery pain in my ass."

Raiden's eyes had gotten larger as I went on, flashing as if trying to tell me something. But I was on a roll and didn't heed the warning even as my throat burned with each lie I spilled. I should have, because as soon as I stopped, I felt the painful tug in my core.

"Is that all I am to you? Just someone to *handle*? Just *Silivia's sister*?"

I spun to see Dalacia standing behind me, her face twisted in disbelief as she bristled. But my stomach sank to my feet with shame and regret, because that was hurt in her eyes. Hurt I'd put there by narrowing down her existence to the very thing that formed the core of all her pain. Only being known as the queen's sister. She'd been kidnapped for it. Trained by the clan and not her father because of it. And now she was a prisoner of Rifka because of it.

"Dalacia, I..."

But she didn't wait to hear what I was going to say. She just stormed away, tears pooling in her blue eyes. I stood frozen for a second, unsure whether to go after her or stew in my stupidity. Why didn't I keep my mouth shut? Yes, I'd spoken mostly the truth, but it was slowly becoming more than just a job, and though I was hesitant to accept it, I knew that.

"You should go after her," Raiden said, a concerned frown on his face. I glanced at him, and he inclined his head. "If only to prevent her from doing something stupider than you just did."

I winced. I deserved that. Swallowing my pride, I rushed after her. I found her marching down a quiet street. "Dalacia, wait!" I called.

"Just go away, Barak!" She screamed back, wiping furiously at her face.

My gut clenched again, and the burning in my core grew worse. I ran until I was close enough to grab her arm and stop her, spinning her to face me. "For gods' sake, stop. I'm trying to apologize," I growled in frustration.

She glared at me angrily, her blue eyes shiny with her tears. "Why? Because lord forbid you lose all your progress with the queen's sister and she goes back to being the evil fire princess you know her to be?"

I winced again. *Gods*, I was an idiot. "No, that's not what I meant. And that's not why I'm here. I really did come to apologize. I was out of line and wanted my brother to get off my back." I sighed. "Not that that's a good excuse for what I said. I'm...I'm sorry, Dalacia."

She stared at me for a few seconds, the pain still painted all over her face, but then her shoulders fell, the fight going out of her. She signed heavily, her eyes on the cobbled streets.

"Do you know why what you said hurts so badly, even though I know you spoke nothing but the truth?"

It wasn't the whole truth, I thought sullenly, but said nothing.

"I walk around this world feeling like I'm alone in a crowd and that I'm powerless to fight it. I just want someone to see *me,* Barak. Not Silivia's sister. Not Fariel's youngest daughter. Not the clan's bait. *Me. Just Dalacia.* Is that too much to ask for?"

It wasn't, and I was a fool. The burning in my core reminded me of that fact as I stepped closer to her. I lifted her chin so her eyes met mine. "No, it's not. And you're more than *just Dalacia* any day."

She sniffled softly. "You're just saying that," she whispered, but a little bit of the fire came back into her eyes.

I shook my head adamantly. "I don't just say things like that, Wildfire."

She gave me a skeptical look. "Okay, I'll bite. Who am I then?"

I opened my mouth to tell her, despite the clenching in my chest, my gaze dropping to her mouth, but screams split the air. I spun back towards where we'd come.

"It's coming from the marketplace!" Dalacia exclaimed and took off running.

I was quick to join her. We raced back to find clan soldiers fighting the royal guards and Resisti, while others attacked the residents.

"No. No. No," Dalacia chanted, staring in horror as the clan that had been concealed worked to reverse all the progress we'd made.

What would it take for Rifka's people to stop supporting the attack on their own people? I could feel the heat rising off her and glanced down curiously at the iron bracelets on her wrists. It wasn't the first time they hadn't worked like they should.

"We have to stop them!" Her gaze shot to mine, and I knew I wasn't going to like what she said next. "You said you want me to prove that I'm on your side. That it was the only way I switched from being a prisoner to claiming my title. To making amends for the suffering I caused." Regret and pain flashed in her eyes as she clenched her fists.

"Let me prove it to you now. I need to stop them, Barak. I need to prove that I'm more than what people think I am. And...I need to prove it to myself, too. That I'm not just another villain in my own story. *Please*."

I knew what she was asking me to do. I also knew the others would have my head, but I was running out of time. We needed to meet Silivia, Ghost, and the others soon, and Dalacia couldn't come if she didn't do something major to show she was on our side. I wanted to do the very thing that no one had ever done. I wanted to believe in her. Believe in her abilities. Her heart. Despite the logical side of me screaming at me not to do it, the burning in my core said trust her, as I wanted her to trust me. So, I reached out and did what could be the stupidest thing I'd ever done...I released her.

The heat between us rose to scorching as fire immediately appeared around her fists. But it was not victory in her eyes, but determination as she turned to face the marketplace.

"Thank you. Now let's fry their asses."

I snorted a surprised laugh as I drew my bolt blade, lightning jumping down it as I spun it one-handed. "Let's."

Then we rained hell. If I thought she was beautiful before, she was a goddess now. I couldn't help appreciating the way she danced through the crowd, her fire controlled and precise as she took out clan soldier after soldier. Their surprise was evident as she knocked them out or burned them to a crisp when they attacked her ruthlessly. They'd likely thought the battle won with her flames released, but true to her word, the fire princess fought for a different side now.

I wasn't the only one who stopped fighting after a while to just watch her work. I heard several appreciative whistles from the other males as they lowered their weapons. One of the changeling guards froze in utter surprise when she saved him from a clan soldier at his back. Dalacia only nodded in acknowledgement before rushing off to stop another, the guard still staring open-mouthed after her.

"She is something else," Raiden breathed, eyes wide.

I nodded, not taking my eyes off her as she twisted and spun as fluid as a flame. In the blink of an eye, the clan threat, along with their supporters, had been neutralized. Guards, Resisti, and residents alike watched as she calmly walked over to me, grabbed the iron bracelets from my pocket, and snapped them on herself. The heat in the air vanished, but not the heat in her eyes. She met my gaze and then my brother's.

"Does that tell you where my loyalty lies?" she asked.

Raiden opened his mouth, but she didn't wait for his answer. Without another look at either of us, she walked away and started cleaning up the marketplace. Raiden and I both blinked.

"Normally, I would be chopping you up into little pieces and feeding you to a grigor for doing something idiotic like releasing what is likely one of the most powerful fire users we've seen in centuries into our city. But I think I'll let it slide. You already have your hands full with that one." Raiden shook his head as a wolfish smirk twisted his lips.

I glared at him. "Gee, thanks. So generous."

But he was right, and she'd done what we'd hoped. Or at least she was beginning to. I had a feeling that there was more to the fiery-hearted princess, and a part of me was looking forward to uncovering it.

"You know what this means, right?" Raiden continued, gesturing at the princess who was being hugged and thanked by the residents along with the rest of the warriors.

"Yeah, I do. It's time to take down a king."

Raiden smirked, and I returned it. "Looks like we're headed to Siron."

Chapter 36

I was the monster in the night.

I burned your dreams when mine shattered.

But pain begets more pain.

And I refuse to live that way.

So now,

I'll be the monster in the night.

And burn our enemies away.

Dalacia

I desperately itched to take off the iron bracelets. The feeling of my fire flooding my veins and rushing out of me was like coming home. There was a part of me that screamed at the fact I'd willingly put it out again. But it was the only way I could show Barak and the others that I was serious about joining my sister's side. I might still have reservations when it came to our sisterly bond, but the people had suffered enough for my jealousy and...

I frowned and stopped stuffing the bag I was carrying to Siron. And...what? There was this feeling on the edge of my consciousness, like I was forgetting something. Something important. A part of me whispered that while this had started with jealousy, it wasn't what caused me to turn against my sister. In fact, Silivia and I had always been close. It wasn't until I'd come to this world that it had changed. Yes, I was envious of Dad's extra attention to her, but had I really wanted the extra responsibility? Extra expectations? Not really. Yes, I was angry that I'd suffered at the clan's hand. That no one had heard my cries. That I'd been taken instead of her.

So why did I feel like I was missing something? Why did I feel like the clan had stolen more from me than my innocence and family? The spark in my core grew warm, reminding me of my fire. It was like it was trying to clear the cobwebs in my head. In my soul. Maybe on this journey to stop a group responsible for teaching me to destroy my father's kingdom, I'll figure out what was hidden there. Maybe it held my retribution. And my future.

Rifka was beautiful. It was little towns that embodied nature and Rifka's love of the winged. It was miles and miles of forest, rolling hills, and mountains.

I'd learned about its geography extensively in the months leading up to the clan's agreement with Queen Isrella to overtake it. In the northeast lay the Valley of Whispers, nestled between the Moran Mountains. Massive, jagged mountains called the Fanged Mountains housed the dragons to the west of the valley. Further west, within the White Mountains, was the Selondian Forest, frozen in a perpetual winter for most of the year. To the east was the Forest of Dreams that led to the Silent Hills. The forest made you dream of that which weighed on your heart, and the hills... they showed you your greatest fears and forced you to face them. Just the thought was enough to make shivers scatter down my spine.

Far to the south, in the western corner, lay the last major landmark of the land of the winged, the Pools of Reverence. From what I was told, it showed you your deepest desire. Whether you went for it was up to you. The southern part of the kingdom itself was protected by the Shielded Forest.

I had seen much of the kingdom in my mission to cause as much mayhem as I could during the time the clan was stationed here, but it was with different eyes I saw it now. Then, it was how I could cause the most damage and flush out our targets. Now, it was with eyes that sought to understand what caused my sister and her friends to fight so hard to reclaim it. I realized now that I'd missed out. On how the red poppy fields looked as they danced in the wind, like little embers of flames. On how the creatures here were unique in their beauty and danger, like the cat-sized deer with wings called a dilek, and the Clydesdale-sized dyrewolves who watched us from the shadows at night, their four ears twitching at every sound.

And maybe I'd missed out on something else, too. I glanced over to where Barak and Raiden laughed with the males occupying us. Two were my personal royal guards as Princess of Rifka...though I'd never made an effort to learn their names. All I knew was the sterner one had long silver hair and black wings, while the other, more laid-back one, had black hair and dark grey wings, and that they were twins. The others were members of the Resisti who had fought with my sister.

They all had this easy camaraderie between them, even though some of them hadn't even known each other a few months ago. The drinks and jokes flowed, and none seemed to worry about exposing their back. They generally seemed to trust and like each other.

It had been different in the clan camps. There were jokes, yes, but laughter was quickly followed by sneers, and I'd seen way too many take a blade to the back for comfort. A suffocating shadow always hovered over them, a darkness that was similar to the ones the King of Shadows concealed, but while Ghost was faithful to his family, friends, and people, the clan soldiers were only faithful to themselves. I still remembered the taste of my fear those first few months.

I shivered, wrapping my arms around my knees as I leaned against a tree, watching them. I knew that while no one's eyes were directly on me, they were still waiting for me to step out of line. I deserved their distrust, but I felt like an outsider looking through a window, desperate to join the warmth on the other side.

"You could join them, you know."

I jumped, not realizing that Raiden had snuck up beside me and now leaned against his own tree. How the hell did he move so quietly? You would think males as tall and built as he was would surely make some type of sound, or at least that hammer of his would make his steps heavy, but no. It was a skill the Fae had that I had yet to fully master.

Remembering what he'd said, I raised a brow in surprise. "You act as if I would be welcomed. I am part of the reason Rifka is as messed up as it is," I answered bitterly.

Surprise flashed across his face. "So, you're taking responsibility for your actions now?"

I bristled at his condescending tone, but he wasn't wrong. I had been adamant about my lack of guilt. I didn't reply, and he continued.

"They saw you in the marketplace. They've seen you care for your people for weeks now. I'm sure you've noticed that they don't watch you quite as severely as the days go by."

"Are they my people?" I asked. "And they do still watch me. I will never live down what I've done."

Raiden gestured at the forest. "So why are you here?"

I scowled. "What do you mean? I have to be here."

He shook his head. "No, you don't. You could have remained in Aurevel, albeit as a prisoner, but you could have stayed. You didn't have to defend its people." He gave me a pointed look. "You didn't have to put them back on."

I glanced down at the iron bracelets. Meaning I could have used Barak's trust against him and destroyed my captors. Except. I glanced at those around the fire again. They were listening even if they pretended not to.

"Maybe I got tired of feeling powerless," I said finally. "Maybe I just got tired of the silence." I hated Raiden's knowing smirk when I realized that I was unintentionally staring at Barak...and he was staring back.

Raiden moved to head towards the other males, but said over his shoulder, "Then maybe you should make some noise."

Chapter 37

The Silent Hills summon your worst fears.
And make you face them.

Ghost

We were tiring and fast. For every grigor or hogar we attacked, two more replaced them. The banshees continued to screech, but thankfully not appear. I didn't want to face off against one, gods forbid several, with so many other creatures besieging us. As if rescuing the griffins from them wasn't hard enough.

The ground was saturated with black and red blood alike. It only seemed to feed the forest's hunger. If you wandered too close to one of its trees, branches and vines reached out to grab you and hold you in place. Precious time was wasted freeing each other and fighting off creature after creature. The changelings refused to leave our sides, but even they sported sliced wings and pained grimaces as they cut down enemy after enemy.

"We can't go on like this forever!" Tess yelled over the snarls, growls, and agonized shouts.

"Then we need to figure out where they're coming from!" Tyrian shot back, dodging a hogar's club before cutting it down with his sword.

I gritted my teeth, sending my darkness to wrap around a grigor intent on attacking Silivia from the back as she held down another. "Silivia, duck!" I roared, moving too slowly to stop the claws coming for her head.

Thank the gods she didn't hesitate, and the attack took out the grigor in front of her instead. She finished both off with shots of ice through the chest before throwing me a grateful look. She was breathing hard and likely in desperate need of a break. Misting to her, I wrapped an arm around her and misted her to the edge of the fight, keeping a wall of darkness up to fend off the trees that immediately reached out for us.

"Are you okay?" I asked, scanning her for any immediate concerns.

She nodded. "I'd be better once this stops," she panted, glancing over her shoulder where our friends still fought. "Where are they all coming from? Surely not all of these creatures live here? How would hogars even get up here?"

I frowned, the thing that had been nagging at me finally coming to a head. "They *don't* live here," I told her, looking at the forest with new eyes. "Does this remind you of anything?"

Silivia frowned and followed my gaze. I studied the grigor that Tyrian fought, noticing that as he cut it down, slivers of darkness seemed to leak from the wound along with blood. Wait. Not darkness...shadows. Like the shadow creatures that I myself could create. The only way this many would be materializing here was if summoned, but Obsidian nor I were to blame. The only other thing strong enough to do so...was fear.

My eyes widened in understanding. Fear that materialized into that which you feared to face, just like a certain Silent Hills. A location that just so happened to lie right below the forest we fought in now. What if some of its power leaked into the sky? Instead of manifesting your individual worst fears, it created creatures who were the worst of the worst. Meaning...

"They're not real!" I shouted as I lowered the wall of darkness around Silivia and I.

She threw me a startled look, but it only lasted a second as she realized the truth in my statement.

"How can you be sure? Their claws sure as hell are," Tyrian shouted back.

"Because darkness recognizes darkness." Silivia threw me a knowing look that said she understood what I wasn't saying.

The darkness's pull had been relentless lately, as if my power was being coaxed out, but that was a problem for another day.

"When snow and shadows bind..." I heard her whisper before her eyes went wide. "Wait! That's it!" my mate exclaimed, meeting my eyes.

I frowned, not following.

"Ghost, we have to work together!"

I threw her a dubious look, but then growled in pain as a grigor took advantage of my distraction and sliced me in the side. "What?" I growled as she retaliated by cutting the beast down with her twin blades.

Our guards flew to our sides, fighting off further attacks.

"We need to use our power together!"

It took a moment for realization to hit me, but then I spun so that she was in front of me, wrapped one arm around her waist, and held out the other. Silivia placed her hand outstretched under my own. Gods, I hoped this worked. If it did, the prophecy wasn't just talking about us taking on the Blood King.

"Ready?" I whispered into her ear, reveling in the rightness of our bodies pressed together, our power rising to answer the other's.

"Yes," my mate breathed, and then with a deep breath, we released snow and shadows.

They weaved together as they often did between us, but this time they formed a wave. A wave that rose and rose before it swept through the entire forest, wiping away the fears that battled us. All beasts turned to dust, and the chill from the banshees disappeared until all that was left was a band of panting, exhausted warriors.

"Whoa," Reece breathed, glancing around us in awe.

"Is everyone alright?" Lorik asked, grimacing as he shifted on his wounded leg.

Confirmations rebounded, but my mate said nothing.

"Silivia?"

She startled in my arms, glancing over her shoulder with wide eyes. "Do you see what I see?" She pointed a shaking finger at the forest to our right.

Following it, I blinked in surprise. Little tufts of pink and purple, like those of the mimosa tree, fluttered over the ground, forming a path. They seemed to shimmer and dance through the air as if asking us to follow them.

"Yeah, hard to miss that," I breathed.

"Miss what? Ty asked, frowning in the direction we watched. "I don't see anything."

I blinked, and Silivia met my gaze again.

"They only reveal themselves during impactful moments. We represent light and dark working as one like the prophecy claims. What is more impactful than that?"

I wanted to deny it, but here was the proof right before us. "Then we'd better get patched up and see if we passed the test."

Once everyone was able to walk with minimal pain, Silivia and I led the group down the shimmering path. My mate tried to explain what exactly we were seeing to the rest of the group.

"So, we're following a bunch of flying pink seeds?" one of the changelings scoffed skeptically.

Yeah, I had to agree it was novel to me too, but hey, when had things ever been normal for our group? We had a prince who grew dragon parts when he was angry. A queen who produced icy cold flames. And I could weave the darkness and shadows others feared. We were most definitely not normal. We'd walked roughly two miles before the trees opened up and changed altogether.

"Oh my god," Silivia gasped.

"And this is why we follow invisible, flying pink seeds," Tess teased, gesturing at the beautiful forest made up of flourishing cherry blossom trees with purple and blue flowers.

Birds fluttered in and out of the branches, twittering to each other. A herd of liocks flicked their lion tails and watched us from where they reclined around a stream. Their ever-changing antlers shifted every few seconds. The snow-white deer utterly unbothered by our presence.

"I could stay here forever," Silivia exclaimed, throwing Tess a grin.

The females giggled, while us males rolled our eyes, unable to fully fight a smile. Where the forest behind us had been dark and full of fears, this one was airy and full of peace. No wonder the Ikari called it home. But where were they?

I went to my mate's side when she'd wandered towards the cherry blossoms. I cocked my head as I watched her hold one of the many flowers to her nose. My heart clenched at the sheer pleasure on her face, her eyes closed as she smiled. She was a goddess and as good as they came. And she was all mine. Unable to stop myself, I pulled her into my arms and lifted her chin so I could crush my lips to hers. She gasped in surprise before melting into me, her hands coming to my waist and pulling me closer as she met the intensity of my kiss. She didn't fight me when I demanded entrance with a swipe of my tongue. Only nipped at my bottom lip before opening like the blooming flowers around us. Her soft moans of pleasure had me losing myself in her, desperate to drink every sigh that fell from her lips. When I finally pulled away, we were both panting for an entirely different reason.

Her lips were swollen, and her eyes, glazed over with pleasure, shone with amusement and longing as we stared at each other, catching our breath. "What was that for?" she asked, making no move to shift out of my embrace.

"I've spent too much time not kissing you when all I wanted to do was pull you into my arms," I told her. "I've decided to stop holding back."

She grinned mischievously as her eyes softened. "You won't find me complaining," she replied, rising on her toes to kiss me again.

"Um, Ghost. Silivia," Tess called. "As sweet as it is to see you both finally walking in your bond, I think you should see this."

We both spun to see everyone staring into the forest. At first, I wasn't sure what held their attention until I saw the space around a tree shimmer and shift. My hand went to the wolf blades at my side, but Silivia's hand stopped me.

"Wait. Look."

Suddenly, the shimmer began to take shape, revealing the most beautiful dragon I'd ever seen. It was covered in iridescent blue and purple feathers that camouflaged with the trees. Its long tail trailed out before curling. Its wings seemed almost like glass but were shaped like those of a butterfly with the same colors as its body. It sported lengthy antennae that trailed behind its long, slender head. I'd never seen the Ikari outside of paintings and books, but no one could mistake the dyrewolf-sized dragons for anything else. And they'd just revealed their presence to us.

"There are so many of them," Silivia whispered as one by one, more Ikari revealed themselves from where they were wrapped around the trees.

The first that had done so was much larger than the others, a curve to the top of her head that looked like a crown. She was a darker blue and purple than the others and eyed us curiously as she stepped closer to my mate and I.

"The Ikari queen," Farek breathed in awe.

No one else spoke as the Ikari walked until she stood directly in front of us. She lowered her head and stared with shimmering, silver eyes before huffing at us. Silivia and I shared a look before she reached out a hand for the Ikari to sniff. The queen huffed again, and smiling softly, Silivia placed a hand on the dragon's snout. A lyrical hum rumbled through the Ikari's chest, but her eyes shifted to mine as if in offer. Swallowing, I hesitated. I was a king of darkness. I had no business touching a creature as pure as this.

As if sensing my doubt, snow enveloped the silver bond, and Silivia took my hand with the one not on the Ikari's snout. "She revealed herself to both of us," she whispered, and then she placed my hand alongside her own on the soft, feathered dragon.

The lyrical hum grew louder, and the Ikari around us joined in until the forest was alight with their welcome. Silivia and I both startled, eyes going wide as a new bond weaved of shimmery blue appeared within our cores. Ever since I'd accepted our spiritbond, I could feel all the bonds she shared with the winged, but had never gained an additional one of my own. Apparently, my mate was correct. The Ikari recognized both of us and had gifted us with a bond I'd never heard of being shared with them before.

I felt their acceptance in every cell of my body. Felt the spiritbond grow even stronger. Shadows and snow trailed around both our feet, rising to dance around the Ikari queen. She pulled away and chortled in the dragon's way, turning to watch as the young Ikari played within it. Unable to fight the smile and joy rising in my chest, I laughed at their antics. Silivia threw her arms around my waist and hugged me tightly as we watched them dance around our friends and family. Soon, the Ikari queen whistled for their attention, and one by one, the dragons disappeared, camouflaging among the trees again. She was the last to go, sending one more hum of acknowledgement to which I inclined my head, before she, too, disappeared.

No one spoke as we made our way back out of the forest. Somehow, returning to the glass castle went much faster, as if the forest had been wiped clean. Soon we were all gathering in the room Silivia and I shared.

"I've never seen anything like that," Ty said in reverence, sinking onto the couch.

I'd held my mate's hand all the way back and now had her back pressed against my chest as I stood against the wall, needing to feel that connection to her.

"It was...I don't even know how to describe it," Reece breathed.

"This is going to be one for the history books," Tess said excitedly. "And we all witnessed it."

I rolled my eyes and smiled at my sister-in-arms. No one loved history like her.

"She bonded with both of you?" Lorik asked from his position by the door. The question was aimed at Silivia, but his eyes were on me.

Trust me, I'm as surprised as you, I thought, returning his questioning gaze.

"Yes," Silivia replied.

"You two are going to turn Fenriel upside down," Farek said, shaking his head in awe.

Obsidian snorted. "They did that the day they were born. This is just confirmation."

The truth in the statement had me tensing, but Silivia gripped the arm around her waist and gave it a gentle squeeze.

"At this rate, you'll hold bonds with all the major winged in Rifka. Talk about embodying your title," Reece smiled as he shook his head. "I'm proud of you, little sister." His eyes softened. "And Dad would be too."

I felt her heartache and hope down the bond and held her tighter.

"He's right," I whispered into her ear.

She shivered slightly. "Thank you, but I couldn't have done anything without any of you," she replied. "I'm not sure what our future holds as we face the other Fae kingdoms, but I have to say, I like our odds."

Grinning, Reece jumped up to pour us all a drink before holding up his glass. "To the King and Queen of the Winged!"

"To the King and Queen!" The others echoed and drank.

But as I held my glass for another drink, I felt a dark knock on my mind. My shadows shifted in my core in answer...but hesitated. Because it was not my own.

Chapter 38

How can a monster of the night
dare to hold the light?
There is only a matter of time
before it consumes it wholly.

Ghost

"What? That's impossible!" Lord Faunus looked more flushed than I'd ever seen him as he glared at the Ikari feathers Reece held.

He'd better watch his tone. I was still very displeased with how he'd spoken to my mate the last time. And with the weird dream I had the night before, I was in a worse mood than normal.

I fought to keep my face in its indifferent mask as visions of nefarious laughter and my mate's screams in the darkness played on repeat in my head. I gritted my teeth to keep from wincing as I once again heard her voice begging in the night...*begging me.* Concern flooded the spiritbond, despite the wall of darkness I was fighting to keep in place. I didn't want Silivia to know that I was being haunted by nightmares of hurting her even worse than before. But keeping her blocked had been easier before we'd both accepted the bond. Now, even though it was muted, she could still tell something was wrong. Just not what. So, despite the berating Lord before us, her attention was on me.

"What's wrong?" she asked. *"You've been off lately. Are you worried about the war or something else?"*

Of course, I was worried about the war to come, but I was just as worried about what *I* would do during it. I couldn't bear to lose her...I'd lost too many of those who I cared about already. I hadn't been able to protect Sicily or my mother, but the gods be damned before I lost my mate too. Even if I had to protect her from myself.

"*Daniel?*"

My heart skipped a beat before filling with warmth. "*I'm...*" I started.

"*Don't you dare lie to me,*" she snarled. "*We've come too far for that BS.*"

I didn't know whether to sigh or laugh. She was the only one who would go head-to-head with the shadows fearlessly...even back when I'd made it my duty to despise her. I had no chance of resisting her now.

"*Okay, I'm...struggling with something, but this is not the place to discuss it,*" I amended. To be able to feel her glare even through a bond was impressive, to say the least. "*Later, I promise.*"

She finally relented, turning to the still raging male in front of us. Alright, I'd had enough.

"Silence!" I snapped.

The room fell silent immediately, the Fae around us freezing as they turned to me. Lord Faunus swallowed audibly as if he'd just realized who he'd been berating. Apparently, they'd forgotten just how short my patience could be.

"You may not like it, *Lord* Faunus, but we are your king and queen. Last I heard, we do not need to prove ourselves to you. In fact, it is you who should be proving to us why you and your mate should remain leading Vedia at all."

His eyes widened in horror as his mate gripped the arms of her chair.

"You know, he makes a good point," Reece said thoughtfully. He raised in brow. "Why *should* you stay as lead? If I remember my history correctly, you have always been nothing but confrontational to the ruling royals, whether in my father's time or now, and yet I fail to remember you offering anything of use."

Lord Faunus bristled, and I could tell Lady Vanadei was biting her tongue to stay silent. Reece turned to me with a contemplative look.

"You know, Ghost. The council has done well with some rearranging. Instead of standing in this stifling, wannabe throne room, maybe we should consider who would be better suited to rule it."

I nodded with exaggerated thoughtfulness, trying to fight a smirk. "You're right. It would make unifying Rifka much simpler in the long run. New rulers would likely be more amiable towards our plans."

Reece nodded. "Exactly! Tyrian, who do you think would fit best?"

We both turned to my brother-in-arms, who wore a severe look that didn't quite mask the mirth in his eyes.

"Well, I know we're short on time," he mused. "We could always place some-one temporarily until after the war." He tapped his chin. "Hell, Sirius would likely rule Vedia better than the current rulers."

I had to swallow my snort of laughter to keep a straight face. Amusement was flooding the silver bond, and I knew Silivia was avoiding my gaze in order to keep her own neutral.

Lord Faunus sputtered in indignation as he shot to his feet. "My King! My Queen! Surely you are not actually considering this! Vanadei and I have ruled this city for many a century. Our people have thrived under us!"

"Yes, they've thrived so well, they stood by while the rest of Rifka dealt with the destruction of the clan," Silivia said smoothly.

Faunus paled.

"You must understand, Your Majesty," Vanadei said imploringly. "We only did what was best for our people. If it had come to it, we would have stepped in where needed."

"The people of Rifka are your people, not just those of Vedia," Silivia snapped. "And you had your chance to step in when we spent days battling to retake Aurevel. Don't you know what would have happened if we'd failed?"

Neither elf answered, and she narrowed her eyes. "You will step in where you're needed? Great. When Ghost and I call upon you to join this war, you will be there. You will start preparing your warriors now because it will likely be sooner rather than later."

Faunus opened his mouth to interrupt, but I held up a hand. "You wanted us to win over the Ikari, it is done," I growled. "The bond between them, my mate, and I is proof of that. The feathers that can never be seen unless gifted are also.

They will come when we call, and so will you if you wish to hang on to that seat you so foolishly think can't be taken away."

He sat down again and inclined his head, if not stiffly. "It will be as you say, King Ghost. Queen Silivia," he muttered.

Silivia smiled. "Great. We will be leaving first thing tomorrow. Ensure that our dragons are not shot at when they arrive."

Both elves' eyes flashed at the insult, but after having it done in Kra, I understood my mate's parting remark. When we'd finally made it back to our rooms, our gazes all met for a second before we broke down with laughter.

"Gods, did you see their faces?" Reece chortled, hands on his knees.

"Priceless!" Farek snorted.

Even Lorik wore an amused smirk.

"Have to admit, didn't expect you to have such a good sense of humor, Ghost," Obsidian snickered.

I rolled my eyes but glared at the females when they broke into laughter again.

"Oh, trust me, it comes out when you least expect it," Tess giggled.

"Yeah, and then you have to decide whether to laugh or run," Silivia added with a grin.

"Hey, dark humor has its place too," I growled.

Tess nodded in agreement. "It does, it does. But you have to admit, even it has been few and far between from you, Ghost."

I grumbled unintelligibly under my breath.

"And look how well you and Reece are getting along! You're basically best friends!"

The prince and I glanced at each other and then spun to Silivia.

"Absolutely not!" we roared in unison.

A new round of laughter broke out, and despite my annoyance, I had to admit it was a nice change.

I stared down at the world at my feet. My darkness, unleashed at last, weaved between those on their knees to gleefully devour those who refused to kneel. The crown upon my head was heavy, but I was finally free to be exactly what they expected...what they called me. The King of Shadows.

"This is how it should be. Listen to their screams."

I turned my head slightly to take in the shadowed figure at my ear. I could not make out any other features but his cruel smile and yellow eyes...eyes only a few shades lighter than my own.

I frowned. Something wasn't right. I was dreaming, right? So, why did it feel like this scene wasn't mine? The male grinned wider.

"Ahh, your mind is strong. Your power...the strongest I've seen in centuries. Even now, you fight me. Fight the vision of what your future could be. But it would be a crime to keep such power leashed. It was meant to be free. To devour. To rule."

He eyed me knowingly, the cries of the kneeled and fallen a soundtrack reverberating through my mind. "You like the feeling, don't you? The idea that you can finally bring those who hurt you to their knees. Who murdered your dear sister and mother. Join me, Ghost, King of the Shadows. Stand at my side and we will rule this world...together."

But my frown deepened at a snow-kissed tug on my core, making me turn so that I looked behind me to where the darkness didn't touch. A figure of snow and blue flames waited for me, and even though I could not see her face, I knew who she was.

"She can come to," the dark male told me.

The shadows around his face thickened even as he turned to follow my gaze. Who was he? Why did the bond in my core beg me to ignore him?

"Your queen, yes?"

I nodded, still confused, still being tugged towards the darkness behind me and the snowy light in front of me.

"Bring her. And if she fails to walk at your side, then she will kneel in the darkness at your feet like everyone else."

I recoiled at his poisonous tone, his hatred evident even as he stared leeringly at my mate. He would have her join us...or die? No.

"No," I said finally, shaking my head. "No," I repeated, gripping my head when his smile fell and the darkness began to roar and devour everyone in sight. I couldn't see my mate anymore. I couldn't find the light.

"You will join me, Ghost. It's up to you whether it's willingly, or on your knees." He smiled again, the darkness thickening around him. "And she will too."

"NO!"

I jerked awake, my heart beating out of my chest as I fought to catch my breath. I couldn't focus beyond the panic, the knowledge that a dark part of me had wanted to say yes. To give in.

"What's wrong?"

I couldn't answer her. Couldn't face her, not when I was contemplating her destruction.

"Ghost?"

The panic in her voice made me freeze. The darkness and shadows I now realized had been roaring around the room, slowed to a stop. Cool hands pressed against my flaming skin as she took my face and guided my gaze to hers.

"Ghost, my love. Breathe."

Who knew such a simple word could hold such power. How many times had I spoken the same to her?

"Breathe," she repeated, her lips pressing to mine as she delivered me a breath directly.

I sucked it in desperately. She gave me another and another until finally my heart rate and panic calmed enough for me to make out her concerned face. Her blue-grey eyes full of love...for me.

"Silivia," I whispered, my voice hoarse as if I'd been screaming. I wrapped both arms around her and pulled her closer to me. I squeezed my eyes shut and lay my head against her chest. "Silivia." I didn't know what I was asking. Couldn't get any other words out but her name, but she seemed to understand what I needed regardless.

"Shhh," she whispered, hugging my head to her. "I'm here. Whatever it is, I'm here."

I don't know who moved first, but then our lips were meeting. I kissed her with a desperation I couldn't voice. I moaned into her mouth, spinning us so that she was beneath me. I kissed along her jaw, down her neck, and her collarbone before kissing her deeply again.

"I need you," I implored her, the space between us barely present, but still too much.

Worry swam in her eyes, but her hands trailed down my bare chest. "Then take me," she breathed.

I groaned and crushed my lips to hers again. I ripped her nightgown from her body, too impatient to take it off properly. I kicked my own sleeping pants off as she opened her legs wide to welcome me. Our gaze remained on each other as I slowly, deliberately sank inch by inch into her until her eyes fluttered with pleasure, and we were as close as two people could be. I withdrew only to push back in with the same torturous slowness that had her digging her fingers into my waist to pull me in.

"Ghost," she breathed, arching as I watched her unravel below me.

"My love," I answered. I wanted to take it slow, to revel in the feel of our connection, but I could still feel the panic racing through my veins.

Silivia frowned, her hand coming up to cup my cheek. "Don't hide from me. Whatever it is, we'll face it together in the light."

I closed my eyes, pausing for a moment as I fought the choking fear, before opening them to meet her gaze again.

"I love you, Ghost."

Gods. And then I was losing control, desperate to keep the love in her eyes forever. I went from slow and agonizing to fast and rough, and she gripped me through it all. Moaning my name and her love for me with increasing volume until neither one of us could take it anymore, and I roared her name in return. I collapsed onto her, burying my head in her neck and simply breathing in her scent of home.

After what seemed like hours, I lifted my head again to meet her eyes.

"Do you want to talk about it?" she said softly.

I sighed, taking in the snow and mist dancing along with the shadows and darkness around us. Even knowing what I was capable of, she looked at me as if I was the moon and stars. Her power caressed mine as if it welcoming the warmth of the darkness. But I knew she was a goddess, for who else could tame the abyss?

"There may come a time when I succumb to the call of the night. When that day comes, I need you to end me before I end the world."

A sharp intake of air shattered the space. I knew it was an unfair request, but I couldn't take the risk that I would finally destroy that which I loved...*who* I loved. I met her shocked eyes.

"You may be the only one who can get close enough to me to do so. I wouldn't be able to live with myself if I hurt those I've vowed to protect. I need you to promise me, Silivia."

She blinked and shook her head adamantly. "If you lose your way, I will guide you back. Your darkness would never hurt me. *You* would never hurt me. And I will never give up on you. I will rappel into the abyss itself and fish you out before I let you lose yourself."

"Silivia..." I needed to convince her, even if her declaration healed a part of my heart I didn't know was broken.

"No, Ghost," she interjected. "Don't you remember? It's you and me against the world. Together. Always and forever."

I smiled at her, resting my forehead against hers with a sigh. How could I convince her when her love for me was the reason I wanted her to promise in the first place?

"I won't convince you then?"

"I promise to never give up on you. To always be the light to lead you back from the darkness. I promise to remind you who you *really* are when you forget. To love everything that you are with everything that I am."

My heart clenched at the reference to her wedding vows, and before I knew what was happening, I was taking her again. When we cried out our release together, I separated only long enough to turn on my side and pull her against my chest, face to face.

"I don't deserve you," I whispered, my darkness finally settled within me again.

She only smiled and kissed me deeply. "That's just it. We deserve each other."

We fell asleep wrapped up in each other, and anytime I felt that darkness knocking on my mind, I pulled her closer and washed it away with snow and icy flames.

Chapter 39

There are secrets I bear
Locked within my mind.
But when the chains fell away
I wondered if they should have stayed that way.

Dalacia

Sleep had been fitful the night before. I'd tossed and turned, memories flashing through my mind any time I drifted off. Time from the last year played over and over. Pieces from my torture. My training. The havoc I'd caused.

And this figure.

He was shrouded in shadows, but I could occasionally make out his yellow eyes. They were sharp like an eagle's and cruel. So very cruel. He reveled in my screams. He would whisper things in my ear, plant seeds of thought I never would have considered, water those I had. He starred in every memory. In every dark corner.

"You will bring them to me," he'd whispered from the shadows. *"Because I will give you no choice. Hurt her. Break her. Destroy her kingdom. But bring her and the King of Shadows to me."*

"Why?" I'd asked from my fetal position on the cot.

He'd only smiled, and I'd almost puke from the fear it inflicted. *"Because I am the Bringer of Blood and Tears, and I will bathe in the suffering of the world. And you, your sister, and her mate will help me do it."*

I hadn't remembered this before, but now, as we traveled, I gripped my horse's reins tightly. My head pounded unbearably as if something was taking a hammer and trying to break its way out. The torment grew and grew until I could barely breathe around it. I couldn't even see. I sat almost bent over my mare's neck with my eyes squeezed shut. I hadn't even realized I'd moaned aloud or that Barak was at my side until I heard his alarmed voice.

"Dalacia! What's wrong?"

I couldn't tell him. How could I explain that it felt like the fissures around my mind were cracking like ice on a frozen lake? I moaned again, and unable to hold on to my horse any longer, I started falling over the side, only to be caught in strong, muscular arms. Electricity skittered along my skin, but even if it hadn't, by scent alone I would know it was Barak who caught me.

"What's happening? What's wrong with her?" Raiden was there beside him.

Gut-wrenching pain sliced through my brain, and I cried out. "Barak," I gasped through the agony. "Please." I didn't know what I was begging for. For him to take away the pain? For him to tell me what was wrong? To end it all?

"Hang on, Wildfire. I've got you."

I clenched his shirt in my fists and then screamed. The world went black.

Slowly, I came around. I became aware that I was cradled in Barak's arms at the same time that he realized I was awake.

"She's back," someone exclaimed, but I focused on the hand brushing hair off my sweaty face.

"Hey, easy. You fainted for a few minutes there, but you're okay," he assured me.

And funny enough, he was right. The pain was gone, and it felt like a wall had disappeared from my mind. With it, though, came knowledge I didn't know I had. I remembered why I started to hate my sister. Why I'd been so determined to destroy her and take a throne I didn't even want. I realized why I'd no longer cared about others' welfare. Why my power had taken a dark turn...or rather, *for whom*.

I sat up suddenly, still gripping Barak's tunic as he stared back at me in surprise. He cradled me on the ground.

"Easy. You just fainted on me, remember."

"I know who he is," I exclaimed, my eyes wide as I realized with horror just who we were all going to war with. My heart rate went into overdrive as I fought the panic. I had to get to my sister and warn her. She was walking into a battle she could never win.

He frowned, and I saw the others exchange surprised glances around us. "Who?"

"He's the leader of the Blood Clan, and Barak, he's *ancient*. He's been planning this for so long. My sister and her mate don't stand a chance. None of us do." It was getting harder to breathe.

"Planning what exactly?"

I took a shaky breath, but I had to warn him. "Everything. What happened to Ghost. What happened to my family. What happened last year. He planned it all. And he's not done, Barak. He's coming for Ghost and my sister. He's coming for Fenriel."

"Breath, Wildfire. Breathe." He gripped me by the nape of my neck, sending a shock through my system that instantly calmed me. "Who is this he, Princess?"

I met his eyes, hoping he could see just how screwed we all were in them.

"Eztil Karlus, the King of Farla. The King of Blood."

Chapter 40

What if your power, pain, and regret
were all orchestrated by another?

Barak

"Eztil Karlus, the King of Farla. The King of Blood."

I blinked and stared at her in shock. Surely, she wasn't saying what I thought she was. Everyone shared confused glances and words.

"Are you crazy? Eztil? You really expect us to believe that?"

Dalacia scowled at the warriors and changeling guards.

"How else would I know his name? He told me his plans and then put a freaking wall around my mind to prevent me from remembering it. Why would I make this up now?"

One of her royal guards shrugged, his dark grey wings flaring as he crossed his arms. "You could be telling us this to convince us to trust you. After all, it probably doesn't feel good to wear iron for so long."

Dalacia scoffed. "I wish my imagination was the problem here, but unfortunately, I'm telling the truth." She glanced at me, her blue eyes pleading. "You believe me, don't you, Barak?"

I swallowed uneasily and gave her an uncertain look. "I want to, but what you don't seem to understand is that everyone believes Eztil is dead."

Her brows knitted in confusion. "That can't be right. Why?"

"Because he was exiled from Farla almost one thousand years ago. He was killed not long after by assassins when the new monarch worried that the late king would retaliate," Raiden explained.

She raised a brow. "You sure he was killed, or are people just assuming that's what happened? Fae are immortal, are they not?"

I nodded. "They are, but not invincible. And he disappeared, Dalacia. There's been no other mention of him in history since."

She jumped to her feet, fists clenched, even as her body wobbled slightly. She quickly regained her balance. "I know who I saw, and if you won't take me seriously, we're all going to die." She paced away and climbed back onto her mare. Without waiting for everyone else to join her, she galloped down the trail.

The others hurried after her, but I put a hand on Raiden's arm. "Wait," I told him quietly, and he nodded.

We mounted our horses and waited until everyone was out of earshot before we followed at a walk.

"What is it?" he asked, glancing at me.

"You realize who we're up against, don't you?" I said, gripping my reins tightly.

Raiden hesitated. "No, but I also didn't spend as much time reading history books as you. What am I missing?"

"The princess likely *did* meet him, Raid. Eztil had a special power; he could manipulate the blood in your body as well as the darkness. He used it to torture those who would not bow to his rule."

Raiden nodded. "Oh yeah, I remember. It was why he was exiled in the first place. He went crazy and almost murdered his entire family."

"Yeah, everyone but his youngest granddaughter and her parents. But Eztil could also see flashes of the future."

Raiden's brows shot up. "What? You think he spared them on purpose? That the assassins failed and he has been hiding all this time because of something he'd seen?"

"Remember how we learned that the Blood King had manipulated Ghost's and Silivia's lives? It makes sense that Eztil was in hiding, using his visions to do so while he built an army."

"Okay, but why the secrecy? So what Eztil is potentially the legendary Blood King? That makes him a formidable opponent, but doesn't provide a reasonable explanation for him hiding this long."

I gave my brother a tight grimace. "Because Eztil was the grandfather to Ceclia, who later became Ceclia Lokswood when she married Gonthar Lokswood."

Raiden jerked his horse to a halt, his mouth opened in horror. "But that's..."

I nodded sullenly. "The Blood King is Ghost's great grandfather. And if we don't want our king to destroy the world in his anger and grief because of it, we can never tell him."

Chapter 41

I wish I could undo the damage I caused
but all I can do
is let the memories tear me in two
so that my heart bleeds for you.

Dalacia

The Resisti and changeling guards were watching me closely as if afraid I'd ride off to rejoin the clan. I wouldn't. Especially now that I knew the reason for my behavior over the last year. Somehow, it didn't make me feel any less guilty about the damage I'd inflicted. I'd earned their looks of distrust. Hell, if I were them, I wouldn't have let me out of Aurevel's dungeon.

Instead, we were only a couple of days from Siron...and the rest of my sister's inner court. The thought was terror-inflicting. I couldn't understand how Silivia had forgiven me so easily. Was it a big sister thing? Or was her trust as tentative as those who tensed when I was near her? I wanted to fall to my knees and spew my apologies at her feet. She was the only family I had left, and I'd tried to *kill her*. I'd almost lost what little I had over amplified jealousy and mind control.

I discreetly wiped at the tears that kept escaping my eyes as I huddled at the edge of the campfire. Gods, I couldn't believe I'd been such a monster towards her. And...I had a brother. A sibling I never asked for but had nonetheless, and his first impression was of me attempting to kill the heir to our father's kingdom. Would that forever be my legacy? Rifka's crazy fire princess who betrayed everything and everyone to the clan?

The tears fell faster now, and I sniffled hard into my arm, trying to fight them. It didn't help that I knew there was no way to conceal my anguish from the sharp

Fae ears all around me. The fact that they pretended not to hear my pain made it hurt worse.

"You know, I was once a prisoner of the Blood Clan."

I froze. Then lifted my head to stare at Barak. His gaze was fixed on the flames. The rest of the camp went silent as focus shifted to him.

"You're probably familiar with their motto, 'Yield, or die.'"

I nodded sullenly. Anyone who'd had their lives ripped apart by the clan knew those words.

"They'd caught me unawares. I was still a young member of the Resisti, and I'd had something to prove. I was still carrying that burden of being from the poorer parts of Rifka on my shoulders. Not to mention, I was already fast friends with Reece since we'd been recruited at the same time. We'd bonded over his desire to prove his worth under the crushing power of his mother. Two males from the slums and a male from the palace. Who would have thought we'd be friends, but being royal doesn't protect you from the darkness of the world."

No, it didn't. In fact, it seemed to only open you up to more. Forget the expectations that came with the title. It was what made my shame doubly heavy. I'd failed as a sister, a daughter, and an heir. The trifecta. Guess I was an overachiever. I grimaced.

"How did they catch you?" One of the changeling guards asked.

Barak's expression darkened as he glared at the flames. "They didn't. I walked right in." My eyes widened in shock, and he threw me a sad smile. "Yeah, I know. Stupid right? But like I said, I had something to prove. Except there were more clan soldiers than I'd anticipated, and instead of taking out the threat, I was caught and tied with iron chains. Days went by with them trying to weasel their way into my mind and force me to kneel. They weren't able to get the information they desired from me, but in my pride, I was brought to my knees and almost lost everything."

I lowered my gaze to the dirt. Pride before the fall. Or in my case, jealousy. Neither was any less destructive when allowed to get out of hand.

"I say that to say that I understand better than most how you feel. To feel like your life was out of your control, and that you are still left to pick up the pieces. But you're not your mistakes. And sure as hell not the clan's actions. And even though these knuckleheads will never say it, the only person you have to prove anything to, is yourself."

He rose then, and I lifted my gaze to his as he strolled over to me and squatted down so that we were eye to eye. There was understanding and acceptance in his gaze that I'd never expected to see. An electric hum reverberated through my core in answer.

"You may have a long road before this is all behind you, but for what it's worth, you earned my trust when you used your fire to protect Aurevel and put the bracelets back on."

I blinked at him in surprise and then gasped when he took each of my hands and removed the iron from my wrists.

"Barak! What are you doing?!" One of the guards snapped. "She's a prisoner of the crown."

"Wrong. She is a member of the crown, and this is not how we treat our royal family, especially when she put herself at risk to protect us," he corrected.

"But the king and queen..."

"Can take it up with me when we get to Siron," he interjected. He stood and faced them, electricity shooting across his skin occasionally as he stared them down. "The queen put me in charge of her sister, and if I say the bracelets come off, then they come off until says otherwise. Any other objections?"

The males glanced at each other, and a couple seemed put out and even furious, but in the end, not one of the five sent to guard me said a word. Raiden only eyed his little brother and then me with a questioning look in his gaze.

Your guess is as good as mine, I thought when he lifted a brow towards me.

The big male only shrugged and went back to munching on the nuts they'd found. "Fine, by me," he replied.

Barak immediately relaxed as if in relief. If his brother backed him, the changelings and Resisti were even less likely to stand against him. As I thought, they grunted or mumbled to themselves one by one, but settled down again.

"Use it wisely," Barak whispered to me as he walked away.

I stared after him and then down at my hands, where flames jumped and danced in joy, but it was the warmth in my core that truly dimmed the chill of my too-long night. That made me feel seen.

Chapter 42

Leave me.

Hurt me.

Betray me.

But no amount of pain will change the truth.

Will dim my love.

So is the burden of the oldest.

Silivia

Siron. I never liked this city, with its corrupt high Fae and clan supporters. It was a cesspool of greed and crime, and with its proximity to the Shielded Forest, it allowed those two things to thrive.

Or at least it used to. Now, it had a different feel to it as I walked the streets. Last time, I was here in secret, planning a sneak attack on Queen Isrella to take back Aurevel. It was here that we'd met in a long-forgotten room with those who became the Resisti Seven. Now we met out in the open in the lord and lady's castle in their council room. Maybe it was because I was no longer just the heir apparent, but the queen. Maybe it was because I'd finally begun walking in my power, my title, and my spiritbond. Or maybe because I'd gone to battle and won.

Regardless, I walked down the cobbled streets like I owned them. Because I did. I greeted those who'd been oppressed by Lord Dolis and Lady Aris and scowled at those who'd supported them. Because why shouldn't I? I did so with the knowledge that this status was hard won and would require a heavy hand to remain mine. Unlike eighteen-year-old human Silivia, I had no qualm with that.

Even though the decision-making didn't get any easier, and I would never get used to ordering executions.

I swallowed my unease as I stood before the people of Siron. A mixture of disdain, gratitude, and begrudged respect stared back at Ghost and I. The lord and lady glared at me from their front row seat of iron chains. Ignoring them, I addressed the crowd.

"People of Siron. Because of the clan and its supporters' actions within and outside this city, and their blatant refusal to repent, I sentence them to death. Know that any who seeks to imprison and harm the innocent within Rifka will be met with the same fate."

"You can't do this!" Lord Doris spat, yanking on his chains even as the changeling guards aimed their blades and arrows at him. "These people resided here longer than you have been born. You have no power here!"

Ghost lifted a brow as he eyed the fuming male coldly. "You sure about that?" Shadows pooled around his feet as he loosened the leash on his darkness. "You think because you've gotten away with your wickedness for so long that you are entitled to it, and maybe under Isrella, that was true. But we are not her and will not allow such practice in our kingdom."

"So says the King of Shadows himself!" Lady Aris accused. "Who are you to judge us? You who could easily wipe this entire kingdom off the map."

I rolled my eyes in annoyance. This argument was getting old. My mate simply cocked his head.

"And yet I stand up here, and you sit there in chains. Tell me, which of us has actually harmed this kingdom? And which has the power to do so and hasn't?"

The people mumbled to each other, but none could refute him. I bit back a smirk and glanced over to see Teslia and Tyrian doing the same. Reece didn't bother to hide his glee at the lord and lady's discomfort.

"Great, now that that's settled." Ghost turned towards the clan soldiers and supporters kneeling on the platforms, fear finally overshadowing their confidence as his darkness slunk towards them. "As said before, for your crimes, the punishment is death."

And the platform was shrouded in darkness.

"Your sister is here."

I shot up from the couch in an instant, all discomfort from the earlier executions dispelling in a heartbeat.

"Really?" I asked excitedly.

Ghost rolled his eyes but nodded. "She's on her way with Raiden and Barak to the castle as we speak. One of the royal guards flew ahead to alert us."

I paused, suddenly nervous to see her. It had been a few weeks since last we spoke, and she had still been against being sisters again. What if nothing had changed?

"Barak and Raiden wouldn't have allowed her to travel to Siron with them if that was so," Ghost reminded me. He wrapped his arms around me.

I hugged him back in return. "What if things between us never go back to the way they were?" I whispered, voicing the fear that had haunted me since that day in Nyri where sister turned against sister.

"They won't," he said blatantly, and I pulled away to glare at him. But his golden eyes were serious as he prevented me from escaping his arms. "My love, you aren't the same person you were back then, and neither is your sister. To expect things to go back is to discredit everything you've been through to become the capable, awe-inspiring female you are."

I blinked at him and cuddled close again. "Nice save," I mumbled against his chest.

He chuckled. "Thanks. I thought so too."

"Silivia! Your sister is here!" Teslia yelled through the door, and I took a fortifying breath.

"Ready?"

Ready to face who my sister and I had become. Ready to learn how we would fit into each other's lives again. Ready to stand side by side, beaten, scarred, and transformed.

"No, but I have a feeling you'll drag me out there anyway," I said, pulling away again.

Ghost looked aghast. "Who me? Why would you assume such a thing?"

I gave him a scathing look. "Says the person who dragged me to the Selondian Forest to force me to face my power and then to Rifka to face my birthright."

The dark male raised a brow. "But wasn't it worth it, though?" Not bothering to give him the satisfaction of an answer, I stalked out the door. "Yes. The answer was yes, Ghost, and I couldn't have done any of it without you."

"If that helps you sleep at night," I singsonged over my shoulder and giggled when I heard him swear under his breath.

I sobered when I entered the council room and met peacock blue eyes, this time void of malice. And wrists void of iron bracelets.

"Clear the room."

Barak glanced at my sister and back at me, an apologetic look on his face. "Silivia, I can explain."

"We tried to stop him, Your Majesty."

I held up a hand to stop the guards and Barak from speaking...and coming to blows.

"It's fine, but I would like to speak to my sister alone." Dalacia actually looked nervous at the prospect and glanced at Barak as if for reassurance. He nodded to her, and she nodded back.

"You sure?" Ghost asked.

I glanced up at him and smiled. *"I'll call you if I need you."*

He eyed my sister warily, but his animosity seemed to be diminished. Was it due to the meaning behind the look between our friend and my baby sister? A knowing smile lifted his lips.

"I'll tell you about it later."

"I'll hold you to that."

He winked but gestured for everyone to leave the room. Farek and Lorik hesitated, but at my determined gaze, they bowed and left us alone. When the door had clicked closed, I turned back to my sister.

"Look, before you say anything, I know I owe you the biggest apology known to man, and nothing I can say will ever come close to expressing my shame over what I've done. You are my big sister, and I tried to kill you. It's the ultimate breakage of the sibling code, and I will spend however long it takes to convince you to forgive me. And don't worry, I've only used my fire to defend the people of Aurevel since Barak took off the bracelets. Please don't be mad at him. I think he was only trying to build camaraderie with me to help me get over my guilt, and well, yeah."

I blinked and stared as she gulped in a much-needed breath. Emotions warred within me. Distrust and Hope. But seeing her almost reduced to tears, she appeared, for the first time in a long time, like the sister I used to know. I didn't have the words to express the pang shooting through my chest, so I simply moved to her and enveloped her in a tight hug. She froze for a second, caught unawares, but then she was burying her face in my neck and hugging me just as tightly.

"I've missed you," I whispered, not bothering to hold back the tears raining down my face.

Dalacia laughed sobbed as she gripped me tighter. "I've missed you too. So freaking much."

And then we were sobbing and hugging. If the council could see me now. My face puffy, eyes glazed with tears, and a blubbering mess, but I didn't care. Not if it meant getting a piece of my family back.

Long minutes later found us catching up on the meeting floor as Dalacia told me about what went on in Aurevel after I left. She told me about the storytelling elder and the way Barak had led the reconstruction across Aurevel. She explained the training sessions they'd had and how he'd released her bracelets when they'd been attacked by clan soldiers. The fondness she spoke about the male had me curious about what else they'd been up to, but I decided to wait to ask until after

I'd spoken to Ghost. In return, I updated her on what happened in Belus and Vedia.

"Wow! So, you really are the Queen of the Winged," she remarked with awe. There wasn't a hint of contempt in her voice.

I laughed. "Yeah, it looks like I am."

It was like old times, when we'd used to talk for hours into the night, and it made me hopeful for the future. Ghost checked in a couple of times when my emotions became elevated as we spoke about some of what happened after our parents died, but mostly he left us to our reunion.

"I really am sorry, Silvee," Dalacia whispered after we'd been quiet for several moments.

"You were under the Blood King's influence. There's nothing to apologize for," I assured her.

"Still, I want to," she insisted. "And I want you to know that I'm wholeheartedly on your side in the journey ahead."

I smiled at her, my eyes watering again. "I'm so glad to hear that, and of course, I forgive you, Daccy. It'll take time for our relationship to heal, but I've always been willing to try."

She nodded, tears pooling in her eyes again. "I..." She swallowed as she wrung her hands. "Thank you for not giving up on me."

Crap. And now I was about to cry again. "Of course. What are big sisters for?" She chuckled at that, and I grinned. Wiping my eyes and jumping to my feet, I held a hand out to her. "Come on. My mate is getting restless, and we have a world to save."

Daccy laughed as she took my hand, and I pulled her to her feet. "You really think the world's ready for two of Dad's heirs?"

I shook my head. "They had two of his heirs, and they weren't ready. Let's see how many waves three of them can cause."

Her answering smile was mischievous and bright.

Part II:

To Bind a World

Chapter 43

Ghost

I could feel it again. That darkness that wasn't my own. It went beyond the shadows of the trees interspersed in the mountain pass of Hyra. It went beyond the blackness of night. No, this felt like swimming through ink as dense as molasses. It felt like a blanket over my mind, my power. My own darkness wanted nothing to do with it, and yet it felt like it was being reeled in like a fish on a hook. It was driving me mad.

It was bad enough that I couldn't shake the rage over being manipulated my entire life. Everyone knew trauma built endurance and character, but if you'd told me that becoming a powerful master of the shadows was dependent on watching my mother and sister suffer, I would have chosen to be powerless. Especially now, when it felt like something was trying to take control of said power.

And what could I say? Who could I tell? Most already feared me and what I *could* do if I were ever inclined. How did I explain that I didn't want to, but that there was this voice in my head that kept whispering that it would be better if I did? How did I explain that it was no longer whispering, but speaking to me as clearly as my mate or Arctic down our bond? Silivia had enough on her plate. She didn't need what was on mine.

"But is that not the point of a spiritbond? A mate?"

I stiffened and tossed a glare up at Arctic, who flew above us along with the other dragons. They would fly us the rest of the way to Hyra, but it was considered less of a threat if you walked through the Fae kingdoms' borders first, so they were alerted of your presence. Less risk of it being construed as an act of war that way. Not that it took much for the royals of Hyra and Farla to construe some insult or another. Farla still held a grudge so unrelenting that convincing them to join our side would only occur if we already had might behind us. Hence, the out-of-the-way trip to Hyra first.

"Ghost?"

I started. Gods, I was out of it.

"I'm fine, Arctic," I told him firmly. *"It's nothing she can help me with. I'm sure I'm just having some kind of power surge or strain from exhaustion. I haven't been getting much sleep."*

I could feel his deep displeasure down the bond. If he were in front of me, he would have surely pinned me with the disapproving gaze of one of his red eyes...and the tip of a sharp talon.

"And why aren't you sleeping?"

Good question. And one I hadn't even answered when Silivia asked. She knew I was having nightmares again, but I'd hidden their nature and frequency from her. How would she react if I told her I dreamed of bending her to my will and killing her? My darkness and I recoiled at the thought.

"She already knows something is wrong. If you don't tell her what, how can she help you deal with it?"

He was right, of course, but what could my mate do? I didn't even know how to reconcile with the reason for my power's existence. Forget my desire to destroy. I didn't know if it was ingrained in me or had always been a part of my psyche, and I never would. All I could do was try to keep this ever increasingly bad mood I was in from infecting anyone else. Already, Obsidian and Tyrian were giving me wary looks. Gods forbid everyone else caught on.

"Ghost."

"For fucks sake. Let it go, Arctic!" I shouted. *"I don't need you or anyone else's help. I have it under control."*

He was quiet for a long moment, and then. *"For now, but what happens when you don't?"*

With that thought, he redrew from my mind and flew up and away from our group. I couldn't fault him for being angry. I was lashing out when I should be asking for help. But this was my problem to handle. I wasn't going to allow anyone else to go up in flames to feed the darkness, even if it meant it consumed me in the end.

Chapter 44

The path to redemption
is long and difficult.

Dalacia

I should be past this. Silivia and I had bonded. She'd forgiven me. My guards had stopped constantly looking at me like I was seconds away from betraying them all. So why did I feel like I was waiting for the other shoe to drop? Why couldn't I stop getting into fights with the others in the group whenever I offered any knowledge I had about the clan? Why did I feel like that at any moment, I could revert to that girl from a few months ago?

"There was a time when I feared my brother would never trust me again. Hell, that I would never even see him again."

Surprised, I glanced up to see Barak watching me from the trees. I'd been sitting here, with my knees pulled under my chin, staring into this tiny pond for I didn't know how long. But surely, I didn't just hear what I thought I did.

"What?"

Barak stalked to my side and took a seat beside me. He sighed heavily, pulling his knees up and hanging his arms off them. "Back when I was a captive of the clan."

I swallowed uncomfortably, remembering his confession from not too long ago.

He gave me a humorless chuckle. "It's why I can understand some of your mannerisms to an extent."

"What mannerisms?" I asked, narrowing my eyes.

"The ones that require you to snap at everyone, even as you try to determine if your reaction is because the clan made you do it, or if it's who you are. The ones that say you feel guilty but don't know how to vocalize it. The ones that say you feared for your family as desperately as you feared for yourself."

I snorted. "You're wrong. I never feared for my sister. I was too angry that no one had tried to save me. That I'd been grabbed because of who my sister was." Barak studied me but didn't interrupt, so I continued. "It should have been her. I thought about it every night. How kidnapping me was only a mistake. *I* was a mistake." Tears stung my eyes, and I fought to hold them back.

"They tortured me so often, I stopped being able to tell night from day," he said quietly. "Every few hours, they would remind me that the pain would stop if I gave up my family and friends. Told them where to find the Resisti. Joined their ranks." He clenched his fists, glaring at the water.

"I had a moment, just one, but a moment nonetheless, where I considered giving in. Where I thought, surely Raiden could handle this better than I. How could he hold it against me for wanting this torment to end? For not being willing to risk my life to protect his? I'd already lost everything and everyone else. Why should I lose my life too?"

Barak grimaced, shame tinging his eyes. He swallowed. "I think that's why I was relieved but regretful that Raiden and Reece came to rescue me soon after. How could I look them in the eyes when I'd considered selling them out?"

"You were in pain," I insisted. "They tortured you!"

"And they were and are my brothers. It shouldn't have ever crossed my mind."

"But it did," I whispered.

He nodded sullenly. "I couldn't forgive myself for decades after. I became reckless, jumping into situations without any regard for my life. It became so bad that Reece, Raiden, and I got into a fight after I'd gotten stupidly drunk and challenged a group of hogars. They'd beaten me until I could finally hear my brother yell that he wasn't going to sit by and let me kill myself because of some misguided guilt."

I blinked in surprise, and he smiled sadly. "Apparently, when I get too drunk, I talk in my sleep. He'd heard me confess what I'd considered doing. Heard me beg him for forgiveness."

'You don't need to ask for my forgiveness, Barak,' he'd growled. *'You were being tortured. I don't fault you for thinking it. You never followed through with it, and that's what matters.'*

'I could have,' I'd told him. *'If you and Reece had been any later, I would have.'* He'd only shaken his head adamantly with tears in his eyes. He'd pulled me from the ground into a bear hug.

'No, brother. You wouldn't have,' he'd told me so confidently, so defiantly, that I'd finally believed it."

Barak turned to gaze at me again. "You are not a mistake, Dalacia. The clan snatching you instead of your sister might have been an accident, but you yourself are not. Your power, your title, is not. You were Dalacia the Fire Princess then, and you are Dalacia the Fire Princess now. Also, how do you know that no one tried to rescue you or noticed you were gone?"

I frowned. "I saw no one. Dad was too busy watching Mom, and Silivia was missing."

But then...that wasn't quite true. A memory surfaced, one I'd somehow buried, and I gasped. I spun to face Barak, my eyes wide.

"There was a moment...when the clan was dragging me away. There was a moment when my dad looked at me, even with all the chaos and Mom's death. It was like time slowed. He smiled and said... *I'm sorry, my little flame. I love you. Be strong.'"*

"And then I was dragged from the house, kicking and screaming, but right before I was knocked out, I heard her. I heard Silivia calling my name. She'd gone looking for me. That's why she wasn't on time to save our parents." Tears slipped from my eyes, and I bit back a sob. "She was making sure to save me." Sobs rocked my body then, and Barak pulled me into his arms.

I let him hold me as I finally grieved the night I lost everything. I'd spent so much time worrying that I was secondary. That I was not seen, but in those dark moments, both members of my family had been focused on me. And I'd repaid them with jealousy and disdain. What an awful daughter and sister I'd been. So, I cried for the lies I'd believed. For the family I'd lost. I cried for little Daccy, who never knew that all along she was every inch the princess she wanted to be. And I cried for what I'd done.

And then I did what Barak's brother had told him to do. I let it go. Slowly, the tears finally came to an end, and I just laid there for a second, reveling in the steadiness of the male against me. I was grateful for his strength. It may take a while before I was fully healed, but I was finally on the way to doing so. And it was thanks to this male who'd understood my pain enough to fight for me even when he still didn't trust me.

I lifted my head to meet his gaze. It was filled with something that almost looked like affection. The electric hum in my core grew warmer, and before I could think better of it, I pressed my lips to his. Barak froze in surprise, but it wasn't long before his hand went into my hair, and he opened his mouth to seek access to mine. This kiss was different from what I would expect my first real kiss to be. It was rough with grief, sharp with passion, and warm like the feelings building between us. I wasn't ready to acknowledge it fully, but maybe someday.

When we finally pulled away, Barak laid his forehead against mine and sighed. He lifted my hand to his lips and kissed my inner wrist. I frowned at him questioningly. He smiled. "For the scars that bind us," he said simply and pressed another kiss to my lips.

My heart warmed at his words, new tears prickling my eyes. "May we heal but never forget," I whispered back.

Chapter 45

I could feel it.

Something bearing down on us.

War was coming.

And it was determined to steal all I had.

Silivia

Ghost was hiding something from me. He thought I didn't notice that most nights he did not sleep. And when he did, he awoke violently partway through from nightmares that stole his peace and strength. Because he *was* tired. And increasingly agitated. But instead of talking it out with me, he insisted nothing was wrong. That I should just focus on getting our allies for this war, but how could I focus on a war I didn't want to fight when one of my biggest reasons for fighting it had blocked me out again?

Of course, he couldn't block me fully down the bond anymore. If he had, I would never have been able to sense the level of unease and restlessness that caused his darkness to writhe around his feet when he wasn't actively reining them back in. I couldn't even send the full extent of my ice and snow to soothe him because he wouldn't let them pass the wall on his side of the bond.

And maybe I would have let it slide as prewar jitters if it wasn't for the fear I could feel leaking out from his mind. He was terrified of something. Something likely to do with the oily consistency I'd been feeling around his power. Something I would love to tell him about if he didn't dismiss me every time I tried to bring it up. Why was it that with everything but this, we could discuss it and get on the same page?

It took over two weeks to travel from Rifka to the border of Hyra, where we'd had to hike on foot through the border mountains before we could continue the journey by dragon. Now we were almost to the Hercule, the capital city of Hyra. We'd landed for a break, yet all I could focus on was the progressively tense male next to me. You know what. Forget this. We were going to talk whether he wanted to or not.

Signaling for the others to go on ahead of us, I stopped Ghost with a hand on his arm. It took him a moment to acknowledge me, a weird glaze over his eyes clearing as if he'd been battling something deep within his mind.

"Ghost, we need to talk."

He lifted a brow, annoyance rippling off him as he eyed the retreating group. "Now?"

"Yes, now," I snapped, but I stopped and took a deep breath. "There's something you're not telling me."

"I'm fine."

I gave him an incredulous look. "No one in history has ever been fine when they said that."

Ghost grimaced, not meeting my eyes. "Yeah, well. I am."

"Look at me." He didn't. "Ghost, my love, please look at me."

Slowly, hesitantly, he did. His eyes seemed off, but I couldn't put my finger on why. He was hanging on by a thread. That I could see plain as day. I needed him to talk to me. Then I needed to ensure he slept, even if that meant I stayed up all night soothing away the turmoil in his mind.

"You're not sleeping. You've blocked our bond. And you're lying to me. I thought we agreed to face things together."

"I have it under control," he mumbled, crossing his arms, but his darkness whipped aggressively around him.

I frowned. "Yeah, no. See, I know for a fact you don't. You're acting the same way you did back when you were fighting our spiritbond, but this time it's worse because your power seems out of control. Why is it when I have a challenge, you're willing to help me with mine, but you won't let me be there for you with yours?"

He stiffened further, his eyes growing cold. "What makes you think you can help me, uh? You, who not so long ago were just learning to accept and use your power. You, who insisted on how human you were, and ran away from your birthright. You, who have yet to come into your full power, if you ever will at all. How can you possibly help me with a power I've had for centuries longer than you've been an idea? Can you suddenly command the nightmares to stop? The darkness to yield?"

Hurt shot through my chest like an iron-tipped arrow. I bit my lip hard to keep from saying something I'd regret. Anger and grief warred within me, but I recognized his response for what it was. Ghost only became cruel like this when he chose to be alone with his pain and struggles, usually in an effort to protect those he cared about...or to protect himself. If he would just let me *in*, the stubborn male would remember he didn't have to battle alone anymore.

The air around us grew cold, and I fought the shiver down my spine. Apprehension warned me to pay attention, but I needed to get through to my mate before I could handle anything else.

"Maybe I could if you would let me," I told him finally, gritting my teeth. "If you would stop attacking me for loving you and let me carry some of your burdens. Why are you being so pigheaded about this? What can be so bad that you would try to hurt me like this?"

Ghost growled and turned away. "You wouldn't be hurt if you learned to stop poking where you're not wanted."

The air grew colder, but I couldn't focus on that when I was trying to keep my heart from shattering.

"Ghost!" But he was already storming away towards the forest edge. "Gods, that hard-headed, dark, stubborn bastard! Why does he do this? Why can't he..."

The air was getting colder still, and I finally noticed the wave of darkness rising from between the trees, blocking out the sun. The larynnx. *Oh no.*

"Ghost!"

He spun back to me at my shrill cry, and I saw the instant regret and horror flashed across his face. Then he was swallowed up by the darkness that enveloped the forest.

"Ghost!!" I screamed, but all I could hear was Ilara's cruel laughter echoing through the mist.

And then we were being ambushed from all sides, too quickly to fight back. Her laughter grew as I heard cries of agony as my friends were attacked.

"No! Daccy! Tyrian!"

No one answered, but moans of pain and clashing of metal echoed. I called for the changelings next, but although I could hear Farek and Lorik roaring my name, I could not reach them. The battle raged, clan soldiers appearing out of the mist to attack before retreating. Grigors appeared out of nowhere with barred teeth and bloody claws to devour. Giant ogres swung deadly axes and clubs that I barely dodged.

It felt like an eternity passed as we fought for our lives with no idea whether we were losing or winning. Or where the enemy had even come from. And then I was being cut down by shadow claws. Crying out, I fell to my knees, my blades outstretched to meet the next attack. An attack that never came. The mist finally receded. The clan and their creatures all gone, leaving their fallen comrades and our men painting the ground with blood.

I sucked in several shaky breaths, trying to figure out how this could have happened. The battle wasn't supposed to be fought yet, and we'd been vigilant. Hadn't we?

I could feel it. That undeniable feeling that something was wrong with my mate. I managed to get my feet under me and scanned the clearing.

"Ghost?" I called. All around me, my friends and warriors were dragging themselves to their feet, but not one was the male I sought. I winced as I took a stumbling step towards the last place I saw him. Nothing greeted me but trees. "Ghost?"

The panic was rising now. The bond sending shards of agony and terror through my core. *Find him!* It screamed. *He needs us!*

Where. Was. He?

"Ghost?!" I shouted, searching the trees desperately for my mate. I could see the truth written on the faces of my friends as they realized that I wasn't going to find him anywhere near us, no matter how much I wished to. Tyrian stepped to my side, his hands held up placatingly, but I shook my head at him, my eyes wide.

"Silivia," he said, his eyes full of grief.

"No," I whispered, barely able to get the words out. It wasn't possible. Yes, the fight was fast, but I'd only lost sight of him for a few minutes. Ghost couldn't be gone. He was too powerful for that. Except he wasn't at his best. And we'd fought, so he'd been distracted.

Tyrian moved closer until he was standing in front of me and gripped my shoulders to keep me from racing into the forest after my missing mate.

"It's her fault," I heard Obsidian growl. "She betrayed us!"

"No!" Dalacia shouted. "I would never do that! I wouldn't! Silivia, you have to believe me!"

But I couldn't focus on her or the now arguing males, not with Tyrian still gripping me like I may run at any moment.

"I'm so sorry," he said heavily, acknowledging that the concern in the clearing was valid.

"No..."

"Ghost...he...they took him, Silivia. He's gone."

"NOOOO!" Anguish I'd only felt once before, back in the Silent Hills, ripped through me. I'd experienced what it would feel like to break the spiritbond and now...now the pain reverberated through me so thoroughly that I slammed to my knees.

Tyrian reached for me. "I'm sorry," he said again.

But I was beyond caring. My icy power rose suddenly and viciously, craving its partner. Unable to stand the feel of my heart breaking, the bond between us utterly silent, I screamed and coated the entire clearing in flames and shards of ice.

Chapter 46

In the dawn of despair
a flicker of hope remains.

Dalacia

I couldn't stand the accusing gazes of our group. The changeling guards looked only seconds from torturing their king's location from me. Only the order from Tyrian and Barak to stand down kept them from flying me high with those dark wings and dropping me to my death. Dramatic? Maybe. But I knew that it was my own damn fault. I was the cause of their distrust. Or at least the me that used to be under the clan's control.

I shook my head to clear it as the memories tried to take over. That was a concern for another day. Right now, all that was important was getting my sister safely to Hyra. Maybe then, someone would be able to reach her in the cocoon of grief she'd shielded herself with.

We'd been lucky not to be seriously injured when she'd unleashed her power. Only throwing up a firewall of my own had kept the ice shards from cutting us to shreds. Afterwards, she'd collapsed into a ball of screaming agony, her blue flames wrapped as tightly around her as the arms clutching her middle. I'd never seen anything like it. She sounded like she was dying, and until she'd finally burned herself out, none of us had been able to remotely touch her to soothe her.

"It's the bond," Master Marcus had explained when we'd called over the mirrors. He'd glanced at Tyrian. "I've seen this occur when those who are spirit-bonded have the bond either ripped from them or their mate dies. Since we know the clan would not kill Ghost, they have likely blocked the bond, mimicking that same feeling." The master had nodded at Tyrian. "You may be the only one she lets touch her."

Tyrian's face had hardened, letting me know there was more going on here than I knew, but he'd indeed been the only one my sister had let pick her up. Wrapping her in a blanket when her body was reduced to shivering uncontrollably, despite her heavy fur coat, Tyrian had transferred her to his dragon. Lorik, Obsidian, and Farek flew close, seemingly afraid to take their eyes off their queen.

That had been days ago, and not once in that time had Silivia said a word. She didn't even seem to hear anyone when they spoke to her. She was a shell, a shivering, agonized shell grieving a mate that had become her world. Tyrian sighed heavily as he glanced over to her huddled form, her back to the fire we'd made just for her. She refused to stay near the group, so a separate fire had been built for her each night, her guards staying as close as she'd allow.

"We have to do something," Farek growled, stomping over to where the others sat. He threw a dirty glare my way as he filled a bowl with stew.

I tried to ignore him as I leaned against a tree apart from the group.

"She won't eat. She won't sleep. And her power isn't working properly."

"You heard Master Marcus," Barak said, gesturing at her prone body. "There's not much we can do except wait for her to come around. For the bond to recognize that Ghost isn't gone."

"We don't have that long," Obsidian growled. "We need to find Ghost now! We can't do that without his mate."

"What would you have us do?" Tyrian growled back. "Smack her around until she comes too? She's not asleep. She's not listless because she wants to be. She lost her mate!" Pain flashed across his lavender eyes, telling me Silivia wasn't the only one missing the King of Shadows.

"It's not her we need to be smacking around."

My eyes shot to eyes darker than night. Everyone turned to me, and I felt my blood boiling, my fire wanting to lash out at the perceived threat. At the accusation.

"I told you. I. Had. Nothing. To. Do. With. It," I snapped, jumping to my feet. "You think I don't wish I could remember more about where the clan held me so I could lead you there? You think I don't want to rescue my sister's mate? I do. *Gods,* I do. And I know I've done plenty to earn that distrust in your eyes. But I swear on my parents' death, I didn't do this." I choked on a sob, glancing at my sister as my vision blurred.

"I'm sorry," I whispered towards her. "I'm sorry that once again that you are left with the wrong daughter to help you." Then, I spun from their accusing gazes and fled into the woods.

I don't know how far I'd gone or how long I'd been at this trickling creek before I felt the charge in the air. I sniffled, trying to see past the tears in my eyes.

"I thought we talked about you being the "wrong sister"," he said in greeting as he sat at my side.

I glanced at his profile, but he stared into the trees. I sniffled again. "Yeah, well, tell that to the males back there who want my head," I mumbled, wiping my face. Ugh, I probably looked like such a mess. A handkerchief appeared below my nose, and I glanced over to the warrior at my side, who still hadn't met my gaze. Grabbing it, I wiped at my face until I felt halfway decent.

"Better?"

I sniffed but nodded. "Yeah. Thank you," I said softly.

"Good, now let's talk. Did you help the clan take Ghost?"

Flames erupted along my hands as I turned furious eyes on him. "No!" I snapped. "I would never hurt my sister like that! Not now, not ever!"

Barak finally eyed me with an unreadable expression. "And yet, months ago, you would have gladly seen your sister suffer."

"Yeah, well, that was before I realized what a lying, cheating group of people the clan was. They *brainwashed* me. Turned me against my family. I would never do that of my own free will."

His hazel eyes held something I couldn't read as he studied me. "And you are running on your own free will now?"

I leapt to my feet. "What is this? You know I am! I've proved it! If I were really on the clan side, would I be sitting in the middle of foreign woods crying because I loathe that the hatred and distrust the others have of me is warranted? Berating myself for being useless to take away the pain in my big sister's vacant gaze?"

A sob broke through again, and I bit it back. "I have so much to make up for, but please don't sit here and make me prove my loyalty to you, too. I can't stand one more person looking at me as if I'm the devil in a sea of angels."

Barak rose to his feet and stepped closer so that he looked down at me. He was quiet for so long, I didn't know whether to crumble under his scrutiny or spit in his face. "I know you didn't do it."

I blinked, sucking in a sharp breath. "You...you do?" I asked tentatively.

He nodded. "That's not what I'm getting at. You need to believe you didn't do it. That you are more responsible for your actions outside the clan's influence than you are under it."

I snorted in disgust. "Tell that to them," I said, gesturing back towards camp.

Barak only studied me. "Dalacia, if you want them to stop seeing you as the princess who attacked her own people, then you need to stop seeing *yourself* as such."

I frowned. "But..."

He shook his head, cutting me off. "No, no buts. How can you expect them to forgive you, to trust you, when you don't forgive or trust yourself?"

I stared at him, at a loss for words. "That's all it takes?" I whispered.

He smiled, lifting a hand to wipe away a tear I hadn't even realized had fallen. "Remember what I told you? About what my brother said?"

I nodded. "He said you didn't have to ask forgiveness for something you never did."

"Exactly. And I'm telling you that you've already apologized for what you did do. Stop seeking forgiveness for that which you didn't. Start walking in the forgiveness you've already gained. Silivia loves you." Barak snorted. "Hell, she was defending you even when none of us could see the good. So, give her faith some credit, and have faith in yourself."

I sniffed. Ugh, I was crying way too much today. "How did you get to be so wise, lightning boy?" I whispered.

Barak snorted a laugh. "Wildfire, I've been living for over two centuries. If I haven't learned anything yet, gods help us both."

I blinked at him, then a slow smile lifted my lips. "So, you're saying, you're not a lightning boy...you're a flickering old man?"

A wicked look passed over his face, sending delicious shivers down my spine. "I'm not those human boys you know back home. I'm a Fae warrior. A powerful male in his prime, and best believe, Wildfire, what I can show you will do more than flicker."

The promise in his eyes had my lady parts clenching and the breath leaving my lungs in a rush. Eyes wide, I had no comeback as he grinned in triumph and walked around me to head back.

"Come on, Princess," he called over his shoulder. "We have a king and queen to sway and another set to save."

Chapter 47

Dalacia

I was still avoiding Barak's eyes as we made our way back to the camp. Apparently, I'd gone pretty far into the woods. Every time I tried to meet his gaze, his answering smirk had me glancing away with warm cheeks. Damn Fae males and their giant egos. I scowled, ready to tell him off when I felt something tug at my core. I halted in the middle of the path.

"What is it?"

"I'm not sure." I scanned the forest, trying to pinpoint what was calling me. "Something is drawing me that way." I pointed to the east of the direction we walked.

Barak glanced between me and the direction I indicated before nodding. "Okay, let's follow it."

Maybe I should have been more nervous to follow a foreign feeling deeper into the woods, but Silivia and I had always felt safe among the trees. So, I let it lead me to a lake. It was quiet, peaceful, and the water only shifted slightly in the soft wind.

I frowned as I took in the serene area. "Why did it bring me here?" I asked, confused.

"Dalacia," Barak whispered. I turned to see awe on his face. "Have you ever traveled to Spirit Mountain?" I shook my head, my brows furrowed. "Meet Spirit

Lake. They sit in the same dimension in the space between worlds. Looking into their lakes reveals that which you are spiritbonded to."

I blinked and glanced around with new eyes. "How did we end up here?"

Barak shook his head with awe. "I don't know. Spirit Mountain always occupies the same location as the Selondian Forest, but Spirit Lake is said to appear wherever it's needed."

I edged up to the greenish water and glanced down at my reflection. "And it's needed?"

Instead of answering, he asked, "What do you see?"

What did he mean? I saw my reflection except, the more I looked, the more I didn't recognize the female staring back at me. This Dalacia wore a tiara of rubies, twin, flaming swords at her sides, warrior gear adorning her. On her right hovered a Chinese dragon made of lightning, its face holding a pair of familiar hazel eyes. On her left stood another dragon. This one of crackling green flames. I gasped, turning to meet Barak's gaze.

"What? What is it?"

I scanned his face, then looked back at the now clear water. "I..." I paused, eyes widening as I watched the water begin to ripple. "Barak?"

retreated to his side as he drew his lightning blade. I glanced at it and noticed for the first time that the outline of a Chinese dragon adorned the metal. A sharp tug in my core made me gasp, but I didn't have time to address it, not when a dragon, the same green as the water it stood in, rose to meet us. It was huge, with beautiful silver eyes, large, almost opaque wings, and a long paddlelike tail.

"No way," Barak whispered, his blade lowering.

"*Dalacia.*" Came a voice in my head.

I jerked. "Wha...what? It just spoke into my mind," I breathed.

"No way," Barak repeated. "I think it's your bonded dragon."

"My what?" But there was that foreign tug again, sitting right next to another that still tugged me towards the male at my side. "But why now?"

"Dragons only reveal themselves when it's time to bond with them." He glanced at me. "I would say it's time."

I continued to study the massive dragon. "But why not before? Back when I was trapped with the clan?" Bitterness coated my tongue.

"Likely because under the clan's influence, you couldn't be reached. And because it would have put him in as much danger as you, giving the clan another way to control you. Trust me, fate knows what it's doing."

"How do you know it's a he?" I asked.

Barak smirked. "Isn't he?"

As I felt the presence of the dragon within me, I realized Barak was right. This dragon at home in water and sky was male, and he was mine.

"I am Aoi. I have waited for you a long time."

A slow smile finally formed, a rightness I hadn't felt in a long time warming my soul. "Welcome to the family, Aoi."

An answering hum flowed down the now crystal green bond within my core.

Chapter 48

My spirit is broken.
My soul cries for you.
But even in this dark pit
They will not let me quit.

Silivia

"She hasn't moved since she went into the room. Hell, she hasn't spoken since she almost killed us all earlier," Lorik growled. "Someone needs to talk to her."

"I don't think she'll hear anything we have to say right now," Tess answered sadly over the vision mirror. "She's too far lost to her grief."

"And whose fault is that?" Obsidian growled.

"Enough! This is not Daccy's fault," Barak snapped. "We need to focus on Silivia. If we can't knock her out of this, Ghost will be lost for good," he said firmly. "How long do you think the clan will wait to try to turn him against us?"

"No, we need to prepare," Sirius said quietly through his mirror.

"Prepare for what?" Reece asked.

"For the chance that he does turn against us. We need allies now more than ever."

Growls and snarls filled the room.

"Ghost would never do that!" Tess growled. "He hates the clan."

"But can he withstand the control of the Blood King directly? The fire princess only broke his hold because we captured her. The Blood King will ensure that won't happen with the Shadow King. Not when he's wanted him for centuries."

They argued back and forth, voices rising and falling, but it was of no consequence. I couldn't focus past the emptiness within me. I couldn't feel him, and without him, I wasn't sure how to move forward.

"I'll talk to her." Everyone went silent. "If anyone can reach her, I can. Just... give us some space."

There was quiet for a moment, and then.

"Let us know how it goes," Tess said softly. "And Ty? Let her know we love her and Ghost, and we're here for them both, no matter what."

Distantly, I heard everyone clear out until only the burly male who'd I'd broken the heart of remained to help piece mine back together. Ironic really.

"Silivia?"

He was standing by the bed now, directly behind me, but I didn't turn to face him. They were right about me not moving. I just couldn't manage the energy to care, not even when they'd decided that we should move to an inn closer to Hercule. My body shivered, my power diminished in the face of my torment.

He sighed heavily and climbed onto the bed, shifting until he leaned against the headboard. "Look, I know we haven't been on the best of terms in weeks...hell, in months, but I hope you know that I've never stopped caring about you."

He paused, but when I didn't respond, continued. "Despite the way I've acted lately, I love my brother. We've been through hell and back, and I hate that I let my pride and selfishness get in the way of that. I know I blamed you for what happened in the end...when you chose him over me, but if I'm being honest, it was as much my fault as yours."

"I knew who you would choose. I knew that my brother wanted you...needed you, but I'd selfishly convinced myself that I should have you anyway. I should have stepped aside as soon as I realized that for the first time in centuries, someone had reached into the dark abyss Ghost had secluded himself in and pulled him back out into the land of the living. I don't think I ever thanked you for that, by the way. He may have saved me, but you, Silivia, you saved him. And I will be forever grateful for that."

He sniffed as if holding back tears, and for some reason, it was enough for me to shift until I was lying on my side still, but now facing him. Tyrian gave me a sad smile.

"I'm so sorry I couldn't protect him," he whispered.

And those were indeed tears on his face. My heart clenched painfully, my power reaching out for darkness that wouldn't answer.

"I'm so sorry I let what happened between us keep me from being the friend to you that I should have been."

"I led you on," I managed to whisper past the knot clogging my throat.\

Ty shook his head. "See, that's the problem. You and Ghost were the only ones who couldn't see what the rest of us could. What *I* could but *ignored*. You loved each other for a long time. And I..." He clenched his fists at his side as he gritted his teeth.

"Gods, you're so easy to love, Cowgirl. And I do still love you. Despite how perfect you and Ghost are for each other, I still do. I think a part of me always will, but I've come to terms with the fact that it's not meant to be between us. And that's okay."

He glanced at me, releasing his fists. "We're going to be okay because our friendship means more to me than a broken heart."

Tears rolled down my face now, but I made no effort to wipe them away.

"And my love for Ghost is greater than a rivalry that should have never gone on as long as it did. So, however you decide to approach this, know that I will follow your lead. If you want to drop everything and go after him right now, I will follow you. And if you decide that we need to finish our business in Hyra before rescuing him, then we will."

He grabbed my hand and interlocked our fingers, our grief mingling along with a growing resolve. "Regardless, you and me? We *will* bring him home."

I swallowed past my tears. Past my grief and broken heart. Past the emptiness in a bond I believed in my soul still remained. Finally, I nodded.

"Whatever comes," I whispered. And then I got out of bed.

Chapter 49

Ghost

Drip. Drop. My ears twitched at the annoyingly constant splatter of water somewhere in the cell. My head was pounding so hard I could barely concentrate, but I still lifted it to take in the cell. I flinched at the low light of the torches outside the bars. Not bright enough to scatter all the shadows, but enough to highlight the irons I found myself in.

Iron. The only reason I hadn't already broken out of this hellhole. Not just any iron either, if the markings on the chains were any indicator. They were meant for someone like me. There was only one group that would dare use such restraints.

My head shot towards the bars framing my cell, the pain shooting daggers through my brain and making me wince, but I focused on the steps I could hear approaching. My darkness roiled in my core, fighting to get out as I watched the group approach. Their long red robes gave them away, as well as the white skinned, red-eyed, horned moon demon next to them. The Blood Clan and their bloodhound, the larynnx. That would explain how they found me, but how did they catch me?

The larynnx flashed a devious smile and blew me a kiss. My darkness roared, but I focused on the robe in the middle. His were black, with what looked like red raining down along the bottom hem... like dripping blood. I felt such a malicious power rolling off of him, I recoiled. An uneasy feeling twisted my gut as he entered my cell. I swallowed past the dryness in my throat. I needed to get out of here and back to Silivia. The thought of this male anywhere near her made my skin feel like it was being cut with a thousand tiny blades. It didn't help that part of my misery came from the feeling of the spiritbond between us empty, as if our connection had never been. It was sheer force of will that was preventing me from succumbing to the darkness the pain wanted to drag me into.

"King of Shadows, we finally meet."

My blood ran cold at his voice. Who was this male who made me want to fully unleash my dark power?

"I would say the pleasure is all mine, but I'd be lying," I gritted out.

He chuckled darkly. "Ah, yes. Just as spirited as they say. It has cost me much to catch you, oh dark one. If only you came willingly."

I scoffed. "And why the hell would I do that? You are the reason for a world worth of suffering and pain. Why would I want to join that?"

"Because that is what your darkness was born from. And it is what it feeds upon." I clenched my teeth tightly. He tilted his head as he considered me from underneath his hood. "You should thank me."

"And why the hell should I do that?" I spat.

"Because if it wasn't for the death of your mother and sister, you wouldn't be the formidable male you are now."

The snarl that slipped from me was born of centuries-old pain and grief, and I hated him for wrenching it from me. "Fuck you," I growled. I knew my eyes had switched to their deadly state, black with a golden ring. If it wasn't for these iron chains, I would have shoved my darkness down his throat by now. More pain shot through my head, but I ignored it.

"Calm yourself. You of all people know that suffering begets strength."

"What do you want?" I snapped, but I knew. It was the same thing the clan had always wanted.

"Your power. It is about time that I called in the gift I'd bestowed upon you."

"You gifted me nothing."

"Nonetheless, it is time for you to take your proper place by my side. Together, we will bring Fenriel to its knees. And once we collect that mate of yours, I will set my eyes on other worlds as well."

My eyes widened in horror. He was insane. Now more than ever, I needed to get out of here. I couldn't let Silivia come anywhere near him. "No," I growled. "I will never join you."

He was silent for several moments. Then he smiled. "The time for you to choose has passed. Maybe we'll reconvene after you've served a few decades."

I fought a wince as my headache grew in intensity. "What are you talking about?" I gritted out.

"Do you not feel the pain getting worse?"

I froze. It felt like a cloud was starting to fill my brain. No matter how hard I shook my head, it wouldn't clear. Out of the corner of my eye, I noticed the chains glowing. Fear, unadulterated fear, flooded my veins.

"No," I whispered, but the fog was getting thicker. My body and my power felt like it was drifting away. "No."

The robed male laughed as I fought against succumbing to my worst nightmare.

"Yes. And when we're done here, you will help me hunt down the Phoenix Queen so I may have the full set."

No, I thought, but I was losing control over my body.

"Who are you?" I managed to gasp out.

He lifted his hood from his head, and I met his yellow eyes. He smiled a dagger-like grin and held his hands out wide. Upon his head lay an iron crown adorned with garnets.

"I am the beginning and the end. I am Eztil, the Blood King. I am your great grandfather. And until you join me willingly, dear grandson, you will bow."

"No," I gasped, horror flooding my veins. It couldn't be. I couldn't be related to this monster.

Suddenly, it felt like an iron cage went down in my mind. I couldn't move my body. I couldn't feel my power to control it. The Blood King smiled and snapped his fingers. The chains holding me fell away, and I stood there, unmoving. I screamed and fought against the bars around me, but no matter what I did, my body would not respond.

"Bow."

I felt my body bend and roared internally as I went to one knee with a fist over my heart.

"Show me your darkness."

The darkness pooled at my feet, touching everything but him. The Blood King walked over to me, the darkness splitting before him. He put a finger under my chin to lift it, his sharp claws cutting into my neck. I met his cold eyes.

"Now summon your mate. I have a world to destroy."

Noooo! I screamed and screamed, but I could do nothing. Nothing as I sent the call down the bond. Nothing as I followed the Blood Clan out of my cell. I was death, and I was unleashed.

Chapter 50

What do you do,
when you hurt so much
you feel nothing?

Silivia

I still felt numb as we finally arrived at the edge of Hercule. I barely remembered traveling through the land. Didn't get to enjoy the oddity of the reversed creatures and plants around us. Trees were small, grass and mushrooms tall. Dragons and dyrewolves were like puppies. Jackalopes and butterflies, the size of wolves and eagles. But I couldn't care less. I just needed to convince King Kratos and Queen Eshara to join our cause, and then I could rescue my love.

"Just a little farther," I promised down the bond, despite its silence. I'd felt a weird summoning yesterday, but it had been nothing like what my mate should feel like. The darkness that usually brought me comfort now felt foreign and malicious, as if someone had doused my mate's power in oil.

I'd broken down in tears when I realized the Blood Clan was likely attempting to force him to lead me into a trap. Tyrian had hugged me close, whispering his promise to help me save Ghost whenever I gave the word. It was his steadfast determination that allowed me to get up again. To journey through each day as if a piece of my soul hadn't withered and died. Now I stood within the castle courtyard, watching the guards gallop towards us on...

I blinked. "Um. Are those dileks?"

The normally cat-sized deer were now the size of Clydesdale horses and were ridden as such.

"Yeah. Horses have to be specially shipped to be ridden, but most Fae use the dileks instead," Farek explained.

"Weird, but okay."

To be fair, everything felt topsy-turvy in Hyra. Celena snorted in agreement behind me. She and the other dragons would have to stay outside the city since it wasn't built for the winged, but they'd insisted on flying us to the castle.

"I wonder how difficult it's going to be to convince the Fae here to ally with us," I mused halfheartedly.

"I've heard the King and Queen of Hyra can be ruthless and stubborn, so it'll likely be a challenge," she answered, glaring at the castle.

I tried not to let the thought send me back into the pit. I had to hold it together long enough to finish up here. However long it took. Celena poked me with her snout, offering what comfort she could.

We both stiffened as the dileks brought their riders to stop before us. The changeling guards reminded me of vikings with their towering heights, broad shoulders, and long hair pulled back to reveal tattoos down their necks and arms. Savage blades and axes hung from their sides or strapped to their backs. Their clothes were the color of black Fae steel and stood out with their long, white wings.

Farek, Lorik, and Obsidian surrounded me, their hands hovering close to their weapons as they stared down the snarling guards. We said nothing as the changelings fought whatever silent battle raged behind their snarls and glaring gazes, but when the lead guardian in front of the group inclined his head to mine, I felt everyone relax.

The guardian dismounted and bowed to me. "Your Majesty, I am Captain Merk. Welcome to Hercule. The king and queen have tasked us with escorting your group to the throne room."

Good. Better I deal with them now before I decided to climb into bed and sleep for a month. I gestured with a hand. "Then lead on, Captain."

He inclined his head before leading us through the courtyard with his men surrounding us. I ignored the stares as we followed him into the massive stone castle engraved with creatures of every type.

We were almost to the throne room when Captain Merk slowed to walk slightly in front of me. Lorik narrowed his eyes but said nothing, his hand still gripping the blade at his side.

"I can finally say I have met the famous Phoenix Queen."

I blinked, glancing over at Tyrian. He shook his head and threw a wary look at the guardian's back. Frowning, I turned back to the captain.

"You speak as if that is a good thing," I replied, too tired for court niceties.

Stark, azure eyes met mine, faint amusement in them. "Forgive our gruff appearance, Your Majesty. We are a hardened group, but we are not cruel. There are many here who knew your father and would consider him a great king and ally. For one so young, you have proven yourself just as capable of holding your own. Tales of the trials have traveled far and wide."

I gaped at him in surprise, and Captain Merk laughed. "I'm sure you have already learned that Fae males can be just as big of gossiping hens as females."

I offered him a small smile. "Yes, I have noticed that now that you mention it." He chuckled again. I studied him curiously. "But I still find it odd that you are telling me this now."

Respect flashed in his eyes as he inclined his head. "See, you have learned quite quickly for one raised in the human world."

I lifted a brow. "If you've been following my journey as you say, then you know that I haven't had a choice." I paused. "But thank you. You still haven't told me why you're telling me this."

Captain Merk grew serious. "I say this because you are going to face opposition from my king and queen. Not because of what you have done, but simply because they will not be so quick to respect a half-human queen. Even if she has proven herself worthy of every one of her titles. The years under Isrella were not friendly, and Fae are not quick to forget."

"Neither are humans," I tell him.

"Touché." We had reached the throne room at this point, but he paused. He scanned our group before meeting my gaze again. "Just remember to walk in your titles and power, no matter your age, and my king and queen will come around."

"Why are you helping me win them over?" I asked, frowning. "Don't get me wrong. We need them as allies, and I thought you were going to start a battle out on the streets a few minutes ago, so your welcoming demeanor is a pleasant surprise. But you have no personal stake in all this."

"Actually, I do."

"Who?"

I glanced at Ty, but he was studying the guardian.

"I have family in Kra who were able to flee when Ghirit was attacked. If it wasn't for the curse being removed from the Valley of Whispers, I would have lost them for good thanks to the clan."

Captain Merk turned to me. "I will be forever grateful to you for that, and it is why, regardless of what my king and queen say, I will be at your back for this final battle."

Surprise rippled through the group, and I expected to see the same in the guardians surrounding us, but they, too, shared that they had family throughout Rifka that had been saved or lost due to the clan. Was it fate that had warriors who sympathized with our cause escorting us in Hercule? Was this an encouragement to persevere no matter what walls we hit in this throne room? Maybe. Regardless, as they opened the throne doors to let our group in, I held my head high and strode in with the knowledge that I had earned my place among the powerful Fae of Fariel.

Chapter 51

Nothing annoys me more,
than pointless politics and posturing.
Say what you mean.
And mean what you say.

Silivia

Did I say I belonged? Silly me. What I meant was, I *should* belong after reclaiming and bringing an entire kingdom to heel. You would think that would count for something, but nooo. King Kratos was a grouchy brute, and Queen Eshara wore her scorn for my presence like a cloak with every look and comment that fell from her painted lips. You would think I was trying to steal their land, instead of helping them protect it, by the way they treated me. It had been over a week of arguing back and forth about whether the Blood King was real and if he truly would come to Hyra.

According to them, attacks had been concentrated in Rifka or wherever my group happened to be – their excuse for the attack we faced within their lands. And while it was true that we had faced more than our fair share of clan members, their claims were refuted when presented with reports from our allies visiting with people throughout Fenriel. To say I was at my wits' end would be an understatement.

With each passing day, I could feel the desperation to find my mate eating away at my sanity. Every day that I lingered here was another he endured under the Blood King's claws. I couldn't let him do to Ghost what he'd done to Dalacia. I wasn't sure the world would survive it. And even if it did, I wasn't sure if Ghost would be able to forgive himself. Especially if he knew the truth.

Barak and Dalacia had called us together a few days ago to share the shocking news of who exactly held Ghost captive. To think his own relative had orchestrated this entire thing. Organized the murder of his grandchildren to encourage the darkness in another. It was unthinkable, and if it had brought me to a screaming rage at the thought, what would it do to Ghost?

"Your mate is not even fighting on your side. How can you ask us to?"

The room went still with silent rage and shock. Startled out of my mental spiral, I raised my head to eye the king and queen sitting at the head of the council table. We'd stopped meeting in the throne room on the first day, and Reece had demanded to be called in on the mirrors after that first disastrous meeting. But surely, they hadn't just said what I thought they just said.

"I'm sorry, what?"

My group stiffened, the guards' hands shifting closer to their weapons as Obsidian echoed. "What?"

Queen Eshara held a hand over her mouth with false surprise. "Oh! You didn't know!"

I narrowed my eyes, but it was Tyrian who growled. "Know what?"

The queen was almost gleeful as she continued to stare at me. "Your mate is part of the Resisti, is he not?" King Kratos stated, ignoring his question.

The condescension in his tone was as thick as a minotaur's skull. Growls reverberated behind me.

"Careful, we may be in your kingdom, but Silivia and Ghost are still the rulers of Rifka," Ty warned in a quiet voice.

The king's eyes darkened as they narrowed. "You dare threaten me in my own kingdom!" he roared.

Well, this was going south fast.

"Forgive us, Queen Eshara, King Kratos, you've caught us by surprise," I said, placing a hand on Ty's arm to calm him.

His eyes snapped to mine, then he stood down. I willed the guardians at our backs to do the same, and surprisingly, Obsidian stopped growling.

I turned back to the rulers. "You were insinuating what exactly?"

The queen gave me a brief look of reluctant respect before she gestured at the doors behind us. "Oh, how about we let your men tell you?"

Frowning, I spun as they allowed one of our Resisti warriors to run in. He kneeled at my feet, fist to his heart, even as he panted with obvious pain and weariness. My eyes widened in shock as I took in the wounds all over him.

"My queen," he proclaimed.

Fearing the worst, I gestured that he should rise. "What news do you bring...?"

"Solis, Your Majesty," the male said, bowing again.

I nodded in acknowledgement. "What news do you bring, Solis?"

His eyes grew somber. "I'm afraid it's not good news, Your Majesty. Our king has been spotted in various locations known to belong to the clan over the last few days. And last night he attacked one of our camps."

"No! He wouldn't!" Ty exclaimed, gripping the arms of his chair.

Solis held his ground despite his obvious discomfort from the bristling male at my side. "Normally, I would agree with you, Warrior Tyrian, but the king...well, he didn't seem himself."

I frowned, fighting the panic rising within me even as I called down a bond still silent as death.

Daccy spoke up. "Were his eyes fogged over and demeanor indifferent to your declarations that you knew him?" she asked softly.

Barak tensed at her side, a pained look crossing his face. My eyes widened as I realized what she was asking, but they couldn't have done that to Ghost. Could they?

Solis's brows knitted together. "Now that you mention it, his eyes did seem to have this glaze over them. We called out his name, but he heard us not. Just sent wave after wave of his darkness to destroy the camp and to attack any who stood in his way."

I fought to hold my composure, knowing the king and queen of Hyra were judging my reaction. I glanced at Ty to see him trying to lock down his own emotions as Daccy nodded at the confirmation. Needing to know, but afraid to ask just in case the male that I loved had turned into the thing he despised, I took a deep breath and faced Solis.

"How did you survive?" I asked.

The male winced, but his eyes were full of confusion and awe. "That's the thing, the king held us with his shadows. We were seconds from perishing, the clan's bloodhound egging him on gleefully."

My blood ran cold at the mention of the larynnx. Meeting her once was one time too many. If she was with Ghost, she was having the meal of her life just like she wanted.

"Then he let us go."

I blinked, shocked out of my musing.

"He did what now?" Reece said over the mirror, startling us all.

I'd forgotten he was there. The Resisti warrior nodded adamantly.

"He was killing us, but then it was like for a second, he regained control. I watched his eyes clear, and we were all released before he misted away."

"He's still in there," I whispered softly. Distantly, I heard Ty send the warrior off to be treated.

"You still seek our assistance, knowing that the King of Shadows has switched sides?"

Queen Eshara's question sent me spinning to face her, my snow misting around my feet and my ice burning through my veins.

"The last thing Ghost would do is join the Blood Clan," I snapped.

"How do you explain his behavior then?" King Kratos barked. "He attacks your allies! What keeps him from attacking us, too?"

"No one hates the clan like my mate does. He would not willingly follow their commands. Some other power is responsible for this."

The king and queen shared a look that I couldn't decipher. "What are you implying?" The queen asked.

I glanced at Tyrian. We hadn't planned on revealing who exactly held my mate, but we may need to. He nodded. I turned back to them and held my head high.

"You may have heard of him. He was exiled from Farla many centuries ago due to his use of dark power to control and harm others in his kingdom." I saw the king stiffen imperceptibly. "It was thought he was dead, but instead we discovered he's been orchestrating certain events so that he may rule over Fenriel once and for all."

Queen Eshara snorted in disbelief. "You expect us to believe some ancient king is controlling the King of Shadows?" She laughed mockingly, but King Kratos gripped his chair with an iron grasp. I raised a brow.

"You believe me, don't you?" I asked him.

He swallowed even as he gave me a dark stare. "The person you speak of was erased from history books. How do you know who he is?" he growled.

"Not all history books," Barak stated, his arms folded as he stared down the king. "I was still able to learn about him, and he is the only known Fae capable of doing what my queen mentioned."

The king shook his head. "But he is dead. How would you even know what he was capable of doing? That is nothing but a myth now."

"Didn't feel like a myth when he held me captive for almost two years," Dalacia said matter-of-factly.

Kratos blinked, but he must have seen the truth of the statement in her eyes because he paled.

The queen scoffed in disgust. "Surely you don't believe them, my love," she stated incredulously, but the king turned to me.

"Speak his name," he said sternly. "Speak it correctly, and I will join our forces to yours."

The queen stared at him in shock.

I only stared him down. "Eztil Karlus, The Blood King."

The king closed his eyes, his face paling even further, even as he took a deep, steadying breath. What had this male done to result in such a visceral reaction?

"We will join you."

"Kratos!" the queen exclaimed.

The king opened his eyes and met mine. "If he has your mate, it will take a miracle to free him, but we may not survive this war if he isn't."

Didn't I know it, but failing wasn't an option.

"I will get my mate back and we'll ensure that Eztil is defeated for good this time."

Hyra's king nodded. "I admire your resilience, Silivia. There are not many who could have done what you have, especially after growing up in the human world. Fariel would be proud."

I fought tears as I inclined my head to the king, surprised that one name had changed his demeanor so much. "Thank you," I managed.

King Kratos gave me a sad smile before waving a hand. "Go, I have much to discuss with my queen and warriors. Rest until we meet again."

Still fighting the emotions trying to take me under, I quickly made my way back to our rooms, my sister and friends following close behind. We were barely through the door before Tyrian was grabbing my hand and sending everyone to the sitting room.

"Give us a minute."

No one refused him as he led me to my room. Lorik, Farek, and Obsidian simply took up guard outside my door. As soon as it shut, Ty spun to face me.

"Let it out," he said softly.

And then I was sobbing so hard, he pulled me into his arms. I clung to him, soaking his shirt as my mind ran wild with what was happening with my mate. The silence down the bond was excruciating. I'd always felt connected to him, no matter what was going on with us, even when we'd loathed each other, but this... Not knowing if he was suffering or not was unbearable. Knowing what he would face if we freed him was too.

"When," Ty whispered.

I hiccupped as I pulled away to meet his gaze. Tears ran down his own face as he wiped mine away.

"I know what you're thinking. You're worried we won't be able to save him. That he's finally succumbed to his darkness, but he hasn't, and he won't. So, *when* we free him, we'll deal with the aftermath."

I sniffled, doubt making my heart heavy. "How do you know that?" I asked. "He's been having nightmares about this for centuries. I have a feeling that they've been haunting him the last few months before he was taken. What if they were just premonitions?"

But Ty was already shaking his head. "I know because he has something he didn't have before."

I frowned, another tear slipping down my face. "What?"

Ty wiped that tear away too, a sad smile lifting his lips as the love in his eyes shone through–love for his brother and love for me. "You. How many times has he told you that you're his light in the darkness? I know you can save him, Silivia, because you two were always made to complement the other. It's why your lives always seemed to be missing something. The Blood King cannot fully control what is already freely given to you."

I felt the rightness in his statement and leaned in to hug him tightly. "You are amazing, Tyrian. And I can't wait until your mate shows herself and convinces you just how much."

He returned my hug, a soft chuckle slipping out. "I can't wait either," he whispered into my hair.

I pulled back and winked at him. "Until then, I'll just have to keep reminding you."

He laughed outright then and pulled me into another hug before releasing me. "Come, my queen. Your subjects await."

Shaking my head, I followed him back out of the room. But just as I entered, my hand flew to my chest as I gasped. Everyone was on their feet and turning to me before I could take another step.

"Silivia?" Farek asked, his eyes alarmed. "What is it?"

I raised my head and met Ty's eyes. "It's Ghost. He's calling me."

Chapter 52

There is no hurt
like hurt inflicted by family.

Ghost

My darkness was on the hunt. Despite the larynnx feeding greedily from it a few hours ago, it still felt endless. Never had I felt it so unleashed. Never had I feared it as I did now. Before, my power and I were on one accord. It fed off the clan I took down as revenge and allowed me to conceal within the shadows. To become someone able to take on the organization responsible for so much suffering like mine. Now, it didn't heed me. Now it felt like a never-ending abyss with no direction except for that given by the Blood King...to devour.

"I am your great grandfather. And until you join me willingly, dear grandson, you will bow."

I'd vowed to never bow or cower in front of one of the clan ever again. I'd trained, strategized, and killed to prevent doing so, and in one moment, he'd not only brought me to my knees but stolen my hard-fought control from me. And...he was my blood. As much as I wanted to refute his claim, I'd seen the proof in his eyes. Eyes so similar to my own. And I knew that name. Seen it in my mother's journal many years ago. Seen the panic in her eyes when I'd asked about the great-grandfather I'd never met.

"Put him out of your head, Daniel," she'd insisted. *"He is not worth knowing. You are nothing like him, and I refuse to let his name and actions poison your mind."*

I understood what she meant now, for more than the eyes and the name, I'd sensed a power similar to my own. That alone terrified me. If I were so powerful that he triggered my abilities, spent the last several centuries trying to recruit me willingly, and his power was already able to do great things, what was *I* capable of? And what would happen if I didn't break this cage before he figured it out?

"Focus sweetness," the larynnx...Ilara crooned.

I cringed internally. Her diet of power, darkness, and blood made my stomach twist uncomfortably, but outwardly, I only eyed her indifferently. She stepped up to my side from the shadows and stroked a blood-colored nail down my chest.

"Oh, don't be like that. We're going to have so much fun, you and I." She smiled maliciously and gestured in front of me. "Now, my dear Shadow King, show us what you can do. Let's not have a repeat of last time, or I'll be forced to tell the Blood King. *Kill them.*"

The command made my skin crawl, but I couldn't stop the darkness' answering pleasure. I turned towards the clearing where some of the Resisti camped, waiting for Silivia and our friends to return from Hyra. I'd been in a similar camp just last night, but even the knowledge of what damage I'd caused couldn't stop me from slipping into the shadows, creeping closer until I was a few feet from the patrolling warriors.

One of the sentries froze, eyeing the forest warily. He could likely feel the shadows hunting him. He called out for backup as the darkness' tendrils started slipping across the clearing towards him. They wouldn't be enough. None of them would. The camp was thrown into chaos as I stepped into the moonlight and met the sentry's gaze. His face went pale, and the darkness growled in hunger. Then I was shooting it throughout the tents.

Shouts of surprise and pain rang through the camp as my shadows took the shape of dyrewolves and grigors and attacked everyone they came upon. Soon, I found myself in the center of camp, my allies, *my men* hanging from the tendrils of my darkness.

"Kill them," Ilara crooned excitedly. "Kill them, Ghost."

I sent darkness down some of their throats and squeezed others, but even as the larynnx fed on their panic and torment, I fought. I fought to break the hold of the fog on my brain just enough to get the darkness to stand down. Maybe Eztil's power over me wasn't complete. Maybe my power recognized that this was not my will, because right before it was too late, I sent a command with all my being.

"Release!"

The Resisti collapsed to the ground as my darkness pulled back, and I quickly misted away, Ilara's screeches piercing my skull. I panted, the exertion of pulling back so much power so quickly jarring.

"Now, Ghost, you know that's not what I commanded you to do."

I spun to find the Blood King stalking towards me. He eyed me, his yellow eyes flickering with malicious interest.

"How you're still able to disobey me at all is a wonder. I'd hoped last night was a fluke, but maybe you need more restraint than I previously calculated."

No, I thought, but it was too late. Pain shot through my skull, and I crashed to my knees, roaring into the night. The fog thickened, the bars holding me captive becoming more suffocating, until I was gasping for air.

"Now, let's try this again." He stalked to my side and yanked my head back by my hair so I met his hard gaze. "You think I don't know that you cut off the call to your mate at the last minute?" Surprise shot through me, and he smiled knowingly. "You're strong, Ghost. It's why I want you at my side, but you will not stop what I have planned. You can't. You see, I was once like you. I let love for another blind me to the adversaries at my back. And then *they took her from me*. I *will* ensure the world burns for it."

He stared down at me with a pensive look that made my blood run cold. "I'm giving you the opportunity to do what I couldn't. Rule the world with your spiritbond at your side."

Understanding flashed through me as my eyes widened in shock. A cruel, knowing smile lifted his lips.

"Now, be a good boy. Call your mate."

I gritted my teeth, desperate to fight his command. Desperate to save my mate, because she would never bow to him willingly, no more than I would, and then I would be forced to hurt her.

"Call. Your. Mate!" The Blood King boomed.

I roared in pain as power I couldn't stop poured down the silver bond, calling Silivia to me. I collapsed to the ground in agony, my vision going in and out. Not even the return of the feeling of my mate at the end of the spiritbond could ease it.

"Good," he said, pleased. "Now we wait."

I succumbed to the darkness of my nightmares, hoping beyond hope that my mate would do what we'd promised never to do...leave me behind.

Chapter 53

Such a lovely, deadly match
to my wicked, charged heart.

Barak

I was a goner. I watched the fiery-hearted princess as she spoke animatedly with a merchant about their wares. Daggers spun expertly in her palm as she examined their balance and complimented the intricacy of their design. The giant male was all too pleased to indulge her, his long wolf tail almost wagging with pride. His tufted ears twitched occasionally, and I laughed at his expression when Dalacia leaned over to croon at a set of black daggers with Chinese dragons woven with red veins decorating them.

"Oh my god, I must have these!" she exclaimed, lifting them up to admire them closer.

The merchant nodded enthusiastically, seeing the potential sale. "Yes, yes. They fit you well, Your Highness."

I snorted, but I couldn't disagree. I was too busy enjoying her openness. Something I wouldn't have had the pleasure of seeing only months ago. Her azure eyes were bright. Her long curly hair fell freely down her back. She'd shed the leathers in favor of a light blue blouse that matched her eyes, black leggings, and dark brown boots that rose to her knees.

Out of respect for the Hyra royals, she'd left her blades at home, but the changeling guards standing a few feet from us ensured she was not without protection. Besides, between her fire and my lightning, that was never a concern. Dropping my gaze, I noticed she wore a new silver bracelet with a thin ring of gold on either wrist. The warmth in my core grew at the sight of the bracelets I'd gifted her a couple of days ago, still being worn.

She'd been rubbing absentmindedly at her bare skin as if she could still feel the constraint of the iron bands. Wanting to give her something good for once, I'd spontaneously chosen the bracelets when they'd caught my eye in the market. I'd wanted to wait until later, but she'd seen me slip them into my pocket and had sneaked a peek when I'd refused to reveal them. The sheen of tears in her eyes and her soft smile told me I'd made the right decision buying them.

"Oh no. I hadn't even thought to bring more than a few coins with me today."

I shook out of my revelry as I returned my attention to Dalacia and the merchant's conversation. A quick glance at the disappointment on both of their faces alerted me instantly to the problem. Daggers like the ones the princess held were no small fortune, and with no time to give her access to the royal vault before we'd left Rifka, she was running on empty.

I didn't even hesitate as I reached into my bag to retrieve several coins. "Here," I offered the merchant, surprising them both. "It would be a shame to leave such beautiful blades behind."

Blue eyes wide, Dalacia stood speechless until I placed the wrapped blades into her palms and walked away. Blinking, she quickly thanked the merchant and hurried after me, but it wasn't until we were on the edge of the market, under the shade of the large sycamore trees, did she place a hand on my arm to stop me.

"You didn't need to do that," she said softly. "You've already bought me these lovely bracelets. And now these daggers..." She glanced down at the blades in her hand, rubbing a thumb across the covered handles. "Both cost a fortune. You don't have to spend such money on me. I haven't earned it." She basically whispered the last part.

I found myself moving closer to her side. I lifted her chin with a finger until those beautiful, fiery eyes met mine. "Wildfire, I wanted to buy them for you. I enjoy seeing your eyes light up when you get something you like, whether it's a sweet treat or a new piece of jewelry. To see you smile, to have that smile be because of me, directed at me...well, I'm finding I will do whatever it takes to trigger it. And for the record...you don't have to earn my admiration. You already own it."

I smirked at her. Causing such a wild female to be speechless is a feat in itself, and here I'd done it twice in a few minutes. "Might want to close your mouth unless you're planning on catching extra dinner."

Her jaw shut with an audible snap, and she glared at me before storming away towards the giant building we'd left Aoi reclining on, much to the city guards' displeasure. We could have easily walked back to the castle, but I had a feeling that neither dragon nor rider wanted to miss a chance to fly together.

The massive dragon raised his head at our approach, his green scales shimmering in the sunlight. We made our way to the roof before climbing onto his back. The royal guards nodded as they shot up into the sky, but before Aoi did the same, Dalacia turned to me.

"Barak?"

"Hmm?" I replied, my eyes focused on the straps on Aoi's side, as I checked that our legs were secured properly.

"Thank you for... just thank you."

I raised my head to meet her shy gaze. Something passed between us in that moment, and I felt it solidify more securely in my core.

"Anytime, Wildfire." And then I pulled her close as Aoi leapt into the air, reveling when she molded into my arms like she was meant to be there. Like she was mine.

Chapter 54

Ghost

There were screams all around me as the shadows and flames danced together. I watched the houses crumble in on themselves. Listened to the cries for mercy as the inhabitants were up lined on their knees in front of me. They recoiled from the darkness spinning hungrily around them, tears painting their faces. Females. Children. Elders. It mattered not. The darkness wanted to devour them. To fill this growing ache in my core that craved something I could not give.

I could feel her. *Gods,* I could feel her. She kept fighting to reach me through the fog around my mind, but I couldn't let her in. If I did, she would know where I was, and they would kill her. Wrong. They would have me kill her if she refused to bow.

Pain shot through me, and the darkness snarled. My eyes lifted to the figure in his black robe, his yellow eyes too similar to my own, staring me down. I waited for his command as I fought the pull of my mate. The Blood King wanted her. Wanted to control her as he did me. To destroy the world that took his mate from him. I couldn't let him get his hands on mine. I had to fight long enough to break this fog cage around my mind. And then I will kill him myself. Silivia will never want me back after what I've done. What was one more death?

"Kill them," the evil king, my blood, ordered, his eyes watching me closely as if he felt the battle raging within me.

I kept my face indifferent, but the darkness twisted gleefully even as pain shot down the bond. Thank god this wasn't Rifka. I didn't think I could mentally handle it if he had me kill my own people. I'd already tortured those at the last couple of villages as he warned them to follow his rule or die, unable to fully resist him after my defiance at the Resisti camp.

He'd had me kill his own men earlier this week as a warning to fall in line to the other clan soldiers. I hadn't minded those deaths. The darkness was hungry, and I still raged for all the suffering the clan caused, so I hadn't fought the command. But these people were innocent. Their only crime was living too close to clan territory. They fought to protect their loved ones. Had refused to bow to the Blood King, and now they forcibly kneeled to me.

"Did I stutter?" I lifted my eyes to the king again. "Kill them, Ghost."

Shots of pain tore through my veins when I still refused to move. I gritted my teeth against it, against the darkness reaching for the villagers at my feet. They whimpered and cried, waiting for their deaths. But I refused to allow it to be. I punched the cage around my mind. With a roar, I punched it again and again. I continued to roar as the pain increased to almost blinding levels. The darkness whipped around us in an unrelenting fury, tearing the homes around us apart.

"Kill! Them!" The Blood King bellowed.

I roared back, sending the darkness to engulf the clan soldiers around me. They screamed as the darkness overtook them, and others ran to escape the weaving tendrils of shadows. Within seconds, the ground was painted in blood.

"Enough!"

The darkness relented. I barely stood my ground, my shoulders hunched over, trying to breathe past the agony burning me from the inside out as the king walked to my side. He stopped in front of me and studied me. I panted but shifted to stand tall.

"I told you to kill them," he said quietly.

"I did," I retorted through gritted teeth.

The king raised a brow. I swallowed, trying not to crumble from the pain of fighting his command. Blackness was hanging at the edge of my vision, telling me I was close to losing consciousness, but I still bit out.

"You didn't specify which of them to kill."

The king's lips lifted in cruel amusement. "Right you are," he said after a few seconds. "A mistake I won't make again, I assure you." He lifted a hand,

My eyes widened in shock, but I was too late to stop him. Screams assaulted my eardrums for a second before every last villager collapsed to the ground dead, blood leaking from every hole. I stared in internal horror, but my face was of cold indifference as my eyes rose back to meet his.

"Next time, do what is commanded of you, Ghost. I would hate to see how well your resolve holds up when faced with those you actually care about."

It was a threat I wasn't stupid enough to ignore. I knew he had avoided pitting me against my friends so far, but it was only a matter of time. He just wanted to make sure he had complete control over me when he did so.

The Blood King walked away, but I once again stood surrounded by blood, ash, and fire. This time, the darkness that had caused it, was mine. I was becoming everything he wanted me to be. Everything I always feared I'd become. I could feel my resolve to fight his control slipping with every attack. Every command. How much longer could I keep fighting it? Wouldn't it just be easier to be the very thing everyone thought I was? The world feared me already. What did it matter if I lived up to it or not?

The darkness wrapped around me, concealing me from the world as it prepared to mist me away. Through the shadows, I noticed a golden bracelet painted in blood and ash. Just like another golden bracelet lost to the flames so many centuries ago. The darkness blocked my view of it, but it was too late. I'd already felt my heart shatter into a million pieces, and I roared my pain to the shadows.

Chapter 55

You are not the monster
he wishes you to be.

Ghost

"Daniel, my Daniel."

The voice sounded so far away. Was it a memory? It was becoming increasingly more difficult to determine what was me and what was the Blood King. I knew his patience was running thin and his frustration growing. How I still managed to keep my darkness from fully following his commands, I wasn't sure, but my control was slipping further and further each day. As did the strength to resist him and the emotional capacity to care.

"Daniel, my son."

"Mom?" I lifted my head from where it reclined against the bars around my mind. I blinked in surprise at the lovely female before me, her eyes shiny with tears.

"My beautiful, dark boy," she said softly, slipping a hand through the bars to place it on my cheek. I startled at the warmth that it held. *"What has he done to you?"*

My gut twisted. *"Is it true?"* I asked, willing her to deny it, but the grief in her eyes only confirmed it. *"So, there was never any hope for me."*

She was already shaking her head. *"There is always hope. It was why I'd kept you ignorant of your great-grandfather, of your potential to carry his dark power. I didn't want his darkness to infect you, to twist you into him. I wanted you to carve your own path. One free from destruction, greed, and death."*

My heart sank with shame. *"Then I have let you down, because I've done nothing but destroy and reap death since that day. And worse, I've enjoyed it."*

"No, my son. You have never harmed the innocent, not willingly, and have fought to avenge and protect them. That has already made you different from him."

"But it wasn't enough, Mom," I insisted. *"Look at me. I'm trapped in my own mind. I have no control over my own power. I'm becoming exactly what I'd feared becoming in the first place."*

My mother shook her head. *"The only way you lose complete control of your power is if you give it up. That is why Eztil is so frustrated. You are more powerful than he is, and unless you relent to him willingly, he will never have access to your full power. It's why he triggered it while you were so young. He wanted to twist it so that you answered to him, but fate protected you and saw fit to place you with the Resisti instead. And then you found your mate."* She smiled as my core hummed in acknowledgement.

I frowned. *"But he manipulated her, too. He killed Fariel and tried to kidnap her."*

"Operative word being tried. For all his planning and manipulation, Eztil has been unsuccessful in what he wants most, to get you and Silivia to bend to his will. Don't give up, my son. You are a better male than you believe yourself to be, and I hope one day you will. Maybe that mate of yours will finally get it through that thick skull of yours."

I snorted a laugh through my tears. *"I'm sorry, Mom. I'm sorry I couldn't stop them,"* I whispered the words I'd been desperate to say for centuries.

Her eyes softened as she considered me. *"Oh, my sweet boy. That was not your fault. You did exactly what you were meant to do, and I'm so proud to call you my son."*

She was fading around the edges, her hand losing its warmth against my skin, and I knew our time together was ending. This was likely the last time I would see my mother until I passed into the next life.

"I love you, Daniel. Hang on tight to that wonderful mate of yours. I look forward to seeing all you do together."

"I love you too, Mom," I choked out. Then I closed my eyes as her forehead met mine for one final moment. My mind grew cold, and I knew I was alone once again.

"What a touching moment." My head jerked up to meet the Blood King's wicked grin. *"Unfortunately, it was too little, too late. You are mine."*

"What..." I gasped as he shot his power through me in a stronger force than he'd ever used before. My head fell back in a silent scream before I collapsed to the floor. I could do nothing as my hold on the darkness slipped from my grasp, and he took the reins. The darkness bulked but settled at his sharp tug, and every care I once had disappeared.

"Now," he said with a dark laugh. *"Let's have some fun."*

Chapter 56

I am King of Shadows.
King of Nightmares.

Ghost

I breathed deeply, inhaling the sweet taste of terror and desperation mixed in with smoke and ash. Their screams were music to my ears as they ran to avoid me. But they could not hide in the shadows. I ruled those.

I stopped in the middle of the square, a frown marring my brow as I tilted my head in contemplation. No. I controlled the shadows...another being ruled it. The darkness roared at that. Not liking that another held its leash. I didn't either, but then, he'd allowed me to freely destroy as much as I wanted, so maybe it wasn't all bad. At least for now.

My eyes darted to the side as movement caught my attention. Smiling hungrily, my darkness shot out, wrapping around the male, trying to run from me. He struggled against my grasp, as the darkness worked its way up, up towards his mouth. The male fought harder, trying to keep his jaw locked, but I pried it open, my darkness slipping in. His eyes widened in horror as the darkness began to eat him from the inside out.

So focused was I on feeding on his terror, I didn't immediately register the attack. An arrow embedded in my arm, and I dropped the male as I spun. I dodged another wave of arrows before coming face to face with a white dyrewolf. He was familiar for some reason. Those blue eyes reminded me of someone...of a memory. Of a camp where a white dyrewolf had fought alongside my shadow ones to rescue...

I shook my head. It didn't matter. They were preventing me from finishing what I came to do. Even now, I could see Resisti warriors ushering the people away to safety. My eyes narrowed. Not if I had anything to say about it. I shot a wave of darkness at them, spearing many of the citizens with it before a wall of wind knocked me into a building. Growling, I shot back to my feet.

"Ghost! Stop this!"

I spun towards the voice. In black leather with an intricately designed staff in her hand, a female with hazel eyes stared back at me in horror. I narrowed my eyes and drew my blades. The dyrewolf growled and leaped in front of the Resisti warrior.

"Get out of my way before I cut you into tiny pieces and feed you to the night," I warned him, spinning my blades.

"Ghost! Please. It's us," the female tried again. "We're your friends."

I scoffed. "I have no friends."

Then, I attacked. I misted to the wolf, catching it by surprise, and kicked it in the side, sending it flying. A pained yelp followed his crash into a building. I spun to slice through the female, but she dodged, parrying with her staff. I ducked, barely missing getting whacked. We parried back and forth, dancing through the ash coating the square, but I could tell she was holding back. I narrowed my eyes. Big mistake.

"Ghost! It's me, Teslia. And the dyrewolf is Reece. You have to remember!" The desperation in her eyes angered me.

I snarled. "Wrong. I do remember you," I snapped. "I just don't care."

Her eyes widened in horror as she realized too late what was coming. Another spear of darkness pierced her in the side, flinging her across the square into another building. A furious howl broke the night, and I turned just as the giant dyrewolf flung me to the ground. Bloody teeth that were likely the reason no clan soldiers had come to my aid snapped in my face as I held him off. I howled as his teeth latched onto my shoulder, tearing through muscle and meeting bone.

"Reece! No, don't hurt him!" The beast hesitated, and that was his downfall.

I grinned wickedly and then shot him with several shadow daggers, sending him flying from me.

"Reece!"

I stood to my feet, one hand trying to stem the blood gushing from my shoulder. I gritted my teeth as I watched the Resisti warrior limp towards the inert wolf. She dropped to her knees next to him, trying to staunch the bleeding. Tears poured from her eyes as they met mine.

"This is not you. You are my brother, and you let them turn you into a monster."

Pain shot through my chest, and I frowned. Why did I care what she thought?

"This is me. You were just too naïve to see it," I told her sharply. I turned away. "Next time we meet, you'll have a choice. Either join the Blood King's cause. Or die." Then, I strolled away, melding the shadows around me until I misted from the village.

Chapter 57

I knocked, I banged.
But you did not answer.
Did not heed my calls to stop.
To remember who you are.

Silivia

"He attacked us, Silivia," Tess breathed. "We barely made it to the village in time, and I thought he simply didn't recognize us, but when I told him who we were, he didn't care. *He. Didn't. Care."*

I felt sick as I took in the pained expressions on my brother's and friend's faces. I shook my head.

"He has to be confused, or maybe Eztil's power is twisting his emotions like it did Dalacia. He's been under his influence for weeks now."

It was one of the reasons the time it was taking to corral Hyra was driving me mad. I glanced at my sister hopefully.

She nodded. "It's possible. The Blood King's power feeds off your negative emotions. He likely grasped onto Ghost's darkness and desire for revenge and twisted it."

"But his own people? His friends and family?" Aux barked. The older male was more worried than I'd ever seen him.

"What are we supposed to do if he no longer sees us as such?" Rose added.

I glared at the mirrors, wanting to shatter them or berate my friends for their doubt, but I understand their fear. Ghost was too powerful a male to have as an enemy, and he knew everything about us and our plans. If Eztil were to get those plans, we'd be done for.

"Reece?" I asked, turning to my brother. I really needed his support right now, but my heart clenched every time I eyed his injuries.

"I'm alright, Silivia," he assured me with a small smile. "Nothing some good old TLC can't fix." He winced slightly as he adjusted in his seat, but continued. "As for Ghost, last I checked, we don't give up on family even when they do things we don't like."

I could see my sister fighting back tears at his words, realizing those words didn't refer to just my mate. She may not have claimed him as a brother yet, but it looked like the prince was well on his way to accepting her.

"For now, we need to focus on what we can control," Ty said. "How goes it with everyone else?"

"Rifka is secure and ready to defend its borders while we're gone. Belus and Vedia have already begun marching to the edge of the Ogre lands to await your arrival. We'll join them as soon as you leave Farla," Tess said.

Oh yeah. I still had another Fae kingdom to visit. That would have to wait until I retrieved my mate, though. There was no way I could risk or stand to leave Ghost in the clan's hands for much longer.

"We were able to recruit a few of the minor lords, and they, too, are preparing to march," Sirius stated.

"Same goes for the major lords," Aux announced. "There was a lot of push back, and unfortunately, we didn't gain as many as we'd hoped. There was some hesitation about facing off against the clan." He scowled.

Rose nodded. "Same for the minor lords. They're worried about the fallout if we were to lose."

"We can't afford to lose. Eztil would kill us all for the insult," Barak growled.

I had to agree. We had to ensure that it didn't come to that.

"Well, better some than none," Ty mused. "I was hoping more would come around, but maybe in the coming weeks they'll change their minds."

"Agreed. Keep working on them. We need all the help we can get," I told them.

Confirmations echoed through the group.

"What of Hyra?" Reece asked. "Are they almost ready to depart?"

I groaned. "Waiting for immortals to move is like waiting for a seed to sprout. There's likely more going on than I can see, but boy, is it torture to wait."

"But at least King Kratos is willing to partner with us at all. His warriors will be a valuable addition," Ty mused. "Hopefully, he will be finished with preparations by the end of this week, and we can continue on to Farla."

"Will you wait until Hyra is ready to march?" Raiden asked, his arms folded as he cringed at the thought.

Ty shook his head. "Not likely, but we'll leave a representative here to ensure he doesn't change his mind. Unless something changes, I say we prepare to head out sooner rather than later."

"And Ghost?" Teslia's voice was soft, and all eyes turned to me. I swallowed uncomfortably.

"I have scouts attempting to determine where he'll head next, but as much as it kills me, there is nothing I can do for my mate at the moment." My heart clenched painfully, and I held back the snow as it tried to slip down the bond. *Just a little bit longer*, I told it.

"Hopefully, we won't be too late," Raiden said.

"We won't." Tyrian and I glanced at each other after voicing the thought at the same time.

He gave me a knowing look, and I offered him a small smile before turning back to the others. "We'll reconvene at the end of the week. Until then, stay safe everyone."

Chapter 58

With each day,
I slip further into the darkness.
Become one with the shadows.
There will come a day
when I don't emerge at all.

Ghost

I stood against the stone wall, arms folded, waiting for the meeting to finally end. While before the Blood King never allowed me to remain for them, the last few weeks he'd deemed me "ready" to be a part of his plans. If I'd known that meant standing around planning when I could be out destroying, I would have violently declined. I sighed sharply. But alas, here we were in another meeting.

Mist twisted at my feet and darkness at my back, both impatient. We'd already been here for over an hour, and yet nothing seemed resolved. I stiffened slightly as milky white skin shifted into my peripheral. I fought the urge to stab her through the heart with my blades as the Blood King's bloodhound trailed a hand down my chest.

"My, my, my. Why so tense, my sweet?" Ilara cooed.

I avoided looking at her as I attempted to focus on the meeting I had no interest in. It was better than encouraging the attention of the larynnx. Plus, it wasn't her touch the darkness craved. No, it preferred the softness of snow, the harshness of ice, and the burn of icy flames. I was tempted to go secure it, if only to wash away the feeling of the cold and poisonous hand trailing further down me. A deep part of me roared, begging me not to reach down the wall preventing me from calling the owner of that welcoming snow and ice to me. I frowned internally, trying to remember why it would be a bad idea. What did that inner presence know that I did not?

Crimson eyes met mine as the she-demon moved in front of me. Her body was almost plastered to my own, her curled horns adorned with jewelry made of bone. Today her gown was blood red to match her eyes and lips. It barely covered her, and the feeling of the silk against my skin should have felt nice. The promise of a good time in her smile should have bent my will, but revulsion raced through me with every interaction I was forced to have with her. Once again, I found myself trying to remember why I couldn't have the queen of snow and ice at my side where she belonged, as my darkness recoiled in disgust. Once again, that inner voice screamed at me.

"My sweet, why do you ignore me?" Ilara pouted.

Damn. I must have gotten lost in my head. One couldn't afford to be distracted with the larynnx around.

"I do not ignore you. I simply do not desire your company," I told her flatly. She frowned, molding her body closer to mine. I gritted my teeth and fought the impulse to strike her.

"You still crave that other female?" Her frown turned into a deep scowl before turning back into a seductive smile as her hands trailed down my abdomen. "Don't you know I can satisfy you like she'll never be able to. Unlike her, I revel in your darkness, in its destruction, and need to feed off terror and pain. We're alike, you and I. We're meant to be together." Her hand trailed lower as she spoke, her lips coming dangerously close to mine. I knew what she sought, but she would not get it from me.

"Let me show you," she crooned across my lips.

My hand shot out, catching her wrist as it went to wrap around my manhood. She gasped, staring at me in surprise.

"Not today. Not ever," I growled. "Go feed on someone else."

Crimson eyes darkened until they were pools of death. Her nails turned into claws as she snarled at me, her teeth now jagged daggers, but I would not relent, not on this. Once the larynnx fed on you fully once, she would feed on you forever. She wouldn't be happy with simply snacking on the tendrils or the fear she produced. I was no fool. I knew exactly what she wanted from me. She could get drunk off the level of power under my skin. What she would do with it, I didn't particularly care, but I was no one's food.

"Ilara, enough," The Blood King snapped.

His bloodhound hissed her displeasure and moved to pull away. I held her still.

"Next time, I won't be so gentle," I warned her.

Her eyes narrowed further, her sharpened claws beginning to dig into my skin. I narrowed my own, daring her to do it.

"Ilara." She hissed again as I let her go, and she stalked to the other side of the room.

"Ghost, come here."

Fighting a scowl at being summoned, I moved to the king's side before his power punished me for disobedience. Didn't need to be writhing in pain for a day when I could be causing it.

He glanced at me, a knowing look on his face. "It is time we start the discussion on how to handle your past acquaintances."

"Handle them how?" I asked with disinterest.

His grin grew wicked as he steepled his fingers. "Well, you've already shown your loyalty to me with the attack on two of them, the Resisti warrior, Teslia, and Rifka's prince, Reece. Well done, my son."

I stiffened. He was no father of mine. He continued as if I weren't contemplating risking his fury to deny his hold on me.

"While your warning was good, I still would prefer they join our side instead. Of course, if they cannot be converted, then they must be removed permanently."

The Blood King watched me closely as he spoke, as if waiting for me to care about what he did to those I used to work with. The only one I wanted was the female bonded to me. My darkness craved her as it did destruction and pain. But as it did at the mention of the snow and ice queen, that inner voice in my head screamed, banging against the walls as if trying to convey something I no longer remembered...or cared about.

"I want you to bring them to me, Ghost. Either on their knees, or in pieces, I care not, but you will bring every one of those who are a part of your old team to me. They are becoming a nuisance. Attempting to raise an army against me is foolish, if not admirable, but I cannot allow it to continue. People are questioning who the true ruler of Fenriel is, and with questions come doubt, and then my orders take longer to implement. I'll be required to kill more in demonstration of my power."

He rolled his shoulders as he sat back in his chair. "That is wasteful, and I do not deal in wastefulness. Do you understand?"

"Of course, Your Majesty," I said indifferently.

He raised a brow. "You will also bring me the Phoenix Queen. I find that I am in need of a new queen, and once I have bent her to my will, she would look nicely at my feet...and in my bed."

Dark wrath like I'd never known shot through every part of me, for once in agreement with the inner presence raging at this order. *She was mine.* The Phoenix Queen was bonded to *me* and *only me*. And the Blood King wanted her for himself? No. I would not allow it. I could not remember why the wall was up on the bond. Nor could I remember why that inner presence continued to implore me to keep the female from the king. But it did not matter. I will obey him without fully doing so. I'll collect the Phoenix Queen, but *I* will keep her...far, far away from the male in front of me.

I kept my face cold as I soothed the darkness with the knowledge. It calmed, ready to go collect what was ours. "As you wish, Your Majesty."

The Blood King studied me for a long minute, but I remained stoic. I could see disappointment in my lack of response in his eyes, but he waved me away.

"Go. It must be done sooner rather than later."

I bowed and then purposedly strode from the room. I will bring the Resisti to the Blood King. But the queen...the queen was mine.

Chapter 59

Fate will not take more from me.

Silivia

"We have to accept the fact that no matter what we do, we may be too late to save him."

The silver bond shrieked in pain at the thought, and I fought the desire to roll up into a ball as I had the last few weeks. Every report of what the Blood King made Ghost do tore me apart. I would save my mate, but what condition would he be in when I did?

"Silivia?"

I turned to face the males and females around me. Some of their images flickered as they watched me with worried eyes through their communication mirrors. Reece still grimaced at the thought of the injuries Ghost had inflicted. Tess did too. We all knew if he had meant to kill them, they'd be dead.

These were my friend –my family. I knew they meant well. I knew it hurt them just as much as it did me to even consider the thought that Ghost was lost to us. But they couldn't feel him like I could. They didn't know about the random flashes where I felt the true him come through. Where he likely fought back against the king's commands.

"Silivia."

"Stop."

Everyone froze. I met each one of their gazes as I scanned the people around me. Tyrian and Teslia had pained looks in their eyes. I knew they weren't ready to quit on Ghost, but this was wearing on them. I looked at Reese next. He hadn't known Ghost as long, but my brother gave a single nod. He would stand by whatever decision I made, even after what my mate had done.

I eyed each member of the Resisti Seven. Each had various degrees of regret and resignation on their faces. Some were ready to give up, others were holding on by a thin thread of hope.

"She won't give up on him." I, along with everyone else, turned to my sister. Dalacia swallowed nervously but sat up straighter. "I was a prisoner of the clan for almost two years. I fought until I could no longer stand to. Then, I did whatever they told me to."

She swallowed again, clenching her hands together tightly. Barak edged closer to her side, and I saw her glance at him gratefully.

"I won't say I didn't know what I was doing because I did. But I had given up. I'd given up believing that anyone cared enough to rescue me. I knew no one here. I had no one, so I gave up."

She cleared her throat, and my heart broke all over again as I realized just how true her statements were. My sister never knew I'd spent all that time attempting to save her. She'd thought she wasn't wanted enough. Loved enough.

"It does not excuse what I've done. But the point I'm trying to make is that Ghost is not alone. He has all of you." Dalacia turned to me. "He has his mate. She knows who he is inside and out. If she says he's redeemable, he is." I fought the tears forming in my eyes, and she turned to scan the room. "You all once said, there was no hope for me. That I should be destroyed. My sister said otherwise. She gave me the second chance I didn't deserve. I tried to kill her, and she still saw past the clan's influence to save me. So, if she says the king can be saved. If she refuses to give up on him, then neither should we. I, for one, trust her judgment."

I'd never wanted to hug my sister more, and a small smile lifted my lips when Barak took her hand in his. I turned to the group around me and took a deep breath.

"I will not surrender my mate to the Blood King. He has attempted to take everything away from every last person in this room. He has tried to destroy a world that is not his to take. I refuse to let him take anything more. I know that you do not know the power of a spiritbond, but I can assure you that Ghost is not lost to us."

"The last report is proof enough. He blatantly went against orders and refused to kill those villagers. It may seem small to you, but Ghost has not fully harmed any innocents despite the control the clan has on him. He may not even be aware of the fact that he hasn't left lasting damage. I don't know how long that will last. I don't know how long we have until he gives up on the hope of being saved, but I, with or without you, am going to save him."

I scanned the room. "I'm not blind and naïve. I know we have a war to prepare for. I know we still need to meet with the king and queen of Farla. That is why I will send you all ahead of me to continue to collect our allies and convince other potential ones. I can't do everything. Can't be everywhere. And right now, I need to focus on getting my mate back. We all know that we cannot allow the clan to keep him. And I refuse to let them do so. Call me young. Call me reckless. But I'm going after my mate right now."

I met each of their gazes. "Any objections?"

There was silence for so long that I fought the urge to squirm. Finally, Sirius stood up straighter and inclined his head.

"We will do whatever the queen needs while she goes and rescues our king."

Shock reverberated throughout the room, but I nodded back to Sirius with a small smile. There were murmurs of agreement as everyone agreed. Relief flooded me as we began to plan.

"I'm coming for you, Daniel," I whispered on a snow-kissed wind down the bond. "Don't give up. I'm coming for you, my love."

It was faint, but a soft pulse answered.

Chapter 60

Hope came on a snow-kissed wind.

Ghost

The darkness had always been my solace. My escape. I was never afraid of it. I never resented it. But now it felt empty. There was no snow to temper it. No coolness to calm the rage. No icy heat to warm my cold, pained heart. I hadn't felt this alone in centuries.

When I'd watched my family being killed by the clan in front of me, I'd been weak and unable to do anything to stop it. Even when Marcus had taken me in and raised me along with Tyrian and Teslia, some measure of that loneliness still remained. It wasn't until Silivia was thrust into my life that the feeling started to fade. I hadn't even noticed at first. I hadn't noticed how I was drawn to her despite the loathing and regret she triggered. How being in her presence, even when we were fighting, just made things better.

Now, sitting here in this cage, all I had left were the memories of her. Every day without her caused the fractured pieces of my heart and sanity to crumble further. I knew what this was. The Blood King was requesting more and more from me. It was only a matter of time before he had me do something I couldn't come back from. Before he succeeded in making me lay a trap for her. I didn't know how much longer I could fight it, but I would find a way to end it before he made me end the love of my life. It was all I could hope for now.

The darkness whirled around me agitatedly, but I had no energy to pay it any attention. I was tired. So very tired. I wasn't sleeping. I couldn't. Every time I did, the same recurring nightmare played. I watched as I killed my mate with my darkness again and again. So no, sleep and I weren't friends right now. No more than I was with the darkness that was supposed to be my solace.

As if in answer, the darkness picked up, whirling fiercely until suddenly it stilled. I lifted a weary head from where it drooped against the foggy cage's bars. I was still in my room at the Blood King's castle, lying in bed, but whatever this was came from my core. Came from... the bond.

"I'm coming for you, Daniel," A snow-kissed wind whispered, stroking the darkness and my cheek, instantly bringing a feeling of calm and peace. *"Don't give up. I'm coming for you, my love."*

A small smile lifted my lips for the first time in a long time. Of course, she was. No matter how hard I fought to keep her away from the clan, did I really think she wouldn't come for me? That our vow was one-sided? I closed my eyes and let that snow-kissed wind soothe the pain, if only temporarily. This time, when I dreamed, I dreamed of my honey-kissed mate, her curly black hair falling into those beautiful blue-grey eyes as she gazed at me with all the love she possessed. If anyone could tame the darkness, break the chains keeping me from her, it would be Silivia, the queen of my soul.

Chapter 61

You knew not what you did
when you imprisoned me.
I've come to claim my retribution.

Dalacia

There was a rightness to sneaking into the clan's town. To using the knowledge they'd ingrained in me against them. There was a pang of guilt, too, because this small, unassuming town had once been lively and under the protection of the Resisti until I'd swept their defenses in a sea of flames during the early whispers of night. I'd been uncaring of the screams and imploring cries to relent. I'd watched with indifferent eyes as the clan rounded up the citizens and bid them bow or die. Silly me for thinking that if I didn't draw the blade across their throats myself or throw the bodies of their loved ones into the still raging flames, that I was absolved of any guilt.

Truth was, I was more guilty than the clan soldiers who laughed as they beat and raped the people into obedience. Unlike them, I was still haunted in my sleep even then by the glassy eyes of my mother lying discarded in the flames next to a father who'd been unable to protect his family in the end. To have such images play in your head and still be a willing participant in others' suffering was an entirely different level of cruelty.

"Except you didn't have a choice," came Aoi's gentle rumble in my head, startling me. *"Eztil's control over you was absolute. What you did under his command cannot be held against you."*

It was going to take time to adjust to having a voice in my head part of a bond and not a cage. But as sweet as my dragon's words were, it didn't change what I'd done.

"I appreciate the sentiment, but I am still responsible for the things I've done," I told him as Barak threw me a questioning glance. I shook my head at him to signal I was fine.

Aoi's growl reverberated through the crystal green bond and my head. *"The Blood King is the one responsible, and I will see his head removed from his body and his entrails watering the land for what he's done."*

Whoa. Between the male at my side and the one flying high above, I was surrounded by more support than I could have imagined back in those early days in Fenriel. Add in my sister and a brother, whom I still struggled to embrace, and one would say I'd lost family only to gain another.

Shaking my head to clear it, I figured arguing with the still bristling dragon would be pointless. *"Then, let me focus so I may bring retribution faster,"* I told him.

An undignified huff had me biting back a chuckle, but I refocused on tonight's mission. Under the sheet of darkness, I led Barak to the center of the once flourishing city to where the robed clan members now resided in a large villa. The lord and his family, who'd once resided in it, had burned right outside on the steps when they'd vowed their loyalty remained with King Kratos. At the time, I'd thought their deviance and loyalty foolish. Now, I knew it to be brave.

The villa was quiet except for the clan soldiers patrolling the grounds, the remaining servants and the clan members already in bed. I paused behind the trees a few feet away, eyeing the soldier who stood between me and the back door to the kitchens.

"You know him?" Barak asked quietly right against my ear, sending a shiver down my spine that I bit my lip to ignore.

"What makes you say that?" I managed, ignoring the heated gaze I could feel concentrated on my back.

"You started growling."

I blinked. I did? Man, being around these Fae males all the time was really doing a number on me.

"Yeah, well, I used to work with him," I said flippantly. I could feel the aggression starting to crackle through the air and from my core.

"Closely?" came a deep growl.

I couldn't help offering Barak a sweet smile. "Does it matter?" I fluttered my lashes at him, and my lady parts clenched and warmed when lightning shot across his eyes and he flashed his canines with a deep rumble.

I swallowed. If he kept this up, it was going to be nearly impossible to deny the truth of what I'd discovered at Spirit Lake. I didn't need that kind of possession, even if the idea of belonging to someone like that made my heart pound.

"Relax, lightning boy, this works in our favor." When his growl rose in pitch, I hurried to cover his mouth with my hand. They stuttered as his eyes widened. "Apologies. I meant relax, oh so powerful lightning warrior, and watch me work."

Amusement filled his eyes as he nipped at my hand. I snatched it away with a gasp, and he grinned, but at least he was no longer about to blow our cover. I took a fortifying breath and stood up.

"What are you doing?" Barak whispered yelled, but I was already strolling through the trees like I belonged there.

"Well, well, well. Look who got the short end of the stick," I said mockingly, strolling right up to the clan soldier on duty. The huge toro was quick to place his broad blade against my throat, but I didn't flinch. "Now, Zerath, I would have thought we had an understanding by now."

Huge canines, sharp and deadly as the curling horns on his head, reminded me just how volatile the male could be if provoked.

"And I thought you were a prisoner of the Phoenix Queen, fire brat," he growled back. "What are you doing here? Does the king know?"

I rolled my eyes, trying to project more calmness than I felt.

"Is there anything the king doesn't know? He's the one who had me pretend to get captured and gain the queen's trust in the first place. How else was she going to give me free rein to be able to come and report?" I gave him a reproachful look. "I'm guessing no one filled you in."

Deep growls were my answer, the blade pressing a little firmer on my throat. I could feel the crackling in the air increasing, and I willed Barak to wait. It wouldn't do for a member of the Resisti to be seen jumping to my defense. With a bold move, I pushed the blade from my throat and stepped around the bristling toro.

"Yeah, yeah. I'm sure they meant to tell you, and it just got lost in the chaos that is the kingdoms right now. How about we head inside, and you can personally hear my report?"

Appeased, it wasn't long before Zerath had led me to the meeting room and summoned the robed clan members from their beds. Several furious males glared at me as they stood around the table.

"What is the meaning of this, Dalacia?" the eldest said, his red eyes flashing. "Zerath tells us you were captured on order of the Blood King. Why is this the first we're hearing of this?"

I scoffed. "I'll tell you the same thing I told him. I have no say over what the king deems to share. I follow orders, same as you."

They spoke among themselves for several moments before finally turning to me.

"Fine. What have you come to share with us that requires you to put your position as a spy in jeopardy?"

I smiled sweetly at them then, flames licking down my veins. "You see, that's just it. It's not what *I* came to share, but what *you* will tell *me*." Confused and wary glances were tossed around the room, but I only crooned. "Ohhh, Barak." Then, I sat back and watched my own personal light show as the Prince of Lightning single-handedly brought the entire room to its knees.

"I should have brought popcorn," I told Aoi, sending him an image of watching an action movie from home.

Deep laughter traveled down the bond.

Chapter 62

Barak

If I'd had my way, we'd have gone in with more obvious force. Instead, we took back the city so quietly and efficiently that by morning, when the original citizens awakened, there was much confusion at the lack of clan soldiers patrolling. Instead of iron whips and blades, they were met with Resisti warriors warning them to act as if nothing had changed.

Business as usual was the decree passed from house to house as the people silently celebrated being liberated. Freedom that would only remain if we won this war. It didn't stop the tears of joy or the vows to join our army from males and females alike. Long live the Phoenix Queen was whispered through the streets. And when it was slipped by one of the warriors that the Fire Princess herself had aided in their release, there was a mixture of confusion and anger, but whispers of thanks to her as well.

But while freeing Fenriel's people was an added bonus, it was not the true reason we'd entered this city. The true reason glared at us from the iron-spiked chains securing their bodies to their chairs. Their red robes, the color of dried blood, had my lightning begging to burn them to a crisp like they'd done to so many others. I held it back, waiting for them to answer the questions of the female I vowed to never allow into their clutches again.

"What makes you think we'll tell you anything, traitor?" spat the eldest of the three clan members still alive.

Not for much longer if they didn't stop looking at my mate that way. I froze, shaking the thought from my head. Even if it was true, Dalacia wasn't ready to accept a bond between us. Not when she'd been forced into one by the Blood King.

"Funny how you all break into people's homes and force them to bow the same as you were once forced to do so, but I'm considered the traitor," Dalacia mused. She spun a dagger of obsidian and silver in her hand as she considered them from her seat at the head table. Her ankle was crossed over a knee, and with her deep maroon assassin gear tight to her body, she looked every inch the fiery princess warrior she was. How anyone had ever doubted she was Fariel's heir was beyond me.

"The Blood King should have killed you. You've always been nothing but a disappointment," spat another, his hair an ugly brown that stuck to the sweat around his neck.

I snarled, lightning shooting across the floor and causing him to yelp in pain.

Dalacia tsked. "I did warn you. Barak here doesn't like when people insult Rifka's royal house. You should be more careful. Now, tell me what we need to know about the inner court, and we'll gladly be on our way. He may even spare you from being fried on a spit by hogars." She smiled sweetly.

If it had been anyone else, I would have been uneasy. But seeing it on her just sent blood rushing south and desire flooding my veins.

The clan members eyed us both warily. "We can't tell you that. You know we can't tell you that," the last one said shakily."

"Oh, but you can. You see, when the Blood King finds out that you not only lost him a city but failed to recapture his prized fire warrior, what do you think he'll do to you? I bet it's worse than anything we could do to you."

Their faces paled, telling me they knew very well how true that statement was.

"Exactly. So, how about you tell me which of the rumored locations actually holds the Blood King's inner court, and I'll be out of your hair to take care of him before he comes after you."

"No one can stand against him," the eldest insisted. Dalacia raised a brow over her still-spinning dagger.

"Want to bet?"

They gulped, but after several hours of torture, they were exhausted. The iron chains sapping their energy didn't help.

"No answer? Very well." She gestured at the changeling behind their chairs, and he moved up and slit the throat of a clan member.

Shocked gasps rang out as the male choked on his blood. Within seconds, he was gone, and the next one had the blade at his throat.

"Wait!" The guard paused, the blade already causing a sliver of blood to trail down the throat it threatened. "The easternmost part of the Ogre lands on the edge of the Black Forest. That's where you'll find the inner courts."

Dalacia's dagger stopped spinning. "You're sure? This isn't just another attempt to mislead us?"

The clan member glared at us. What good does it do to mislead you? This is all part of the Blood King's plan. You're playing right into his hands. Soon, Fenriel will belong to him."

Dalacia stared at him blankly, then nodded and stood to her feet. "So be it." She strolled out of the room, and I followed her.

I nodded at the guard before doing so, and gurgled cries of surprise followed me out. Dalacia was already halfway down the hall when I caught up with her.

"What now?" I asked her, noticing her tightly clenched fists.

"They confirmed our conclusions, and now my sister knows for certain the location of our last stand," she said bluntly, fiery rage simmering just below the surface. She paused when we made it back outside as she called for her dragon. Then she met my gaze, with eyes full of flickering flames.

"Now we take down the king in his own domain."

Chapter 63

Silivia

Two months. Two torturously long months had passed since I'd laid eyes on my mate. We'd never been apart this long, even in the early days when we still loathed each other and he had to go on missions. A part of me hated how strong our bond was because feeling his dark emotions seep through as he swept through Fenriel was torture.

But then, I could feel him...the real him. The male who lived in the shadows but loved his people. He reveled in destruction, but only of his enemies. And his enemies kept forcing him to do the opposite. I felt the battle in him, even as it weakened every day. If I didn't hurry, I was going to be too late. I could only pray that he knew I was coming for him. That I would always wake him from his worst nightmare. Even if I could no longer sleep peacefully without him.

I was getting closer. Following the bond of a male who could mist from place to place when the bond was mostly blocked wasn't easy. It would have been faster if we could have taken the dragons, but we couldn't chance the clan realizing how close we were to their territory. But I was getting close. I knew I was. He just had to hang on a little while longer.

We'd been following behind him for days when I felt a tug on the bond. Spinning, I halted those at my back. Lorik and Obsidian signaled for the guardians to wait. Tyrian moved to my side, scanning the horizon.

"What is it?" he asked, his hands tight around his reins.

"I think he's here."

He glanced at me quickly, and then around us. "We're near Cerrock. It's right over the hill. He must be headed there."

I swallowed past the lump clogging my throat. I signaled the patrolling dragons, telling them to make their way to us, but to remain out of sight. I couldn't afford to miss this chance.

"I travel alone from here." Protests immediately crescendoed from around me. "Stop," I ordered. They quieted. I met their gazes before stopping on Ty. "It has to be me."

He stared back, understanding in his eyes. He gritted his teeth but inclined his head. "Bring him home, Silivia," he said in a pained whisper.

I could hear the plea in it. None of us could stand the alternative. I nodded and then rode to Cerrock. It was eerily quiet as I entered the city. No guards stopped me at the gates, which just stood open. I gulped, not liking where this was headed. Slowly, I rode down the streets, eyeing the homes and businesses around me for any sign of people. There were none, windows and doors shut tight. My horse whinnied and pawed anxiously at the ground, but continued on when I soothed her. The closer to the center of town I became, the greater the dread grew. It was too quiet. The calm before the storm.

And then I saw the clan soldiers. They were stationed on the roofs, their weapons casually at their sides as they watched me pass by them. They didn't bother to attack me. No. That was the job of the male I sought, but where was he? It became apparent when I could suddenly make out the screams and moans of people the closer I came to the center of town.

I rounded the buildings and gasped as I took in the city residents on their knees or sides. Clan soldiers had some females by their hair and arms, dragging them away to do what I could only guess. Others were beating and yelling at those who did not comply, putting down those who attempted to rescue the females. Horror twisted my gut as I contemplated how I was to save those around me.

Then, I saw him. He stood in the middle of the chaos, his arms folded, uninterested as he scanned the crowd. They were placing people before him, his mist and darkness spooling around him, waiting to devour those who denied the clan. I could barely breathe. My chest clenched in pain as I tried desperately to call down the bond to him. To stop this. I reached for the bond, expecting to run into an impenetrable wall. What I felt was a million times worse.

No. I could feel his darkness–it was a raging inferno–but I couldn't feel *him.* I couldn't feel the cage Dalacia had described. As if sensing me, his gaze turned to meet mine.

"Ghost," I called his name, but he stood before me, his eyes almost wholly dark with the smallest ring of gold I'd ever seen. It was barely present. I could see he recognized me. He just didn't care.

"Ghost, don't let him do this." I stepped towards him, the clearing quieting as the soldiers stepped out of my way. I watched the way the darkness and mist whipped around his feet. The way it rose as a dark wave behind him. He could destroy the world, but I had to believe his darkness would still refuse to do so to me.

"Is it letting them do it if I'm already darkness?" He scoffed.

"You are the King of Shadows," I reminded him. "No one has the right to your darkness. No one can force you to yield it." If I could keep him distracted, maybe I could use my snow to wash away the cage around his mind. I drew my dragon blades. I couldn't beat him, but I could hold him off.

"They wanted you to destroy the villages and cities, but you didn't, Ghost. You scared them. You ripped apart their homes. You injured them, but you didn't kill them. A part of you still recognizes who the enemy is, and it's not Rifka. It's not Fenriel."

With a wave of his darkness, he flung everyone, friend and foe, to the side out of his way. He drew his wolf blades and shifted into an offensive stance, his eyes narrowed.

"Don't make this more difficult than it has to be. Just agree to join the clan, and I won't cut you down where you stand."

I summoned my snow and ice until they spun around my feet–the light to his darkness. "I am your spiritbonded. Your other half. You won't hurt me, and I'll prove it to you."

I ran at him, ducking to the side at the last second to avoid the slash to my left side. Spinning around him, I met his swords against my own, using my momentum to whip from under him before he could pin me down. Meanwhile, I sent tendrils of snow down the bond, twisting but avoiding touching his darkness just yet. If I could just reach the center. I turned to face him, but then he misted behind me, holding his blade to my throat.

"Give up, Phoenix Queen," he whispered in my ear as his darkness started coiling around my legs. "Give up and come be my dark queen."

I sucked in a sharp breath before misting away from him. "I'll never give up on you. Same as you wouldn't me," I reminded him, sending the snow corralling faster down the bond. "As soon as we're back on the same page, we'll take down Eztil."

He snorted. "You are naïve. You don't know who you're dealing with. The Blood King is not to be trifled with. He will burn down everything you care about if he has to. Why don't you go ahead and surrender now?"

He moved faster than I could see. Suddenly, I had a gash opening up on my right arm. I hissed in pain but parried and dodged his next attack. Spinning, I caught him across the chest and then jumped away.

"You, better than anyone, know about the burning of homes. Do you not remember how the clan burned yours? What they did to your sister and mother before they tossed them into those mourning flames?" I saw him tense, and for a brief second, I swore I saw grief and pain flash across his eyes. Saw him see the connection of what the clan soldiers were about to do around him. Only a wave of darkness prevented them from interrupting our fight.

"Don't you remember that we are the same? The clan burned my home and parents too. In both cases, he awakened the power within us." I held a hand over the gash until it slowed to a drizzle and stopped. "He destroyed our worlds to create weapons to rule Fenriel." I stood taller and held out my dragon blades on either side of me as the snow rose into a wave.

"But this power is mine and mine alone. He cannot have it."

"He *will* destroy all you care about," he snarled.

I smiled knowingly at him. I could finally feel the iron cage wrapped around his inner mind now. Could feel him barely hanging on within it. But when iron freezes...it breaks.

"No, they won't, because we're going to wipe this world clean. Starting now."

With that, I released the full extent of my ice and snow, both through the bond and physically, wrapping him in a blanket of white. His darkness roared, but it had always been soothed by my snow. As I stroked it and wrapped around it in a bear hug, I also engulfed the iron cage in blue flames. Ghost dropped to his knees before me, his darkness whipping in a frenzy around him as he gripped his head in his hands. I gritted my teeth as I pushed against the power I could feel wrestling me for control.

"*Come on, Ghost*," I pleaded with him. I could feel a presence fighting to rise from the floor of the cage. I met his golden eyes as he dragged himself closer to me.

"*Silivia*," he groaned. "*I can't control it. Run, before I hurt you.*"

I narrowed my eyes in defiance, the strain of the power struggle making my head pound and my muscles clench. "*No*," I snarled at him. "*No, you* will *fight. You* will *come back to me. You* are *stronger than he is.* You are my spiritbonded."

I put my hands on the bars of the cage at the same time as I struggled through the snow tornado to wrap my arms around the male on his knees.

"You *are* my mate," I whispered, both out loud and down the bond, then glared. "*He's taken enough. So, fight Daniel. Fight!*"

There was a pause before his eyes filled with determination, and he gripped the bars right above where I held them. Then he gritted his teeth and pulled. The flames roared higher, the snow wrapping tighter until we both screamed. All the glass windows around us shattered as the mental cage did.

We both gasped as the shadows and snow once again blended down the bond and around us. I could feel Ghost trembling in my arms, but tears blinded me as his arms came around to hug me tightly to his chest. He lifted my chin to meet his eyes, tears of his own pouring down his face.

"My queen. My mate," he muttered in reverence. "You should have run." He laughed in relief. "But gods am I glad you didn't."

I smiled through my tears and kissed him. His grip tightened as he returned it. When we finally pulled away to catch our breaths, he lowered his head, so our foreheads touched.

"Silly male," I sniffled. "Have you forgotten? Whatever comes."

He chuckled softly. "Together. Always." He sobered and frowned, turning to stare around us.

Somehow, the city folks had been spared and had disappeared in the chaos. The clan soldiers weren't as lucky. Their bodies lay sprawled around us, unmoving, some of the glass having impaled them. I could feel and see the guilt and shame shoot across the bond.

"That could have been so much worse," he said bitterly.

"But it wasn't, because I was right all along," I insisted. He turned to look at me, a brow raised in question. "Even with the clan controlling your power, you didn't do what they wanted you to do. You've always feared that they'd make you wipe the world out, but you saved people instead." I smirked at him in triumph. "I think you should give yourself more credit."

He laughed softly, stroking my cheek. "You have always been the one to see the good in my darkness. I'll always be grateful for that...for you. The luna to my dark wolf." He smiled slightly. "Only you could have wiped away my worst fear."

I shrugged. "I only assisted. Your fear was always just that, a fear. You're a better male than you believe yourself to be." I jumped to my feet and watched as he joined me. I smiled wickedly, anger turning my eyes stormy. "With that said, I think it's time we end the Blood Clan once and for all."

Part III:

To Fell a King

Chapter 64

Ghost

I should be asleep. Instead, all I could do was hold my mate close to my chest and bury my nose in her hair. Fresh snow and spring. The calming hum of a spiritbond finally whole. A lightness I had almost forgotten burying through the darkness still haunting my mind. It was no wonder I was afraid to close my eyes. What if I opened them again to see that the one who meant home to me wasn't actually in my arms? That I was still confined in that cage in my mind. That I was still doing the Blood King's bidding.

Restless despite my mate's presence in my arms, I carefully extracted myself from the bed and slipped out of our bedroom. Not before I threw one more look at the beautiful, resilient female sleeping peacefully. A female who, against all odds, still believed in a dark soul enough to save it. I could see the strain my absence had caused her, the shadows from sleepless nights still under her eyes. To see her so relaxed now, simply because I was here, was a blessing. Once again, I didn't deserve her. And I didn't deserve her or our friends and family's forgiveness...but for my sanity, I needed it.

"Shouldn't you be resting?"

I glanced up to find Tyrian leaning against a tree, watching me. I'd thought taking my energy out on invisible adversaries would stop this desperation under my skin, but all it did was soak me in sweat and dirt. I eyed my brother-in-arms, unsure where we stood or how to speak to him with everything hanging over us.

"Couldn't sleep," I answered, turning away, unable and unwilling to see the loathing in his eyes. Gods, when had I become such a coward?

"Or simply afraid of what'll happen if you do?"

Tensing, I didn't turn around even with the undercurrent of a threat in his voice. My shadows stirred at my feet, but I held them at bay.

"Maybe I just have too much to atone for," I replied instead.

"You would if you were actually at fault."

Surprise had me spinning to meet his eyes. There was nothing but understanding, relief, and...love in them.

"How can you say that? Was this not what we'd been afraid of? Was this not the very thing you warned me would happen way back when I'd wanted to fight for Silivia?"

Regret flashed in his eyes as he stalked closer. If he decided to take a swing at me now, I wouldn't stop him, and maybe that's why I wasn't prepared for him to pull me into a tight bear hug. Startled, I froze for a second, but then I was hugging him to me just as tightly.

"I spoke out of jealousy," Tyrian said when he finally pulled away. He shook his head, sadness tinging his gaze. "I'm sorry I let it cloud my judgment. I'm sorry I said things I will never mean. And I'm sorry I gave you any indicator that I didn't trust and stand by you no matter what."

I stared at him in shock. Gone was the animosity that had besieged us for months since Silivia entered our lives. Gone was the wall between us that prevented us from being the brothers we were. Had my own doubts and pain prevented me from seeing the full extent of the love around me?

"I'm the one who owes you an apology," I said finally. "For many things. I'm sorry for what I put you through these last few months...and I'm sorry for not fighting for us instead of against us. You will always be the brother I can't bear to live without."

Ty blinked in surprise and then grinned at me. "Look at us. Getting soft in our old age."

But I could see the shine in his eyes. I grinned back. "Who said we were old?" I snorted. "I like to call us well seasoned."

There was a pause, and then we both laughed uproariously. A lightness that I hadn't felt between us in too long settled in as we finally pulled ourselves together.

"Gods, it's good to have you back, Ghost."

I pulled him into another hug, because maybe I *was* going soft. And if there were tears shed from both of us, maybe it could be blamed on the dust in the air. "It's good to be back," I said quietly. After a long minute, I sighed as I pulled away again. "Can I borrow your mirror?"

Ty gave me a sympathetic look but nodded. "I'll leave you to it."

Feeling heavy with the emotions I didn't know how to express, I sent a call out to Rifka. Tears were already in her hazel eyes when she answered.

"Tess," I breathed past the lump caught in my throat.

She showed no signs of the wounds I'd inflicted, but I knew better than some how it was the ones that couldn't be seen that were the worst.

"Oh my gods, Ghost. I was starting to fear I'd never hear the real you again," my sister-in-arms exclaimed, tears streaming down her face.

"Tess..." I started.

"No, I want to say something first," she interrupted. "Before you fall down whatever guilt trip you're headed on, I want to let you know that no one holds you responsible for what happened. We're all fine and happy to have you back. Even Reece. Right, Reece?"

I startled as the prince's sincere gaze met mine. He eyed me as if searching for something, but he must have found it, because he grinned broadly.

"Right. It's damn good to have you back, Shadow King. Try not to get captured again, will ya?"

I stared at them both in utter disbelief. "But I attacked you. I attacked our allies. Our home. And you're just...forgiving me?" How could I be this blessed?

Tess's eyes softened as more tears escaped. "I've never been more afraid than when I heard they took you," she whispered. "Not because of what you'd do, but what they'd make you believe was your fault. You don't deserve to suffer for the Blood King's sins, Ghost. We've all suffered enough because of him, so regardless of what shame you feel right now, it's not yours to bear."

"I might not have known you personally as long, but I'm with your sister," Reece added. He studied me for a second and then added. "But I understand if you need time to accept that."

Accept that not one member of my family was holding my actions against me. Accept that the Blood King had been wrong in all aspects. I may have been born in the shadows, but thanks to the very people he sought to destroy, I lived in the light.

"I'm still sorry," I said. "And I will make it up to you, both of you."

Reece grinned again. "Make it up to us by helping us beat the Blood Clan's ass once and for all."

Tess snorted and smacked the prince on the arm. "Despite Reece's less than elegant way of saying it, I agree."

I smiled, glad to see the bond between them had grown in my absence. But if the prince were to hurt her, I would make his life a living hell. A knowing look passed through his eyes, and he gave me a slight nod of acknowledgment. *Likewise*, his gaze said, and I knew exactly who he meant. Before, I would have said he had reason to doubt, but when your darkness refuses to hurt your mate, you start to believe wholeheartedly in the depths of a spiritbond.

"On another note, are you all finally headed to Farla?" Tess asked, growing serious.

Right. Silivia had taken care of the Hyra royals in my absence, but had spent the last couple of weeks hunting me down.

"Yes. We should be there within a few days. I believe Eztil placed me in Silivia's path, knowing the plan was to go to Farla next. It works in our favor now."

They both nodded.

"I don't know if you've had a chance to be updated on the progress here in Rifka and across Fenriel."

When I gestured for him to continue, Reese and Tess spent the next hour catching me up. To say I was proud to hear how much had been accomplished was an understatement. It was still going to be a close battle. One that would determine the direction of Fenriel forever, but I knew with every fiber of my being that I was on the right side of this war.

Chapter 65

The clan stole parts of me,
But slowly, but surely
You're piecing me back together.

Dalacia

"Is he going to be okay?" My question startled my sister out of wherever she was. Wide eyes turned to me.

"Uh? What?"

I smiled sadly at her before nodding towards the dark male strategizing with Tyrian and the Resisti Seven over the mirrors. Obsidian stood close to his side as if afraid that if he took his eyes off him, his charge would be gone again.

The king and queen of Farla had refused to see us, but we'd decided to wait them out as long as we could. Our group was trying to plan the best course of action once we entered the ogre lands and the clan's territory. I knew it was stressing everyone out not being able to determine what Eztil would have waiting for us, but it was the haunted look I could see in the Shadow King's eyes that worried me.

"He's struggling, isn't he?" I asked my sister.

Her shoulders slumped, too worried or tired to deny my claim. "He still believes it's his fault," Silivia admitted. "I thought the fact that all of us forgave him would help. Hell, even our allies and the Resisti, after ensuring he was truly back on our side, moved past it, but I almost think he *wants* us to hate him. Like that would make what happened more palatable."

I nodded in understanding. "I get that. I felt the same way when I finally realized what I'd done. It's hard to imagine that anyone could forgive you when you can't forgive yourself."

Silivia eyed me carefully. "Do you still feel that way?"

I shrugged. "Less and less every day. It helps to be surrounded by people who care about me and remind me regularly. Being able to do something to bring the clan down helps, too."

My sister bit her lip as she studied her mate again. "I should be over there helping them, but all I can think about is how to help *him*," she admitted. "He barely sleeps. He barely eats. He trains like he has a vendetta against the very shadows he rules over. I don't know what to do."

I hated seeing her so unsure, but I admired her strength. She'd had to be unimaginably strong as she held together a kingdom while grieving her mate and planning for a war. I wouldn't want to be in her shoes, no matter how much past me thought I could handle it.

"Just keep doing what you're doing now." Silivia eyed me questioningly. "Loving him. Being there. Reminding him that it wasn't really him who did the despicable things haunting his mind. It takes time to erase all the tendrils of the Blood King's influence, so just be there for him in the meantime."

"When did you get so wise, little sister?"

I gave her a sorrowful smile. "When the world decided that we both needed to grow up."

She snorted a mirthless laugh. "Understatement of the century."

We smirked at each other before growing somber again. "He'll be alright," I assured her. "He has you, and I believe that's stronger than any darkness. I should know." Tears pooled in her eyes, and she drew me into a tight hug. I closed my eyes and hugged her fiercely back.

"Silivia, can we borrow you?" Tyrian called.

She quickly wiped her eyes before she fell into the role of queen that suited her so well. She winked at me before strolling over, but I met golden eyes who studied me with camaraderie before he nodded, and I nodded back.

"Why do I feel like you're hiding?"

I turned from the flowers I'd been studying to see Barak strolling through the forest towards me. My guards were nowhere to be seen. They tended to disappear whenever Barak and I happened to be alone together. I wondered if it was out of respect for our budding relationship, or just confidence that he would protect me.

"I'm not. I'm just taking a moment to enjoy the vast number of flowers that Farla seems obsessed with. I mean really. How many different plants can one place have?"

Barak laughed. "Thousands actually. Hence the title, Land of Flowers."

I smiled. "Touché."

He sobered as he studied me. "For real though. How are you doing?"

I gestured at the green dragon frolicking in the lake surrounded by marigolds. Sometimes I wondered if Aoi was more water dragon than sky. "I have an amazing dragon. An amazing sister. I'm getting to know my brother. I'm making friends. And I'm not a prisoner of the clan. I think life is good."

"Wildfire." I sighed, unable to meet his gaze as I stroked the purple, star-shaped flowers before me. "Dalacia, what is it?"

"What if we fail?" I whispered the fear that had been plaguing me. "What if I lose it all again?

Warm hands that shot ripples of electricity through me encased my face and lifted my gaze to his. There was something in his eyes I couldn't read, but the unspoken bond between us hummed with energy.

"We won't."

"But what if we do?"

"We won't."

"You can't know that."

"But I do."

"How?"

His gaze grew impossibly warmer. "I choose to believe that fate wouldn't bring us together to tear us apart."

Was he saying what I thought he was saying? What every part of my being was desperate to be true.

"But I have so much more to lose this time," I told him, unwilling to leave it unsaid when I could feel that final battle on the horizon. One where I might not get a chance to tell him the truth. I'd made that mistake once before. Taken for granted what I'd thought would be there forever. Now my parents were gone.

"Like what?" he asked.

We were breathing the same air. It wouldn't take much for one of us to close the distance between us.

"You, Barak. I'm afraid of losing my sister. My new brother. Even my new friends and family. But most of all. I can't bear to lose *you*." Did he feel it? Did he know what I'd understood after Spirit Lake? The crackling of lightning in his eyes and around us told me he did as his answering smile sent butterflies fluttering in my stomach.

"Good, because I can't bear to lose you either, Wildfire. That's why I know we won't fail, because I refuse to do so. Not when I just found my spiritbonded mate."

And then he was kissing me. I gripped his shirt tightly, afraid that if I let go, this would be nothing but a dream. But as he kissed me deeper, as we learned each other's taste, felt each other's skin, I could feel that bond within warming, crackling, until it fully formed into an unbreakable crimson strand. I could feel his power and mine intertwined. I could feel every rising emotion, including one I'd never expected to have.

Barak pulled away from me, only leaving a sliver of space between our lips. Just enough to make my heart shatter and remold again. "I love you, Wildfire. With every electron of lightning in my veins, I love you." And then he lowered me into the sea of flowers to show me just how much. He kissed every bit of exposed skin as he slipped first my shirt, then my pants, and everything in between off. I returned the favor, reveling in the feel of all the taunt muscles his body was made of.

When he finally slid between my legs, he paused, a question in his eyes. I nodded, desperate to feel the fullness of the connection growing between us. I gasped with first surprise and then pleasure as he entered me slowly, his gaze never leaving mine. And when I had adjusted to the feeling of being one, I lifted my hips towards him, begging him to continue. He did. Slowly. Gliding in and out as he made love to me. I'd never felt so complete. So loved. With every kiss, every stroke, every thrust, I felt the darkness, the cold, withdraw until I was unable to hold back the rippling flames as I came.

"Beautiful," he whispered before kissing me again.

And then he was thrusting again, losing himself in me as his hip movements became frenzied and harsher. The world stuttered and stopped, flames dancing alongside the electricity charging the air particles around us. And then we were coming together, his roar of pleasure shaking the forest. When we were too tired to move, we lay in the flowers facing each other, his arms holding me close. I lifted a hand and traced the scar on his face.

"I love you, too, lightning boy," I told him. Laughter echoed through the field, and I smiled, feeling complete for the first time in a long time.

Chapter 66

Ghost

I'd never leashed my power as relentlessly as I did now. But then I'd never trusted myself so little either. I could feel the darkness tugging, restless with my refusal to even allow the shadows to spin at my feet, but it had harmed those I cared most for. I couldn't trust it not to do so again. I couldn't trust myself not to let it. And maybe that's why it didn't fully fight against the restraints. The darkness had never liked the idea of harming Silivia. So it sat in regretful, restless silence.

I couldn't hold it forever. My power couldn't go that long without release, but I wanted it to be against those who'd made me a threat to those I loved. I needed retribution. I needed revenge. Or maybe I just needed to forgive myself, as those around me had forgiven me. As *she* had forgiven me.

"Daniel?"

I jerked my head up to meet her concerned gaze. The sound of my name was bittersweet. That part of me died so many centuries ago. And after what the Blood King had forced me to do...I've never felt so far removed from Daniel as I did now.

"My love."

I jerked out of my revelry. Gods my focus was trash. I couldn't stop the thoughts, the guilt, from reverberating through my mind. I didn't know if I wanted them to.

Cool hands framed my face, focusing my gaze on her blue-grey eyes. Eyes that were full of understanding and love. "Let me be your light," she whispered, and the darkness froze. "Let me hold your hand. Remind you that no matter what the Blood King made you do, I see *you*. I know *you*. I trust *you*. And you are worthy of forgiveness, of love. Nothing that gods' forsaken, manipulative bastard does or did will ever change that."

Only my mate could reduce me to tears this easily and not make me feel like any less of a male. Hearing her vows made my heart hurt even as I desired to pull her close.

Silivia wrapped her arms around me tightly as if afraid I would run from her again. "I love you," she whispered.

I returned her hug, burying my nose into her hair. I closed my eyes as I breathed in that scent of fresh snow and spring flowers. She was right. I was letting what my great-grandfather did prevent me from moving forward. I'd escaped the cage around my mind, but I was still walking as if he held me in chains, but no more. My family was right. I'd fought it as hard as I could. I'd prevented the clan from killing those I cared about. And I was free. It was time I moved on and focused on that. Stop living in fear of the worst thing that could happen. I'd already done it and I'd survived. My family and friends had survived. Now I had a monster to destroy, and by some twist of fate, it wasn't me.

I pulled back and lifted her chin, staring down at the female who made the darkness quiet. "Thank you," I whispered. "For saving me. For loving me. For trusting me even when others told you not to. I don't know how you've always been able to see through the shadows to the male underneath, but I'm eternally grateful for you every day."

She gave me a watery smile. "It's only fair," she teased. "You saved me first. Who needs a superman when I have the Shadow King?"

I snorted, leaning down to place my forehead to hers. "I love you," I whispered against her lips. "For now, and forever."

"Likewise," she whispered back, and then she kissed me.

It wasn't hurried; it was tearful and tender, filled with the words we couldn't find. It was a healing kiss, one that I felt piecing together my broken bits one by one, binding us even closer together. I now understood why the prophecy called for the shadows and snow to mix. If doing so healed a male lost to the darkness, how much more could it heal a world bathed in blood and tears?

Chapter 67

You are my home.

Silivia

"We're wasting time!" King Kratos growled over the mirror.

Projections of our allies stood in an arc around where we sat at the meeting table, either sitting or standing wherever they were.

"Even now, the clan is rallying around the ogre lands. They know we're coming, and if we don't move soon, we'll lose our chance to gain a foothold in this war."

"King Ivar is a stubborn brute. He and his mate Magnolia have had a grudge against Rifka for centuries that isn't likely to be resolved anytime soon," Master Zephia added. Her sharp eyes narrowed as she eyed Ghost for some reason.

I really hope this grudge had nothing to do with him, or this impossible task was going to become even more difficult. We'd already been in Farla for more than two weeks, and I agreed with the uneasy allies around me that we couldn't afford to wait for much longer. I'd already spent weeks searching for my mate–something I will never regret–but in doing so, put us further behind.

"They're not the only ones rallying," Aux reminded Kratos. "Our allies and warriors have already started heading to the south, the Resisti Seven with them. We'll be ready by the time our king and queen reach us. Just make sure your army is."

"Don't have the pretense to tell me how to move my warriors," Kratos barked in return. "I have been at this just as long, if not longer than you, Aux. I have an entire kingdom under my command in case you've forgotten."

"Which is all well and good, until they're not in position when they need to be," Tyrian cut in.

Snarls echoed throughout the room, and if they weren't separated by the mirrors, I had no doubt they'd come to blows.

"Enough!" Ghost commanded, silencing the room.

I found myself increasingly glad he was back at my side. Wrangling a bunch of Fae warriors with testosterone poured in was beyond exhausting.

"Kratos, no one is questioning your ability to rule your kingdom. Is or is not your army on the way?"

The brutal king glared at Ghost for a long moment before relenting. "Yes, we are on our way."

Ghost nodded in acknowledgment.

"It still won't matter if you don't arrive yourself before the armies are apprehended," Master Kure pointed out. "And without Farla, there is a slim to no chance that this battle will be in our favor."

I gave him a scolding look. "Oh, and you're suddenly concerned about that when it was the masters who deemed our mission to fight the clan an overly ambitious one. Have you suddenly decided to take part in the battle itself, or do you simply wish to sow doubt?"

Raiden whistled appreciatively, throwing a grin Reece's way. My brother looked proud even as he tried to hide his own grin. Even Sirius looked amused. There was a pause.

"You should remember that the rest of the Resisti are still under our command, young queen," Master Astral said gently.

Her warning was noted, but this went beyond them. "And you should recall that those in the Resisti remember quite well why they joined in the first place," I replied. "I have no doubt they will fight with or without your approval."

"Understand that your being in this meeting was a courtesy, one born of the centuries being raised, trained, and then working for the Resisti, but if you still will not stand with us, then I suggest you say so now."

The room fell silent again at Ghost's words. For a moment, I was afraid we'd lost much-needed allies. Something we couldn't afford to do, but then Master Marcus inclined his head.

"We stand for Fenriel. Do not doubt that."

"*Pretty words, but we both know what that means,*" Ghost spoke down the bond.

I fought to keep my face neutral. "*Yeah, just a friendly reminder that they're still not a fan of us going above their heads,*" I replied.

"*The masters will always have their own agenda, Silivia. It's just a matter of whether they align with ours.*"

"*When they don't, I won't hesitate to walk away.*"

"*Nor will I. But I doubt we'll be alone, and I think that's what's driving them mad.*"

Amusement shot through the bond as I eyed everyone around the circle.

"Look, we all know that we're running short on time, and while it would give us a leg up to have Farla join us, we will make do without them if we have to. We'll give them a few more days to answer our call to meet, but if by the end of the week there is no reply, we will make our way towards the Ogre Lands to meet you."

There were disgruntled nods of agreement, and I sat back exhausted as discussions switched to numbers and how much gold would be required to continue to sustain the vast number of warriors. Unfortunately, money didn't grow in trees, not even in Fenriel, and keeping our allies and armies fed and housed without them being picked off by clan soldiers was a feat all in itself. One I'd never thought I would have to conquer. Thank god for my friends and family. Where I lacked the knowledge, they stepped in. But I looked forward to the day when discussions of war and betrayal were not so commonplace because I was weary to my very bones.

"I want to take you somewhere."

I stopped my furious attack on the training dummy to find Ghost leaning back against the training wall. Panting heavily, I turned to face him. I was still reeling from the frustration of knowing Farla's royals ignored us, and the fear for the safety of those waiting for us near the clan's territory. I desperately needed a distraction. Or some good news.

"Where?"

He smiled. "A place that means a lot to me."

Curiosity piqued, I nodded. "Okay fine. No good staying around here anyway."

Ghost held out a hand, and I gladly accepted it. I lifted a questioning brow as he wrapped an arm around me. With a knowing smirk, he misted us away. When we reappeared, we were at the edge of a meadow covered in...

"Fairybells," I breathed in wonder, taking in the sea of cerulean flowers with splashes of purple. They went as far as the eye could see, a path of green moss the only thing disrupting their flow. I turned back to Ghost. "I thought they only grew in the snow of the Selondian Forest."

His smile was bittersweet, one of love and grief. "I also told you that my mother had an affinity for flowers." He gestured to the field. "This used to be a field of spiky, reed grass."

I turned to take in the sea of flowers around us. They swayed in a gentle wind, their sweet aroma reminding me of lavender and the cleanness of the air after a good rain shower...or the first snow of the year.

"What happened?" I asked, feeling that ache for home, for Ghost's cozy cabin in the middle of the Selondian Forest.

My mate sighed, wrapping his arms around me from behind, and buried his nose into my hair. He did that a lot lately, and it filled me with warmth to know he could draw comfort from me like I could him.

"My mother, Ceclia, brought us to visit her childhood vacation home as often as she could so she could visit her parents in the city. They left her the house once she decided to marry my father. They didn't agree with her choice to marry a changeling and move to Rifka, and made it known every time they spoke." His arms tightened around me, and a hum went down the spiritbond. I smiled as I clung to him in return.

"They left her the house in hopes that it would encourage my mother to come home. To remember her roots. When...Sicily was older, she complained to my mother that she got too homesick when we were here. That she wished we could bring a piece of Rifka with us. To my sister's delight, my mother did this." He waved a hand to indicate the meadow. "And then wrapped the house with them."

I followed his gaze to a beautiful, small stone cottage wrapped in lush green vines with more fairybells growing between them. It looked like something out of a storybook. Pulling gently out of his embrace, I wandered up to the house, trailing my hands down the ancient wooden door that depicted a dyrewolf lying in a field of flowers. I glanced back to see Ghost smiling at me. He'd followed me down the path and raised a hand to lay on the dyrewolf.

"And this she engraved for me. Said she wanted my spirit animal to protect our home until I was strong enough to do so." Ghost snorted with sad mirth. "I had no idea then that it was indeed my spirit animal, nor that I would become strong enough to summon an army of them."

"Your mother was very wise then," I said softly.

He glanced down at me and smiled. "Good mothers usually are. Shall we?"

I nodded, eager to view one of his childhood homes. It was cozy inside. Large windows illuminated the living space with a fireplace and chairs on the right and a small kitchen on the left. The hallway branched out into three bedrooms, each depicting a different array of flowers from summer hibiscus to fall marigolds.

But the master bedroom held my other favorite flowers painted across the wall, because they represented the shadows that so dearly held my heart. Moonflowers, four o'clocks, evening primroses. All flowers that bloomed at night.

When I finally made it back to the main living space, I found Ghost holding a quilted blanket in his hands as he stood in front of the fireplace.

"I have so many memories of listening to my mother tell us stories by the fire while she quilted. Even if I never got to know my father, she made sure that I heard about Gonthar at every opportunity. And when he passed..." He hesitated, his mournful eyes not leaving the fabric in his hands. It was my turn to wrap my arms around him and squeeze him tight. "I'd never seen my mother so heartbroken," he whispered. "She told me later that it was I who kept her going. My sister, yes, but it was I she saw so much of my father in.

'*As long as you live, Daniel, then my love can never truly be gone.*'"

"Were they spiritbonded?" I whispered.

Ghost shrugged, dropping the quilt onto the sofa. "Maybe, but I hope not."

I frowned, but he turned in my arms to face me. His big hands framed my face as his golden gaze bore into mine. They were filled with such love for me, and his love and grief for the family he would miss always.

"Don't misunderstand. A spiritbond is a blessing I never thought I would have, but it is also, in a way, a curse. I pray that my parents were not spiritbonded because after having one, after feeling what it was like to have it cut off. I wouldn't wish that kind of pain on my mother. I can't bear to think she had to learn to live with a shattered heart and soul because I know that I would not survive it."

Tears escaped my eyes then, and as his lips led mine in a slow, sensual kiss, I felt his own mix with mine. His hands lowered to pull me close, and I gripped him just as tightly back. I understood what he could not put into words. I, too, would rather die than feel the absence of our bond. I sniffled as he pulled far enough away to lay his forehead against mine.

"I want you to have it," he whispered onto my lips.

I frowned. "Have what?"

He gripped me tighter. "My mother's cottage."

I blinked up at him in surprise. "But it's one of your family homes," I insisted.

Ghost just smiled at me. "You're my home, Silivia." My heart jumped, and more tears rose to my eyes. "What's mine is yours, and I want to give the most important female in my life the home that meant the most to the females of my past. I don't need it to remember them anymore. I have you."

And I was crying again. Ugly, gut-wrenching sobs. He pulled me close and let me bury my face into his chest.

"Of course, the cabin is still mine. A male needs his cave." I snorted a laugh through my sobs. "But you're welcome there anytime," he whispered.

When I could finally breathe without breaking down again, I pulled away and wiped my face. "You realize that I lost one home and gained three new ones?" Between the cabin in the Selondian Forest, Aurevel, which was slowly becoming home, and now here at this cottage.

"Only three?"

I knew what he asked, but there was no contest. I pulled him down into a deep kiss. "I thought it was a given," I whispered. "I'd thought I'd lost everything, but then I found you. I will gladly accept any of the homes in Rifka or Farla you give me, Ghost." I smiled at him, hoping he could see his love reflected back at him. "But all I need is you."

The sheer joy on his face was enough to make my heart ache, and I laughed as he spun me around. When he put me back down, his hand gripped mine.

"Ready to demand an audience with Farla's knuckleheaded monarchy?"

I grinned back at him as we headed out of the cottage. "With you by my side, absolutely. They won't know what hit them."

Ghost laughed and wrapped us both in his mist, the scent of the fairybells on a gentle wind, wishing us well.

Chapter 68

We can't choose who shares our blood.
But we can choose our family.

Ghost

A couple of days after I took Silivia to the cottage, we were finally called into the throne room to speak to King Ivar and Queen Magnolia. I stared them down as we stopped in front of the dais, refusing to offer the respectful bows owed them. Ivar glared back as if by will alone he could force me to relent. He should know better than that.

"So, you finally deemed to see us," Tyrian stated evenly, his arms folded over his broad chest.

Apparently, I wasn't the only one whose patience ran thin.

"Forgive us, I fear that bad habits are difficult to break," Queen Magnolia offered.

She glanced at me, but I ignored her. Obsidian glanced between us before his eyes went wide. I threw him a warning look, but he only smiled mischievously. Damn guardian. He had definitely reached a conclusion I didn't want to face today. Silivia wasn't having it, though.

"Oh, and what bad habits would that be?" she asked, making me think she'd figured out the connection between the royals and I. Maybe she had finally pieced together what their grudge was about. The anger in her eyes didn't match the innocent tone of her question.

I stiffened as King Ivar narrowed his eyes. "So not only did our grandson fail to invite us to his coronation, but he also failed to share that he was already heir to *this* throne."

The room went silent as death, and I bit back a groan. With the pain of knowing the Blood King was my relative, I'd dismissed who else was.

"So, you were already a lord in Rifka and a prince of Farla? Collecting titles left and right, aren't we?"

I glanced at my mate to find her blue-grey eyes twinkling. I snorted a laugh despite myself. I should have known. Only she could be this nonchalant about my past. I mean, she was the same one who looked at my power with awe.

"Yeah, well. You know I don't do titles," I gave her a secret smirk, and she shook her head.

Tyrian chuckled at her side, mirth plain as I met his gaze with a grin of my own. "Except for ruler over the shadows, it seems," my brother teased.

We grew somber as a growl reverberated from the throne. The smile fell from my face as I glared at King Ivar. He only glared back as he leaned forward with a rising sneer, but I saw a hint of something else behind his angry gaze.

"Don't, my love." The king glanced at the female at his side before relaxing against the throne again. "Despite the bad blood between us, we've decided to fight the Blood Clan alongside you," Queen Magnolia declared.

I scoffed. "You're the ones who dismissed my mother because she decided to marry a lord and move to Rifka. It was you who said that she was no longer welcome, only to then extend gifts to try to coax her home. Not once did you recognize me as your grandson. Not once did you reach out after she lost my father. After I lost her and my sister."

I was shaking now, anger and grief a potent mixture stirring the mist and darkness at my feet. "And now I'm expected to believe that you've suddenly had a change of heart? Or are you embarrassed that your father is the reason Fenriel is at risk in the first place?"

Surprise encompassed the room, and my companions stiffened at my side.

"Watch your tongue, boy!" my grandfather growled, his silver eyes flashing, but my grandmother laid a hand on his arm.

"I understand why you would doubt us. We have not been there for you in the past, especially when we should have been." Her eyes darkened with sorrow alongside the king's.

But I still bristled, unable to reconcile their dismissal. They should have been the ones to take me in when the clan stole everything from me. Instead, I'd found my own family.

"Give me one good reason why we should trust you now," I snarled, ready to find a way to fight this war without them.

It was my mate's turn to calm me, her hand resting over my heart, reminding me that I wasn't alone. I glanced at her and felt the darkness settle as snow wrapped around our bond. I met Ty's gaze over her head, and he gave me a knowing nod. It didn't matter if my blood family had let me down. This family, standing with me, never had.

When I glanced back at my grandparents, they shared a look before turning back to us. "We can give you two."

I blinked, and Silivia frowned in confusion. "What do you mean?" she asked.

Queen Magnolia waved a hand, a shimmering mist rising over her fingers that reminded me of the darkness at my feet. I blinked again in surprise. "I have the gift of foresight. I'd like to show you a piece of your future."

The others stared at me. I turned my back to my grandparents, and the group circled around me.

"We need them, Ghost," Obsidian whispered as his eyes watched the king and queen distrustfully.

I gritted my teeth. "We can manage without them," I growled back.

"Sure you want to risk that?" Barak asked, eyes going to Silivia and then Dalacia.

My darkness snarled at the implication, but I inclined my head. We turned back to the royals. "Fine, show us what you must."

Magnolia eyed the rest of our group. "Are you sure you want them here for this?"

I stiffened. "Those here are more my family than you have been my entire life. They can see whatever you show me."

Another flash of regret went through her eyes, but she inclined her head. "So be it. Watch."

The world went black for a minute, wisps of shimmery mist weaving around us until an image slowly took form. I felt my heart stop, and then start pounding uncontrollably as Silivia gasped at my side. Another vision of her stood before me in a flowy blue top and black pants, her silver crown of sapphires reflecting the sunshine peeking through the trees. We were in the Selondian Forest, back at the cabin.

But it was who made her laugh with such joy that had my heart clenching. A little Fae girl with long, curly black hair and beautiful blue-grey eyes, wearing a silver tiara of her own. She was weaving little dragons out of shadows. Then she was calling for someone on the other side of the cabin.

My heart stopped again as I saw myself. My eyes upon the Fae boy learning how to wield a dagger in front of me. His black hair fell into his eyes, and when he lifted his gaze, I met golden eyes the exact shade of my own. He turned at the call of the Fae girl, made a face, and then with a wicked smile sent vines out of the ground to trip her. Cries of outrage pursued. I watched with awe as the girl misted with shadows, and the boy with snow, as they chased each other through the trees.

Their laughter played in my head as slowly the images faded until we were once again in the throne room. I couldn't find the words to express the emotions rushing through me. No one in our group spoke, but I could feel the awe radiating off them. Finally, my grandmother offered me a soft smile.

"Now you see why we will fight at your side in this war. Fenriel depends on it, but most importantly, so does Farla and Rifka."

"What are you trying to say?" Silivia insisted, but she sounded as breathless as I was.

I'm glad she'd asked, because I needed them to say what I was too afraid to dream of. What I never thought to desire. But now I found myself wanting the future they'd shown me.

"We're saying that one day you will have twins, and one will rule Rifka and one Farla."

Chapter 69

We fight for a future
I never thought to hope for,
But now can't live without.

Silivia

We'd done it. We'd bonded the three Fae kingdoms together against the Blood Clan. Things moved quickly after the meeting with Ghost's grandparents. Messages were sent to all our allies to rendezvous. With no time to return to Rifka, we took a shortcut through the Kamuna Desert to the Ogre lands.

It had been well over two years since I'd first set foot on that side of the world, but I was no longer the lost girl who'd walked through a birch tree to save the only family she had left. I was a queen, a friend, a wife, and someday...a mother. Images of the twins with the shadow infinity of their father played through my head.

I wanted that. That slice of happiness that I never knew I would. I wasn't ready for it yet. I wanted a few more decades of just Ghost and I before then. Give us a chance to learn how to live outside of war and heartache for a while. But someday. Someday, I wanted them to love the cabin in the Selondian Forest, the cottage in Farla, and both kingdoms overall as much as my mate and I. I wanted them to be best friends with the children of Tess and Reece, Barak and Dalacia...and Ty and his mate. I wanted to have giant family dinners and come together for family vacations and holidays. I wanted peace and never-ending happiness for all of us.

But before any of that could happen, we had one more piece of the prophecy to complete. To say I was afraid was an understatement. I stood to lose so much if we failed. But as I looked back at all I've been through in the last couple of years, I couldn't help wondering if my parents would be proud.

"They would be."

I spun from the window of the inn to see Reece standing at my door.

"Reece!" I threw my arms around him.

He laughed as he hugged me back. "Hi, little sister. You act like we didn't just speak over the mirrors a few days ago."

I pulled back to grin up at him. "Yeah, but it's been months since I've seen you in person. I'm allowed to miss you."

Surprise and joy showed in his face, reminding me that my brother hadn't always had someone who cared about him in his life.

"I missed you, too, Princess," he whispered.

I snorted. "Um, I'm no longer a princess. Remember? You were there."

He laughed and then tugged on my curls. "Yeah, yeah. Let me be a big brother, please. I have too many years to make up for."

"Room for one more?"

We both turned to see Daccy hesitating at my door. She threw Reece a shy look before glancing at me.

I smiled. "Of course, sis. You're a part of this family, too." I pulled her into the room and over to Reece.

They studied each other wordlessly. They hadn't really had a chance to get to know each other once Dalacia had switched to our side. He'd remained in Rifka, and she'd traveled with me, but I hoped they could eventually become close like I was with both of them.

"I'm sorry." Her declaration startled both of us.

Reece blinked. "Why?" he asked.

Daccy glanced down at her feet, fiddling with her hands nervously. "I hurt you too, when I was attacking Rifka, and I said some things I didn't mean."

There was a pause, and then.

"We both said things we didn't mean, but that's what siblings do, right?" She glanced back up at him in surprise, and he gave her a tentative smile. "I know we haven't had much of a chance to be brother and sister, but when this is all over, I would like us to get to know each other better. If that's what you want."

My heart clenched as she returned his smile, her eyes lighting up. "I would love that."

I sniffled, and they both glanced at me.

Reece lifted a brow. "Are you crying?"

I sniffled and waved at my eyes. "What? No! My allergies are acting up."

Daccy gave me a dubious look. "You don't have allergies."

I glared at her, and Reece laughed. "Okay, okay. I think this calls for a group hug."

Daccy turned her dubious look to him. "Really? We're going to be *that family*?"

I snorted a laugh, and he grinned. "We already have matching blades. I'll say it was preordained."

Before we could retort, he pulled us both into a hug. Giggling, we returned it and stepped back.

"If only he could see us now," Reece whispered, glancing at both of us. "He would be so proud."

Okay, now those were tears in my eyes.

"Yeah? Even in me?" Daccy whispered.

He pulled her into another tight hug. "Even you," he assured her.

I smiled as I watched them. Yeah, failing wasn't an option. I had too much to look forward to, and we were all long overdue for our happy ever after.

Chapter 70

May this war rage.

Silivia

I couldn't shake the feeling of dread that being within the clan territory filled me with.

"They'll attack at dawn," Queen Magnolia warned, that freakishly familiar mist wrapping around her fingers as she gestured.

I'd thought Fenriel was done with its surprises, but lo and behold. Only Ghost would refuse to acknowledge not one but two titles of power. At least he didn't shrink away from the one that bound him to me.

"We can't get a good read on their numbers, but we have to assume that there are multiple power users hidden within their ranks. They account for several soldiers all on their own," Ty warned.

"We need to watch our backs as much as our front," King Kratos warned. "The land east of the Ogre Lands may be the only part of Fenriel marked as theirs, but the clan has a hold on everything south of the Kamuna Desert. I wouldn't put it past them to surround us."

"What are the odds that the ogres and hogars will stay out of this?" Rose asked, her flowing hair pulled back in a tight braid for once.

We were all dressed for battle. Reece and Teslia had brought Ghost and I new armor. This time, they appeared to be made of dragon scales. Mine was a dark blue and black to match my crown, and Ghost's all black. While I would have preferred never to don it again, the lightweight armor was a relief to have.

Heavily decked out warriors filled the meeting tent. The changeling guards all wore more weaponry than I'd ever seen on them as they lined up against the wall. The Resisti masters had even gifted us armor for our bonded dragons when they'd arrived a couple of days ago. We had weapons. We had allies. We had the drive. Now we just had to make sure it was enough.

"Slim to none," Hemera said, startling everyone. "The clan mobilizes them as we speak. Promises of blood are all it takes."

We all blinked at the female assassin twin for a second.

"Great, as if we didn't have enough to contend with," Sirius scowled. Barak threw him a warning look, and the yellow-eyed male threw up his hands. "I'm just not relishing the idea of being roasted on a spit by smelly, rat-tailed, hybrid bastards."

"Agreed," Aux said, disgust twisting his face. "So, we ensure we keep an eye out for them as well."

"I want to send a messenger to the clan," I interjected.

"Silivia," Ghost warned.

We'd argued about this at length last night, but if I could stop this war before it started, it would be worth the effort.

Faunus and Zerc exchanged a look. The two Rifka lords probably still saw me as some naïve human female. A lot of the incredulous looks around the tent probably did. And maybe it was my human side that dared to hope, but I couldn't help it.

"For what purpose, Your Majesty?" Zerc asked carefully, even as he eyed Ghost.

My mate narrowed his eyes at the male as he sent waves of displeasure down the bond to me.

"I want to give them an option for a ceasefire."

Kratos snorted a laugh. "That won't go well."

Reece threw him a scathing look but turned to me. "I don't think that'll make a difference," he said sullenly.

"Well, we won't know unless we try, will we?" I said stubbornly.

Ghost growled under his breath, his arms folded against his chest, and a scowl marring his face, but he said nothing.

"You're wasting time on pointless human sentiments when we should be making our move," Ivar insisted.

I glared at him, my snow twisting at my feet. "Is it only human sentiments that make me want to prevent bloodshed when I can?" I challenged.

"It is if all it does is avoid the inevitable or provokes more bloodshed," Faunus pointed out. "Your mate agrees."

Said mate still said nothing but scowled at the male.

"Regardless, I have already sent a messenger to the clan," I said.

Outrage rung out threw the tent.

"Without speaking to us?!" Kratos roared. "You foolish human!"

Metal sliding against metal and bows being drawn could be heard as every guardian reacted to the threat in the tent.

"Put your weapons down for gods' sake!" Reece snapped. "We're on the same side."

When no one complied, he glared at Lorik. We all knew, regardless of what the others thought about it, Rifka was leading this show, meaning our side needed to stand down first.

"At ease, Lorik," I told him calmly, even as the shadows and snow wrapped around Ghost's legs and my own. Despite his agreement with those around me, he would protect me from their wrath in a heartbeat.

"You too, Obsidian," Ghost ordered.

As one, the guardians at our backs lowered their weapons, and the others did the same.

"I know you don't agree, but it didn't hurt to try," I told them. "The messengers should be returning soon."

"That's where you're wrong, young one," Master Astral said.

I frowned, but a call shot through the camp. Suddenly, an elf with green locs and bark brown skin slipped through the tent flaps. He bowed to Ghost and I before glancing at me with wide eyes.

"Your Majesties, a messenger rides to see you."

I glanced at Ghost, unease worming through me. "One of ours?" I asked, turning back to the male.

He glanced at Ghost before shaking his head, and my stomach dropped. "No, my queen."

Swallowing past the dread I could feel clogging my throat, I gestured beyond me. "Lead us to them."

The messenger rode on a blood-red horse with a mane of rippling night. I'd never seen one like it. The soldier riding it wore the customary gear of the Blood Clan, a bleeding B on his bicep. Our warriors snarled and growled, their hands on their weapons as I ordered the uneasy winged to stand down. Our bonded dragons were barely holding back from ripping this male apart as they stood at the edge of the crowd with deadly teeth bared and bristling bodies.

"The Blood King sends his regards," the male said, his voice oddly projecting through the camp.

I stepped forward with Ghost at my side and our allies at our backs as I faced off with the male. "What says he to my request? Where are my messengers?"

An evil grin of jagged teeth that sent a cold chill through me was my answer.

"He says bow or die. There is no other option. Either you join him, or this land will be watered with blood and tears. As for your warriors." He reached around his saddle and tossed a bag at my feet.

At first, I didn't register what was spilling out of the now open bag. Then I noticed a finger. A toe. An arm. A head. The Blood King had sent my men back in pieces.

"Bow or die," was the clan soldier's final warning over the cries of outrage before he and the demon horse rode away.

I could barely hear over the whooshing in my ears. Distantly, I heard Ghost order the bag and pieces burned properly. And he must have led us to our tent afterwards because suddenly I was surrounded by fabric, but all I could see was the pieces of the males I'd sent to their deaths on a misguided attempt to stop a war.

A wall of darkness surrounded me as the world went silent, and then Ghost was standing in front of me. He didn't touch me as I met his gaze. Pain and rage were reflected back at me.

"Let it out," he said, and that was all the permission I needed. It bubbled up within me, rising, raging until with screams of ice and blue flames I lost it.

It wasn't dawn, but that moment when night and day meet, when the alarm shot through the camp. The clan was here. I was on my feet in seconds, pulling on my boots and weapons as Ghost did the same at my side. We said nothing about what had happened yesterday. There would be time later to grieve properly. There would be many other casualties if we didn't win this war.

Right before we left the tent, he stopped me and lifted my chin so that our gazes met. "No matter what happens today, I want you to know that it is an honor to call you my mate, my queen, and my friend. We will not lose. There is too much living I still want to do with you."

"And I with you." Determination grew within me as I sent every ounce of love I could down the bond. "With shadows and snow," I whispered.

His eyes flashed in recognition. "We'll wipe this world clean," was his answer, and we strolled hand in hand to meet the clan.

Chapter 71

I will not yield.

Silivia

I thought I knew what war was. I thought I'd experienced all it had to offer when I fought to take back my kingdom. But the battle for a world was unlike any I could have imagined. The fear was almost debilitating when Ghost and I looked across our hill to the hill parallel hosting our enemy. Ogres, grigors, hogars, and clan soldiers on and off more demon horses stretched as far as the eye could see.

Figures in blood-red robes were far and many, and right between their army and ours was a valley that had no idea how much blood was about to saturate its dirt. Crows already cried out their warnings in the sky, heedless of the many winged flying above and behind me. The Fae royals watched with grim determination in front of their armies. Resisti stood behind each of the elders, ready to fight with everything their name represented. I could taste the fear, but also feel the resolve of those at my back.

I gripped Ghost's hand tighter in mine, and he squeezed back in return. I could feel his worry pouring down our bond. But also his trust that I was more than capable of standing at his side and surviving. Dalacia stepped to my side, swallowing as she gripped her dragon blades and eyed the vast army before us.

"What now?" she asked.

I stood taller, shaking off the anxiety that impelled me to turn and run. This was it. Everything that I had been taught, every decision that I'd made, came down to this moment right here. This was the determining factor of whether I'd live to see the future Ghost's grandmother had shown us. The future I dreamed of for my family and friends. I will not yield.

"Now," I said resolutely. "We fight."

"Archers!" Tyrian called. At his demand, bows were drawn back and arched towards the sky. "Fire!"

Arrows flew through the air, fire and lightning thinning out the enemy as our power users struck true.

"Shields!" came his next order when the clan retaliated.

Cries of pain and death broke out as some of the attacks hit home. Then, with a battle cry heard for miles, the armies raced down their respective hills and collided.

It was pandemonium. Death struck hard and fast on both sides. Our warriors evenly matched by those of the clan. Even the winged were struck down by enchanted spears, arrows, or power users. Unlike with Aurevel, the battle went on nonstop, the lines being rotated back to allow some to rest for a few hours before rejoining the fight. The field was draped in death. The infirmaries overflowed with cries of pain and grief. The tang of blood in the air was so thick that I swore I could taste it. The battle had been going for five days, and while the bodies kept piling up, there was still no sign of the Blood King himself.

"He's waiting us out until we're too exhausted to fight back," King Kratos had warned the day before.

I'd been too busy trying to wash the taste of blood and death from my mouth to retort. There was only ever enough time to wipe the blood from my skin with a shallow bowl and stuff my mouth with bread and wine before we were discussing plans for the next day. A servant was nice enough to wipe off Ghost and my armor each night, but what I wouldn't give for a hot bath and a real meal.

"If we don't find a way to convince him to reveal himself, we will be," Reece said, exhaustion having him slump in his chair.

"Are we even sure this king exists?" Faunus had asked. "Or are we chasing a phantom?"

"He exists," Ghost and Daccy had said in unison.

"Unfortunately," King Ivar had added.

I couldn't help wishing it was as simple as a phantom, but the truth of the matter was, we were tiring, and the clan's ranks showed no sign of diminishing. It would take defeating their ruler to defeat them.

It was time for a rest. My mind was wandering. My limbs heavy. But it was hard to rest when the battle seemed never-ending.

"Silivia!" Ghost's terrified cry had me throwing up a wall of ice.

Somehow, we'd been separated by the last wave of soldiers, and we hadn't made it back to each other's side. Even the changelings were having a difficult time staying at our side with the sheer number of enemies attacking. We'd been trying to conserve our power as the battle progressed, and it was my saving grace.

"Hello, sweetness."

Crimson eyes met mine as I took in the creature dressed in black silk and blood. Her milky white skin, long spikey tail, and spiraling horns told me exactly who she was.

"Ilara," I breathed, eyeing the larynnx and the Blood King's bloodhound. I could feel Ghost racing to my side, but I didn't take my eyes off the female in front of me. My changeling guards would keep anyone else from getting to me. This monster was mine.

She grinned wider as she took a deep breath in. "Mmm, someone has come into their power since we last met. Smells delicious. I bet it'll taste even better."

I raised my twin blades, so they were pointed at her chest. "I've been hoping to run into you again," I replied.

She laughed. "Oh, someone doesn't like sharing. Heard I got to feed off your shadow mate, uh? Don't be jealous. One can't expect to hold that kind of power all to her lonesome. It's rude not to share."

"His power is not yours to take. Nor is mine." I bared my teeth at her, my ice flooding my veins. "And I will make you pay for every tendril you ate." I attacked, and she danced away, her sharp claws quick to counter.

We danced back and forth, Ghost still fighting to reach me through the throng of people fighting between us.

"Hang on, Silivia! I'm coming!"

But this wasn't his fight. I was going to be the one to end the blight that haunted some of his nightmares. I screamed as I was too slow to avoid her claws slicing down my right arm before she kicked me in the ribs. I fought to catch my breath as the armor absorbed most of the damage and my healing abilities knitted the skin together along my arm, albeit slowly. Celena roared from above and took out a swarm of clan soldiers trying to overtake me from the side. Heat rolled off my skin, but I barely felt it as the ice in my veins grew. Arctic did the same, closer to Ghost, working to clear the path so that he could reach me.

"Silivia!!"

Ilara laughed gleefully. "Come now, pet. Surely, you're not giving up so soon."

I growled at her as I gripped my aching ribs with one arm. "Wouldn't dream of it." And then I attacked her with renewed energy. Back and forth we went, neither of us making any progress.

"Ooo, here comes the Shadow King," she teased when I pulled away to catch my breath. "I can't wait to taste him again."

I quickly glanced to see that Ghost was only a few feet away. His widening eyes had me snapping back to the larynnx just in time to avoid her claws. I needed to end this before he arrived.

"You. Will. Never. Feed. On. Him. Again." I punctuated each word with a strike until finally I misted right through her.

When I reformed, the larynnx face was wide in shock. "What?" she gasped, frozen.

"He's mine," I growled. Then I watched with satisfaction as the larynnx shattered like ice.

"Silivia!"

Ghost reached me just as I sagged from exhaustion, the guards allowing him in as they pushed the clan soldiers back. Farek and Lorik threw me concerned glances, but I nodded to assure them I was fine.

"Are you okay?"

I gazed up at Ghost with a small smile. "Never better," I answered.

He chuckled, shaking his head. "Gods, you're going to be the death of me, you know. Come on, it's time for you to have a break."

He put an arm around my waist, but before he could lead me back towards camp, cries of terror and pain tore through the battleground. A cloud of darkness that was nothing like that of the male at my side rolled in from the clan's hill.

"Silivia!" came my sister's cry as she raced to our side. Her eyes were wide with terror as she pointed above us.

They were falling from the sky like rain, dead before they even hit the ground. Dragons, griffins, even the Ikari.

"Oh my god."

Daccy's choked whisper had me staring in horror as enemy and ally alike screamed as blood poured from their eyes like tears before they crumbled to the ground. And then fear like I'd never known froze every cell in my body. Ghost tensed where his body held mine close. Pain and panic flooded down the bond as his darkness rose to protect us. But I couldn't take my eyes away as a figure in a bottomless black robe with crimson red raining down its hem rose from the hill. My gaze met one of amber and sheer evil, right before his lips lifted in a slow smile, and the world went black.

Chapter 72

My nightmares had been given flesh.
But I am the master of my fate.

Dalacia

He was here. All around me, there were cries of pain. Blades slid against blades. Arrows shot through armor like it was nothing but silk. And death permeated the air like ash. But I couldn't take my eyes away from the one who ruled over all of it. The Bringer of Blood and Tears. The Blood King himself.

His robe billowed out behind him as he strolled through the battlefield. Fire did not touch him. Blades aimed his way were melted with darkness without even lifting a finger, their welder swallowed into nothingness.

I was a trained warrior. Wielded power over the very flames he walked through like smoke. But in his presence, I was reverted to that little girl who'd been jealous of her sister's training. Who'd thought her parents didn't love her as much. Not realizing what they were trying to spare her from. A girl who'd shivered and cried herself sick over her dead family as she was beaten relentlessly for not being her sister. Hopelessness. Grief. Terror. That's what had made my body heavier than concrete. My soul too weak to fight back, until I'd had no choice, lest I died in a pool of blood and mud.

Those same emotions threatened to overtake me again. I didn't even bother to summon my flames. What good would they do? I hadn't been strong enough then to stop him from taking over my mind, my will. I sure as hell wasn't strong enough now. I just stood frozen, waiting for the inevitable. I didn't even respond when, with a wave of his hand, he sent a fresh wave of beasts to attack us, separating me from Silivia and Ghost. I felt that same darkness infiltrating my mind, stealing my control away.

"Dalacia!!"

Barak's terrified call somewhat jerked me out of my stupor, but it was too late for me to stop the grigor bearing down on me. My guards had been separated from me, and just over the massive monster's shoulder, I saw the Blood King's lips lift in a smile.

Then jet-black wings were fanning out in front of me as Lorik cut the half-dragon beast from the sky. His canines bared, he continued to do so for every grigor that came my way until, with a jolt, Barak's hands framed my face, forcing my gaze to his wide hazel ones.

"Wildfire! Don't let him make you doubt yourself. You're not helpless. You're not alone. And you are not to be underestimated. He doesn't get to take anything more from you. Stand up to him!"

"I...I can't," I told him through gritted teeth, terror making the darkness spread faster through my mind. "Barak!"

"I have you." And then he kissed me, sending tendrils of lightning down the bond and throughout my body, sending the darkness scurrying. Barak pulled away, his eyes on only me, even in the midst of the chaos all around us. "Burn. Burn like the wildfire you are," he told me.

With a sharp exhale, I felt my power answer his call. My eyes narrowed as my fists clenched at my side. Barak saw it and grinned wickedly at me.

"Ready?" he breathed, lightning dancing along his skin to mine.

"Ready." And I picked up my twin blades and rejoined the fight. I threw Lorik a look with a whispered thank you. The male inclined his head in answer, and although I expected him to rush back to my sister's side, he and Barak remained at mine as we conquered the wave of enemies together.

Chapter 73

And those who are winged

shall answer her call.

Silivia

I'd lost count of how many had fallen because of my blades. Or even to the icicles I threw like daggers. But no matter how many I killed, there were always three more to take their place. I no longer knew whether the blood painting my skin was my own or the enemy's. But with every cry that came from our side, my heart grew heavier, my blades slicker in my palms. Even Ghost had taken some hits he'd normally be able to avoid. We were exhausted before, but with this new sweep following the Blood King's arrival, there was no opportunity to rest. We were losing. And unlike before, if we lost here, it wouldn't be only Rifka that suffered, but the entire world and the worlds beyond.

"Silivia to me!" came my brother's desperate order.

Gritting his teeth, Ghost threw a look towards him before moving closer to me. "Go! I'll follow you."

He and Farek protected my back as I spun to rush to my brother. He leaned against a tree in a surprisingly quiet spot. At least for now.

I panted heavily as Ghost and Farek fought to my side, their chests heaving as they continued watching the battle. Ghost's gaze hardened, and a hateful growl rumbled from him as he eyed the Blood King across the field. We were shielded from his gaze for the moment, but I knew it was only temporary.

"What is it, Reece?" I panted, startling as Tyrian and Teslia joined us.

They, too, were covered in blood and wore exhaustion like armor, but at least they were still standing.

"You have to end this," my brother said, cringing with pain as he shifted his left shoulder. "We are holding our own, but if you don't do something now, we're going to be wiped out."

My gut dropped with dread.

"He's right," Ty added, and my gut fell farther. "It's time for a last stand. It's now or never."

I gazed at my family, stared out at the battlefield of chaos, and then finally back at Ghost. He nodded sullenly. He knew what we had to do, even if it killed us.

"We have one more play," I told them. "But if it goes sideways..."

"Silivia," Ty contested.

I shook my head. "No, I need to say this." I took a deep breath. "I want you to know that no matter what happens next, I'm forever grateful to have met all of you. I came to this world to save the only family I had left, and instead, I found you all." I met each of their gazes, including Farek's. The changeling lowered his head in acknowledgment, sadness in his eyes.

"I couldn't have asked for a better family, friend, guardian...or mate." I took Ghost's hand, and he squeezed back in response. "If this is the end, at least I know that it wasn't in vain. That it wasn't because we didn't claw with tooth and nail to prevent it. So, thank you. Thank you for everything. I love each and every one of you."

"Oh, Silivia, we love you too," Tess cried, pulling me into a hug.

When she released me, Ty was next to pull me close. "I refuse to believe this is the end," he said gruffly.

I smiled sadly at him before leaping forward to wrap arms around my brother's neck. He hugged me tight and buried his face in my shoulder.

"Father would be proud," he whispered. "As am I, to call you sister."

I sniffled as I stepped back to smile and embrace Farek next.

"Silivia," he said softly.

I moved back to Ghost's side and gripped his hand again. He eyed those around us, determination and grief warring in his gaze.

"May we meet again on the other side," he said.

Tess tried to smile past the tears threatening to fall, and Ty bowed to him. "Go. We'll distract him."

With no other words to say, I watched as our friends and family threw themselves into the fray once again. They signaled to our allies to head towards the Blood King so we could sneak around to his other side.

I turned to my mate. My throat closed up, unable to release the words that would never be enough to tell him how much I loved him. So, I sent every emotion I was feeling down the bond between us. He pulled me close, his lips devouring mine for several seconds in a desperate need for connection. When he pulled away, we were both panting again.

"I know," he whispered against my lips.

I took a deep breath, and when Ghost nodded, I sent one final call down every bond within me. It rippled outwards until even the trees bowed backwards as it passed, and then we were running.

We'd skirted all the way around the valley at this point. I could still hear the battle raging as Ghost as I ran to avoid the clan members on this side of the hill.

"Almost there," Ghost breathed as we made our way to the top.

If we'd calculated it right, we would come up right behind the king and catch him by surprise. I was panting heavily but paused briefly with Ghost before fully ascending.

"Ready?" I nodded, and we raced up the hill to see...the king was gone. I blinked and spun to scan the field.

"Fuck," Ghost swore, immediately drawing his blades.

I did the same, searching frantically for the black robe that should be right in front of us. "I don't understand. Where did he go?" Then cold dread flooded my veins, and I knew.

Ghost froze beside me, his eyes going wide.

"It is truly a beauty when plans come together so perfectly."

We turned slowly to meet cold, amber eyes. A long, crimson blade was held in each hand, shadows seeming to swim within the metal itself. The Blood King smiled as he eyed us hungrily. He paused on Ghost, and his smile grew wider.

"I see you still brought me the queen as I asked, oh grandson of mine. Well done."

"You will not touch her!" Ghost seethed, his darkness and shadows spilling out of him to wrap around our legs.

Eztil just laughed. "Such wrath. One would think you were still upset about that little cage mishap." He shrugged, managing to look sorrowful as he said. "If only you'd relented, I wouldn't have had to resort to such methods. I would have much rather had you standing by my side."

"Never," Ghost growled, shifting so his blades pointed at the king. "I'd rather die first."

The Blood King uttered a long-suffering sigh before turning to me. "And you? Will you join me, or are you just as stubborn as your mate? Haven't you had enough of the bloodshed and suffering?"

"You mean what *you* caused? What *you* orchestrated over centuries? *That bloodshed and suffering?*" I scoffed. "Yeah, no. I think I'll pass."

The king tsked. "Children. So little respect these days. No matter. I'll just have to teach you to kneel."

Then, shots of dark power were coming at both of us. I dodged out of the way as blue flames roared up between us. I threw ice daggers through their tendrils, but he tossed them aside like toothpicks. Ghost shot waves of darkness at the king, misting away when shards of obsidian were shot in return.

"The quicker you submit, the less your friends suffer. Or do their lives mean so little to you?"

His sinister grin made me freeze, and I shot a horrified glance at Ghost. He, too, was frozen, but his gaze was fixed on the battlefield behind me.

Twisting, I shouted in horror, "NO!"

Everyone, clan and otherwise, was encased in darkness, writhing in pain. Even the winged were not spared. Those on the ground roared and clawed at the cages pinning them, while those in the sky roared their panic as they slammed against the bars holding them in place. Such power. Such evil. And the Blood King was killing them all.

I spun to face him again, my face twisted in a snarl as snow and ice whipped around me. Rage twin to my own roared down the bond as Ghost growled at the grinning male before us.

"They're your people, too!" I screamed at him. "You would kill those loyal to you? A world's worth of people, for what? Just because you can?"

He laughed. "Child, when you become as old and powerful as I, you do not worry yourself with the feelings of ants. They are like any soldiers, disposable." He opened his arms wide to encompass the destruction as his gaze met Ghost's. "Look what I'm capable of, and I'm barely breaking a sweat. Join me, and I'll teach you what it means to hold true power."

"Never!" Ghost snarled, shooting a wave of darkness that Eztil knocked aside.

"You're holding back, Shadow King," he tsked. "Maybe this will be motivation for you."

Before I could consider what he meant, darkness shot through the flames and ice protecting me and wrapped around my throat. My hands shut up to pull at it as I started to choke.

"Silivia! No!" Ghost threw himself at the Blood King. "Let her go!"

Each word was paired with a deadly strike of his wolf blades, but none made contact. Instead, he cried out as he was sliced by blades of pure darkness he didn't manage to block in time. I tried to scream for him, but I could barely breathe around the grip on my neck.

"Better. But you're still holding back. What will it take for you to unleash?" He tilted his head, cruel calculation playing behind his gaze as he examined me. "Maybe...her death."

I gasped as I felt the coldness of iron sliding into my side. I choked as the tendrils gripped tighter, my power winking out as I fought against the black starting to blur my vision. No. It couldn't end like this.

"Either submit and get her to kneel, or watch me kill her. What is your choice, grandson?"

I could see my mate wavering, his love for me overpowering his desire to fight back against this tyrant.

"Don't you dare give up!" I growled down our bond, fighting to ignore the iron scalding my side, the burn of my desperate lungs. *"Don't you dare submit to this bastard!"*

Fear, rage, and darkness were a tornado on his side of the bond. *"I can't lose you. I won't survive it,"* he bit back. *"If I fight, you fight. Whatever we do, we do together."*

Distantly, I could hear the cries and screams of those dying below. I could feel my heartbeat starting to slow, just as I could feel his desperate determination as he struck at the Blood King again and again, each strike stronger than the next. Stronger, because we'd always found our true strength, our true power, in each other. In our friends and family. Every challenge we'd faced the last couple of years always came down to us conquering them...as one.

My eyes grew wide as I felt an answering hum down every bond within me, but most importantly, the spiritbond.

When the land shudders and is watered with blood and tears...

"We fight together or not at all," Ghost growled aloud. "Choose Silivia!" He would yield if I did.

...only then will she be born.

"Fight back!"

But I was not born to yield no more than he.

Risen from the ash as ice and flames...

I could feel my power rising, rumbling like a tsunami, and without looking, I knew a blue phoenix had appeared behind me. Darkness and shadows roared in answer as Ghost's power rose to meet it.

...all that is winged will answer to her call...

The call of the winged grew louder, more focused, more vicious. And over the horizon, I could see a sea of Ikari, dragons, griffins, and more flying to our aid. Shadow dyrewolves and shadow winged joined their ranks.

And only when the shadows and snow bond as one...

The Blood King's hold on my throat stuttered and loosened as he was bombarded by the Shadow King's power and wrath. He would get his wish. Ghost's eyes were the darkest I'd seen with a tiny golden ring, but he was more in control than he'd ever been.

...will the land be healed again.

"You. Will. Let. Her. Go!!" He released a wave of power so powerful, it broke through the king's defenses.

The Blood King called out in pain and surprise as he was thrown several feet into a tree. His tendrils fell away from my throat, and I sucked in several breaths of air as Ghost rushed over and pulled the iron dagger from my side. He dropped it to the ground before gripping my face and searching my eyes. I nodded, and he moved to stand at my side. Shadow creatures of all sizes surrounded us. My phoenix screeched its rage to the sky.

A wicked grin twisted the Blood King's mouth as he rose to his feet, discarding the shredded robes of the clan. "Yesss. Now this is a challenge. This is power. Show me what you've got."

"With pleasure," I retorted, and we attacked.

Chapter 74

Long may he burn in hell.

Ghost

There had never been a time that Silivia and I were more on one accord. Each attack was executed like a graceful but deadly dance, giving back just as hard as we received. With every attack, I could feel our power growing, shadows replacing those destroyed, winged divebombing from the sky alongside icy daggers. Never had I fully unleashed my power like this, not even when held by the Blood King himself. But instead of out of control, I felt centered, determined, and it was all because of the spiritbond balancing my darkness with the very light that would be the Blood King's end. Yet, despite every attack, he was still standing.

"Enough of this!" he roared, sending a wave that wiped out several winged and shadow creatures and pushed us closer to the edge of the hill.

We paused, chests heaving as he stared us down. His eyes were more maniac than I'd ever seen, his power writhing around him like beheaded serpents.

"This is your last chance before I send everything at my disposal to destroy you. YIELD!!"

I noticed a light next to me and turned to see my mate stand tall, her eyes glowing as they whirled with stormy power. I felt it when the bonds within her grew stronger than iron. I felt it when the dark bars caging her winged shattered. And I felt it when my queen came into her full power, and she smiled and pointed beyond the king.

"Not if I turn them against you first."

Confused, he turned to see where she pointed, and my eyes widened in surprise as my chest grew tight with pride. Half dragon, half lion creatures dressed in bloody armor stalked from between the trees. Some were easily the size of a full-grown dragon, claws as thick around as saplings. They growled as one, but unlike before, they weren't here for us. The Blood King cried out in alarm as they attacked.

All I could do was watch in awe as the creatures, infamous for killing plenty of our warriors, turned against the one said to control them. But this wasn't over. Too soon, the grigors were dwindling under the Blood King's power, but finally so was he. It would only take one coordinated attack to end this.

I turned to meet her gaze, impeding every inch of pride and love I could in one look. I didn't look away even as the largest creature alive rose behind us, his black and purple eyes upon us. I simply summoned his shadow twin. When she summoned her blue phoenix to her side, I called my shadow dyrewolf to mine. Snow and darkness spun all around us. Icy flames and shadows danced at our feet. It was always meant to end this way. It was always going to come down to us.

"Let's wipe this world clean," I told her, a wicked grin on my face as I lifted my wolf blades, shadows dancing down the metal.

Love and equal mischief shone in her face as she lifted her own dragon blades, now lined with blue flames.

"Let's."

With a roar that shook the forest, the King of Dragons, its shadow twin, Silivia's phoenix, and my shadow dyrewolf attacked. We jumped in between their attacks to deliver one of our own. Dodging away when the Blood King's power struck. His shouts of anguish rang in response for several moments until we finally sensed his power dwindling. When they were called off, the Blood King fell to his knees. Blood gushed from multiple cuts and burns scarred his body, but his power still worked feverishly to heal him. He wasn't going to get a chance.

As one, Silivia and I stalked to him, and I glared down at the male who had orchestrated so much of the pain and destruction each person down in the valley and beyond had experienced.

"Do you yield?" Silivia demanded as she glared down at the fallen king.

He laughed manically as he wiped the blood from his mouth. "Feels good doesn't it. Holding so much power. You have many centuries to live. To grow to be great like me."

I growled. "Do. You. Yield?" I reiterated.

My great-grandfather only turned to me with a twisted smile. "You can't kill me," he said. "I created you. Both of you. You are nothing without me."

"Wrong," Silivia said with narrowed eyes. "We are despite you."

A whisper down the bond, and we struck as one, our blades shredded through the Blood King's heart as the shadows and ice weaved throughout his body, destroying his power. His eyes widened in horror as his darkness went out, leaving only mine twisting around us.

"This... is...impossible," he breathed, blood bubbling from his mouth. "You...were... supposed...to... kneel...to...me!"

Silivia scoffed. "Foolish king, when are you going to learn?"

"We kneel to no one but each other," I finished, and we buried him in darkness and icy flames.

His screams echoed across the hills until the clan leader was nothing more than ash on an icy wind. As we turned away and stood on the hill looking down at the valley, our spirit animals and the winged roared our triumph. The darkness holding everyone captive had disappeared with the king's defeat. At the sight of us wounded, but standing tall, shadows and snow still whipping around us, clan soldiers and robed dropped their weapons and fell to their knees. Those who didn't were immediately cut down by our allies until we were all who stood.

"We won." I eyed my mate, disbelief in her eyes as she turned to me. "We actually won."

I snorted. "As if I ever had a doubt," I answered, crossing my arms."

She blinked at me in surprise before laughter broke from her. It was sheer joy and relief manifested, and I'd never heard a more beautiful sound. Unable to resist, I pulled her into my arms and kissed her deeply, desperately. For a moment, I'd thought I would never get the chance again. And now I could look forward to doing so much more for many, many years to come.

Epilogue

Silivia

"We've come a long way," Daccy said, staring up at the clouds.

She lay to my right on a patch of grass in Selondian Forest. I smiled, remembering that not too long ago, I sat in this exact spot trying to learn how to embrace the power within me.

"Ooo, look! It's a unicorn!"

Reece snorted a laugh. "Yeah, we have. To think I used to be an only child and didn't have time for mundane things like cloud watching. Also, that's obviously a grigor."

"Eww, why would you visualize something like those gruesome beasts, brother?"

"Um, those gruesome beasts helped our sister defeat Eztil, remember?" Reece replied, sounding affronted. "And don't blame me for your lack of vision."

"Lack of vision! What about the dragon over there? Surely you see that."

"Looks more like a mountain to me."

Daccy scoffed. "Now, who has a lack of imagination?"

"Children. Children," I scolded, fighting a smile. "Remember, we're all family here. Plus, you're both wrong. That's obviously an Ikari."

"What!" They both demanded, and there ensued another furious debate over dragon versus Ikari. It was so painfully and wonderfully normal.

It had been three months since the Battle of Blood, as it was being called, and it would take time for things to settle. A lot of Fae and creatures had been killed, a lot of enemies imprisoned, but we'd gained a stronger bond with both Hyra and Farla.

Despite some grumbling, Rifka had accepted and welcomed Dalacia after she'd so ruthlessly defended them. The Resisti Seven had been given permanent citizenship and land in Rifka, along with the positions they already held as my inner court. The masters of the Resisti will never fully give us the credit due, but we'd departed without hostility. Many of our allies had left with either begrudging respect or a vow to continue to support each other in the coming years. Our last meeting had been the most cordial of all of them, giving me hope that future dealings would be more tolerable.

It wasn't clear what the future held, but so far, it felt full of promise. We'd all decided that a vacation was in order, and after the males had updated the cabin to fit our expanded family that now included Raiden, Barak, Daccy, and Reece, we'd all decided to take a week off to just enjoy the peace. Even our changeling guards were taking the time to recharge and enjoy the fun, even if they were never far from us.

Currently, Reece and Teslia were taking their turn cooking–and enjoying each other-and the rest were off on some male fun in the forest. And my siblings and I were learning how to be just that.

I smiled as I eyed them on either side of me. Both would likely be getting married soon. Reece had confided his desire to propose to Teslia during the winter solstice. And Ghost had told me with amusement how Barak had begged him and Tyrian for advice on how to propose to Dalacia. Even Raiden was toying with the idea of asking Rose, although he said they'd both agreed to wait a few more years first.

I sighed. Now, if only I could find Ty's fated mate, our group would be complete. Speaking of mates. I smiled up at the sky.

"Hi Ghost."

Daccy and Reece stopped arguing long enough to glance around us. They shot me confused glances, but I was already jumping to my feet. I winked at them as I skipped towards the trees I'd seen the shadows disappear behind.

"Bye, you two! See you at dinner!"

Reece snorted. "As if you plan on leaving your bed once you enter," he called after me.

"You're one to talk," Daccy shot back. "At least the rooms are soundproof. I do *not* need a reminder of how loud you are when you come." She shivered in horror.

"You sure you want to go there, little sister? Barak and Daccy, sitting in a tree..."

I giggled at their banter as I raced through the forest, chasing the shadows. I frowned when I reached the Spirit Mountains, but found no one. Spinning in place, I shrieked in surprise when a warm arm wrapped around me from behind.

"Ghost!" I scolded, turning in his arms.

Amused, golden eyes grinned down at me. There was still darkness there, hidden behind his smiles and jokes. And there likely would be for a few years as he healed, but at least we would get the chance to do so together.

"Hello, my queen," he said softly, lovingly as he held me against his chest.

I melted against him as I always did. "Hello, my king," I answered.

"Missed me?"

"Desperately."

He'd been in Azalea visiting his grandparents, who unfortunately still held firmly to their dislike of Rifka. Guess saving the world together didn't erase centuries of prejudice. Oh well. Maybe eventually we'd get to family dinner level, but at least for now, Ghost had to visit them occasionally to maintain our alliance.

I'd hardly slept, unwilling to go without his arms around me at night. I knew all too well what it was to think I'd never feel his heartbeat against mine again. I had no desire to do so again.

"Next time I'll take you with me," he promised, leaning down to kiss me deeply.

"I'll hold you to that," I whispered against his lips, pulling him closer by his tunic.

In answer, he wrapped me up in darkness and misted us to our rooms. Except when the darkness receded, we were also lacking our clothes. I lifted a brow as I eyed him with amusement.

"New trick. Someone's eager."

Ghost laughed as he tossed me onto our blankets and crawled over my body. "I missed you desperately, too."

He kissed me again, our tongues dancing as our hands relearned each other. He kissed down my jaw to my neck as I traced down the strong, flexing muscles of his back. I sighed with pleasure as his mouth gravitated to my chest, sucking on a nipple as he twisted the other. I ground against him impatiently.

"Ghost," I begged, gasping as he nipped me in answer. "I don't have the patience for foreplay tonight."

A rumbling groan was his answer as I took hold of his length, boldly meeting his gaze as I guided him into me. We both moaned in pleasure as we came together. I gripped him around his taut waist as he gently and thoroughly made love to me, his gaze on mine the entire time. It was torturous and deliciously slow. It was like coming up for air. It was life.

I watched as he gradually lost control, his eyes growing darker with a golden ring. His breaths coming in sharp gasps of pleasure. I felt the desire pooling in my stomach. Spreading until I could barely stand the orgasm rushing to overtake my senses.

"Ghost!" I cried out. It was too much. Too good. I needed to come. I needed it to last forever.

"Let go, my love," he whispered, grinding against me. "Let me see how beautiful you are when you come."

I gasped, and then I was aflame, literally and metaphorically. I screamed as he wrenched my pleasure from me, leaving me clenching around him so hard he bellowed his own release as the shadows and darkness wrapped around us in a loving embrace.

When I returned to earth, I found him gazing deep into my eyes, his hips already slowly rolling against me.

"See. Beautiful." And then he proceeded to make love to me all over again.

Hours later, we lay in each other's arms, my head against his chest as I traced his scars with a finger. Peace and contentment like I'd never known filled me, and I could tell he felt the same way. He kissed my hair and pulled me closer with a pleased sigh.

"I could have never imagined what my future held when I kneeled in the ashes of my home. I'd lost everything. Everyone. I'd never thought that what I would gain would be so much more."

I lifted my head to meet his gaze. His eyes were a golden river, flowing calmly for once.

"If you could go back and change anything, would you?" I asked, curious despite myself.

His fingers trailed up and down the bare skin of my back as he contemplated. "If you'd asked me that a few years ago, I would have told you yes without hesitation, but now..."

"Now?" Love flowed down the bond, wrapping me in a dark embrace.

"Now, knowing in the end it brought me to you? No, I wouldn't change a thing." I sucked in a surprised breath, tears prickling my eyes. "Would you?"

Would I? I loved my dad and mom. I missed them desperately. But I had gained so much. I had a brother, and I was even closer to my sister than before, but I'd also found a bigger family in Ty, Tess, and Barak. I had more friends than I could ever dream of, in males like Farek, Lorik, and Raiden. And... I had the love of my life, just like my dad had escaped to the human world to have. I'd lost a lot, but I'd found so much more.

"No, I have everything I could want or need right here." A pleased hum came down the bond, and he pulled me close again. After a few minutes, I couldn't help asking. "What do you think the future holds?"

"Whatever we want it to," was his answer.

"Like twins?" I whispered and peeked at his expression.

Pure elation shone in his eyes as he smiled at me. I could see how much the idea delighted and terrified him. Good, we were in agreement.

"And so much more." And then he hummed his mother's lullaby, sweeping us away into a future of love and peace encased in snow-kissed shadows.

Afterthoughts

There were so many times when the characters almost reduced me to tears while writing this book. This was my debut series, and so in a way it will always be my favorite. And I have to admit, from the start, I have *always* loved Ghost. Watching all the characters heal and find happiness was cathartic. I know what some of you may be thinking. The characters in this book are not real people. But I would beg to differ. I'm sure many can connect in some way with their scars and struggles, and putting their stories on paper makes them real in a way.

Regardless, this is the end of an era, of Silivia and Ghost's story. It is bitter but oh so sweet. No one deserved their happily ever after like these two. I can't say I won't return to Fenriel to visit other characters' stories, but at least for now, I'm moving on to other worlds, other adventures, and other love stories just waiting to be told.

I hope you have fallen in love with this series as much as I have, and even if you haven't, thank you for taking this journey with me.

Check out my new Romantasy series, The Forces of Nature. This is a series of interconnected standalones with a guaranteed HEA. See how the series begins in Heart of the Forest.

The Four Princes of Nature are cursed with the power over life and death, but one being was never meant to carry both. As the princes succumb to the darkness flowing through their veins, the kingdoms reflect their changing hearts. A flicker of hope still remains, but only the Princesses of Disaster can reverse the curse and restore balance to the forces of nature.

Ember stopped believing in fairy tales a long time ago. It's hard to believe in such things as royalty or knights in shining armor when you're busy trying to survive your abusive father and save the family legacy. But some things are just too much for one person to handle. When things escalate to dangerous levels, Ember decides to fight for her life and escape, but she doesn't expect to end up in another world where princes and princesses do exist. Except, they are not like

the royalty you know. They are Fae gifted with the power over life-and-death....
and she's one of them.

Thatch is the Prince of Forest, heir to the Forest Kingdom. He should be
preparing to take over the throne from the King and Queen of Nature, but
instead he is battling an ancient curse given as punishment for a crime his parents
won't admit to. Instead of giving life to the forest, the curse twists his power into
something deadly. He's meant to protect, but with his power becoming darker
with each decade, Thatch has lost hope that he can be cured and decides the only
way to save his kingdom would be to remove himself altogether. It is prophesied
that only a Princess of Disaster can balance out the curse, but after trusting the
wrong person, Thatch finds it hard to believe that an act of love could reverse
centuries of death.

**Will a journey to save a kingdom bond and save two souls, or will they
succumb to the darkness?**

About the Author

Shaquilla (shuh-kee-luh) M. Lunsford, or better known as the **"Dragon Queen"**, is known for writing fantasy worlds full of romance, magic, and majestic creatures. She enjoys the complexity and creativity required to develop an entirely new world with its own set of rules and characters. With her love of dragons, they usually make an appearance in her writing or daily life. She also draws inspiration from Greek and Roman mythology to create some creatures and characters, and sheer imagination for others. Despite Shaquilla's passion for fantasy, poetry is her first love, and those incorporated in her books are usually her own.

Shaquilla currently lives in North Carolina with her "mini zoo", consisting of reptiles, a cat, and a dog.

Did you enjoy reading Downfall of the Blood King? Please leave a review and share. That is a great way for indie authors like me to reach other amazing readers! Subscribe to my newsletter for updates on upcoming releases and giveaways: https://shaquillalunsford.com

Or follow me on Social Media!
Instagram/Facebook: @ShaquillaLunsford
Goodreads: Shaquilla Lunsford
TikTok: @authorshaquillalunsford
Pinterest: @shaquillalunsford